# THE SLEEPLESS

# FIRST INK

Published 2025 by First Ink,
an imprint of Pan Macmillan
The Smithson, 6 Briset Street, London EC1M 5NR
*EU representative:* Macmillan Publishers Ireland Ltd, 1st Floor,
The Liffey Trust Centre, 117–126 Sheriff Street Upper
Dublin 1, D01 YC43
Associated companies throughout the world
www.panmacmillan.com

ISBN 978-1-0350-5804-4 Hardback Main Market Edition
ISBN 978-1-0350-6940-8 Hardback Open Market Edition
ISBN 978-1-0350-5803-7 Trade Paperback Edition

Copyright © Jen Williams 2025

The right of Jen Williams to be identified as the
author of this work has been asserted by her
in accordance with the Copyright, Designs and Patents Act 1988.

All rights reserved. No part of this publication may be reproduced,
stored in a retrieval system, or transmitted, in any form or by any means
(electronic, mechanical, photocopying, recording or otherwise),
without the prior written permission of the publisher.

Pan Macmillan does not have any control over, or any responsibility for,
any author or third-party websites referred to in or on this book.

1 3 5 7 9 8 6 4 2

A CIP catalogue record for this book is available from the British Library.

Printed and bound by CPI Group (UK) Ltd, Croydon CR0 4YY

This book is sold subject to the condition that it shall not, by way of trade or otherwise,
be lent, resold, hired out, or otherwise circulated without the publisher's prior consent in
any form of binding or cover other than that in which it is published and without a similar
condition including this condition being imposed on the subsequent purchaser.

*To Pete, for giving me the most unexpected of stories*

# PROLOGUE

The sun was rising, and the serpents had been screaming all night.

The girl had lain awake listening to them, unable to sleep, just like every other citizen of Addersport. She'd pushed her dormitory bed right up against the windowsill, so she could hear them especially clearly; their voices were high and eerie, a sound like a wet finger dragged across glass. Addersport sat next to and within the sea; waterways invaded the city like veins through a leaf, and the smaller sea serpents had swum up these convenient thoroughfares until every canal glinted with scales of blue, green, yellow and black. To cross a bridge in Addersport these days was to run the risk of feeling a set of serrated jaws close around your ankle. The footpaths that ran along each waterway were positively lethal. The city was under siege.

That morning over breakfast, the orphanage was rife with the rumour that the city officials had brought in an actual magpie to deal with these rogue monsters – a mage, dedicated to one of the twelve gods, able to ask a boon and banish the serpents. The girl looked into her bowl of porridge and considered: which god? The Hooded Crow, perhaps. The god of death could turn all the serpents into so much seagull chow with a wink. Or the Pack, the god of the chase. They could bless the city's whaling ships with the ability to hunt the beasts.

Outside, the screaming continued.

In the afternoon, while the children were packed into the dusty schoolroom for their lessons, a group of men in city guard uniforms arrived, their faces closed and grim. Sitting at her desk by the door, the girl couldn't hear what passed between the guards and the bursar of the orphanage, but she caught a glimpse of a small bag being handed over. It looked heavy, and it clinked when the bursar put it in his pocket. When the guards left and the bursar turned away from the front door, he glanced up and caught sight of the girl. To her surprise, his normally sallow face flushed crimson, and he quickly moved out of sight. The girl, staring at the dusty floor where he'd been standing, felt a cold tremor move through her. Something was happening, and it wasn't good.

So when they came for her, she wasn't particularly surprised. It was the middle of the afternoon by then, and the orphans were busy at work, darning clothes for pennies. A boy and a young woman came into their workroom and stood for a moment, surveying the children. The pair were so richly dressed that, as one, the orphans fell silent. They rarely saw visitors at all, let alone ones in burgundy silk and golden thread. The boy was perhaps only thirteen or fourteen years old, and he was handsome in a cold sort of way, with black hair pulled back from his face in a braid. His eyes were hazel, almost tawny coloured, and they seemed to hungrily consume everything they looked at. The woman looked nearer twenty years old, with brown skin and hair hidden under a swatch of embroidered cloth. In the centre of their chests they both wore a solid gold pin in the shape of a lion; rubies spilled from its claws like blood.

The girl, who at twelve summers was the oldest in the room, stood up from her pile of cloth. Her heart was beating too fast and the air felt thick with danger. *Meet it head on*, she thought.

'Who are you?' she asked. There were no staff present. The bursar had made himself curiously absent. 'What do you want?'

'Impertinence,' said the woman, although without any heat. If anything she looked bored. 'Can't you see who you're talking to?'

'Acolytes of the Bloody Claw,' the girl said, her eyes drawn to the lion pin. She could feel the other children staring at her. She cleared her throat. 'That's my guess. But what does the Bloody Claw want with orphans?'

'She's clever, this one,' said the boy. He half turned to the young woman. 'You know Mother likes it best when they are clever, Dalesh.'

The girl blinked. Could these two be brother and sister?

The woman grunted. '*What use is a sacrifice if you're not really losing anything?*' The words had the tone of something she had spoken many times before. 'Our lord likes His food to plead eloquently as well as squeal deliciously.' Dalesh sighed. 'But she told us to look them *all* over. Mother has entrusted us with an important task.'

'Ah, it's fine.' The boy waved his hand, swatting away the woman's concerns like flies. 'I've got a feeling about it. And you know that Mother trusts my feelings.'

The woman grimaced. 'Fine.'

'It's decided then.' The boy smiled – a sharp, brittle thing with no warmth in it at all – and gestured impatiently at the girl. 'Come along, you. We don't have all day. You're coming with us.'

The girl took a step backwards. Around her, the other orphans had all drawn back, as though afraid that they might catch her fate from being too close.

'I'm not going anywhere with you.' She balled her hands into fists. 'The bursar can't just sell children. This isn't some backwater village where you can wander in and do what you want. This is Addersport.' She took a breath. 'You'll have to drag me out.'

The boy sighed.

'If you insist.'

★

Out under the summer sun, the air rang with the sound of serpents. Members of the City Guard dragged the girl through the narrow streets, taking care to avoid the main waterways until they came to the Tumble Stone, a huge piece of natural rock that thrust up from the seabed at the very edge of Addersport. Over hundreds of years the city had built its port around the stone. They had carved steps into its side and a smooth platform at its summit. Once, the elders of the city had used the Tumble Stone to watch for pirates and raiders; on special occasions people were married there, and flowers thrown into the water on festival days. When the girl arrived at the stone, it was surrounded by a great crowd of city folk. They were quiet, watching either her or the figure that stood at the summit of the stone. The girl could barely make it out herself. The bright sun stood behind the person, whoever it was, carving them into a thing of shadow.

'What's going on?' She'd asked the question all the way through the streets, in varying tones of outrage and fear, and with every curse word she knew thrown in, but none of the guards had responded. Now, the boy with the cruel eyes and the woman called Dalesh took her from them.

'You've been given a very great honour today,' said the boy. He took hold of her arm and began walking her up the stone steps. He was taller than the girl and had little trouble moving her. Dalesh walked on the other side, her grip even tighter. 'You will shortly meet Mother Maura, one of the most celebrated mages in all of Tlevrae. Aren't you lucky?'

'A magpie?' The girl threw herself backwards, trying to wriggle out of their hands. 'You're taking me to a bloody *magpie*?'

Dalesh squeezed her arm viciously. 'You don't want to say that in front of Mother,' she said evenly. 'She doesn't approve of that particular nickname. You'll show some respect or you'll regret it.'

'Although,' added the boy, half laughing, 'you won't regret it for very long.'

By now they had come to the top of the Tumble Stone. The sea stretched away in front of them, a deep dark blue in the very distance, but a churning white and green below the stone. The figure came forward and a pale hand with red fingernails reached out and closed around the girl's wrist. She felt all resistance leave her body. She was powerless here.

'This is the best you two could do? A scruffy little ragamuffin? It's barely a snack for our lord.' The woman's voice was rich and deep, like the purr of some great, lethal animal. 'To give Him anything less than what He desires is dangerous. I shouldn't have to say this to you.'

The girl summoned all her strength to lift her head and look at the woman whose fingernails were digging into her flesh. She was tall and imposing, with high cheekbones and a vast amount of auburn hair that cascaded down her back, both loose and bound in plaits and braids. A single streak of white began at her temple and was lost in the larger chaos. She wore scarlet robes and across her forehead there was a golden band with a single ruby claw set in its centre. Her eyes were a sharp yellowish green.

'She is the right choice,' the boy was saying, his voice full of confidence. 'I'm quite sure of it, Mother. She's bold, clever, just *brimming* with piss and vinegar. Plenty of fight in her. If she'd been left to live her life, she certainly would have made something of it, and won't our lord find that delicious? All that potential, offered up to Him. It'll be more than enough to fuel this spell.'

'I will be the judge of that,' Mother Maura snapped, dragging the girl over to the edge of the Tumble Stone. Below them, the sea serpents churned the water in a hungry frenzy, their shining hides flashing gold and silver in the sun. 'You see them, child?' Mother

Maura peered over the edge, her lips pursed. 'Dirty jih beasts. Filthy monsters. They've done nothing but disrupt this city's trade for weeks. Not to mention the number of lives lost. Eleven dead, I believe.' The woman grinned, revealing white, neat teeth. 'Eleven lives used for nothing more than to line a wyrm's belly. A waste. But you, darling girl, *you* get to save the city. Your life won't be a waste. When the serpents pull you to pieces, your life will be devoured and savoured by my lord and then He will give me a crumb of His power to banish them.'

The girl opened her mouth, willing the words to form on her tongue.

'Let . . . me . . . go.'

Mother Maura chuckled. She took hold of the front of the girl's shirt and shoved her so close to the edge that she could feel the emptiness at her back. The mage leaned forward, her arm held out straight, and the girl trembled all over. All the mage had to do was let her go, and she would be gone, dropped into the sea like a pebble lazily cast into a pond. She looked behind Mother Maura to see the acolytes watching closely. Dalesh looked faintly pained, as though the whole thing was distasteful, but the boy was watching raptly, his hazel eyes eager.

'My lord, the Bloody Claw,' Mother Maura was saying, her voice lifted above the roar of the sea and the screaming of the serpents. 'Take this life of potential, feast on it and grant me a boon.'

There was a shimmer around the woman, something like the heat haze on a road on a very hot day. Maura's eyes flashed like a cat's, and the girl had a fleeting sense of something else being there with them; something huge and powerful, that reeked of blood.

'What's your name, girl?'

'Elver.' For a moment the girl wondered if speaking her name would save her somehow; if once she was named, the mage would show her mercy.

The woman laughed.

'Goodbye, Elver.'

Mother Maura let go, and the girl fell into the sea.

There was an awful, yawning sense of nothing, and then she struck a mass of hard, cold bodies. For a moment it was as though the sea itself had vanished; she had fallen instead into a country made of serpents, a solid land of hissing and scales like battered silver coins. Elver saw her sandal come off, saw blood in the water, and then a pain like nothing she had ever imagined seized her around the midriff. A huge, yellow sea serpent had its jaws around her and was sinking its long, barbed teeth into her flesh. There was no breath or room to scream. Another moment and she was tugged down, under the black sea water and the writhing bodies, the dappled light of the sun speeding away from her, the human world left far behind.

*I'm dead*, she thought. *I'm dead.*

And then something else began to flow into her veins, something cold and dark that ate up her own red blood and replaced it with poison. The girl's eyelids fluttered once or twice, a strange hiccupping tremor that moved through her whole body as her final breath left her. When she opened her eyes again the inner life of the sea was revealed in a flickering corona of colours, and the vast head of the yellow serpent hung before her. When the creature spoke, its voice rang inside her head like a bell.

*Welcome home, poison child.*

# CHAPTER 1

*Five years later*

The dawn bells of the Golden Tower of the Perpetual Morning were loud enough to make the ears ring; loud enough to wake the dead. They had to be, since it was vitally important that every Sleepless currently inhabiting the monastery was absolutely, thoroughly awake.

And, all at once, Artair was.

He awoke as he always did, sitting upright in a chair in front of the small, barred window of his cell, with no memory of sitting there or even moving the chair. The *other one* had done that. The clay cup that Artair used to drink water and tea had been smashed, shards lying on the floor. From the damp patch on the plaster wall, he guessed the other one had thrown it in one of his wild moments of rage.

Grimacing at the familiar ache in his back – just once, he'd like for the other one to have spent the night in the narrow bed instead of pacing the room or sitting in the chair – Artair stood up, stretched and washed his face in the basin of cold water. He'd been waking at dawn since he was a child, and he was used to the punishing schedule of the Golden Tower. Even so, he glanced longingly at the bed with its undisturbed blankets and pillow. Perhaps he could just lie down for a few moments, resting until Brother Benzin came to do the morning checks . . . But lying down and resting was forbidden to the Sleepless outside of authorized hours. There was always a chance, after all, that he would forget himself and start to doze, and then the other one would come forward. If that happened, there was no predicting what he might do.

Never very far away, a dark memory flickered in the back of his mind: the choking smell of smoke, the taste of burning flesh in the air . . . Artair splashed more cold water on his face to banish the thoughts.

'The foundation of the tower is vigilance,' he murmured.

There was a tiny mirror over the water basin, warped by the years and slightly discoloured in one corner. Artair looked into it, searching his face for signs of the Other, as he did most mornings. It seemed impossible that just moments ago someone else had been looking out of his brown eyes – that some other intelligence had moved his mouth and made it smile, or frown, or shout. His face remained familiar: long straight nose, sharp jawline, the narrow slash of a scar that cut through his right eyebrow – not the result of the other one's violence, that, but an accident with the wooden staffs the novices trained with each afternoon. Brown eyes looked back at him, full of their usual uneasy combination of curiosity and determination. His dark hair was wild and tangled, as though the Other had spent the night tugging his hands through it, but that could be fixed with a comb and a brush. At least the Other hadn't been pulling it out, as he had on other occasions.

'Morning, Artair!' Brother Benzin's face appeared at the small aperture in the door. He was a gentle, florid man with a grey beard, the white robes of his order always marked with grass stains. Where possible, Benzin preferred to be working in the gardens. 'Are you with us?'

Artair presented himself in front of the door to recite that day's line of poetry. Every day they were given a new one, so that the Brothers and Sisters of the monastery could be sure of who they were dealing with.

'The silver fish flits where it will, the badger digs deep under the hill.'

'Yes, yes, fine.' There was a rattle at the door as Benzin unlocked it with the keys he kept on a ring at his belt. 'A little simplistic for my tastes, but Sister Rosea has ordered in a new book of poems from a shop in Addersport and I'm afraid she's quite taken with it.' The door swung open, and Brother Benzin stood to one side. 'Brace yourself for many more stirring uses of *cat* and *bat*, or, the Twelve save us, *river* and *slither*. Goodness, look at the state of your hair. I assume we had a rough night?'

Artair knew it wasn't a real question. After all, how could he know what the Other got up to? But he felt his cheeks flush anyway.

'Was there any noise from my cell?'

Brother Benzin shrugged, then patted Artair on the shoulder fondly. 'There is noise from every cell every night, my young friend. Don't let it play on your mind. After your morning meditations and exercises I will want your help out in the orchards. Is that alright?'

When Benzin had left to continue his circuit of all the cells in the tower, Artair ducked back into his chamber, wet his comb and spent some minutes trying to tame his hair. There was a shadow of stubble on his jaw, but not enough yet to go to Sister Rosea for a shave – sharp blades were expressly forbidden in the cells of the Sleepless. When he'd done all he could to make himself presentable, he paused to sweep up the remains of the broken cup, depositing the shards on the small wooden table in the corner of the room. It was only then that he saw that one of the sharp pieces of clay had been used to carve a message into the tabletop. The words were jagged and rough, as though the author had had only minutes to carve it and not an entire night.

> LET ME OUT

'Never,' Artair said. He rubbed his fingers across the carved words, thinking: *My hands did this*. 'I'll never let you out.'

# CHAPTER 2

Elver broke the green ice on the top of the pond with her bare foot, savouring the brittle crack as she sank in up to her ankles. There had been a cold snap overnight and in this deepest, darkest part of the Jih Forest rarely a day passed without something freezing. She waded in deeper, letting the frigid black water envelop her up to her chest. Since the Queen of Serpents had swapped out her blood for poison when she was a child, cold water did not particularly bother Elver. She was jih now, a monster spirit in the forest of monsters, and the natural world could offer up very little to cause her discomfort.

In the middle of the pond, which was one of the smaller hidden watery places of the forest, there was a ragged island made of reeds, and mud, and stunted weeping willows. She headed towards it slowly, not wanting to startle its residents, but they were even more attuned to the forest than she was. She'd made it less than halfway when a bristly head stuck up out of a thicket of reeds. Large eyes flashed with blue-green light, briefly illuminating the island.

'Hey, it's only me,' Elver called softly. 'Just come to see how the cubs are getting on. I've brought treats!' She raised the bag she held in one hand, and the watching creature made a low whistling noise of satisfaction.

Seen only in silhouette, the keltraxia looked a little like oversized foxes, with their long snouts and bushy tails, but seen up close, their bodies were covered in tiny blue scales, except where they sprouted red and orange feathers. Their ears, covered in these feathers, looked like little bursts of flame, giving them the name by which humans knew them: fire-listeners. Elver thought the human name was stupid. The Queen of Serpents had told her the true names of all the jih spirits in the forest.

In the water around her, Elver could sense the movement of other things: frogs and fish and water snakes, but jih spirit creatures too, things with which she shared a kin-bond. Something with silver gossamer fins and eight red eyes brushed against her leg and was gone in an instant. Elver held the bag a little higher and continued.

The edge of the island was ringed with thick black mud, which Elver gamely stomped through until she was on what could charitably be called dry land. Just beyond the wall of reeds, mosses and heather, she could see a large nest of mud and sticks, and standing over it, the keltraxia vixen. The creature opened her mouth, letting her tongue scent the air, and the long scarlet feathers on her ears flickered open like a bird taking flight.

'You can smell these from the other side of the forest, I'm sure.' Elver placed the bag on the ground by the nest and opened it up so the vixen could get her snout inside. Green Lady snails were only found in the far west of the forest, and knowing how much the keltraxia enjoyed them, Elver always made certain to collect a big bagful whenever she was near. While the vixen munched and snorted her way through the bag, Elver carefully peeked over the edge of the nest. Inside was one as yet unhatched egg and three healthy-looking keltraxia cubs. Only recently hatched, they still had more feathers than scales, but their eyes were open and glowing with a softer version of the light their mother displayed. Elver reached a hand down to them. The nearest stuck his snout into her palm and licked it with a rough tongue.

'They're doing well.' She looked again at the egg and felt a little of her good mood slip away. 'Shouldn't that have hatched by now?'

The vixen turned to regard her, the fiery feathers on her ears lowered.

*Not that one*, the keltraxia said in the voice only Elver could hear. *She is still and cold, and did not have the strength to break the shell.*

Elver nodded. She understood – not everything that lived in the wood thrived – but it seemed unfair. From the southern slopes of the forest, on the foothills that marked the beginning of the mountains, it was possible to see the roads that led to Addersport, and on them there passed a steady stream of human life: travellers, traders, wanderers. They came with carts and caravans, on single horses or on foot. There seemed to be no end of human life souring the world, yet this one little keltraxia cub had not had the chance to live.

*We will eat it*, the vixen continued. *When the others are old enough to stomach it.*

Elver grimaced. She rubbed her hands through her hair – bone white since the Queen of Serpents had bitten her – and stepped away from the nest. The vixen came closer and briefly laid her head on top of Elver's; a greeting between kin.

*The snails are tasty*, she said. *Thank you, human-sister.*

'Not human any more,' said Elver. 'But you're welcome, my friend.'

Elver made her own home by another source of water: the great Serpent Lake that nestled in the centre of the Jih Forest. She had found an abandoned hunter's hut at the edge of the treeline and over the years had transformed it into a place she could shelter. There was a bed of fur and feathers, donated by the kindly, lumbering forms of the kartesh, monsters with the stocky, furry bodies of bears and the avian faces of owls; there was a mirror, brought to her by a roch, a vast bird with four fiery wings. On a single shelf there was her beloved collection of books, stolen from travellers or found and brought to her by the other jih spirits of the forest – they knew that their sister had a fondness for the human habit of reading. From the lake she caught fish, and washed herself, and drank, and every now and then she would find messages from the Queen of Serpents. On rare occasions, the god herself would appear, a huge golden shape coiling through the green water. Elver was not a mage – the Queen of Serpents had none – so she could not call the god to her or ask it for a boon, but as a jih spirit she was one of the Queen's own and, consequently, the god liked to visit. Elver had the vague sense the god had taken a special interest in her since saving her from being sacrificed in Addersport. The idea made her uneasy, as though it were all part of some larger painting, of which she could see only a tiny corner. But she knew the Queen had brought her back from death, while the people of Addersport had been all too eager to see a child thrown into the sea to save their own hides, and that was more than enough to earn Elver's loyalty. She thought then, as she often did, of the red-haired mage who had sacrificed her to a hungry god. Humans were duplicitous, selfish and bloodthirsty. The jih were all the company she needed now.

It was an hour's walk back to the Serpent Lake from the keltraxia nest. Elver moved through the forest like a creature that had been born there, slipping through the undergrowth silently, noting the signs and marks and songs of the birds and small animals. She paused at the edge of a stream as a platynus passed by, a vast monster whose reptilian head cleared the tallest treetops in the canopy. Elver could see only its enormous flank, muscles as big as tree trunks clenching and releasing under leathery purple and yellow skin.

When she arrived at the lake, she stripped off her clothes – scavenged or crafted by her own hand – and washed quickly in the water, cleaning the black mud off her feet. When she was dry and clothed again, she headed towards her ramshackle home, thinking to fetch her fishing spear and catch something for that night's supper. If there were plenty of fish about, she could start putting some by for the long winter that was beginning to breathe its cold air on the back of her neck.

But as she was picking up the spear she caught the scent of something acrid and sour against her tongue.

Woodsmoke. A human fire started with a splash of something else – oil, perhaps.

Elver turned and saw, on the far side of the lake, a point of buttery yellow light and a thin line of black smoke that poked above the tops of the trees. There was a figure there, sitting by the campfire, its head down as it looked at something in its lap.

'Intruder.'

Elver felt the poison in her blood churn. A filthy human, here, in this place that was her home.

She left the spear by the hut and instead retrieved her knife, which she pushed through her belt. Rather than following the edge of the lake around, she went back beyond the treeline, circling until she could see the human framed against the green water of the lake. It was a woman in her middle age, her limbs long and rangy, and she wore a wide-brimmed hat. There was a sword, still in its scabbard, lying on the sandy ground by her feet. The interloper's hair was short, and from her vantage point, Elver could see the bare skin on the back of her neck. All it would take was her cold, pale hand pressed to that section of skin and the woman would quickly regret ever coming into the Jih Forest . . .

But that wasn't enough.

Elver stepped out of the treeline, letting her feet crunch over the autumnal leaf litter, and watched with satisfaction as the human woman startled and turned, her eyes wide. She pictured what the woman was seeing: an alarmingly pale girl of seventeen years with a shock of white hair and yellow eyes, a line of blueish scars marking her neck and shoulder and arm – the places where the Queen of Serpents had bitten her. A monster girl dressed in leather and bone and feather, with a knife in her hand. Of course, she wouldn't know that the knife was the last thing she had to worry about.

'Who are you?' Curiously, the woman did not reach for her sword.

'I am the guardian of this forest.' Elver walked towards the woman boldly. It made her heart thunder in her chest, to be this close to a human. 'And you aren't welcome.'

The woman stood up slowly. On the ground behind her there was a well-used bedroll and a battered tin cup filled with soup.

'I've heard of you,' the woman said. 'The ghost of a girl is supposed to haunt this place. But you're no spirit. Are you living out here by yourself? How are you alive?'

Elver laughed. 'This is my home. Nothing here will harm me. But you? You've made a very serious mistake, human.'

'Listen.' The woman raised her hands slowly, palms facing out. 'I'm just a traveller. Passing on through this place on my way somewhere else. There's no need—'

'You thought you could just *pass through* the forest of the jih?' Elver grinned, and for the first time the woman looked truly unsettled. 'Humans, you think that everything is a road for you to walk on. That everything deserves to be beneath your feet. A dung beetle has more sense than you.'

'Now then.' The woman scowled. 'I'll not have such attitude off a scrap of a thing like you. You've gone mad, living out here by yourself.' Incredibly, she took a step forward, reaching out as though to bring Elver towards the fire. 'You need some hot meals inside you, a bloody good bath and then maybe you'll know to speak to your elders with some respect.'

'It's you who needs to show some respect.' Elver took the woman's arm and pressed the flat of her hand against her skin. The woman jumped as though she'd been bitten, the hat falling off her head with the force of it, and she gave a little shriek. Elver saw the shape of her own handprint on the woman's arm, the skin already blistering, and then the woman folded to her knees, falling down next to her own campfire. Her eyes had rolled up to expose the whites.

'I told you. Idiot human. Talking to me like I'm some lost child. The monster forest is my *home*.'

Elver knelt to feel for the interloper's pulse. It was there, light and fast. When she took her hand away, there were two more livid marks on the woman's skin in the shape of her fingertips. She wiped her hand on the back of her trousers. Touching humans made her feel dirty, but even worse was the painful curiosity it roused in her. What would it be like to touch a human safely? What did skin feel like when the person you touched didn't recoil in pain and horror? The memory of that sensation had long been lost to her. *You're not human any more*, she told herself fiercely. *And you never will be.*

'You're not dead,' she told the unconscious woman. 'Which is more than you deserve.'

It would be easy to end it, though. A longer touch from her poison skin should do it, or if she didn't mind making a mess, her knife would do the job.

Elver looked up to see another of the forest's monster inhabitants peering at her from the treeline. Slowjorns were some of the more talkative of the jih spirits, and she knew this one well.

*Greetings, forest guardian. One of your kind?*

Elver felt heat prickle across the back of her neck, but she swallowed down the annoyance like a sharp stone.

'No, not my kind at all. Since you're here though, will you do me a favour?'

The slowjorn crept forward. Out of the shadows, it looked like a human-sized bipedal snail, its limbs tentatively picking their way across the ground. The bulbous shell on its back was formed of a great spiral.

*Perhaps.* The antennae on its head expanded curiously, questing towards the body on the ground.

'Drag this idiot back towards the road. You don't have to go near it, just get close enough that she'll see where she has to go when she wakes up.' Elver smiled, imagining the look on the woman's face if she woke up during the journey and saw what had a sticky tendril around her ankle. And of course there were lots of dangers in the Jih Forest. She might not make it to the road at all. 'Don't worry too much about bumping her over brambles and puddles. She needs to learn not to ever come back here.'

When the slowjorn had gone, dragging the human behind it like a sack of bones, Elver picked over the traveller's possessions. She drank the cold soup, savouring the taste of herbs and spices from outside the forest, and took a notebook with a few empty pages left from the fallen pack – there had been books in the orphanage and they were one of the few things she truly missed. This one looked as though it had been used to keep track of the woman's travels; there were notes on Addersport, a town called Tarflin she had never heard of, and a detailed section on a mage dedicated to the god Tisk. There wasn't much else, but the sword was decent enough and had a sharp edge. Elver took it back with her to the other side of the lake.

# CHAPTER 3

The monastery clung to the side of the mountain like a cluster of oyster mushrooms on a tree. From its walls it was possible to see the Jih Forest spreading away across the foothills below, a dense carpet of trees that at this time of the year burned yellow and orange and red – and beyond that there was the ever-shifting sparkle of the sea. Between the two lay Addersport, hidden by the rise and fall of the land, the only clues to its existence the trails of smoke that rose from its industrious buildings and the steady arrival and departure of ships of all types. The monastery itself grew out from the central tower, where the Sleepless were housed during the night; buildings with green and blue tiled roofs crowded around it like children around a nursemaid. Behind its sea-facing walls, there was an interior garden so sheltered from the mountain weather that the monks and their charges grew most of the things they consumed there, from apples and cabbages to herbs and medicines.

Artair liked to look at the view as he made his way from the meditation hall to the garden, peering out of the many tiny windows that marked the corridor. If he ignored the bustle of activity that gave away the existence of Addersport, it was easy to pretend that the Golden Tower was all alone in the world; there was just the mountains, the forest and sea, with no people to make things complicated. If the world was empty beyond the monastery, then it would be safe for him – for all the Sleepless – to leave the tower behind.

But it would never be safe. As long as the Other dwelt within him, he was dangerous. And thinking about the world beyond was dangerous, too. Brother Elthem believed that such thoughts of freedom originated with the dark spirit, because what the dark spirits wanted, more than anything, was to get out into the wider world so they could cause chaos. The monks taught them to keep their minds and their bodies occupied – with meditation, physical training and simple chores.

*Vigilance*, thought Artair.

Down in the orchard the apples were ready to drop, and Artair spent much of the day with some of the younger novices, picking the fruits and carting them away in crates to the monastery kitchens or the cold cellars dug into the raw rock of the mountain. In the afternoon, the monks gave them a couple of hours of leisure time, so they went to the natural spring at the edge of the gardens. Over thousands of years it had carved a small pool into the rock, fed by a bubbling waterfall. It was a good place to sit and talk, with their bare feet dangling in the freezing water. To be Sleepless was to be constantly seeking ways to stay awake.

'My parents say they will visit after the next harvest,' said Reah. She had arrived at the monastery only six months ago. She looked down as she spoke, apparently examining the freckles on the backs of her hands. 'Which isn't so long now. But . . .' Reah shifted on the grass, her posture awkward and stiff. 'I can't believe I'm not there with them, helping them with it. That I'm going to be stuck in this place . . .'

She didn't say it, but Artair could hear the word in her silence anyway. *Forever.* Stuck in this place forever.

'It's harder for you,' said Chessun, in a matter-of-fact tone. He was one of the older novices, a broad lad with sunny blond curls. 'Most of us found out we were Sleepless when we were little. How old are you? Fourteen? Fifteen?'

Reah frowned at him. 'Fourteen.'

Chessun shrugged. 'There you are then. You were too used to having a normal life. Didn't know you had a *monster* creeping around inside you. Now you're wondering why you can't just wander into town and buy a loaf of bread, or sleep in a room that doesn't lock from the outside. It's a rude wotsit. Awakening.'

'It will get better,' said Artair. He remembered being brought to the monastery five years ago, and the sense of dislocation that came with it. 'You'll get used to the place. The monks keep us busy. And we can go where we want in the gardens.'

'At home, our farm was twenty acres,' said Reah sulkily. 'I could catch a cart to Addersport if I wanted to. I used to go and look at the markets. I'd save up my money to go.'

'At least you don't need money here,' said Artair.

'I didn't even do anything bad, not really,' Reah continued obliviously. 'Nothing permanent, anyway. I can't believe my *parents* would do this.' Her voice wobbled and she looked away from the rest of them, keen to hide the expression on her face. 'That they'd just leave me in this place. In a prison.'

'You didn't do it,' said Artair.

'What?' Reah looked at him. Her eyes were too bright, only moments away from spilling tears.

'Whatever it was that happened, it wasn't *you*.' Artair gave her a smile. Reah was only three years younger than him, but in that moment she looked painfully young. 'The evil spirit inside you, the thing that comes out when you give into sleep. *That's* what did those things, not you. We can't control the spirit that waits inside us, but we do what we can to limit the damage it causes. By living here, in the Golden Tower, away from the world.' He thought of the view from the monastery windows, that open sea that could lead to anywhere, and he felt a dull ache in his chest. But close on the heels of that thought was the memory of what had happened when the Other had first shown itself. *Smoke and blood and ruin.* 'It's safer for everyone this way.'

'I know it wasn't me,' said Reah, although she didn't sound certain. It was, Artair knew, one of the hardest lessons of the Golden Tower – that the Other was something separate, something evil, even though it lurked under your own skin. Even now, after five years in the monastery, Artair still carried the queasy guilt of what the Other had done.

Chessun chuckled. 'You sound just like Brother Benzin, Artair. Come on, the sun is still out and I'm sticky with apple juice.' He stood up in the freezing stream and waded out deeper into the water, soaking the bottoms of his rolled-up trousers. All of the novices wore soft white trousers and yellow shirts, with a mustard-coloured half robe over the top. This last he pulled up over his head to make a rough hood. Artair laughed.

'Thank you,' Reah said quietly. 'This place is just so . . . far away from everything.'

'It'll feel like home eventually,' Artair said, wondering if he even knew what home meant any more. 'Come on, before they find other work for us to do.'

The afternoon was passing pleasantly enough until Chessun decided that he wanted to climb to where the waterfall started, which meant shimmying up a number of slippery, moss-covered rocks. Artair had begun wading out towards him, trying to talk him out of it, when the big novice slipped, falling back into the spring with a sizeable splash. Some of the other novices gave out cries of alarm, and a few of the more skittish ones ran back across the gardens to fetch the monks. Artair, strong and lean after years of martial training and exercise, dragged his friend out of the water and onto the grassy bank. Chessun had grazed his temple on a rock and blood was running freely from the wound, turning his yellow robe scarlet at the shoulder.

'Twelve save us. Chessun, you idiot.' Artair gave his friend a little shake, but the boy's eyes rolled back into his head. Dread seized Artair. 'No, don't – don't do that . . .'

Reah appeared next to him, her face so pale that the freckles stood out like spots of ink.

'Is he alright?'

'I don't know. I think he's passed out, and if he has . . . Reah, get back into the monastery, I'm not sure that—'

Chessun's eyes snapped back into focus. For a split second, they looked to be a shade paler than they had been moments before, and the broad, kindly shape of his face was transformed into an expression of fury. In that instant, the Chessun that Artair had known for years vanished. He was leaning over a complete stranger.

'Chessun, wait—'

Artair scrambled backwards, his bare feet sliding on the wet grass, but Chessun moved faster. He reached out with his big brawny hands and grasped Artair by the throat.

*'That's not my name.'*

Artair gasped for air. He was a few inches taller, and even with Chessun's greater bulk he normally would have had no difficulty in throwing his friend off, but Chessun's strength was coming from a different, darker place. The Other had taken over the moment the novice had lost consciousness.

'I am outside!' The being inhabiting Chessun looked around at the spring and the gardens in apparent wonder. *'Finally.* I can get out of this stinking, pish-ridden hole.'

With a grunt, he stood up and threw Artair back into the freezing water. When Artair had scrambled back onto his feet, soaking wet, he saw that Chessun was heading for the Red Gate. The other novices had fled and a number of Brothers and Sisters had appeared from the buildings, moving swiftly towards the rogue Sleepless. Artair heard them calling his friend, telling him to wake up, to come back to them, but he knew it wasn't going to work. The spirits were at their strongest when they had just taken control – it normally took an entire night's worth of sleep for the novice to be close enough to the surface to return.

Even so, he called his friend's name, a rising flutter of panic in his chest.

'Chessun! Come back!'

The Red Gate was one of the oldest structures in the monastery, dating from before the Order of the Perpetual Morning had moved in. It was made of iron, the scarlet coating of paint that gave it its name now mostly flaked off, and it had a row of wicked points running along the top. It would be locked – the gates of the Golden Tower almost always were – and it stood a good ten feet in height. That wouldn't discourage an evil spirit intent on escape, though.

Artair began to run.

'Chessun!'

On either side of the Red Gate were two small towers. Artair glanced at them as he ran and what he saw made his stomach turn over. There were monks at the battlements, already notching arrows to their longbows.

No one could be allowed to escape the compound.

'Chessun, stop!'

The rogue novice had reached the bottom of the Red Gate and was running his hands over the pitted surface, looking for handholds. One of the monks, Brother Elthem, had reached Chessun and tried to pull him away, but as Artair watched, his friend struck the monk in the face with one big fist, instantly breaking the man's nose and sending him to his knees before returning his attention to the gate. The other monks were looking at each other, grim expressions on their faces.

'They'll shoot you, Chessun!'

The rogue novice spared him a glance over his shoulder.

'Go back to your cell, you little fool, or I'll break your face too.'

Artair didn't have a clear plan in his head, only a vague idea that if he were next to Chessun, blocking the archer's line of sight, they might not fire on them both. Still running at full pelt, he crashed into his friend and threw them both against the Red Gate, which made a deep, discordant clang and shed a flurry of paint flakes and rust.

'Get away from there!' Artair recognized Sister Rosea's harsh voice. 'Artair, come away this instant, there's nothing you can do.'

Face to face now, Artair grabbed his friend by the shoulders.

'Chessun, wake up! Come back!'

The thing that was inhabiting Chessun grinned slowly. Blood from the graze on his forehead had smeared across his face so that he looked fresh from some terrible battlefield.

'There's no Chessun here,' he said. 'I've consumed him. And now I'm going out there, and the first person I meet I'll tear into pieces.' He raised his voice, shouting hoarsely. 'Do you hear that, you bastard monks? *All this blood will be on your hands—*'

Artair shook him, his arms aching with the effort of it. 'They'll kill you, you idiot!'

The creature inside of Chessun met his eyes, and something passed through them that shocked Artair. Was that sadness? Resignation?

'Better that than a slow death looking at the same four walls for the rest of your pointless life.' Artair thought of how he had woken up that morning, his eyes on the single tiny window of his cell. 'The one inside you, *he* knows.'

Artair opened his mouth to reply, not sure what he was going to say, when Chessun jerked violently in his arms. A long wooden shaft had sprouted from the young man's neck, the fletching feathers pointing up to the blue sky.

'No . . .'

The rogue novice sank to the ground. Around them the monks drew closer, talking in low voices, although Artair couldn't hear what any of them were saying. His eyes were locked with Chessun's, who looked like he was trying to speak.

'What is it?' asked Artair. He thought that the young man's eyes had changed again, becoming more familiar. 'Are you there, Chessun?'

His friend opened his mouth and said nothing. The blood that had been pumping from his neck slowed to a trickle as his heart stopped.

That night, when Brother Benzin led him back to his cell, Artair paused in the doorway. The evening had been an especially solemn affair. Before the Sleepless had eaten dinner together, the monks had buried Chessun's body in the far north of the garden, in the place reserved for their charges.

'They could have hit me.'

Benzin carried on trying to find the correct key, fussing with his belt.

'What's that, dear boy?'

'The arrow.' Artair waited for the monk to look up at him. 'It was very close. They could have killed us both.'

'Nonsense.' Brother Benzin shook his head. 'They spend hours training with those bows. Months. You were never in any real danger, Artair.'

★

Later, when the moon had risen high over the sea and Artair had slipped from the waking world, another presence filled his body and opened his eyes. The being that was not Artair rose from the bed, fetched the chair from its place by the table and set it down in front of the window, where he sat, his eyes trained on the tiny patch of starry sky. It was his habit to look at the sky at night, to imagine what distant lands the starlight fell on. The Twelve knew there was very little else to do in this gods-forsaken cell.

The anger began, as it always did, as a hard knot inside his chest, a feeling of constriction that pulsed and grew, fed by the panic of containment. These four walls, this prison – it was all *wrong*.

His hands, where they lay on his lap, curled into fists.

He knew three things for certain. That his name was Lucian. That the face he saw when he looked into the tiny, scratched mirror was not his own. And that something had been done to him, some monstrous injustice, and when he finally got out of this prison, he was going to tear his captors to pieces, he was going to burn the world down, he would force the gods themselves to do his bidding, he . . .

Lucian found that he was standing, rage trickling through his body like sour wine. There was very little he could do in this cramped cell to express his anger – smashing the cups or tearing the bedding became boring after a while – and if he injured this body, he would only have to suffer the pain himself. But perhaps, tonight, the mirror. It wouldn't be easy to break with his bare hands, but it might be worth it. For one night at least, he wouldn't have to look at the face of a stranger. He crossed the room in a few steps, desperate to break a precious thing, anything to alleviate the fury, when the sense of something new flooded the room. A flush of warmth, as though he'd moved into a patch of sunlight; a sharp, familiar scent that made his heart beat faster. The empty landscape of his memory seemed to shimmer and quake. He knew this sensation. He had felt it before, once, another lifetime ago.

And it was dangerous.

His fury banked down to embers, Lucian sat back down on the chair, a rare grin on his face.

*Something is coming,* he thought. *And I will use it.*

# CHAPTER 4

Late the next afternoon, when the sun was painting the mountain red, Brother Benzin walked into the meditation chamber to find a woman washing blood from her arms in the sacred font.

One of his tasks, at the end of each day, was to clear away the straw mats and clean the clay pots in which they burned incense. It was a job he usually found relaxing. The scent of spiced rose oil clung to the room, and it was blessedly quiet, the view from the windows looking out over the interior gardens. But at the sight of the woman, he felt a small measure of panic. If they were due a visitor from outside, he had completely forgotten about it, and the dawn abbot had already retired to his room for the day. Immediately, Benzin was thinking of where he might put the woman until he could rouse the abbot. The day room, where they normally saw outsiders, was currently being used by Sister Rosea to sort through old robes. His eyes just skipped over the blood, not quite taking it in.

'Oh my goodness, forgive me, I had lost track of time.' He bustled over to her, giving her his sunniest smile. He didn't recognize her as a relative of any of their current novices, and she was dressed most unusually for a pilgrim: a lush scarlet gown of silk and velvet, embroidered with leaping cats. On her feet she wore golden slippers. He wondered how she had made it up the mountain path in such garments. 'Were you here to see the abbot, my dear?' Benzin glanced at the white marble font, the water in it stained pink, and then at the woman's hands, now dripping wet. Her nails were red. Disquiet bloomed just behind his breastbone. He shifted his weight so that he would be able to move quickly if he needed to. If she made a move for the door, he would stop her. 'Did you come through the Red Gate?'

The woman was watching him with sharp, yellow-green eyes.

'Yes,' she said after a moment, 'you'll do.' From a pocket in the skirts of her gown she produced a dagger with a curved blade, the golden hilt studded with rubies. 'Lord, taste this death on your noble tongue so that I may bring your loyal acolytes to this distant place.'

Benzin moved instantly, calling on a lifetime's worth of training without a thought, but even as his foot flew through the small space between them, his heel aimed squarely at the hilt of the dagger, the woman blazed with sudden ruby light. His foot stopped some three inches from its target, curtailed by an invisible barrier. In that brief moment, Benzin saw a kind of shield around the intruder, a construction almost like stained glass leaded with red fire, and then it was gone. He almost fell, his balance thrown off by the unexpected collision, but he managed to keep on his feet.

The woman stepped forward briskly and thrust the blade into his guts, twisting it in a sharp movement that seemed designed to undo something inside him, and indeed he sank to the floor as though he were a puppet with severed strings. Benzin clutched at his stomach, amazed at the heat of his own blood.

'... No ...'

Even through his pain and confusion, he caught the scent of something terrible and wild in the room. Benzin lived with danger every day – it was his calling, to watch over the troubled souls of the Golden Tower. But the presence in the meditation chamber felt beyond anything he had encountered from a Sleepless man or woman. Whatever it was, this was a thing of wild appetite; a thing that could consume for ever and never be satisfied. And what it ate would be alive and screaming.

'It's done,' the woman said. She wiped the blade on her exquisite gown, staining the golden threads red. 'The monks of the Perpetual Morning are rare enough to please Him, I should think.'

From where he lay on the stone floor, Benzin saw the space around the woman waver and shimmer, like the air over a heated brazier. There were shadows within the shimmer, figures that appeared to grow more solid even as Benzin's vision grew dim. There was a rustle of fine fabrics as the woman stepped over his body.

'Quickly. We have a lot of work to do.'

Artair was out at the northern edge of the gardens, in the small place where the Sleepless buried their dead. Chessun's grave was marked by a piece of grey slate, his name and the date he arrived at the monastery scratched into it with a careful hand. Someone, probably Reah, had placed a handful of yellow daisies on the raw earth.

He had known Sleepless who had died before – mainly through escape attempts – but it seemed impossible that cheerful, practical Chessun was gone. Artair kept thinking of his friend's eyes, how they had grown briefly paler when the spirit had taken him over, and the sharp look of fury that had narrowed them. Chessun had never once been so angry, in all the years they had known each other. It was a painful reminder of how unknowable the spirits were, and how dangerous. One slip-up was all it took.

Artair reached down and touched his fingers to the cold slate.

'Sleep well, Chessun.'

It was when he heard the birds singing that he realized just how unusually quiet it was. The monastery was never a loud place, but it had its own subtle sounds that were the background tapestry of Artair's waking hours: the ringing of the bells calling them in to eat, or meditate, or be locked away in their cells; the laughter of his fellow novices, the sound of them chanting or singing; the bellowing of the abbot when he had found something not to his liking. But there was none of that. Only the high lonely call of a mountain buzzard somewhere far overhead, and closer, the chatter of the little black-capped sparrows that haunted their garden. The bells for sundown, he realized abruptly, should have rung a good half an hour ago. He was already deep in shadow.

Artair stood up straight and looked back at the buildings. He could see no one in the towers by the Red Gate, and no one else in the gardens or dawdling across the grass. There was a single light burning from a window on the ground floor. He had the sudden feeling that he was alone in the Golden Tower of the Perpetual Morning – but that was unthinkable.

Filled with a growing sense of disquiet, he began to walk across the gardens. Eventually, he began to run.

In the entrance hall, Artair stepped carefully over a bowl of porridge on the floor, the clay shattered and the porridge smeared across the tiles by a booted foot. Nearby, a chair had been overturned, but he found no monks and no Sleepless. When he came to the room with the single burning lamp, he opened the door, half expecting to be chastized for being out in the gardens after dark, and instead found himself rooted to the spot.

'Ah, here he is. I was starting to wonder where you'd got to. You can't go far in this place.'

The woman who spoke was statuesque, a shock of white running through her untidy auburn hair. She was in her fifties perhaps, and she stood tall and straight, one hand on the shoulder of Reah, who looked tiny and somehow drained next to her. In the room were a number of other people, none of whom Artair recognized. They wore black and red clothes, with silk masks over the lower halves of their faces, and many of them had knives in their hands. There was a long, wide smear of blood on the floor, and there, at the end of it, a crumpled shape. A body. Artair could see a hand lying against the flagstones, blood dotted across the palm, and he was almost sure it was Sister Rosea's. Hadn't those hands wielded the scissors when his hair got too long? Hadn't they passed him bowls of food, or mended the holes in his robes?

Artair swallowed hard, a knot of fear and sorrow in his throat. Nothing he was looking at made sense.

'Who are you?'

The question seemed to amuse her.

'I am Mother Maura of the Bloody Claw, child.'

'A mage?' Artair had heard of mages, of course, but he'd never seen one. He tried to remember what he knew of the Bloody Claw, one of the twelve patron gods, and a series of worrying images leapt into his mind: blood, lethally sharp teeth, a lion. He shook his head. 'I don't . . . Where are the Brothers and Sisters? The novices?' His eyes skittered back to the body he was fairly sure was Sister Rosea. 'What have you done to them?'

'They're gone,' said Reah. Her voice wavered. 'They're all gone.'

'What?'

'This one is being overly dramatic.' The woman calling herself Mother Maura shook Reah by the shoulder, as though they were great friends enjoying a joke. 'Your fellow novices are perfectly safe, Artair, they're just not in the Golden Tower of Perpetual Morning any more. Let's be honest, it's probably an exciting little treat for them.'

'You've taken them somewhere beyond the Red Gate?' A new layer of dread settled over the panic churning in his stomach. 'That can't be. They're— We're Sleepless. We can't be out in the world, it's too dangerous.'

Maura chuckled warmly. 'Oh Artair, you know very little about danger. Listen to me. Your fellow novices are not here. They are not anywhere on the mountain. They are in my sanctuary, Prideful Leap, which lies some distance to the north of Addersport. If you want to see them again – and I can have them back here in an instant – you will need to do a little job for me.'

'She killed the others,' Reah said flatly, as though Maura hadn't spoken. 'The abbot and Brother Elthem and Brother Benzin. All of them.'

Artair looked at the crumpled body on the floor. He found that he couldn't speak.

'It's powerful magic, to move so many people so far, and the Bloody Claw demands his price.' Maura smiled. 'Are you listening to me, Artair? Because it looks as though you are not, and let me be clear, the lives of your little novice friends depend on you paying attention. They are safe in my sanctuary at the moment, being cared for by my acolytes. But that could all change.'

With some difficulty, Artair lifted his gaze and looked Mother Maura in the eye.

'What do I need to do?'

'*There* you are. That's good.' Maura tightened her grip on Reah, gave her another little shake and let her go. A portal ringed in red light opened up behind the girl. Through it, Artair could see another place entirely, a cavernous chamber of stone lit with guttering torches. A shifting pattern of light on the ceiling suggested there was a pool of water somewhere out of sight. There were stone steps in the background stained with something dark and clustered in front of it were the other novices. They looked lost and terrified, and just as Artair was thinking to run to them, Reah gave a small shriek as she was drawn back through the portal by an invisible force. Artair saw the look of pain and shock that passed over the novice's face and then in a blink she and the portal were gone. The hot stink of wild animal filled the room. 'She's at my sanctuary now too. I wanted you to see that, Artair, as I think it's only fair you know what you're dealing with. That you know the extent of my power.'

'I do. I understand.' He took a deep breath. 'Please, tell me what I have to do.'

'So pliant. So agreeable. How things have changed.' Maura grinned. 'What I need you to do, Artair, is go to the Jih Forest, which is conveniently located just below this mountain. I want you to go into that place and retrieve something for me.'

'I can't leave the monastery,' said Artair, the words escaping his mouth before he even knew he was going to say them. 'I am Sleepless.'

'Do I need to show you the blood on these knives?' Maura said sharply. 'Do you need me to cut a few more throats today?'

'No,' Artair said hurriedly. 'No, I don't.'

'Good. You will go to the Jih Forest and retrieve for me a keltraxia cub. Alive. That part is very important – a dead thing is of no use to me or my lord. Retrieve the cub and then bring it to me at Prideful Leap.' Maura nodded to one of her acolytes, and they came forward with a tightly rolled piece of parchment, which they passed to Artair. 'That,' continued Maura, 'is a map to my sanctuary and a description of the keltraxia – I don't know what they teach you here, but I doubt it's the true names of monsters – and another map that will show you the locations of several known keltraxia nests. I could go and fetch the cub myself, but, firstly, I do not want to, and secondly, the Queen of Serpents makes her home there, among her monstrous children, and it is well known that she does not tolerate mages, especially those dedicated to my lord. So I need a good little monk to go and collect the creature for me. I assume my instructions are clear, Sleepless?'

'Why do you need a monster cub?'

Mother Maura nodded thoughtfully, as though she had only just considered the question herself. 'You know, Artair, I have plenty of your little novice friends, and it matters very little to me how many of them actually see this place again. How about we say, for every question you ask I will give one of them to the Bloody Claw? How does that strike you?'

Artair held himself very still.

'I thought that might clear things up for you. Good. You will bring the cub to me before the next full moon, which is twenty days away. Arrive after the full moon and you'll find a lot of dead friends. Do you understand what you have to do?'

Through the open window, Artair heard the call of a snow eagle, high and clear and lonely, and it seemed incredible to him. How was the world outside continuing to exist when his whole world had been torn apart?

'I do,' he said through numb lips. 'I understand.'

Mother Maura nodded once, satisfied. She looked for a moment as though she were going to say something else, then shook her head slightly, apparently thinking better of it. She reached into a pocket in her gown and removed a small glass globe filled with a shifting lilac light. She threw it onto the floor where it shattered, and when she raised her hand, a ruby-red fire flowed over her and her acolytes, covering them in a bloody heatless blaze. There was a deep rumbling noise that made the hair on the back of Artair's neck stand on end and then the mage and the acolytes vanished, leaving him standing alone in the room.

# CHAPTER 5

Elver opened her eyes onto a thick blanket of near-dark. The greyish light that filtered through the small window of her hut told her that it wasn't quite dawn, yet something – some noise or movement – had woken her up. She lay for a moment in her kartesh-fur blankets, the familiar shapes of her belongings crowded around her in the cramped space: the collection of chipped cups and bowls, the chair she had made from a wooden crate that had been left on the road, the sword she had taken off the traveller.

Had it been a noise that had woken her up? Or something more subtle?

She lifted her head, and there it was: a golden, flickering light that moved across her window, painting the back of the hut in glitter, before vanishing again.

She knew what that was.

Outside the hut, the night sky was fat with stars even as the horizon to the east pinked at the edges. The lake was as still as a mirror, although there were no stars reflected in it: instead, the flat surface was as black as ink, a darkness that looked like a hole in the world, and within it, a long golden shape twisted and curled in on itself.

'I'm here,' said Elver.

The Queen of Serpents glided through the water towards the girl, her long narrow head breaking the surface of the water without causing a single ripple. She turned her head and opened her jaws. Row upon row of serrated golden fangs glittered wetly.

*Child.*

Elver waited. It wasn't that unusual for the Queen of Serpents to visit her, but a visit before the sun had risen suggested some new flavour of urgency.

*There is a trespasser in the forest, child.*

'The traveller?' Elver cursed herself silently. She shouldn't have trusted the slowjorn to take the woman to the road. She should have taken her herself, regardless of how uncomfortable she found human company. Or, better yet, she should have just killed her and left her carcass for her jih friends. 'I'm sorry, I thought I'd dealt with her. I can find her again, and this time I'll make sure she's gone.'

*No,* said the Queen of Serpents. *This is a new face, and he has thievery in his heart and a bow on his back. Blood will be spilled in the dawn light, child.*

'If that's what you want.' Elver thought of her knife, and then the sword.

The great golden serpent rose up further out of the lake. Her head was adorned with whiskers and horns as fine as glass, glowing with their own inner light.

*I made you and I brought you here to be the guardian of my forest, poison child,* she said. *If something is taken from here, I expect you to retrieve it. Do you understand?*

'I . . . Yeah. I understand.' Although she didn't, not really. 'Do you mean if something is taken out of the Jih Forest I have to . . . leave? And go after it?'

*When you fell into my domain, and I pierced your flesh with my teeth, I tasted a little of your destiny, child. And it has finally arrived for you.*

'My destiny? What are you talking about?' Elver took a step forward. The sun had crested over the eastern portion of the forest, turning the tops of the trees silver and orange. 'I can't leave the forest. This is my home.'

*If this thief steals from the forest, you will retrieve what was stolen. And bring it back before the next egg moon. That is your task, poison child.*

'You're a *god*.' Elver wouldn't normally be so blunt with the Queen of Serpents, but the thought of leaving the Jih Forest, of venturing into human territory, was pushing her feelings to the surface. 'Why do you need me to do this?'

The glistening coils of the god's body tensed and swirled under the black water. She was becoming irate.

*You expect me to scurry after a human like a beggar? To drag myself landwards on some errand?*

'Fine.' Elver pushed a hand through her white hair, making it stand up on end, then shrugged. 'That's fine. I'll find this intruder before he leaves, and I'll make sure he's in no fit state to steal from us again. I'll just get to him before he's gone and then I won't have to leave the forest. Where is he heading? Do you know?'

The Queen of Serpents didn't answer immediately. In the lake, the long coils of her body turned and slid through the water silently, and Elver imagined her reaching out across the forest, touching each body of water with her mind as she searched.

*He is heading towards the keltraxia nests in the south,* she said eventually. *The thief is close to taking what he wants, Elver.*

'Then I'll go now.' Elver turned her back on the serpent, already calculating how long it would take her to reach the nests – too long, she thought, and that wasn't good. 'I'll stop him.' The face of the traveller rose in her mind. 'Permanently,' she added.

*One more thing, child.* Elver glanced over her shoulder to see the Queen of Serpents watching her closely. *Beware of the Faceless One. His priests will not tolerate our kind, out in the wider world.*

Beyond the Red Gate, the night was utterly still. Artair paused for a moment, breathing in the cold air. He hadn't stood on these stones in five years, not since they had brought him to the Golden Tower, and that had been a bright day, full of cheery sunshine that had made the misery in his heart all the worse. In front of him now was the whole world, with no gates holding him back. He thought he'd never been more frightened in his life, not even when Chessun's throat had been opened by an arrow while he held his friend's shoulders.

He took a few steps down the mountain path, pausing to adjust the unfamiliar weight of the longbow on his back. Before leaving the Golden Tower, he had crept into the places that had previously been forbidden to him: the armoury, the rooms of the monks charged with watching the Sleepless, the abbot's quarters. From the latter, he had taken all the coin he could find, loading the money into a sturdy-looking pack he'd found in Brother Benzin's closet. He had no idea what he would find on the road to Prideful Leap, but he knew he would need coin to survive. He'd taken some food from the stores too, although it had made him wary. It was said that the monsters of the Jih Forest could smell such things from leagues away and would hunt you down for it.

The path that wound down the mountain was well maintained by the Brothers and Sisters, and despite the darkness of the night the stones under his feet seemed to drink up what little starlight there was, making it easy enough to follow. Eventually, the tops of the trees came up to meet him and the path curled away towards the north, towards Addersport, and the dark maw of the forest awaited him to the south. A single step into the darkness was all it would take and he would be in the realm of the monsters. Unhelpfully, he remembered the scent of wild beast that had accompanied Mother Maura's magic, a scent that summoned thoughts of teeth and claws.

*Here and now, in this moment, I am safe, I am alive,* he told himself. *The Other that lurks within me is contained.*

He retrieved the small travel lamp from his pack – another item scavenged from Brother Benzin's rooms – and lit it. Part of him insisted that carrying a light was a fast way to get found and eaten by a monster, but the thought of blundering around in the dark, groping like a blind man towards a broken ankle or a snapped neck, caused a rising panic that even his mantra couldn't banish. No, he would have to walk in the light, at least until the sun rose.

'Here and now, in this moment, I am safe.'

Artair stepped off the path and into the Jih Forest. The trees rose up all around him, ancient and tall, the light of the oil lamp seeping into the deep creases of their bark, falling softly on the bulbous shapes of fungus that clustered on trunks and under branches. There was a rich green scent that almost made him feel dizzy, and he had the sudden thought that the ground underneath him was dense with life – this was a living place, a world that existed and thrived without the need of human presence or thought. *There could be dozens of eyes watching me right now*, he thought, *and I would have no idea.*

Still, there was a map to follow, and a job to do. He pulled the piece of parchment Maura had given him from his pack and held it up to the lamp. In his previous life, he had been good at reading and understanding maps – all of his people had been. Moving around the landscape had been an integral part of their lives, until . . .

Artair squeezed his eyes shut.

*Here and now, in this moment, I am safe. The Other is contained.*

And that was a small mercy, he thought, as he put the map away and headed deeper into the Jih Forest. It was late, and he was already exhausted, yet sleep felt a thousand leagues away.

# CHAPTER 6

Artair paused, his heart hammering in his chest. He had been walking through the Jih Forest all night, surrounded by sounds and movements he couldn't identify, convinced that at any moment one of the nameless creatures that lurked in the trees would snatch him up and disembowel him. It wasn't making for an especially relaxing stroll in the woods.

He was at the edge of a creek – the same creek on his map that led to a wider body of water, he hoped – and he crouched by it, letting his fingertips brush the ground. He closed his eyes and recalled Brother Benzin's voice as he led the Sleepless through the morning and evening meditations. *In this moment, in this place, you are safe.* It was hard to believe himself safe when he could hear something that had to be the size of a house grunting and snuffling in the copse of trees behind him, but the words calmed him, his own deliberately measured breathing slowing his racing heart and bringing him back to a place of focus.

'I have a task,' he murmured to himself. 'I will do what is asked of me, and I will bring the novices home. And then we can all forget this nightmare ever happened.'

An image of Sister Rosea's body lying on the monastery floor flashed across his mind – some things could not be undone, after all – and he pushed it away. *Focus.*

Artair stood. One of the benefits of the training of the Perpetual Morning was an ability to tap into this focus – it allowed him to step away from fear and pain, even if it was only temporary. He touched his fingers to the bow slung across his back, drawing strength from its solidity, and began to walk along the side of the creek. Dawn was coming, touching rosy fingers to the edge of every leaf, every twig and wrinkle of bark, every bloom and bud. And as the light returned, and he walked, he found that his fear was receding of its own accord, to be replaced by something else: wonder.

*I am out in the world*, he thought to himself. *Yesterday morning, I couldn't have pictured this future for myself. And now here I am. I have never seen this creek before. Or this tree. I have never stepped on this piece of ground before. Everything is new.*

A surge of something like joy clouded his chest, and he reached for the focus again to clear it away. There was no time. He'd have to work fast if he wanted to save his friends.

The creek grew rockier, and wider, until it spread out before him in a small lake – small, but much larger than the tiny pool that curled around the back of the monastery gardens. In the centre of it, on a reed-pocked island, there was a keltraxia nest; according to the map the red-haired mage had given him, at least. There was movement in the reeds, a flash of vibrant orange and red among the muddy greens, and after a moment he saw an animal around twice the size of a large wolf come to the edge of the lake to drink.

*Not an animal*, he reminded himself. *A monster. These creatures belong to the Queen of Serpents. They are touched with magic.*

But it was a beautiful thing, all the same. Blue scales glittered like sapphires in the dawn light, its long scarlet and orange feathers like splashes of paint. This was a fully grown keltraxia, the parent of the cubs that must be hidden beyond the reeds, and it hadn't spotted him. Artair held his breath and waited, wondering if he should circle around the island and cross the water in a different place, but the vixen abruptly lifted her head, scenting something on the wind, and slid into the water as swiftly and smoothly as a swan. She swam, to

Artair's relief, not towards him, but directly to his left. Once she was across the lake, she leapt up in a brief shower of water droplets and was gone, lost to his sight in the wider wood. She must, he thought, be going to hunt, or pursue some other monster business.

The sensible thing would be to wait. There might be another parent animal on the island, watching over the cubs, or the vixen herself could return abruptly. Better, probably, to stay here until he was sure she was gone.

But he thought of Reah's face, how it had been contorted with fear. If he wanted to get to Prideful Leap in time to save the novices, he had to act now.

*Other jih live in this forest too*, he reminded himself. *Anything could blunder along and decide I'd make a decent breakfast. I have to be quick.*

Without waiting to lose his nerve, Artair slipped the bow from his shoulder and, holding it over his head, waded out into the lake. Cold green water rushed into his boots, soaking his trousers and chilling him to the bone. Silty mud, kicked up by his passage, swirled up all around him, turning the water opaque. When he climbed up the bank on the other side, he held the bow ready, an arrow nocked and his shoulders tense. Fear lapped at the back of his throat again, so he paused to refocus. *The Other is far from me. Here and now, I am safe.*

Just ahead he could see a place where the reeds parted and what had to be the nest, built from sticks and dried mud, caught in a ring of pawprints. There were sounds too, little yipping barks and the odd snuffling noise. He wondered for the first time how big the keltraxia cubs were – he'd brought a sack from the kitchens, but he'd never seen such creatures before and had no idea whether they'd struggle and bite. Belatedly he wished he'd brought a pair of Brother Benzin's leather gardening gloves.

There was no time to worry about such things. Eager to get it over with, he strode across to the nest and peered over the muddy wall. Inside there were three cubs, each no bigger than a large house cat, much to his relief. They were mainly feathers, ears and gangly legs at this stage, and each of them looked up at him with large green eyes; not at all afraid, but curious. One of them opened its mouth and yawned, exposing a bright pink tongue and two rows of sharp white teeth.

'Hey. You're not so bad.' Artair lowered his bow. 'Just don't bite me, okay? I don't mean you any harm, I promise.'

The blood-curdling howl that rose from behind him turned his neck to ice.

Artair swung, the bow raised, to see the keltraxia vixen at the edge of the reeds. Her eyes were glowing brighter than the moon and she was crouched, shoulder muscles bunched up ready to spring, teeth bared. Fury and fear radiated off her, and instinctively Artair took aim and loosed the arrow.

It struck her in the shoulder and knocked her neatly back into the water with a yelp.

For a second, Artair was frozen in place, a sick sensation flooding through his chest and stomach. He'd never willingly injured anything in his life. The keltraxia vixen was lying motionless in the water.

'Twelve damn me.' Familiar memories threatened to surface again: waking up in a ditch, the scent of roasted flesh all around, smoke coating the back of his throat. No, he'd never *willingly* hurt anything living . . .

Artair ran over to the creature. She looked stunned. Her eyes had rolled back into her head, which was partially under the water, and blood, red as the gown of Mother Maura, was swirling away into the lake. He grabbed her front legs and heaved her back onto the mud so that her head was out of the water, before examining the arrow. It had partly passed through a meaty section of her shoulder, leaving the arrowhead and stem streaked with gore, and the fletch feathers – which were yellow – untouched. He took the knife from his belt and cut the end free, letting it drop into the mud.

'Be still for me now,' he murmured. 'I promise I'm trying to help.'

Bracing one hand on her shoulder, he slowly pulled the rest of the arrow out, wincing as it came free and fresh blood spurted over his arm and onto the mud. He shrugged his shirt off, all the while watching the vixen closely to see if she were about to regain consciousness and savage him, then tore off one of the arms. Fingers covered in blood, he ripped the fabric into strips and made quick work of a bandage. He was used to tending the wounds of other Sleepless, and he assumed the principles were the same: slow the bleeding, keep it clean. When it was done, he stepped away and realized he was sweating, despite the chill of the morning.

'That will have to do.' That feeling of sorrow threatened to swallow him again, so he repeated his words – *the Other is not with me, in this moment I am safe* – and turned back to the nest. The cubs were making more noise than they had been, perhaps sensing that their mother had been harmed in some way. When Artair leaned over the nest wall, they were clustered there, looking up at him.

'I'm sorry,' he said again and, leaning down, plucked the one in the middle from its siblings and put it in the sack he'd brought with him. He tied it up carefully, experimenting with ways of carrying it that wouldn't discomfort the creature too much. Already, he realized, the morning was marching on, with the sun inching towards the centre of the sky, and very soon he would have to face the next problem – how he was going to keep the Other from harming anyone now they were both free in the world. He needed a room with a lockable door, a place with no windows. He needed a prison.

The monastery and his small, bare cell were far behind him, halfway up a mountain and in the wrong direction. Addersport was the closest city, but he had no real idea how long it would take to get there on foot, and exhaustion was already weighing on him heavily.

'Time is against me, either way.' He glanced back at the keltraxia vixen again, who had raised her head an inch or so off the ground. 'Forgive me.'

Artair set off across the island.

Elver arrived around an hour later, her pale face flushed with a rare splash of pink across the tops of her cheeks. She had heard the vixen's cries some distance away and started running, a growing fury boiling in her throat. She pictured arriving to find the thief in the middle of his crime, grabbing hold of him so that her hands were pressed against his hated human skin, watching him scream and writhe until enough of her poison was in his system that his heart gave out. But when she staggered onto the island, soaking wet and breathing hard, it was to find only a scene of devastation: blood in the dirt and splashed against the reeds, the vixen crouched in her nest, her nose buried in her remaining cubs, who were crying and keening pitifully.

'What did he do?' Elver scrambled into the nest herself, to be immediately beset by the distressed cubs. One of them climbed into her lap, and she gently lifted him back out again. 'Is that a bandage?'

The vixen's shoulder had been bound with yellow cloth, although much of it had been soaked with her blood. She licked at it once, then nosed mournfully at her cubs again.

*The wound is slight*, she said in the voice only other monsters could hear. *The human pulled out his arrow and bound it. But he took my littlest, child of the serpent. And I cannot run to save him.* Her eyes glowed once, then faded, as though she were in too much pain to maintain her anger.

'I will go,' said Elver. 'I will bring him back to you, my friend. I promise on my life.'

She stepped back out of the nest and looked around. There, on the ground near the water, was a broken arrow with yellow fletching feathers, and a trail of human footprints heading north-east.

'How long ago was he here?'

*The shadows say an hour, Elver. Why are humans so cruel?*

'I wish I could tell you.' Elver went back to the nest briefly, placing her hand along the vixen's snout. The scales there felt very smooth and cool against her skin. 'I'll bring you back your child, and the thief's head.'

The thief was easy to track, as most humans were in the Jih Forest. They didn't know its secret paths so they created their own, tearing across the wood like a knife pulled across skin. His footprints were as clear as day, sunk into the rich black mud, and even when they weren't, she saw his presence in the broken twigs, the trampled bush, the silence of the smaller animals who had been run off by his blundering weight. Once or twice she passed a jih creature and asked if they had seen a human pass that way; if they hadn't seen him, they had certainly smelled him. She was swift, moving through the woods like a ghost, not pausing to eat or drink or catch her breath, but it still wasn't enough. He had had too much of a head start.

Elver came to the edge of the road as the sun passed over the highest point in the sky, a flat heat radiating down on the white stones. It was a wide, well-maintained road, that dipped down the hill and bore east towards Addersport. From her vantage point, she could see the highest spires and roofs of the city, and beyond it, the glittering, ever-shifting light of the Queen of Serpents' larger domain, the sea. She could also see, at the very bottom of the hill, so small he was practically ant-sized, her thief. The yellow of his torn shirt was the same yellow as the bandages the vixen had worn. He was heading towards the city.

'Of course he is from that stinking pig hole,' she muttered.

What she had to do was run after him. She had to leave the forest – her forest – and venture back into the human world. There was no choice. He had stolen a cub from its mother, and even if the Queen of Serpents hadn't commanded her, Elver would have been furious enough to chase him to the ends of the world.

And yet . . .

She turned back to look the way she had come, the cool greens of the forest giving way to oranges and reds and yellows. She rested one hand on the bark of a hornbeam, letting her fingers trace the rough patterns, the whorls and ridges as unique as any fingerprint. A few feet away, animals moved through the undergrowth, oblivious to the problems of the wider world, their days filled with simple concerns: eating, hunting, sleeping, warmth. She longed to join them.

This was the place that she loved, the place where she was safe from humans and their betrayals. Out in the world, she was not safe. And the world was not safe from her. The idea of being in Addersport, of all places, made her feel sick to her stomach.

Yet every moment she waited, the thief was getting further and further away.

Elver squeezed her eyes shut, spoke aloud every curse word she could think of, then stepped out onto the road.

# CHAPTER 7

The cub was not easy to carry.

At first, Artair slung the sack over his shoulder and concentrated on keeping his eye on the road – carts and coaches were moving up and down it frequently, often at quite a pace, but the baby monster wriggled so much that it was constantly dislodging the sack. When he held it in his arms, the creature almost seemed to become a heavy liquid, rolling out of his grip and almost tumbling onto the ground. Eventually, Artair took the sack to the edge of the road and opened the neck to peer in. A pair of big green eyes stared back up at him, blinking owlishly. For a second, they appeared to flicker with light. Was that the cub's magic making itself known?

'Listen.' Artair lowered his voice as a coachload of travellers passed behind him. He strongly suspected that talking to sacks would be remarked upon as strange. '*Listen.* I'm sorry about all this, I really am, but I need you to be still. Maybe just . . . go to sleep? Can you do that?' He sighed. 'I have no idea if you can even understand me.'

The cub yawned enormously, then playfully closed his jaws around Artair's hand, little teeth digging into his skin. Artair smiled. Back in his life before the Golden Tower, his people had raised shepherding dogs – tough, clever animals with lean bodies and wiry fur. This creature reminded him of the puppies that were often scampering around the tents, yipping and chasing each other. The thought gave him an idea.

He took off his pack and transferred some of the food he had taken from the kitchens into the sack with the cub. He didn't know what the cub would eat, so he put a little of everything in there, and as he had hoped, the monster stopped wriggling and set to trying to eat everything at once. Taking advantage of the creature's distraction, Artair closed the sack and put it carefully over his shoulder again. He'd have to buy more food soon, but that seemed a small price to pay for an easier journey.

Around him, the day had moved on. Addersport itself was steadily growing on the horizon, a slow reveal of the place he'd thought about almost every day at the Golden Tower. It was much bigger than he'd imagined, with all manner of buildings crammed in together, intertwined with twinkling lines that had the quality of light on water. There was a constant stream of humanity coming and going from the city, and as he grew closer, there was a distinct rumble of noise too. He initially took it to be the sea, but eventually he realized it was simply the sound of a great many people in one place, living their lives.

The thought was unnerving. Even in his previous life, he'd never been in a place so busy, and now he carried the evil spirit within him, a threat to every single human living in that city. What would the Other do when it realized it was free of the Golden Tower? And who would pay the price? And there was also the issue of the cub. Jih creatures, with their link to the Queen of Serpents and their own unpredictable forms of magic, were considered dangerous enough on their own. Bringing one into the city was a crime that could get him locked away, with no chance of saving the novices.

'Here and now, I am safe,' he murmured aloud. 'The Other is contained and I hold the power to keep it from escaping.'

As if in response, the cub gave a single, fluting snore. Artair smiled a little and headed on down towards the city.

★

Elver pulled her hood up and hunched her shoulders as another cart full of humans rattled past. She felt their eyes on her like tiny knives and a wave of hatred rose up inside her in response. She half wanted one of them to call out, to pass comment on the strange pale girl that walked on the road alone, or for one of them to throw something. It would give her an excuse, a reason to attack. But nothing happened. *They wouldn't be so inattentive if they knew what I was*, she told herself.

One of the coaches that rolled by on her right was brightly coloured, and her eyes were drawn to it: someone with a fair amount of skill had painted a series of red lions leaping along the wooden boards, their manes burning orange and yellow like flames. She remembered dimly from her days growing up in Addersport that people would often decorate carts, houses, clothes, streets, even their faces, with images of the twelve gods. They believed it kept them in their good graces, as though the Hooded Crow would look down on their elaborately painted roof and decide not to visit them with plague. The owner of this coach owed something to the Bloody Claw perhaps, or hoped for something from the god.

*All you can hope for from that one is death, you fool*, she thought. Mother Maura and her acolytes had worn lions on their clothes. For a brief second she wanted to run after the coach and drag the driver from his seat, letting her hands seep their poison into him. *Did you know that your god has children thrown into the sea in his name?* she would ask him. *Did you know that he feeds on human blood?*

Once the coach dedicated to the Bloody Claw had disappeared around a corner in the road, she found she was briefly alone. She took a deep breath, savouring the absence of humans and their stink. It was hard to fathom that she was heading to a place where there would be hundreds and hundreds of humans everywhere she looked. They would press in on all sides, and if she touched any of them, they would scream or faint or possibly even die. The idea was already exhausting.

Ahead of her, a small patch of the road seemed to shift, the white of the stones catching the sun at a different angle. Curious, she headed towards it, only to see one of the stones rise up slightly and a shape peek out, tiny black eyes like beads of ink.

'Hey,' she called out. 'Are you lost?'

These monsters were called froudians, and mostly they kept to themselves. They were tiny creatures, no taller than an apple, with a certain rodentness about their features and clever, flexible hands and feet. Elver had spotted them most often in the undergrowth of the Jih Forest, and occasionally in the boles of old trees. She had the impression that they lived dramatic lives in vast communities just underfoot.

The froudian that had peeked out scampered fully into view, while more of them held the stone up. She could hear their tiny voices piping at each other, but only the one who had crawled out spoke to her directly.

*Certainly not*, said the creature. *Are you, long shanks?*

Elver sighed. She certainly felt lost, but she suspected that wasn't what the froudian meant.

'This is a human road. You're liable to get squashed by a hoof or a wheel. And that's if one of them doesn't spot you and decide you're dangerous.'

*Dangerous? Us?* The froudian seemed to find this amusing. *Humans barely look where they're going, let alone under their feet.*

Elver crouched. It was good to speak to something she understood. She already missed the cover of the forest, that soft green roof overhead. The other froudians had lifted the stone out of the way and were climbing out.

'What are you doing here?'

*Hunting.* The froudian gestured to where the other creatures were scurrying. *Humans drop interesting things on their travels. Food, sometimes.*

The group were scurrying back to the hole in the road, a bread roll carried between them. It had started to turn mouldy on one corner, but Elver doubted that concerned the froudians. Together they wrestled it down the hole and out of sight. There was a rumbling sound growing louder as another cart approached, and the creature that had spoken to her returned to his hunting party as they began to manoeuvre the stone back into place. Elver found she didn't want them to go.

'You should be more careful,' she told them, although she had to admit they seemed quite at ease on the human road. 'If they catch you, they'll kill you.'

*Pft, humans are just big dumb animals,* said the froudian. *And if they give us trouble, we'll bite their knees off.*

The stone settled back into place, and it was as if they had never been there at all. Elver stood up as the cart trundled past. A blunt-faced young man sitting in the back caught her eye and he grinned and pointed her out to the person sitting next to him. There was a smattering of laughter, and he threw something, which hit her on the foot and skidded off to the edge of the road. It was a half-eaten apple.

'Cheer up, love,' he shouted. 'It might never happen!'

Elver watched the cart go, imagining what it would be like to poison every human in the world. Was it possible? Perhaps the Queen of Serpents would be able to do it. An entertaining thought.

She picked up the apple and placed it close to the loose stone, then continued on down the road.

# CHAPTER 8

It was dusk by the time Elver finally caught up with the thief in Addersport. She passed the signs that lined the water gates – announcing to every visitor that jih monsters were strictly forbidden within the city and anyone caught trading or harbouring the creatures would be arrested on sight and taken to the Temple of Trilot the Faceless – and spotted him walking no more than fifty feet away, a sack held in his arms. He seemed oddly dumbstruck by the place, wandering the edges of the waterways with a rapt expression, constantly looking this way and that, as though he'd never seen a marketplace before or a group of musicians plying their trade outside a tavern. He was tall and lean, with dark brown hair that tumbled to the nape of his neck, and he had expressive brown eyes that seemed to be widening in surprise at every mundane sight. Elver watched him from the edges of buildings or the dark spaces in alleys, her hood partially covering her face. There was the question of what to do next. She couldn't attack him in public, with all these stinking humans around – they had rules about that sort of thing, and guards stood on the corner of every street, ready to enforce them. And besides which, she was jih. Her kind were not welcome. If they knew what she was, she'd be imprisoned, or worse.

She guessed that the keltraxia cub was in the sack. Every now and then he would bow his head over it, his lips moving, as though he were talking to it. Threatening it, perhaps?

*What is this fool doing?*

He wandered down street after street until he came to one of the larger taverns. On the upper balconies, men and women in advanced states of refreshment were calling and laughing to each other – a number of them appeared to be only partially dressed. The thief stood outside this place for some time, as though trying to make his mind up about something, until finally he stepped up to the entrance and vanished inside.

*He is selling the cub*, she decided. *This is where he will meet the buyer.*

She couldn't think why a human would want to buy a jih spirit, but then guessing the motives of humans was a pointless activity. Perhaps keeping such a 'dangerous' creature as a pet made them feel important. Humans were pathetic like that.

Elver also paused on the doorstep, her skin crawling. Inside this place, humans would be pressed in close, they would be loud, and she'd be overwhelmingly aware of their stench. Quite aside from her own discomfort, there was also the chance that one of them could brush their filthy skin against hers, and that would be it. There would be screaming, the guards would be called, and she'd be caught. Trapped in this place.

*The cub is more trapped than I am.*

She sighed and stepped over the threshold.

Inside the tavern it was just as she feared. Humans were everywhere, lounging at tables, standing at the fireplace with foaming tankards. At the back of the room, a group of women were playing a card game Elver vaguely recognized from her days at the orphanage; they had played with scrounged pennies and the odd crust of bread. The women laughed uproariously, one of them casually throwing her arm around the shoulders of another as the cards failed to go in her favour. The thief, at least, was easy enough to spot: he stood at the bar, his back very straight, and he was having a conversation with the barman that the old man apparently found quite confusing, judging by the expression on his whiskery face. On the bar itself there was a neat stack of silver coins.

*The* barman *is buying the cub? What use does a tavern have for an illegal monster?*

Elver sidled up to the bar herself, leaning against it in what she imagined was a casual way, her head down so that the hood covered her white hair. She was close enough to hear them speak.

'. . . there's the cellar, I suppose,' the barman was saying. 'I can lock that from the outside, certainly, but there's no bed in it, young man. Are you sure you don't want one of our actual rooms? Like I say, we're busy tonight but there's still one available, and it has the biggest bed. From the looks of you, I reckon you could find someone to share it, if you felt like some company.'

'Thank you, no.' The thief's voice was quiet, and almost earnest. It was not what she had been expecting at all, and something about it intrigued her. She considered the barman's comment. Now that she was this close to the thief, she could see for herself that he was strikingly handsome. There was a tiny slash of a scar through one dark eyebrow. She found herself wondering how he'd acquired it – through some dubious deed, no doubt. 'I need somewhere with no windows, and one door. And I need you to lock it after me. And unlock it again in the morning.'

'Ah well, there *is* a window in the cellar, a small one at ground height, you see, but I can get my son to shut it up for you if you like.'

'Yes, please.' The thief nodded.

Elver frowned. Why would a thief need a locked room?

'You're not planning anything . . . *unnatural* in there, are you?' The barman leaned forward, a steely look in his eye. 'Because I won't tolerate any funny business.'

'No, I'm just a very private person.' The thief reached into a trouser pocket and placed two more pieces of silver on the bar. 'Please.'

The barman eyed the coins and then shrugged. 'No skin off my nose if you want to spend your night in a damp cellar and pay for the privilege. Come on then, let's get you set up in there . . .'

Elver watched the pair of them leave the bar and disappear through a shabby door, which she presumed led to the cellar. She left the tavern, darting around a drunken man who wanted to lean on her for support, and once outside she walked briskly towards the back of the building, looking out for the window the barman had spoken of. She found it quickly; it was wider than it was tall, and it clearly hadn't been cleaned for years. Elver knelt by it and scrubbed at some of the dirt with her sleeve until there was a tiny clear patch that she could see through. The barman and the thief were already in there, still talking away. It was dark, the only light coming from a single oil lamp on a rickety table. There were barrels and crates and a dirt floor. As she watched, the barman put a plate of meat and cheese down on the table, along with a jug of water, and then he left, shutting the door firmly behind him. The thief put the sack down and ran a hand over his chin, deep in thought.

Elver kicked the window open and slid through it, her monstrous nature helping her move eerily fast. In moments, she was in the cellar, running at the thief with her bare hands outstretched. The thief – younger than she'd been expecting, now that she was closer to him – backed away hurriedly, his eyes very wide.

'I'm sorry,' he stammered. 'Is this your . . . cellar?'

Elver growled and leapt at him, wrapping her hands around his neck. To her surprise, several unexpected things happened.

Firstly, he did not fall down onto the dirt floor. Instead, he caught her and stood his ground – it was like leaping onto a tree, solid and immovable, and not sure what else to do, she clung to him.

Secondly, he did not scream with agony. Instead, he looked down at her in a perplexed but vaguely polite way.

'Um . . .'

She pressed her hands to his neck as hard as she could, but the familiar reddening would not come. Desperate, she slid one hand up to his jaw, then down to his breastbone. Nothing. Instead, she could feel her own face turning red.

'What are you doing?' he asked. This close, she could see the dark shadow of stubble on his jaw, and there was a scent, too: soap, and the lingering greenness of the Jih Forest. It was not unpleasant.

'What *are* you?' she snarled. She wriggled out of his grasp and he let her drop to the floor.

'I am just a normal person,' he replied. 'A normal city person staying at a tavern.'

'No you're not,' she said hotly. 'First of all, this is a cellar, and normal people don't sleep in cellars. Second of all, there's a monster in that sack, stolen from my forest.' She pointed at the sack. The keltraxia cub was poking his nose out of the gap at the top of the bag, nostrils flaring at all the new smells. 'You shot his mother with an arrow.'

'Believe me, I had no choice—'

'And my touch is poisonous to humans. You should be in hideous pain – in fact, with the amount of time my hand was on your neck you should be dead. Instead, you're just standing there looking gormless. So. What are you? Because you're not human.'

He looked at her for a long moment, then cleared his throat. 'My name is Artair,' he said eventually. 'And I am one of the Sleepless.'

Elver snorted. 'I don't believe you. Those are just stories.'

'I did not believe there were such things as people who can kill you by touching them, but according to you I am wrong about that.'

Elver took a jerky step backwards. 'You really are one of the Sleepless? When you go to sleep, you become someone else?'

'A dark and terrible spirit inhabits my body,' Artair said solemnly.

'His only thoughts are of escape and chaos. At night, I must be locked up for the safety of—'

'I suppose this would make you jih too then.' This was a problem. If this boy was jih, a monster spirit, then, technically, he too was one of the Queen of Serpents' children. Elver couldn't kill him. Or at least she'd have to get permission. She went to the sack and pulled it open, allowing the keltraxia cub to tumble out. He made a keening noise and rolled over onto her feet, his eyes flashing in the gloom. 'Being jih doesn't give you the right to just take creatures from the forest. What were you going to do, sell him on? You should be ashamed, betraying your own kind, slinking around a human city like you belong here.' She reached down and picked up the cub, who licked her face with a dry tongue. 'I'll be taking him back to the forest now.'

'No!' For the first time, the young man looked truly alarmed. 'You can't. I need him.'

'Why?' Elver held the cub to her chest, the feathers tickling her nose.

He told her. It took him a while, and he kept stopping as he remembered a particular detail that disturbed him – the silence of the monastery, the face of his friend as she was ripped back through the portal. For Elver, it was the colour of the robes the mage wore. The name of their god.

'So you see,' he was saying, 'I have to take the cub to this mage or she'll kill the other novices.'

'That magpie,' Elver spat. 'Don't you see? She'll kill the cub. He'll be fuel for one of her spells. The Bloody Claw only grants magic when a blood price is paid. You can't take him to be sacrificed on some altar somewhere. You should never have taken him from the forest at all – that's his home.'

'I should have guessed . . .' Artair looked down at the floor for a moment. 'She killed Sister Rosea and the rest of the Brothers and Sisters. But all this means is that the novices are in even more danger than I thought. I have to try to save them. I have to.'

Elver carried the cub to the single chair and sat in it. She picked up a slice of meat off of the plate and fed it to the animal, who snapped it up greedily.

'Twelve curse us,' she muttered.

Artair must have seen something of her thoughts on her face because he asked her, 'Will you help me?'

The idea filled her with equal parts fear and rage. All she wanted was to go back to the forest and spend her days with her own kind, never seeing another human face.

'Why would I help a thief like you?'

'Because you know it isn't right.'

'Ha.' Elver gave a short little snort of laughter. 'Outside of my forest, I don't give a fig for right or wrong. It means nothing to me.'

'What's to stop this mage from taking another monster from your forest? She must need a jih spirit for this particular spell.'

Elver glanced up at the young man. He was sharper than he looked.

'Shit,' she said bitterly. She put a piece of meat in her own mouth, chewed and swallowed. 'The Bloody Claw is powerful. You'd need the help of another god. Someone on your side.'

'Are *you* a mage?' he asked. His eyes flickered to her white hair, the scars on her face and arms. She turned her face away a little, so the oil lamp's light did not reach her.

'No, I'm just a simple jih. But I know how the gods work.'

'So, you will help me?'

Elver looked at the cub and sighed. She couldn't kill this idiot boy – not easily, anyway – and she couldn't create a situation where she or the cub was exposed. Neither of them were supposed to be in

Addersport, and she doubted he would let her take the cub without a fight; he was more reasonable than she had been expecting, that was true, but there was something steely underneath the surface too. Perhaps that was the dark spirit she was sensing. No, she'd have to wait until they were all somewhere quieter and take the cub then. Maybe the Sleepless would survive that, maybe he wouldn't.

'I'll help you,' she said. He was practically human, she told herself, and lying to humans didn't matter at all. 'As much as I can, anyway.'

'Thank you.' To her surprise, Artair came and knelt in front of her and took her hand. He looked her in the eyes, and there was an expression there that made her uneasy. He was trying to decide whether to trust her or not, she realized. 'Thank you for helping me with this, poison girl. Can I ask your name?'

She glared at his hand, but he didn't seem to get the message.

'My name is Elver.'

'Elver, can I ask you one more boon?'

'Sure, why not? You've already ruined my day. How much worse can it get?'

He nodded as though this were a reasonable comment.

'Elver, would you please use these ropes to tie me up?'

# CHAPTER 9

Elver sat in her corner of the cellar, her back against the wall, and watched the sleeping monk. She'd tied him up as he'd instructed, hands bound at the wrists behind his back, and his ankles too for good measure, and when he'd thought they were still too loose, he'd asked her to retie them, as tightly as she could. He'd also tried to convince her to leave the cellar for the night, but she'd refused. As uncomfortable as it was to be in the same space as this young man, it was still infinitely preferable to being out in a lively human city.

*I could just kill him and go. Now is the perfect time.* Except that they were locked in the cellar. If the barman opened the door in the morning and found her and a dead body in it, she suspected she would get reintroduced to the Addersport City Guard faster than she'd like.

When she had bound Artair to his satisfaction, he had lain down on the dirt floor and closed his eyes. He'd told her that one of the things they learned very early in the Golden Tower of the Perpetual Morning was that sleep could not be resisted; in fact, it was dangerous to try to avoid it, because if you stayed awake for too long, sleep would simply claim you without asking, and you might not be prepared. So now she listened as his breathing grew deeper, and slower, the light of the oil lamp lying softly on his face. He had very dark, thick eyelashes, that lay like soot against his cheek and her eyes kept returning to the small scar that divided his eyebrow. For reasons she couldn't name, she found herself wondering what it would feel like to brush her thumb over that scar.

Elver stood up and went over to the cub, who was finishing up the cheese and meat – neither she nor Artair had felt like eating, so she'd put the plate down on the floor for him.

'I'll take you home soon,' she said quietly. 'I promise.'

*This is good, this yellow stuff,* said the cub. *What is it?*

'It's cheese.'

*We don't have it at home. Who is he? Why did he put me in the dark?*

'He is . . . Artair. Some idiot human. Well, mostly human.'

*Huh.* The cub had hoovered up all the crumbs on the plate and was licking his lips. *I will bite him. Rend him with my teeth.*

'Maybe when you are bigger.' Elver crouched down next to the cub and scratched him behind the ears. 'Technically, the fool is jih. Can you believe that?'

The cub snorted. *Smells human to me. We should eat him. You've tied him up so I can eat him, right?*

'He is one of the Sleepless. He's himself all day, but when he falls asleep, someone else inhabits him, someone bad. And then when that person also falls asleep, Artair comes back. I've tied him up so that when the evil spirit comes, he won't be able to leave this room.'

*Makes him easier to eat,* the cub commented.

'Are you still hungry?'

'Who are you talking to?'

Elver startled. Artair had sat up awkwardly, twisting his body around to look at her. His voice was sharper, more direct, and although it was difficult to see in the darkened cellar, for a brief second Elver thought his eyes were a different colour – more hazel than brown. She stood up, her hand on the knife at her belt.

'You are the dark spirit.'

'I have a name, which is Lucian, and I'd thank you to use it. Being referred to as the dark spirit gets incredibly tiresome.' His words and tone were relaxed, but something in the way his eyes glittered made Elver consider escape options: except, of course, that the tavern keeper had locked them in, and not long after she'd made her dramatic entrance the tavern keeper's son had blocked up the window.

*Perhaps I should just take my chances and cut his throat here after all,* she thought.

He was still looking at her closely, his eyes travelling up and down her slender frame.

'You're not human,' he said eventually. 'What are you?' Elver was struck by the similarity of the conversation she'd just had with Artair. While the monk's interest had seemed born of genuine curiosity, Lucian's interest was as sharp as a blade. 'You've been touched by a god is my guess, but you're no mage.' When she didn't reply, he gave a short bark of laughter. 'I'm guessing that you're not having a conversation with that table about cheese, which means you're able to communicate with this juvenile monster. You're not a mage, but you have some small spark of magic, and that makes you a jih spirit. Am I right? A monster girl. And from that I would have to conclude that the god who made you is the Queen of Serpents herself, she who has dominion over all monsters. That is very interesting indeed.'

During this little speech, the cub had come over to Elver and pressed himself to her ankles. He had not been afraid of Artair in the slightest, but clearly Lucian was another prospect.

'You're jih too,' she said, although she found herself wondering. This Lucian wasn't human, that seemed certain enough – he was a parasite inside another's body – but Artair had every appearance of one. Did that make him less jih?

Lucian shrugged. 'I feel no kinship with you and that little creature down by your feet, if that's what you're asking.'

'You have a lot to say for yourself.'

Lucian smiled. 'You didn't expect a dark spirit to be so eloquent? The truth is, monster girl, I don't often have anyone to speak to, so this is quite the treat. The monks that keep this idiot locked up,' he nodded at his own chest, 'like to keep us isolated.' He looked around the cellar. 'Which rather begs the question, what are we doing here? And where is here?'

'My name is Elver,' she said. 'Not monster girl. And I'd thank you to use it.'

He laughed delightedly at that. 'Elver. Fine. And where are we, Elver? Why are you here with us? Not that I'm complaining.'

Slowly, Elver sat and crossed her legs. The cub jumped into her lap immediately, his feathery ears drooping.

*I don't like it*, he said. *I don't like this one.* She put her hand on his head to calm him.

'Everyone knows that the spirits that live inside the Sleepless are evil,' she said. 'Chaotic, violent things. Creatures so full of trickery that they should rightly belong to Tisk, the god of lies and mischief.' There was nothing obviously dangerous about this young man, but as soon as he had opened his mouth she had felt a tension in her body similar to the one she felt when a violent storm visited the Jih Forest. 'I don't think I'll be telling you anything.'

Lucian shifted on the floor and sighed. 'Being tied up is new, and I have to tell you, I don't like it. At least at the tower I had a bed to lie on, or a chair to sit in. I don't suppose you would consider cutting these bonds?'

She smiled. It was a cold and icy thing on her lips.

'The only thing I will consider cutting is your throat.'

'Very good, monster girl, very good.'

'What are you, really?' she asked. Despite herself, she found that she was curious about him too.

Lucian shrugged. It was remarkable, she thought, how he could look like Artair and yet not look like him at all. He held himself differently, moved differently. His face was haughty and almost bored, his eyes narrowed and his brows drawn down as though he were examining her somehow.

'Tell me where we are, Elver, and I will tell you everything there is to know about myself.'

Elver frowned. Above them, in the busy tavern, someone had started singing off-key, and several other voices began to join in against a background of general laughter.

'We're in a city,' she said.

Lucian nodded. 'I guessed that myself. And from the sound of that din above, we're in the cellar of a tavern. Of all the places a prissy little monk could find himself . . . I bet the boy is pissing his breeches.' He sounded very pleased at the prospect. It was interesting, Elver thought, that this Lucian clearly thought Artair was weak, when presumably they could never have met. Whatever her opinion of Artair's actions, a weak person did not enter the Jih Forest with the intention of confronting one of its monsters.

'In a city, in a tavern. That's where we are. So, who are you?'

'That's the question, isn't it?' The spirit called Lucian grinned at her, sharp and full of self-satisfaction, but it felt as though there was something else behind it, too. Desperation, perhaps. 'My name is Lucian, and I know I'm not supposed to be here, and that is about all I know, monster girl. Where my past is supposed to be, there is a fog so dense it's like being blind. But if you let me out of here, perhaps I could go out into the world and find out.'

'You haven't told me anything at all.'

He shrugged. 'I told you I would tell you everything there is to know about me, and I have done that. Now, how about you use your clever little knife to open one of these barrels, and we could have a sip of whatever happens to be inside them? When I am locked in the cell at the monastery, I never get to eat or drink. The monk keeps those pleasures for himself.'

'I don't think so. And I don't think I'll be answering any more of your questions, or performing any other tasks for you.'

'You will not talk to me further, Elver?'

Elver did not answer.

The dark spirit inhabiting Artair's body tried a few more times to get her to speak – asking her where she lived, if humans were frightened of her, and where the keltraxia cub had come from – but she went back to her corner and sat with the cub, one hand on her knife hilt, until he eventually gave up and fell into a simmering silence.

*I don't think we should eat that one,* said the cub as he dozed in her lap. *I think he will taste bad.*

*I think you might be right about that,* thought Elver.

Tiredness tugged at her, but the idea of sleeping with Lucian watching her was uncomfortable. Instead, she put the cub down onto a pile of empty sacks and crossed the room to where Artair had left his pack. They had agreed to place it out of his reach, just to be on the safe side. When she picked it up, Lucian raised his eyebrows.

'That belongs to the monk, doesn't it? The Brothers who keep me prisoner have robes made of the same scratchy hessian. What are you doing, monster girl?'

'Nothing that concerns you,' she told him without looking up.

The pack contained enough silver to make her raise an eyebrow, and some food: apples, half a loaf of brown bread, dried meat wrapped in grease paper. This last she took a piece of and chewed on thoughtfully as she pulled out two tightly rolled scrolls. The first one was a map of the Jih Forest, the locations of keltraxia nests marked with circles of blue ink, and the second was a brief description of the monsters, written in a sloping, spidery hand. At the bottom of this, there was a signature.

Mother Maura.

'What is it?' Lucian shifted, craning to get a better look at her face. 'I'd have said that you couldn't possibly get any paler, yet you just proved me wrong.'

Elver stared at the signature. In a horrible, stupid way, it made sense. The mage that Artair had described was bloodthirsty and ruthless, and she had acolytes willing to do her bidding. More than she'd had in Addersport, but it had been a while. Mother Maura had clearly gained more followers since she'd thrown Elver into the sea.

*This doesn't change anything,* she told herself. *I have to return the cub to the forest before the next egg moon.*

Yet here was Mother Maura, intruding on her life again. Causing more pain and suffering when she hadn't even answered for the horrors she'd already inflicted. How sweet would it be to disrupt her plans? To look her in the face and let her know that Elver had survived after all? There were many things she could do if she got close enough to touch the mage.

'Care to share what it is that has given you that steely look, monster girl?' said Lucian.

Elver shoved the rolls of parchment back into the pack, her heart racing.

'Be quiet,' she told him, 'or I'll gag you as well.'

# CHAPTER 10

It was a busy Addersport morning, hideously crammed with human noise and scent. In Elver's arms, the keltraxia cub wriggled inside the sack, already eager to get back out again.

*The smells! I want to see what they are!*

She lowered her face until her lips brushed the fabric of the sack.

'Remember what we talked about? While we're in the city, you have to hide. If we're caught with you here, we're in big trouble. Try to be still.'

*I don't see why I should sit in a sack while you get to walk around a human city. Just because you've got two legs and look like them or whatever.* After that, the cub grew quieter. Elver could sense him busily sulking.

Artair, meanwhile, was having the opposite of a sulk.

'Isn't this place incredible?' he said. They were walking east, away from the tavern, following one of the many waterways that sliced through the city in every direction. It was a bright autumn day, the morning sun dancing on the water and sending sinuous patterns of light over the walls of the buildings around them; they made Elver think of the serpents that had invaded Addersport when she was a child. 'I've never seen so many people in one place.'

'I know. It's awful.'

He shot her a surprised look. 'I used to dream about what it would be like to come to this city. I never thought I'd actually get to do it. I suppose, living in the woods, the city must be very overwhelming.'

Elver scowled. 'I was born in this cesspit. And I lived here until I was twelve.'

'You did?'

The streets were growing busier and busier the deeper into Addersport they ventured. Elver pulled up her hood and used one hand to tug her sleeves down so that they covered much of her hands.

'Let's just get out of here as quickly as we can. The cub isn't happy about being in this sack and I'm not happy about having to smell all these humans.'

He raised an eyebrow at that. 'You're not wrong. A lot of people in one place creates an . . . interesting smell.'

They turned a corner, passing shops with open fronts selling all manner of goods – clothes, fabric, jewellery, spices, a great deal of salted and fresh fish – and then they were in a market square, filled with a large crowd of people. They were all standing around, some of them eating foods that Elver dimly remembered from her childhood – sticky buns on sticks, hot cinnamon bread and spiced lamb wrapped in thin pancakes – and overhead there were strings of red and gold bunting. Everyone appeared to be looking at a raised dais in the centre of the square, which was partly covered with a crimson sheet. There was a man up there too, dressed in fine velvet and silk, a big gold chain around his neck. When Elver had lived in Addersport, the mayor had been a woman; this bearded man was apparently her replacement. Without discussing it, they both stopped to listen as the mayor began to shout over the crowd.

'I'd like to thank the Addersport Orphanage Fund for raising enough money for this fine tribute. It's taken us some time, and I know it wasn't always the case that everyone wanted this monument . . .' There was some muttering from the crowd at this, but the mayor carried on regardless. 'But now that we are here I think that ultimately we can all agree that the sacrifice should be marked and we should have a way to remember her every day.'

'What are they talking about?' asked Artair. He was craning his neck to look at the dais. 'What's under the sheet?'

'I don't know. More human nonsense, I expect.' But Elver had a cold, creeping sensation on the back of her neck.

'Only five short years ago, Addersport stood on the brink of ruin. We had lost many lives and a great deal of money to the monstrous serpent threat.' The mayor paused and dabbed at his sweaty brow with a handkerchief. 'And Elver, brave child that she was, stepped forward to save this city. I give you, the Hero of Addersport.'

He swept the sheet away dramatically and Elver blinked, shock like a splash of cold water on her face. She wasn't sure if she was going to laugh or be sick.

Underneath the sheet was a bronze statue depicting a child, standing with her shoulders back, her chin held high and one foot resting on the body of a serpent that lay on the ground below her. The bronze shone like embers under the sun, and the crowd cooed appreciatively.

'This child died for us,' the mayor continued, his voice solemn and heavy. 'To fuel the spell that freed Addersport. Now, with this monument, we can give thanks to her every day.'

Elver wanted to run up to the mayor and press her hand to his sweaty skin until he screamed with agony. The statue didn't even look like her.

'Are you alright?' asked Artair. 'You've gone a funny colour.'

'The cheek of it. The brass neck of it! I knew this place was a grasping midden full of selfish, mindless fools, but *this*?' Elver was pushing through the crowd, heading to the far side of the square and away from the statue. 'These humans should be ashamed, and instead they've built a bloody great celebration of it!' She wanted to scream at the surrounding crowd, ask if they knew her name. She knew that they didn't. They would know *Maura's* name though, and this made it all the worse. All at once, the idea of facing the mage and making her pay for what she'd done felt irresistible.

'Elver, wait.' Artair caught up with her with one easy stride. He stood close so that he could speak to her in a low voice. His scent, she realized, was different to the humans around them. He smelled of a cool autumn morning. 'What is it? What's wrong?'

He was looking at her very directly. To him, this was a simple question: was there something wrong? Could he help? She remembered his voice as he described what had happened at his monastery, the pain it had clearly cost him to recall it, and she remembered the other voice that had come out of him at night: the sly, slippery tones of Lucian. One body, two entirely different spirits moving through it.

'There's no time. Let's get out of here before I decide to poison some idiots just to cheer myself up.'

Before long they found themselves in the Twelfth district, the place dedicated to the temples of the gods. Most cities and towns large enough had a Twelfth district, where acolytes, priests and mages could ply their wares. As a child, Elver had had no use for the place and avoided it, but Artair dawdled, his eyes caught by every detail. There was the Temple of the Hooded Crow, the god of death, medicine and secrets, the cold black marble of the archway strung with pungent herbs. And there was the colourful Temple of Vilon the Many Limbed, the god of the arts; always popular, men and women streamed in and out of it, talking animatedly about the inspiration they had been granted within. Barleycorn, the god of the hearth – amongst other things – was even more popular, probably because his temple took the form of a well-stocked tavern and the priests were sunny-faced men and women who would come out and merrily chat at you if you weren't careful. Artair wandered too close and a priestess nabbed him.

'Won't you come in and take a load off, son? Barleycorn tells us we should seek out the good times, because what else are we here for?'

'Thank you,' he said. 'Thank you so much. That is very kind of you.'

Elver steeled herself and took hold of his arm to pull him away.

'We don't have time for this . . .'

'Your girl is welcome too, of course,' beamed the priestess. 'Nothing Barleycorn likes better than a young couple rolling in the hay.'

'Rolling in the what?' Artair laughed, and the woman grinned back at him.

'Come *on*.' Elver dragged him away.

At the end of the street was another temple, quieter and more austere than the others. The lintel over the doorway was hung with white masks, and long runners of white silk hung in front of the portal. This, Elver knew, was the Temple of Trilot the Faceless, god of purity and truth. Trilot was significantly less popular than Barleycorn. There was a single priest standing on the steps, watching them as they passed. Elver spared him a quick glance. He wore the long gloves and high-necked gown of the order, though he wasn't masked, so he wasn't one of the high priests. Priests of Trilot were forbidden to touch or be touched and at this thought Elver felt a strange moment of sympathy, which she quickly brushed aside. Trilot despised the Queen of Serpents and all her children, seeing them as the ultimate embodiment of the impure, and it was under his advisement that humanity abhorred monster kin. The Queen had warned her to be careful of the Faceless One.

'There's just so much to see,' said Artair. 'The different faces, the colours of the stone, the food . . . I have never seen a river that runs through a city before, and here they're everywhere.'

'Technically, they're waterways. Not real rivers. Not like you get in the forest.'

'I've spent years only ever seeing the same stone corridors, the same view of the forest, the mountains. The same garden growing the same plants.'

His voice sounded strange, and when she looked at him, he had a slightly glassy expression. The compulsion to ask him if he was feeling well rose up in her, but she swallowed it down, and in the next moment he seemed to shake off his discomfort.

'It's all necessary though,' he said to her emphatically. 'Our sacrifice is necessary. Without it, the whole of Tlevrae would be in danger from the spirits that hide inside us.'

'I don't know. It seems to me that people who are very keen on sacrifice are often the ones not losing anything.'

'No, it's not like that at all,' said Artair, although he sounded thoughtful. 'Listen, we should start thinking about where we're going to spend the night. If we leave the city, there won't be any rented rooms to stay in. I can't risk the Other having the same freedom I have right now.'

'You've got your ropes, haven't you?' Whatever she decided to do about Mother Maura and this Sleepless spirit, she had to get out of Addersport; the hypocritical statue was a step too far. 'I can tie you up outside as well as I can tie you up indoors.' Elver paused. The cub was abruptly wriggling in her arms, threatening to make her drop him. 'Ugh, what is it?'

*I need to go . . .*

'I've told you, little one, we can't let you out of this sack until we're well out of the city . . .'

*No, I need to go now. Normally, I go outside of the nest.*

Elver's heart sank. Carrying around a pee-soaked sack was a level of misery she wasn't keen to endure.

'What is it?' asked Artair. They had left the temple district behind and were in a shabbier section of the city. The waterways here were narrow and clogged in places with discarded garbage. The people here were dressed in clothes that looked as though they'd seen better days. As an orphan Elver had been quite familiar with handed-down clothes.

'The cub needs . . . He needs the toilet,' she replied. Artair raised his eyebrows. 'I'll take him down this alleyway here, where he won't be seen.'

Elver went to the very end of the alleyway, where it was dark even on such a bright autumn day. There were windows high up on the walls here, but they were thick with dirt or patched up from the inside, so she thought it very unlikely anyone would be looking out at them. She opened the sack and the cub tumbled out, frantically sniffing the air and scurrying about. In the grime of the alley, he looked incredibly bright, a beautiful piece of the monster forest let loose. His eyes flashed ghost-green. Despite herself, she smiled.

'Listen, just hurry up and go. It's dangerous for you to be out in the open here.' She glanced back to the mouth of the alley. Artair was there, looking off down the street. He was caught in a beam of sunlight, turning his brown hair almost coppery. Viewing him from a distance, it was striking how tall he was, how perfect his posture – he was straight as an arrow. *Like the arrow he shot this creature's mother with*, she reminded herself.

A few feet away from where the cub was sniffing, the alleyway came to a dead end. Otherwise, she could have picked up the cub and slipped away without Artair noticing. Of course, if she did that . . . She realized that the prospect of facing down Maura was growing more attractive.

She turned back to the young creature.

'Hurry up.'

*I can't go if you're looking.*

'Oh, for the love of the Twelve . . .'

Elver rubbed a hand over her face. The day had only just started and already she was desperate for it to come to an end.

The cub trotted over to a discarded crate and began sniffing it.

*This smells interesting. Do you think it had cheese in it?*

'I don't know. Please do your business.'

She turned away to give the cub some privacy and was startled to see a figure heading down the alleyway towards her. He was tall and dressed in white, and she recognized him immediately: he was the priest who had been standing outside the Temple of Trilot the Faceless. Of Artair there was no sign. Elver moved to stand in front of the cub, but it was already too late.

'What's that you've got there?' the priest barked. 'Does it belong to you?'

'*He* belongs to no one,' she said, standing her ground. Now that he was up close, she could see that the human was handsome in an obvious way, his eyes an icy blue and his hair the colour of ripe wheat. He was in his thirties, she thought, and there was an intensity to his gaze that was deeply unnerving. He did not blink often enough.

'You remarkable idiot. You've brought a monster into the city. Don't you know that these filthy creatures are banned from civilized places?'

Elver laughed, shook her head. She thought of the statue. 'Calling this place civilized is rich. Listen, priest, I don't give a fig about the rules of Addersport, or your holy order, so I suggest you back off.'

Her hand drifted to the knife at her belt.

He loomed over her. 'How *dare* you.'

'I dare alright.' The cub was nosing at the back of her legs. He wanted to know what was going on.

'That creature must be confiscated. We have ways of dealing with the children of the serpent at the temple. If I . . .' Something in his face changed. His nose wrinkled, and suddenly he had hold of her sleeved wrist, squeezing it tightly enough that it hurt. Elver couldn't reach her blade.

'Get off me! I thought priests of Trilot weren't allowed to touch other people.'

'*What are you?*' The force of his grip increased. 'I can smell . . . You're not human! I knew it when you walked past the temple. Dirty jih scum. Walking into the city, bold as brass.' His nostrils flared and he glanced up at the sky. 'Trilot, thank you for sending me this test. I will deal with her as you have bid me in my dreams.'

'Let go of me right now or you'll regret it.' She tried to yank her arm away, but he was surprisingly strong, his fingers like a vice.

The priest grinned, exposing too many teeth.

'Oh my girl, monster kin don't have any rights here. In fact, you could scream until the City Guard came and they would still give you to me. You and the little creature belong to Trilot now. My name is Kantor Witt, and I am a faceless priest of the seventh order. There's a place for you in the temple that's just perfect for what I have in mi—'

'I warned you.'

Elver reached up and placed the flat of her free hand against the priest's face. There was a second of confusion and then he shrieked, yanking his head away – but Elver clung on, feeling a fierce satisfaction as the skin beneath her hand grew warm and then hot. He grabbed her arm and yanked her away, revealing a livid red imprint of her hand on his left cheek. Blisters were forming as she watched.

'What have you done?'

Elver reached down and scooped up the cub and the sack before pelting down the alleyway to the far end. Kantor Witt, the priest of Trilot, was cursing her, screaming oaths of vengeance, and all she could think about was the unmissable red mark that marred his handsome face. His superiors would be able to see at a glance that he had been touched – that he had betrayed his holy orders. She grinned.

When she reached the street, she saw Artair some distance away, frowning at a bakery window. He straightened up as she approached.

'Should we buy some bread for the journey? One of those loaves should last us at least—'

'Run,' she shouted as she sped past him. 'We need to get out of the city, *now*.'

# CHAPTER 11

They had lost the priest, but they were rapidly losing the day as well.

Artair found himself glancing at the sky repeatedly as they wound their way through the narrow streets. They were on the outskirts of Addersport, and the shadows were deepening. Darkness did not necessarily mean sleep, but he was aware that thanks to a night spent running through the jih wood and another night sleeping on an uncomfortable cellar floor, he felt dangerously tired. He had spent all of his life training to be able to go long hours without sleep, yet there was no avoiding the fact that he was exhausted, light was leaking from the sky and a large part of him yearned to lie down and close his eyes.

'Can we not find another tavern? I have the coin for it.'

'Yeah, I saw the amount of silver you were piling up on that bar. Where did you get all that from, anyway?' And then, before he could reply, 'And no, we can't find another tavern. That Trilot priest will still be after us—'

'After *you*.'

'—and we're close to the edge of the city. We'll be able to camp tonight under the stars.' Clearly Elver couldn't wait to leave Addersport.

'I took the silver from the abbot's room. And some gold, too,' said Artair. 'I did what I had to do. I don't have anything of my own.'

'Well, from what you've told me, he won't be missing it.' The buildings were thinning out around them, the waterways becoming more frequent. The setting sun lent its deep orange light to the lines of water, turning them into fiery patterns, and in the distance it was possible to see the road that led to the east. 'There, look.' Elver pointed at a group of long narrowboats that sat low in the water. There were people climbing on and off them, their arms full of goods. A tall man with a large moustache was lighting lamps on each boat as the daylight receded. 'Look – a market. We can buy some food there with your ill-gotten silver, then disappear into the wood off the road for the night.'

A green narrowboat with golden moons on the side appeared to sell all manner of food, so they cautiously climbed on board. Immediately, they were approached by an older woman with a wide-brimmed hat. The glance she gave them was distracted, half impatient, but not unkind.

'Well, what can I do for you? I have to go with the tides, my loves, or I won't make the morning market in Sarancester.'

Artair stood in the prow, watching as Elver rattled off an order to the market woman, the sack containing the cub held securely in his arms. The boats sold food mainly, but he saw swords being sold too, and on one boat, a portly man that reminded him of Brother Benzin was selling charms that supposedly kept you in the good graces of the Twelve. Many of them were made of glass and crystal, and they winked and sparkled in the ruddy light of the sunset.

It was the people, though, who drew his eye: they stood and chatted with each other, laughed at jokes, picked up their children when they ventured too close to the edge of the waterway. He saw men and women holding hands; saw one man peck another on the cheek fondly before slinging his arm around his partner's waist, and an older woman kiss her shorter, balding husband fondly on the top of his shining head. In the monastery, such affections were never spoken of. Not because it wasn't allowed, exactly, but because they had all agreed not to, without ever having discussed it. The idea of wanting to spend time with one person alone when your life must always be separate – it was too painful.

'Are you ready?'

Elver had reappeared. She had also bartered a second sack off the woman and had it slung over one shoulder. Her hood was pulled low over her face and he noticed that she stood turned away from the humans, as though looking at them hurt her, too.

'I am,' he said.

By the time they made it to the woods, it was full dark and Artair felt ready to drop. He followed where Elver led – she could see in even the deepest shadow, she had told him – the weight of the cub becoming more and more difficult to bear. It was almost funny, he thought. All that training to control his body's weaknesses and one full day in the real world had near wrecked him. Elver had fallen into the silence that she was apparently used to, and all at once Artair found he needed to hear her voice. It would help keep him awake.

'Tell me about Trilot,' he said. 'Tell me about this priest.'

'You don't learn about the Twelve in your monastery?'

'We do, but only the basics. I imagine you know more.'

'Hmm.' In the safety of the wood, Elver had thrown back her hood and her white hair shone under the moonlight like the lamps on the boats. She had a heart-shaped face, he noticed, countered by the sharpness of her cheekbones, and her yellow eyes had a darker line around their edge, making him think of the gold coins in his pack. 'Trilot the Faceless is the god of justice, truth, purity and travel. They're a powerful group, usually the hidden hand behind things like the City Guard, the magistrate, schools. In Addersport, they used to keep a few sticky fingers in the ports as well as under the guise of travel priests, and the ports in that city are rich. Trilot deals in secrets: mages dedicated to Trilot must give him secrets in order to perform magic. And . . .' She frowned. 'There are rumours about other things their god will accept, but I don't know how true they are.'

'What things?'

Elver tipped her head to one side, then shrugged. 'It doesn't matter. Trilot's priests take a vow of purity when they enter the temple and that means that they are forbidden from human touch, both giving and receiving. With each year of service, they earn a new piece of priestly garb to cover up their skin – a hood, a pair of gloves and eventually a mask so that they are entirely covered up. Touching another human, skin to skin, is the worst thing they can do. It loses them their connection to their god.'

'So the fact that you touched that priest's face . . .'

'It will have caused him all sorts of trouble.' She grinned.

'He'll not stop coming after us, then.'

'No,' she said, although he noted that she didn't sound wholly certain. 'Priests are too fond of their cosy little temples to leave them for long. And he's just a priest, not a magpie. He can't use magic, he can just, you know, do whatever priests do. Mewl around their gods' skirts like kittens, I suppose. What can he do to us?'

'At the tavern, you said I would need the help of another god to save my friends from the Bloody Claw. I'm guessing Trilot won't do.'

Elver gave a brief snort of laughter. 'Trilot would rather see both us and your Sleepless novices burned to a crisp. No, what you need is a lie. A powerful lie. An illusion to fool . . . to fool the mage.'

There was a spark in the girl's eye that hadn't been there the night before. Artair wondered what had changed.

'You're suggesting I give her an illusion of the cub instead of the real thing?'

Elver nodded. 'And to get an illusion, you need to deal with the god Tisk. I happen to know there is a mage dedicated to Tisk near a village to the east of Addersport. You can go there and buy an illusion spell and then give the thieving magpie a version of this cub convincing enough that you can get the novices out before she notices.'

'The god of mischief and lies.' Artair frowned. It felt risky. 'How do I know Mother Maura won't just see straight through it?'

The girl seemed to wince, but turned her face away before he could figure out why.

'I guess you don't. But I still think it's your only plan.'

He cleared his throat. 'And will you come with me? Will you help me, Elver?'

Her glance was sharp and piercing; it was, he thought, like being watched by a bird of prey.

'What do you need my help for?'

'I know very little about mages, or gods. I'd never even been in a city before. You're right, maybe I could manage this alone, but I think my chances are better with company. And I need someone to keep watch over me at night so the Other doesn't escape.' He took a slow breath. 'I can't fail. People are relying on me.'

Elver looked around at the darkened trees, as though seeking their counsel.

'I'll come at least as far as the mage,' she said eventually. 'I know where the temple is, and she will need the cub in order to make the illusion. After that, I'll be taking him back to the Jih Forest. Where we both belong.'

They eventually chose a clearing on the edge of a stream to make camp. Elver made a fire with the ease of someone who performed such tasks every day, and they let the cub out of the sack. Elver spoke to the creature in a low voice – Artair caught the odd snatch of their conversation, phrases like 'behave yourself' and 'soon be home' – and then they unpacked some of the food they'd bought at the waterway market.

'He's saying he wants some of what you're having,' said Elver.

Artair looked down at the pastry in his hands, which was filled with chunks of beef, gravy and carrots. It was probably one of the best things he'd ever eaten.

'Oh.' He broke off a chunk and threw it to the cub, who caught it in one snap of his jaws. 'Does he have a name?'

'He said he's thinking about getting one. Something like Strongest-in-all-the-forest, or Cruncher-of-human-bones.'

The cub was pushing at Artair's ankle with his nose, and he found he didn't need Elver to translate his intent. He broke off another, larger piece of pastry and passed it to the cub, who this time snaffled it straight off his palm.

Artair finished the pastry – with liberal help from Cruncher-of-human-bones – then ate another, followed by three apples and a thick wedge of hard cheese. He was drinking a cup of water from the stream when he realized that his eyelids were drooping and although Elver had been talking, he hadn't heard a word of it. He jerked upright, his heart racing.

Elver blinked at him. 'What's bit you on the arse?'

'I was nearly asleep!' He stood up, startling the cub, who had been lightly dozing on his foot. *In this place, in this moment, I am safe. The Other is contained.* He cast around for the ropes and gathered them up before holding them out to the monster girl. 'Please, quickly. Bind my wrists and ankles as you did before and then run a rope from me to that tree there.' *The Other is contained, and I am safe.*

Elver sighed, but she did what he asked, looping the rope around his wrists as he held them behind his back, and then his ankles too. Artair tested the bindings, and when he was happy, she tied another rope around the sturdy pine tree that stood closest to their small fire.

When everything was done, Artair let himself relax a little. He lay down on the ground, and as uneven and hard as it was, he felt himself beginning to drift immediately into sleep. Elver had gone back to the far side of the fire, the cub now in her lap, and she was talking to the creature in a low voice. Without her hood, and without the threat of humans nearby, she looked peaceful, the habitual angry crease in her forehead smoothed away. Addersport made her angry, he realized, while the wood – any wood, perhaps – was her home.

He went to sleep thinking about this, the murmur of her voice becoming another soft sound of the forest.

Lucian woke up with a jerk, entirely disorientated. It took him a moment to realize what it was that was so strange, and then he was up and trying to run – *he was outside, that was the feeling of fresh air on his skin, all he had to do was run . . .*

The rope pulled taut and he fell back into the dirt.

'Good evening,' said the monster girl. 'Let me reintroduce you to the concept of being tied up.'

Lucian growled at her, the scent of dirt filling his whole head. He pulled himself up into a sitting position. He was aware of a leaf sticking to his cheek, so he shook his head until it fell off. Everything ached.

'Let me go,' he said. He swallowed, trying to gather his thoughts. They were outside, in a wood, and it was night-time. A small fire burned between them. The monster girl – Elver, he remembered – was sitting on the far side, watching him closely. As well as the dirt, he could smell autumn, a powerful scent of rotting leaves and ripening fruit that he'd almost forgotten. A thick wad of some emotion he didn't care to think about threatened to close his throat. He hurriedly swallowed it down. 'If you wouldn't mind, I would really appreciate it if you could untie these ropes and let me go, Elver.'

'I'm not going to do that.'

He sighed. Despite the bindings at his ankles and wrists, it was extraordinary to be outside. Just the movement of air against his skin felt like a gift. As it always did, the anger inside him began to build. What use was a breeze when you were still trapped?

'I have no memory of being outside,' he said. 'The idiot whose body I share never sleeps outside, so I have never experienced it. Yet, I know that isn't true. I know I had a life before this *imprisonment*. I have no memory of food either, yet I know I have eaten. Can you imagine what that is like?'

'My heart bleeds for you, evil spirit.'

He laughed, a hollow sound in the open night. 'A jih spirit calling me evil. A child of the serpent, no less. Why are we here, and why is the monk spending his time with a monster girl?'

She seemed to consider this. 'We are going to visit a mage. She has taken something, and he's trying to get it back.'

'Taken something from him? He doesn't have anything.'

'He had friends.'

'And who is this mage? What god is she dedicated to?'

Elver shook her head, indicating that she would say no more. On the ground by the fire, there was an open sack of food and Lucian could see a bright green apple. Food was a rare sight; the idiot monk never ate in his cell, after all. Yet he knew what it was, and even had an idea of what it might taste like: a ghost of his forgotten life. 'Give me a bite of that apple. Please, Elver. I ask you this as one jih creature to another. If I must be imprisoned, then let me at least experience a couple of simple pleasures. I'm tied up. I can't hurt you.'

She looked at him for a long moment and then slid the knife from her belt. It was a wicked-looking blade, the firelight moving across it in a liquid flash. Lucian grinned unhappily. So that was it then. She'd slit his throat rather than deal with him. At least he would be free of this endless torture – surely it would be better to be dead than trapped.

But to his surprise, she picked up the apple and cut it into slices, popping one in her own mouth before bringing one over to him. She crouched, some distance away, and held out a single slice. Lucian leaned forward as far as he could and took it carefully between his lips before crunching it between his teeth.

It was incredible – sweet and sharp and sour, the juice filling his mouth with flavour and sensation.

'Thank you,' he said, and he found that he meant it. 'Thank you. You can't know . . .' He shook his head. He felt oddly ashamed. 'So much has been kept from me.'

She leaned forward with another slice and he craned his neck to meet her. Something soft brushed his jaw – her hand, he realized – and in that instant—

*A flash of impossible colour. He was young, his head not quite reaching the altar yet, and the space around him was silent and sacred. Red candles were burning, dripping wax like blood onto the walls and the stone pillars, and somehow this was appropriate, somehow it excited him. There was a smell, a wild and untamed funk tempered with spiced incense. Someone began talking in a low voice. There were windows overhead of red glass, letting in an unholy light—*

And it was gone. Elver had jumped back from him, her eyes wide, the slice of apple forgotten in the dirt. Instinctively, Lucian lunged after her, desperate.

'What was that?' he demanded. 'What did you do to me, monster girl?'

'Nothing! I . . .' She had her knife in her hand again. 'My touch is poisonous to humans. It shouldn't hurt jih spirits. It doesn't hurt Artair. But you just seemed to . . . pass out for a few seconds. Perhaps you are different?'

Lucian let his breath hiss through his teeth, his mind full of the images that had just been gifted to him. He *knew* that place. It was a place he had been. Which meant that he had just recovered a memory.

'Do it again,' he demanded. 'I think your poison revealed something. Woke up a memory, or, I don't know, burned away whatever obscured it.'

'No.'

The monster girl retreated to the far side of the fire again.

'You *have* to,' he spat. 'Do it now, you hideous creature, or I'll . . .'

'Or you'll what?' The girl's face had hardened, and when he held her gaze, she didn't flinch or look away. 'Fall over at me again? I think you've forgotten who is tied up and who has the knife.'

He fell quiet, his mind racing. So she wouldn't touch him again right now, but her guard couldn't stay up for ever. The important thing was he had seen his past life. Just a single moment, a brief shining glimpse of something he'd thought he'd lost entirely. Perhaps everything could be regained. Perhaps all was not lost to him after all.

Lucian grinned wolfishly in the growing dark.

# CHAPTER 12

'If you've lived in the forest since you were twelve, how do you know where we are going?'

Elver frowned. 'I just do, okay?'

It was the next morning and they were walking through the wood, following a deer trail that Elver had picked up, heading east. It was no jih wood, that much was obvious – the signs and marks here were all those of animals you found anywhere: foxes, rabbits, badgers, squirrels, the usual cacophony of birds. The only monster here, aside from her and Artair, was the cub, and he was trotting along at their heels. His protests about the sack had finally worn her down, and after he had solemnly promised to not go out of their sight, she had set him free. They were in the woods, and reasonably unlikely to run into any humans. What could go wrong?

'This is an important task, and I don't want to head in the wrong direction. I have a map to Mother Maura's sanctum,' Artair said and tapped his pocket, 'but this Temple of Tisk could be anywhere, as far as I know.'

'Well, *I* know. I'm sure there's plenty you have no clue about, being stuck up there in the Golden Tower of Perpetual Boredom or whatever it's called, but I know things.'

'I just don't see how . . .'

Elver briefly considered attempting to poison him again, in the vague hope that her power would work on him after all, then discarded the idea. She thought of Lucian, whose experience of her touch had been very different, and entirely unexpected. What did it mean, that he recovered memories when her skin touched his? It was another complication on top of an already complicated situation.

'I collect books. Alright? I pick them up from people passing through the Jih Forest. Or on the road that passes by it. Sometimes, the Queen of Serpents will bring me ones she thinks I will find interesting. One of the books I found on the road was a big book of maps with all the roads and towns and rivers marked out.'

'When you say you picked them up, what do you mean?' Artair was looking at her keenly.

'Kind travellers donated them to me.' She glared back at him.

'You mean you *stole* them.'

'Don't get your robes in a twist. I left most of those people unharmed.' The cub had scampered on ahead, shouting something to her about squirrels. 'I've gathered quite a collection. And when things are quiet and there are no fool humans stomping through my forest that need scaring off, or no monster that's got itself caught in a trap or lost, then I read my books. I've read them a lot, over the years. I know most of them by heart.' She felt a little stab of pride. She knew that the humans that caught sight of her thought she was a ghost, or a wild creature, but the reality was she was probably more educated than any of them.

'Huh,' said Artair. 'That sounds lonely.'

'What?'

'Reading books instead of talking to people. It must be miserable, living out there all alone. At least I have my fellow novices to talk to.'

'Shows what you know,' said Elver sharply. 'Most monsters are vastly more interesting to talk to than any random human you care to name.'

'Brother Benzin knew all the names of all the plants in the garden, and he knew all their uses too.'

'I think you just proved my point.'

Artair looked at his feet and said nothing, and Elver remembered what had happened to Brother Benzin.

'Look,' she said eventually. 'If you don't believe me, I'll show you.'

She broke a stick from a young elm tree and then knelt by a clear patch of dirt. The cub was shouting at her again, about something else he'd seen in the trees, but she ignored it.

'Here.' She drew a small circle in the dirt. 'This is your monastery.' She drew a much larger section near it. 'This is my forest. This little turd here is Addersport, and the line of the coast goes like this. Now, over to the east there are several roads . . .' She took a moment to sketch these in while Artair watched closely. 'There's another city inland, smaller than Addersport, and then just beyond that is the Temple of Tisk. See? I'm not making it up.' She straightened up, pleased with her ability to recall the map so clearly. 'Did they not teach you any geography at the monastery?'

'They did,' Artair admitted. 'But I suppose it didn't seem very important. I was never going to see any of it.'

'Now *that* sounds miserable.'

Elver half expected him to argue with her, but instead he nodded. 'There are a lot of things I have missed.'

They began walking again, leaving the dirt map behind. Elver thought of the spirit that inhabited Artair when he went to sleep. Lucian had said that he never got to eat or drink, because Artair never left any food in his cell; she supposed that if he was never allowed outside, he barely knew what it was to feel a breeze on his face, or to sink his feet into an icy stream. It seemed to her that both of them were half a person, closed off from so much.

'I have heard about carriages, although we didn't have them where I grew up,' Artair said after they had been walking for some time in silence. 'Some of the novices have family that will travel to the monastery to visit them, and they talk about getting the carriage along bumpy roads. It doesn't sound comfortable, but it sounds fast. Faster than this, anyway.'

'I've seen them on the Jih Forest road,' said Elver. 'Cramped, stupid things, pulled by horses.' Around them, the day was growing warmer, building up into the kind of sultry heat that autumn sometimes liked to pull out of its hat. 'I suppose you have family? Who come to visit you in the Tower of Perpetual Boredom.'

'I . . . No. I don't have any family.'

She glanced at him, noting a change of tone in his voice. He was a striking figure walking next to her; broad-shouldered and narrow-waisted, with his bow and his ropes slung over his back. His hair was growing increasingly untidy, although she supposed she was hardly one to judge. And there was a shadow on his jaw, a darker splash of colour against his skin. She thought there was probably more to know about this family Artair claimed not to have, but when she opened her mouth to ask, she felt a sudden surge of annoyance with herself. *He's closer to human than monster. Why should I care if there are things he wishes to hide?*

'Anyway,' she said instead, 'a carriage is a stupid idea. Can you imagine this little pain in the arse in a carriage? We wouldn't last half a morning before he bit someone or weed on someone . . .' She stopped and looked around. The cub was nowhere in sight.

'Where is the cub?' asked Artair.

'I thought you were watching him!' She cast around and called for him. 'Where are you? I told you not to go wandering off!' There was no reply. 'If you don't come back now you'll not get any lunch!'

Nothing.

'If we've lost him . . .' Artair looked alarmed, which only made her angrier.

'Curse you and curse the Twelve, we'll have to retrace our steps.' Elver moved back up the trail. 'The last time I saw him I . . . No, wait, I didn't see him, I heard him, and he was talking about something in the trees, but I was drawing that map for you.' *Idiot*, she told herself. *The cub is your priority, not this half human boy.*

When they reached the patch of dirt still scrawled with images of the local area, she cast about and quickly found his pawprints sunk into the mud under a small gathering of hawthorn. On the gnarled bark of one such tree, she found a single crimson feather – the cub had brushed against it on his way somewhere.

Artair picked the feather from the bark and ran the pad of his thumb over it.

'He can't have gone far.'

'Worried about your precious novices?' snapped Elver. 'Don't worry, we'll find your bargaining chip.'

'That's not . . .'

But she wasn't listening. Now that she had found it, the trail was easy enough to follow – she spent most of her time in the Jih Forest tracking creatures, and the cub was no master of stealth. Beyond the copse of hawthorn, the wood began to thin out, and soon they were travelling over a more open area, green fields and yellow gorse and grey stone hedges lining a landscape that rumpled and bumped like a discarded blanket. This was not good news. Small roads snaked through this place, bringing travellers – bringing *humans* – any of whom could spot the cub and raise the alarm. Would they capture him? Drive him off? Or worse. The Jih Forest was a haven for a reason. Elver sped up, her heart in her mouth.

'I can't go back to the Queen of Serpents and tell her that I lost the cub,' she muttered, more to herself than to Artair.

'What's that?' Artair had stopped, one hand over his eyes to shield them from the glare of the sun. 'A tent?'

Elver lifted her eyes to the hills in front of them and spotted what he was looking at: not a single tent, but one large one surrounded by smaller versions of itself. They were striped purple and yellow, like garish pieces of candy dropped in the grass, and there were swarms of brightly dressed humans moving in and out of them. She wondered if this was what the cub had spotted through the trees. And, even worse, just ahead of them she could see new footprints in the grass and dirt. Human ones. And here the cub's trail ended.

'Someone has grabbed him.' Elver straightened up. 'Someone from that fair, I expect.'

'A fair?'

They began walking faster. 'They're things that humans do for entertainment. There will be loud music and men and women performing strange tricks, like . . . throwing balls at each other.' Elver tried to remember what she'd read about them. Sometimes, smaller fairs made their way through Addersport, but as an orphan she'd rarely had the coin to visit such things.

'Throwing balls at each other?' Artair sounded puzzled.

'And catching them. I don't know. Some of the humans will paint their faces to look funny, and wear large trousers.'

'Truly, the world is a strange place.'

'There's a sign, look.'

They were close enough to be able to read a banner hung on the largest tent. Each word was painted in elaborate, curling letters, purple and yellow and green. Artair read it aloud:

'In the name of Vilon the Many Limbed, Booster Barnham presents her World-Famous Cabinet of Monstrous Curiosities, Featuring Fearsome and Fascinating Jih Creatures from Every Corner of the Continent – All Legally Obtained and Restrained for Your Safety and Entertainment.'

'Oh,' said Elver. 'Fantastic.'

# CHAPTER 13

Inside the main tent, it was hot and stuffy, a strong smell of sawdust and sweat assaulting Artair's nostrils. The place was packed with people talking and laughing, while on top of three small stages elaborately dressed people shouted over the crowd. As they neared, Artair stopped to listen to one.

'Step right up, my good people, and witness the magic of my Lord Barleycorn this morning, the god that's closest to your hearts, no doubt.' The man on the stage wore a tall hat with a flat top and a long, patched coat that was sewn all over with tiny dolls made of corn and twigs. 'For the coins in your pockets I will bring you his bounty, magicked out of the air in front of your eyes.'

'Magpies,' Elver said darkly. She had pulled her hood up and was glowering from beneath it at the press of humans. 'What sort of mage performs tricks at a fair?'

'I did think magic was used for grander things.'

Someone from the audience was passing up a handful of change to the mage, who closed his hand around the coins before kissing his fist. When he opened his hand again, the coins were gone.

'My Lord Barleycorn has accepted your boon! Now let's see what he gives us in exchange.'

The mage picked up an empty glass from off the stage, and as his fingers brushed it, a ruddy liquid began to swirl up from the bottom, quickly filling it to the rim. He passed the glass to the member of the audience who had given him the coins, and she took a sip.

'It's beer!' she said, to general cheering.

'Embarrassing,' said Elver, 'that they're impressed with this nonsense. Who's to say it's really magic? He could have palmed those coins. Maybe that's a trick glass. He might not be a magpie at all.'

'It looked real enough to me,' said Artair. It was strange to think that a few days ago there had been nothing in his future but the same four walls and the gardens of the monastery, and now he was seeing magic performed in front of his eyes. The woman from the audience was passing the beer around for other people to taste, but Elver was dragging them away.

'Come on, this is just the preamble. The monster exhibits are on the other side of the tent.'

They passed the other two stages at a distance. On one, a tall mage dressed in black robes, a wide-brimmed hat and a skeletal crow mask was standing with their head bowed and one pale hand held out in a flourish. Next to this figure was a shifting shape of uncertain light. Artair could just about make out a face, the eyes much too hollow, lips moving soundlessly. The crowd here was hushed, their awed faces painted with ghost-light.

'Daft,' said Elver.

The third stage featured a portly, older woman, her grey hair loose over her shoulders. She was seated on the boards, and from her cupped hands a constant stream of tiny white mice flowed. They scampered down her leg to the stage, where they joined a growing pattern of mice circles, to the delight of several children in the audience.

'A mage of Milik the Small,' commented Elver. 'You don't often see those out in the wild. Here, look. I can see the cages.'

This part of the tent was darker. A striking woman in a short red leather coat was speaking in a hushed voice that somehow still carried. Her face was wide and expressive, with a large mouth ringed in lipstick that matched the jacket she wore. She had a wooden staff by her side with a silver hook on the end of it. This, Artair assumed, had to be Booster Barnham herself. He and Elver approached, standing slightly apart from the human audience.

'What you are about to see, my good fellows, is not for the faint-hearted,' the woman with the staff was saying. 'Each of these cages contains a child of that most fearsome and loathed of the Twelve, the Queen of Serpents.' Artair glanced at Elver to see if this had angered her, but her expression had not changed. *I'm jih too*, he thought. *Or the thing inside me is.* 'Captured from all over Tlevrae by our expert hunters, any one of these jih could end your life in an instant – *if*, that is, they weren't held back by the bars of our steel cages, blessed and reinforced by a mage of John Barleycorn, the god of blacksmiths. Do you dare to enter my Den of Monsters?'

There were mutters and gasps from the humans around them, and many of them held back, afraid to venture any further. Barnham struck one of the cages with her stick, and the creature inside, a great hairy spider as big as a dog, raised its mandibles and hissed. One of the children that had been standing in the front of the crowd suddenly turned and ran blindly, colliding with Elver's legs. The monster girl took a startled step backwards, as though the boy was made of hot coals, but it was too late. Artair saw the kid's pudgy little hand briefly grasp hers – the unthinking action of a child looking for comfort – and then he was crying, holding his burned hand to his chest. The child's parents scampered after him, their eyes wide.

'What did you do?' snapped the father. 'Did you fall?'

They hadn't seemed to connect the injury to Elver, and the mother picked up the wailing child and took him back to the tent entrance. Elver shoved her hands in her pockets, scowling.

'That wasn't your fault,' said Artair. Elver transferred her scowl to him.

'I know it wasn't,' she hissed. 'Stupid human nearly got himself killed. Little idiot. The sooner we're out of here, the better.'

Booster Barnham had moved on to the next cage, explaining to the audience what each creature was and where they'd captured it.

Elver strode towards the cages and Artair had to move quickly to keep up.

'I can't see the cub,' she said in a low voice.

'Perhaps he's near the back.' What if Elver was wrong, and the cub had wandered off somewhere else entirely? They might never find him again, and Mother Maura wouldn't hesitate to kill the other novices if he failed to give her what she wanted.

'I know. I'm sorry.'

'What?' Artair blinked. Could Elver read his mind? But then he realized she had gone over to one of the cages, and she wasn't speaking to him at all. The creature behind the bars was a lithe, cat-like monster, with huge eyes like saucers and shaggy, bat-like wings along its back. Elver passed her hand through the bars, and it came closer, pushing its snout against her fingers. From behind them, Artair heard more than a few gasps from the audience members that had spotted her.

'You have to understand,' Elver was saying, 'there's nothing I can do. I'm as out of place as you are . . .'

'Elver.' Artair tried to stand between her and the gathering crowd. 'People are looking at us, Elver.'

She stood up, and to his alarm he saw that her eyes were very bright, as though she were holding back tears.

'I can hear them all,' she said. 'Some of them have been here for months. For years. Why has the Queen of Serpents allowed this?'

'Maybe she doesn't know.'

In the next cage, there was an oozing, shifting creature with too many eyes; the next, a coiled serpent with long, spiralled horns like a deer. Little flickers of blue fire played around its nostrils. In the biggest cage, a monster with dark blue fur stood on two legs, a long wolfish face half hidden in shadows. All of the jih now were agitated, hooting or growling, pacing or even driving themselves against the bars.

'Here,' said the woman in the red coat. 'What are you two doing to get them all riled up like that?' She came over, brandishing the staff with the hook on the end.

'I see him,' said Artair. At the very end, in a shiny new cage, the keltraxia cub was spinning in circles, yapping. Artair found that he could well imagine what he was saying to Elver. He also realized that they had no plan on how to get the cub out of the tent, or even out of its cage. A seed of panic bloomed in his chest. How had this already gone so wrong?

*In this moment, I am safe,* he told himself. *And Elver needs my help.*

'All of these jih, trapped, kept prisoner by humans, for other humans to gawp at. All their voices . . .' Elver was pushing her hands through her hair, her hood falling back to reveal her yellow eyes and her scarred face.

Artair heard one of the humans near them turn to another and say, 'Looks like that girl should be in a cage too.' He clenched his fists.

*The Other is contained,* he reminded himself. *I will not do anything rash.*

'We have to get them out,' said Elver in a low voice. 'All of them. Now.'

'How?' Artair leaned his head towards hers so that only she could hear him. Next to them, Booster Barnham was poking at the furry blue creature with her hooked staff, pushing it back from the bars.

'I don't know, I just . . . I don't know.' For the first time since he'd met her, she sounded completely lost. He considered for a moment putting a hand on her shoulder, but knew it wouldn't be welcomed.

'Perhaps these humans can be reasoned with.'

Elver made a low noise of disgust. 'Then you don't know humans. All they care about is themselves, their coin and their comforts. Jih spirits? We're less than nothing to them, unless they can exploit us for money.'

'Surely not all of them are like that.' But when he looked at the cages, he found himself thinking of the monastery. He was jih too. And wasn't he also supposed to be kept in a cage?

Elver was flexing her hand in a meaningful way. 'I could grab the woman in charge. Poison her.'

'Then what? Poison everyone else?'

'Why not? They're all as bad as the woman with the stick.'

Artair frowned. 'There has to be a better way. I think I have an idea.'

Artair turned to Booster Barnham.

'My good woman! I would like to buy all of your monsters.'

The statement was met with a thunderous silence. At the back of the crowd of humans, someone laughed.

'Sure you do,' said the monster keeper. 'Do you have a death wish? I'll tell you what, why don't you buy my tame mages, instead? Much safer, and it'll give us all a laugh.'

The audience laughed obediently.

'I'm serious.' Artair reached into his pack and pulled out the bag of coins he had taken from the abbot's room. He had no real idea how much was in it, or even what it was worth, but it was heavy enough. He crouched, opened the throat of the bag and began to carefully pour its contents onto the sawdust-covered floor. Gold and silver coins poured forth, thick and heavy, and very quickly the laughter from the audience dried up. The demeanour of Barnham had changed too. Her eyes flickered from Artair to Elver and back again.

'What's this? Have you two robbed a merchant or something?'

'All of this, for all your monsters,' Artair offered grandly. 'That should be fair, I think.' He had no idea whether it was, but the keeper was shaking her head, a tight little smile on her face.

'I don't know what you're playing at, lad, but even that tidy sum of money is no replacement for the profit I make parading these creatures from town to town.' She raised her voice a little, addressing the crowd. 'What I do is a public service! It's education, rightly.'

'Then what about just that one.' Artair pointed at the keltraxia cub, who had pushed his snout through the bars and was sniffing madly. 'One cub, not even grown yet. For all this coin. That's got to represent a reasonable profit?' Artair was struck with the sudden urge to laugh, which he swallowed down. He was attempting to buy the freedom of a jih spirit when he himself contained a monster. 'What do you say?'

The woman tapped her staff on the ground, perplexed. In that moment, the cub decided to go to the toilet in a loud and dramatic fashion on the floor of the cage.

'Sold,' said the monster keeper. 'Haven't had time to get attached anyway. Get it out of my sight.'

# CHAPTER 14

'We have to go back. Get the others out.'

'What?' Artair looked at her, blinking as though she'd suggested they both sprout wings and fly the rest of the way. Around them, the day was coming to an end, the sun ducking out before its shift was truly over, as it often did in autumn.

'The rest of my jih kin. I can't just leave them to that fate. To be entertainment for gawping humans. You saw how they were being treated.'

'It was awful,' agreed Artair. 'But I have no money left. And I don't think even you could poison all the people without getting caught. How do we get them out?'

'I don't know.' Elver bit her lip, frustrated. 'We have to try.'

'It's too dangerous. What if they figure out that we're jih spirits too? I don't think that woman in the red coat would need to think too long about sticking you in a cage.' He frowned. 'And then what would we do?'

'I'd kill her before she ever got me inside a cage,' Elver said darkly. She glanced at Artair's face: he looked troubled, his brows pulled down low over his eyes, but she could tell he wasn't convinced. He had his people to save, after all. What did it matter if she also had kin she needed to rescue, if those kin had fur and feathers and fangs? A hot flare of anger roused in her chest, and she wished again that her poison would work on him. *Kill him, take the cub, go home.* It would be the easiest thing in the world.

'I'm sorry,' he said, and to her surprise he touched her shoulder briefly, as though reassuring a friend. 'Perhaps we can get something from the Tisk mage to help save them. And we can get them out on the way back.'

Elver moved away from him so that touching her shoulder again wasn't a possibility. 'Yes,' she said shortly. There had to be another way, and perhaps Artair didn't need to know about it. 'Let's do that.'

That night, when Lucian opened his eyes, he found that he was still outside, in a makeshift camp that looked more or less the same as the one they'd been in the night before – trees, bushes, a stream. Standard outside things. But when he heaved himself into a sitting position, his hands bound behind his back, it was to find the monster girl standing over him, her dagger in hand.

'Good evening to you too,' he sighed. 'The monks might have been pompous, pious prigs, but at least they didn't greet me with sharp blades.' He shifted on the grass. 'They didn't greet me at all, to be fair.'

'I have an offer for you,' said Elver. 'One I think you'll want to listen to.'

'Oh? More apples, perhaps?'

'How about . . .' She pursed her lips, as though speaking this aloud cost her in some way. 'If you help me with something, I will help you get your memories back.'

'You'll touch me?'

She nodded shortly.

'Oh, that is interesting. And what would I have to help you with, monster girl?'

'There is a fair near here with a load of jih creatures held captive. I want to get them out.'

He sat up a little straighter. 'The monk wouldn't help you?'

Something passed over her face that he couldn't read and then it was gone. 'He got the cub out. Used all the money we've got to do it. But he won't go back for the others. Whereas I think you're desperate enough to get your memories back that you'll do as I ask.'

Lucian grinned. 'I would say you are a very observant monster. I have one more request though.'

She scowled, but he sensed that she needed this badly, and for the first time in a long while he had a small advantage.

'What is it?'

'If I help you, you'll tell me what is going on here, and why our sweet little monk is on the run from his monastery.'

Elver paused. He could tell that she was still very far from trusting him. But in the end she shrugged.

'Fine. It's not like it matters to me.'

'Then I agree to your terms. Let's go.'

'There is one last thing.' She brandished the knife in front of his face. 'If you try to touch me without my permission, I will cut exciting new holes in you. Do you understand?'

'I wouldn't dream of it! I might be an evil spirit, but I am also a gentleman,' said Lucian. 'Now, let's get these ropes off me so we can go and cause some trouble.'

# CHAPTER 15

'I can't believe they've only left one guard here at night,' whispered Elver.

Lucian leaned in close, so that his mouth was only an inch away from her ear. 'I imagine he's just here to make sure the cages don't spontaneously collapse. Who would be unhinged enough to be breaking in here to steal monsters?'

'A dark spirit trapped in the body of a monk, for one. And step away from me. There's no need to be that close – I know what you're up to.'

Lucian grinned in the dark. He was unbound. He had walked under the night's sky, had seen the stars, had felt the gathering wind on his cheek. And now he was crouched behind a wall of crates that smelt suspiciously like spoiled meat, next to a jih girl who was ready to stab him if he so much as brushed her hand with his, while they watched a beefy man in his early middle age tease a monster in a cage. For the first time in a long while, it felt good to be alive – even if he was trapped in a borrowed body.

'Did you have a plan, monster girl?'

'The beginnings of one. Do you see the creature in the pen right at the end of the row?'

Lucian did. It looked like the last possible thing you wanted to stumble across in a dark wood. It resembled a large, armoured lizard, orange leathery skin covered in hard plates like giant thorns. It had a sizeable crest ringing its head like a halo, and even in the gloom, Lucian could see the muscles on its broad chest and legs. Yet it was curled up on itself as though it hoped no one would notice it. Outside, the wind was growing louder, and somewhere a flap of tent hadn't been tied down properly – it snapped like a boat sail caught in a gale.

'I see it. Quite a brute.'

'The Coshod. They're docile enough, and very social – they live in big groups, and when they hunt, they have the ability to grow much larger. Bigger than that cage, certainly.'

'Ah.'

'He hasn't done it himself because he's alone, and they are always in packs when they hunt. Maybe I can tell him he's not alone.'

'So the monster breaks out of his cage – and then what?'

The guard had a long staff with a hook on the end, which he was reaching through the bars with. He prodded at a furry blue creature that was already crouched at the very back of the cage. Lucian felt something sharpen inside him. Meanwhile, Elver shrugged.

'It's a distraction, isn't it? One monster out. While the guard deals with that, we can find the keys for the rest of the cages. Open them up.'

'Chaotic, full of holes. As plans go, I like it.'

She shot him an angry look. 'Do you have any better ideas?'

Annoyingly, he didn't. He nodded to the cage in question. It was in the deepest shadows, and furthest from the guard at that moment, but that could change very quickly if the man got bored of tormenting the blue monster. 'You'd better get to it. I'll watch your back.'

Elver crept behind the crates and over to the Coshod cage. She moved silently, without even the slightest rasp of boot against the sawdusted floor, and with her dark hood up she was almost invisible. All that gave her away was the flash of a pale hand or a section of her still, unsmiling face. When she was close to the cage, she reached out and carefully slid her arm between the bars so that she could place the flat of her hand against the leathery hide of the monster. Lucian saw the creature shift with surprise at the touch and raise its head cautiously. He saw Elver's lips moving as she spoke, but could not hear what she was saying over the sound of the wind. He glanced back at the guard, still too absorbed in tormenting his own monster to notice them.

It wasn't long before Lucian's anger began to rise, as it always did. He thought of the cell at the monastery, so many years spent staring at the same four walls, watching the face of the monk change in the mirror, grow older, his hair growing longer, the shadow of stubble at his jaw appearing. All while being unable to remember his own face, until *this* face – this hated image of the person who kept him prisoner just as much as the Brothers and Sisters did – this face became . . . his own. It was a vicious kind of torment, not so dissimilar from being poked with a stick when you had nowhere to escape to.

Elver was still talking to the animal, a desperate expression on her face. The Coshod had shifted towards her, big wet eyes blinking in the low light, but as far as Lucian could see, it didn't look any larger. The guard, though, had straightened up and was moving to the next cage, the hooked staff at the ready. Lucian thought they had a handful of minutes before they were discovered, at best.

*Hurry up, monster girl.*

Yet, despite himself, he realized he wanted them to be discovered. There was a power within himself, as yet untapped, that he needed to reignite. He knew it. And he wanted to use it on this guard. He wanted to make him pay.

Lucian half rose from where he crouched, and he saw Elver glance at him in alarm. She shook her head slightly. The Coshod, Lucian now saw, *had* in fact grown – its head was closer to the ceiling of its cage, and its broad shoulders looked even more threatening. *It's working*, Lucian thought, a perplexing mixture of relief and frustration washing through him.

The guard was at the next cage, his staff worrying at a creature that looked like a large, winged cat, its fur covered in dark spots. The jih batted at the staff with one heavy paw and in retaliation the guard thrust the hooked end into the creature's soft underbelly, causing it to hiss. Elver looked up at the sound, an expression of pain flickering over her face.

That was enough. Lucian stood up and walked out from behind the crates, not troubling to move silently as Elver had. The guard spun to face him, withdrawing the staff from the cage. Lucian smiled. That was a start.

'Who are you?' demanded the guard.

'I suppose you'd say I'm a concerned citizen,' said Lucian. 'What have those creatures ever done to you?'

'They're monsters. Jih.' The guard half laughed, shook his head. 'Evil, wretched things. Dangerous things.'

Lucian nodded, delighted. Yes. This was what the monks called him and his kind, too.

'They don't look so dangerous. Locked away in these cages, they look pretty sorry for themselves, actually. Yet here you are, poking them with a stick, tormenting them for kicks.' He moved closer to the guard, making sure to keep the man's eyes on him. 'Does it make you feel powerful, little man? I'm genuinely curious.'

'Cheeky little swine. You're not supposed to be in here, you know that?' The guard squared up to him. 'You can visit the monsters during opening hours, same as everyone else. And you can pay the fee, same as everyone else.'

Lucian laughed. He could sense the shape that was Elver, her eyes on him.

'What I'm going to do,' he said, 'is take that staff from you and find an inventive new place to store it. How about that?'

The reaction was everything he'd hoped for. The guard scowled and came at him, and when he was close enough, Lucian yanked the staff from his hands, surprised at the strength in his own arms. He lifted the staff, too slowly, as it turned out, and the guard punched him squarely on the jaw – hard, but not so hard he went down. Lucian staggered back, his free hand going to his face. His eyes were watering.

'You're going to regret that,' he told the guard. At that moment, there was a shattering, splintering noise, and barely a second later the Coshod crashed into the older man, sending him flying. There was an unpleasant crunching sound as he hit the wooden boards that served as the floor.

Elver appeared, her hood pushed back. Her yellow eyes looked like a pair of moons in the half-light.

'Is he dead?' she asked. She didn't look particularly concerned.

Lucian went and stood over the guard, who was groaning. The Coshod, meanwhile, was stomping around the tent in what Lucian assumed was a victory lap.

'No, more's the pity. He's broken his wrist though, and given his head a good knock. Ah.' He crouched and went through the man's pockets. 'I've got the keys to the other cages.'

They made short work of it, releasing all of the monsters and unlacing the main entrance so that the larger creatures had space to leave. Once, the jih that looked like a spotted cat rounded on Lucian, fangs bared, and Elver spoke to it in her quiet, considered voice – quite different to the voice she used to speak to him, Lucian noticed – and it turned away, mollified.

'That's quite a skill you have, monster girl,' he said as they were walking back over the fields to their camp. The wind had died down, leaving a strange hush to the countryside. 'Speaking to jih. And they listen to you.'

'A gift from the Queen of Serpents.' She was taking care to walk with a sizeable gap between them.

'And not your only one.' He held out his hand to her, palm turned towards the sky. 'Will you let me have a glimpse of my past, Elver?'

'When we get back to the camp. I'm still not sure how all this works, and I don't want you keeling over into the grass. I don't fancy dragging you back to camp.'

'Then you'll tell me why the monk is spending his days with a monster girl and not a bunch of yellow-robed fools.'

'I don't see why I should.'

Lucian felt his anger rising again and smothered it with some effort.

'I've helped you free your monstrous siblings, and received a punch in the jaw for my efforts. And I could have run to the hills at any point. I could have turned you in to that monster jailer and they could have had a new exhibit the next day.' He raised his hands, as if framing a sign. 'Monster girl from the Jih Forest, touch her and die! Eyes like a snake, an abomination—'

'I'm curious. Is this how you get what you want from people?' She cocked her head towards him, as though she really wanted to know. 'Does this usually work?'

Lucian stopped, gritting his teeth. For a few seconds, there was a tense silence between them.

'I claimed to be a gentleman earlier,' he said eventually. There was a need to be careful here, after all. The monster girl could give him access to his past life. He couldn't throw that away just because she was unbelievably irritating. 'Clearly I have forgotten what one of those is.'

'Yeah, I thought that. I thought, this evil spirit is remarkably rude.' To his own surprise, he smiled.

'Quite. Elver, I don't expect you to be my friend. I know what I am.' She glanced up at him, a new expression on her face. Yes, he knew this would work. A monster girl had to be lonely, and she'd naturally have sympathy for the isolated and the unwanted. He gave a sigh and set his features into a faintly wistful expression. 'I only want to know what's going on. I've spent years locked away, Elver, and this is my first glimpse of the wider world. Of course I want to know why I'm suddenly here.'

For a long moment, Elver didn't say anything. When she did speak, she didn't look at him, as though by staring out across the shadows she wasn't giving in to him. 'Look. There is a mage called Mother Maura. She wants the jih cub for a sacrifice to the Bloody Claw and she kidnapped the other novices to force Artair to steal him from the forest. We're going to get an illusion spell from a mage of Tisk so that he can get them back without giving up the cub.'

Lucian raised his eyebrows. He had the strangest feeling that these names should mean something to him, and yet clarity danced just out of reach. Perhaps the next memories he unlocked would reveal something. There had to be more to it.

'Ah. That is . . . quite the quest. Have you come of your own accord, desperate to please our young monk, or did the Queen of Serpents order you to track down the monster cub?'

Elver didn't answer for a moment, and when she did her voice was colder than it had been.

'That's enough questions.'

Later, after Lucian had consented to be tied up again, he'd turned onto his back to face the stars and considered what he had seen, his jaw throbbing faintly.

A glimpse had truly been all it was, yet it was still an unbearably tantalizing thing. When she had taken his hand in hers, he had seen a room full of books and the faces of other young people, fierce with concentration. They were studying something, he knew, the same thing he was studying, and in that memory he had felt the sharp edges of his own ambition. He would be better than them. He would beat them.

And then it was gone, and all he had was the cold hand of the monster girl held in his.

But it was something. If he could gather enough pieces of his fragmented life, he could build them into something that gave him sense and meaning and, eventually, a path. All he had to do was keep travelling with the girl until he had enough pieces and then he could discard her.

Lucian smiled to himself in the dark and closed his eyes.

# CHAPTER 16

When Elver untied Artair the next morning, he sat up a little stiffly, rubbing at his jaw. It felt tender to the touch and mildly swollen on one side. He gritted his teeth; he had the impression they'd been given a good rattle. A cold sensation passed over him as he watched Elver kick dirt over their fire.

'What happened last night?'

'What do you mean?'

'Did he . . . Did the Other give you trouble?' He stood up hurriedly. 'Did he hurt you?'

The monster girl looked at him blankly for a moment, then seemed to note how he had his fingers pressed to his jaw.

'Oh. Yeah. No, he didn't hurt me. But I had to . . . hit him. Sorry about that.'

This was his nightmare come true. The evil that was inside him was hurting others. *In this moment, I am safe, and the evil is contained*, he told himself. But the words felt hollow.

'What did he do? Did he get free? Did he try to run?'

Elver frowned, no longer looking at him. Oddly, she seemed vaguely embarrassed.

'It was nothing. He kept asking daft questions, so I had to hit him to get him to shut up.' She looked up at him then in a slightly challenging way.

'I am sorry,' said Artair. 'Really sorry.' His face suddenly felt warm. What kind of questions was the Other asking? Whatever they were, they had clearly made Elver uncomfortable. 'Perhaps tonight you should gag me as well as tie me up.' Elver shot him a look, and his cheeks grew even warmer. 'I just thought—'

'Maybe I should gag you today as well.' But there was a quirk to the corner of her mouth as she said it, as though she were trying not to smile, and that made him feel a little better.

In the morning light, she seemed to have put the business of the other trapped jih spirits behind her and that made him feel a little lighter, too. She really was going to help him.

'Wait . . .' She stalked over to their bag of food and lifted it up by the end. The cub rolled out of it, making happy snuffling noises. He was followed by a cloud of crumbs. 'Twelve save us, the little turd has eaten all our food!'

'And we spent all our money yesterday.' Artair winced. The cub looked a little bigger than he had, certainly around the tummy area, and he had fewer feathers and more blue scales. Artair supposed he was growing up.

'*You* spent all of our money,' pointed out Elver. She sighed. 'Come on. Let's pack up and go. Maybe we can find some food on the road.'

After the wild weather of the night before, the sky had been scrubbed clean, revealing a bright cold day filled with birdsong. As they got ready to leave, Artair thought he heard something in the wood, back the way they had come; a cough maybe, a shuffle. He had the peculiar sense, as he stood there staring into the trees, that something was staring back at him – and he had the distinct impression that it hated him.

*You're being ridiculous,* he told himself. *There's no one out there. No one even knows you in the wider world.*

The idea was meant to reassure him, but instead it made him think of the time before the Golden Tower of the Perpetual Morning. Once, there had been people who knew him. Had cared about him even. And what had happened to them?

He closed his eyes briefly, summoning the words of his mantra. There was a task he had to finish and he couldn't afford to be distracted from it. Dredging up his old, fragmented memories would not help him.

When Elver called him a second time, he slung his bow on his back and followed her back onto the path.

They walked until midday, and between the pair of them they found a handful of edible things: Elver discovered a colony of blackberry bushes that had mostly been picked clean by birds and some underripe nuts on a tree Artair didn't recognize, while Artair picked some wild tubers that were good to chew on.

'How long until we reach this mage?' asked Artair, after his stomach had performed a particularly loud and musical rumble.

'A few days at least,' said Elver gloomily. 'By which time I'll be ready to eat this grass. Or the cub will be ready to eat us.'

Eventually, they emerged from the wood onto another man-made road; this one, in Artair's opinion, much prettier than the last. It was paved with smooth white stone, and on its borders pink and yellow flowers were growing in abundance, filling the air with a sweet, heady scent. The road trickled off into the distance like a fine ribbon. Despite himself, Artair smiled. The view from the monastery walls had nothing like this.

'What are you smiling at?'

The cub, perhaps sensing that he was already in trouble, had consented to be put back in the sack and Artair could hear him snoring lightly from Elver's arms.

'It's a fine day,' he said simply. 'And I'm in a part of Tlevrae I never expected to see.' He glanced down at her. She had pulled back her hood and the light bounced off her white hair like a beacon.

He could see the blue mark of one of her scars, stark against her collarbone. 'I suppose I'm seeing a lot of things I never expected to see.'

'I'm glad you're having such a lovely time,' said Elver. 'But I feel like I shouldn't have to remind you that you're only here because Mother Maura – may her face shrivel up and fall off – has kidnapped your friends.'

'Ha.' He knew that she hated the mage because she had orchestrated the theft of one of the jih spirits, but the idea that she was on his side in some way made him feel better than he had in days. When he'd left the Golden Tower he'd been afraid of being alone. And now Elver was with him. 'But we've got a plan, right? We're going to get them back.'

Elver snorted. 'A plan feels like a very grand word for what it is. But if we can get that illusion spell, we've a chance.'

Artair nodded. 'I'm glad we're taking it. The chance, I mean.'

The pair of them lapsed into silence for the next hour or so, until a shape emerged from the trees ahead of them. It looked like a tall, covered cart with a pair of oversized wheels, and it was being pulled by a figure in a wide green hat. The cart itself was painted a deep green, with curling, looping patterns picked out in white and pale blue. It turned on the road and started heading towards them.

'A walking shop,' said Elver. 'This might be our chance to get some coin. If you keep him talking, I will sneak up on him and give him a little taste of poison.' She saw the expression that passed over Artair's face. 'Only a touch! Enough to knock him out.'

'So your first instinct is to steal.'

'Monk, the sooner you realize that humans don't care about us, that they hate us, actually, the easier things will be for you.' She snorted. 'They barely even like themselves, let alone monsters. We're nothing to them. If the situation were reversed, this human wouldn't hesitate, believe me.'

'We could sell him something instead,' said Artair quickly.

'And what have we got to sell?'

'My bow,' he said, although his heart sank as he said it. The bow belonged to the monastery, and it was a beautiful thing, carved with sigils of the Perpetual Morning's holy order.

*And they used one exactly like it to kill Chessun*, whispered a traitorous voice in his head.

'Oh sure, go and face Mother Maura with no weapons, that sounds like a great plan,' said Elver.

'I'm tricking her, not fighting her,' he replied. 'I imagine we could get a good price for the bow and then in the next town we can get some food. Maybe a room for the night. And, if I'm honest, every time I look at the thing I think about the cub's mother. I'd be glad to be rid of it.'

As they had been speaking, the thing Elver had called a walking shop had been approaching them and, as far as Artair could tell, speeding up. The man pulling the cart was a cheerful-looking chap with long red hair, a sharp nose and a lean physique – no doubt from pulling his cart about everywhere. He smiled warmly as he approached. Artair suspected that if he hadn't been holding the poles of his cart he would have been waving madly.

'What ho, young lovers!' he called. Elver sighed. As they drew up to the cart, he lowered the poles and stepped forward to shake their hands. Artair watched, bemused, as his hand was pumped enthusiastically, while Elver drew away with her arms folded. 'Not a shaker? Fair enough. You don't know where I've been, do you?' The trader grinned at them. 'Lorian Owllight is my name, a humble magicar performing spells in the name of our Lady Dusk.' He sketched a quick bow.

'Another bloody magpie,' said Elver.

'Not a fan of the magical arts either? Child, you wound me.' But Lorian remained positively cheerful, Artair noted. 'Would you care to buy or sell this fine afternoon?'

'You can do magic?' Artair glanced at Elver, who was shaking her head slightly. 'Could you . . . make something look like something else? Or hide things?'

'Oh now, those sound like the sorts of spells you'd want to be getting from Tisk the Trickster,' said Lorian. He used one finger to push back the brim of his green hat, and in the bright sunshine Artair saw that he was younger than he'd initially thought – barely older than he or Elver. 'My Lady Dusk doesn't go in for that sort of thing, I'm afraid. She will take your poems and your songs and in return she will give you a glimpse of your future. An extraordinary deal, don't you think?' He leaned towards them, as though imparting a secret. 'They have to be ones she hasn't heard before, mind. Easily bored, easily changeable, that's our lady.'

'We have a bow to sell,' Elver said shortly. 'How much will you give us for it?'

Lorian raised his eyebrows so they disappeared under his hat brim. 'Oh well, let's not be hasty. Here, have a wee look at my wares first. Perhaps we can trade rather than get dirty old coins involved.'

He flicked a hook on the side of his cart and the blind it was holding in place clattered up. Beneath it was a compartment lined with many shelves, and all the shelves were packed with things: wooden whistles, jars of silver buttons, a stuffed crow, paintbrushes, clay pots with faces painted on them, a brass trumpet, various figurines of the gods, a velvet swatch pierced all over with copper needles, rolls of blue and yellow silk and a crystal ball.

'We're just looking to sell the bow and be on our way,' said Elver.

'I see this one drives a hard bargain,' said Lorian. 'Let's have a look at it, then, this mysterious and mighty bow.'

Artair unslung the weapon from his back and passed it to Lorian, who turned it over and over in his clever fingers. He was nodding.

'Fine, very fine. The Golden Tower of the Perpetual Morning. Interesting. And where did you get a thing like this?' The trader's expression was still friendly, but there was a new edge to his glance when he looked at Artair. 'Those monks aren't exactly known for being open or friendly, and who can blame them, given what they guard?'

Artair felt his skin prickle with heat. He opened his mouth to reply, but Elver spoke over him.

'We found it. How much coin will you give us?'

'Straight down to business. Fair enough, fair enough.' He turned it over once more, then nodded. 'I will give you five gold coins and thirty silver. Will that do you?'

'Sold,' said Elver. 'Hand it over.'

'Ten gold coins,' said Artair. He was thinking of the gold and silver he'd taken from the abbot's room and how he had poured it out onto the sawdusted floorboards to buy back the cub. 'And thirty silver.'

'Oh ho! I do like a bit of sweet back and forth under a sunny sky.' The trader grinned. 'Six gold and forty silver.'

'We don't have time for this,' said Elver.

'Eight gold, fifty silver.'

'Six gold, forty silver, and this fine necklace for your lady.' Lorian plucked a narrow chain from his wares – it had a blue stone pendant hanging from it carved into the shape of a crescent moon. 'It carries a blessing from *my* lady. Which is no small thing.'

'You can keep your trinkets,' said Elver sharply, and Artair felt an odd pang of disappointment. It might have been nice to give her a gift. 'We just need the coin.'

'Seven gold,' said Artair. 'Sixty silver. That's as low as I'll go. It's a very fine bow. I reckon you won't see another like it on this road, or any other.'

Lorian nodded ruefully. 'Alright, my good sir, I think you have me there. Seven gold and sixty silver it is.'

Artair smiled. Back in his previous life, the one he didn't like to think about too closely, he had often watched his parents haggle on market days and sometimes he would be allowed to throw in his own suggestions. Being able to touch those old days, even in a small way, brought him both pleasure and a sense of dread.

Lorian passed the bow back to Artair and then opened a small compartment on the cart with a key around his neck. There were coins in there, which he quickly counted out onto his hand, then filled a small canvas bag with them. He tossed the bag to Elver, who snatched it out of the air easily.

'I have a poem,' said Artair. The words were out of his mouth before he even knew he was going to speak them. 'I'll give it to you if the Lady Dusk will tell me my future.' Out of the corner of his eye, he could see Elver glaring at him, but Lorian looked delighted.

'This is more like it!' Lorian beamed at him. 'It's a deal, my young handsome friend.'

Artair closed his eyes briefly, trying to remember. All those years he had been reciting lines of poems to Brother Benzin through his cell door. There had to be loads that the Lady Dusk hadn't heard before.

'Fallen is the star,' he said. 'The sky grows darker at night. Our mistress moon smiles on.'

'Ah!' Lorian straightened up as though moved by some unseen hand. 'She does not know that one.' He smiled widely and his eyes filled with a shimmering mauve light. He raised his left hand and traced on his palm was a strange symbol a little like a star. 'Listen carefully: I see . . . I see . . .' The trader's smile faltered. 'I see a future fractured, a destiny tugged in two directions. I see blood in the water and poison both expected and unexpected. A terrible bargain and one heart replaced with another.'

'You see what I mean?' said Elver. 'Typical magpie. Promises all sorts but gives you gibberish.'

Artair thanked Lorian regardless and they took their leave, feeling a little lighter for the lack of the bow but more certain where their next meal was coming from. As they made their way down the road, Artair turned back once to see the trader standing with his cart, watching them leave with a troubled expression on his previously cheery face.

# CHAPTER 17

They arrived at the gates of Ashingdown just as dusk began to melt into true evening, a sharper note of cold on the air. *The first touch of winter*, thought Elver. Winter was always a difficult time in the Jih Forest, when it was harder to hunt and fish and there was little in the way of greenery to eat. But now that she was out in the human world, the thought of winter in the forest was a comfort: the peace of a heavy snowfall versus the cacophony of human company.

Ashingdown itself was a walled town, and as they approached the gate, she felt a stirring of disquiet: there were red stone pillars to either side of the gate, tall as a man, and on the top of each was a lion carved from grey stone, their jaws open to display brightly burning torches. The dirt road of the gate jumped with shadows full of teeth.

'We're entering enemy territory.'

'What do you mean?' asked Artair. He'd been quiet since he'd wasted time with Lorian.

Elver nodded to the stone lions as they passed them. 'It looks like the Bloody Claw is a big deal in this place. We might want to keep our heads down.'

Artair's eyes widened. The guards on the gate, Elver noticed, had leaping lions embroidered onto their leather tunics.

'Let's find somewhere to stay and get something to eat,' said Artair, 'and we'll leave as early as we can. Just to be safe.'

'Agreed.'

Inside, the town was a place of narrow, jumbled streets, with buildings that looked as though they'd seen better days – blinds hung off windows, piles of broken crates filled corners, and the cobbled stone paths were grimy and smeared with mud. There weren't many people around and those that did walk the streets walked hurriedly, their collars turned up to the night air. And here and there, dotted on corners or leering from the corners of windows, there were statues of the Bloody Claw. To her surprise and annoyance, Elver found herself missing the bright sparkling waterways of Addersport.

'Think about it,' she said. 'If you only have to give that mage a poem to get him to tell you your future, how good is the prediction really going to be? Why did you even bother?'

Artair was quiet for a moment. Inside the sack, the cub was asleep in Elver's arms, snoring ever so slightly.

'When this is all over, I will return to the monastery with the rest of the novices and I suppose we will attempt to rebuild the order. While I am out here in the world, I want to try all the things it has to offer.' He paused.

Elver found she was slightly put out by that. 'You mean you really intend to go back to your cell? Just . . . spend the rest of your life shut away from everything?'

'It is my duty,' Artair said gently. 'If I don't, I am putting the rest of the world in danger. The Other that is inside me can't be allowed to roam freely.'

Elver thought of Lucian, how he had walked right up to the guard in the fair and got himself punched.

'Don't you intend to return to the Jih Forest when this is done?' continued Artair. 'You are also shut away from the world. You just do it among the trees.'

'That's different,' said Elver, frowning.

'Because I think you could live among humans if you wanted to,' continued Artair. He lowered his voice as a woman in a long coat strode past them. 'Your golden eyes are very striking, but you could explain them away, say that it runs in your family or something. They might never know unless you told them. Or touched them.'

'That's the whole point! Why would I want to live among the people who had me . . . the people who hate me so much? I choose the forest because . . . because that's where I belong.'

'I suppose that's the difference between us,' said Artair. 'You have a choice, and I do not.'

Elver opened her mouth, sure she wanted to argue with him on this but not quite sure how. She closed it again when a tall man emerged from a side street ahead of them. He had blond hair and a face half hidden under a dark scarf, and he was walking stiffly to her eye. Half a second before he reached them, she realized who it was.

'Wait—'

The priest of Trilot removed what looked to be a shuttered lamp from inside his long coat and, using his other hand, pulled a cord. There was a blinding flash of light, searing white, and before she knew where she was, Elver found she was lying on the dirty cobblestones. She felt as though she'd run full pelt into a brick wall. The sack containing the cub had rolled to one side, and she locked eyes with the startled monster.

'Run!' she told him.

Artair, who had largely missed the blast of light, stumbled backwards in surprise as Kantor Witt crouched over Elver. From another pocket the priest produced a knife, which he pressed to her throat. The scarf had fallen down and Elver could see her own livid handprint emblazoned on his pale cheek.

'The light of Trilot burns you, monster,' he hissed, before looking up at Artair. 'Move even slightly, Sleepless, and I'll open her throat right here on the street.'

'How did the other priests like that pretty mark on your cheek?' she asked, before reaching for his exposed face, but Kantor Witt pressed the blade closer and she felt it bite at her skin. A hot trickle of black blood traced a path down her neck.

'Stop! Stop it, please,' said Artair. He had his hands held up in front of him. 'We'll do what you ask.'

'Good. Get up.' Kantor Witt put his lamp down on the ground, the shutter having fallen back into place, and with his gloved fist took a handful of her hair. Gritting her teeth, Elver got to her feet. The sack on the cobbles was empty and the cub was nowhere to be seen. That was something at least. 'You're both coming with me.'

The magistrate's premises looked in better condition than the other buildings they'd seen so far, and it also had the largest statue of the Bloody Claw; he prowled over the stone lintel, his mane caught in an imaginary wind. Kantor Witt had summoned the town's guard, and so they had quite an entourage as they were escorted up the steps. To Elver's annoyance, the guards wore leather gauntlets and made short work of binding her hands behind her back in tough steel manacles.

Inside, the place was deep in shadows, lit with the odd oil lamp here and there – presumably due to the late hour – and Elver only got brief impressions of this main room as they were hurried through it: a raised pulpit and rows of chairs facing it; a structure not unlike the cage the cub had recently escaped, made of polished brown wood; a stone altar carved with deep runnels across it that led to similar recesses in the floor. Elver frowned at those.

'We shouldn't have sold your bow,' she said.

Artair glanced at her and she caught a rueful expression on his face, but the guards shoved them on before he could reply.

Beyond the main room, some of the town guard split off, and they were left with Kantor Witt and two burly young men who looked like they had been pulled away from the important business of downing ales at the local tavern. One of these opened a heavy wooden door onto a much cosier room. The walls were lined with books – despite herself, Elver found her eyes widening – and there was a fire burning in a hearth. In front of it were a pair of comfortable chairs with two figures sat in them. One of them rose as they entered, standing with her hands clasped behind her back. Elver's gaze glanced over her face, then snapped back, suddenly unable to look away.

'You.'

The woman frowned at her. She was older than she had been, of course, and a little thicker around the waist, but her skin still shone with health, and her hair was braided beneath a red cloth cap. Elver waited for the moment of recognition to come, and there was something – a little flicker in the creases around the woman's eyes – but then the woman turned her attention to the figure sitting in the other chair. This was clearly another priest of Trilot, although one of higher rank than Kantor Witt. He wore a featureless ivory mask lined with silver filigree, white robes and long white calfskin gloves.

'This is what I'm dragged away from my dinner for, Faceless Isnere?'

The priest shrugged. 'What am I to do with reports of two jih spirits loose on the streets of Ashingdown, Magistrate Dalesh? Or would you rather I let it go and your people can learn about them when they've killed someone?'

'We're not the ones killing people,' said Elver. To her own horror, she was finding it increasingly difficult to speak. Looking at Dalesh, all she could think of was the fall from the Tumble Stone, the slippery thump of landing on hard serpent flesh, and the dwindling light as she was dragged down into the lair of the Queen of Serpents. She'd never forgotten their faces, the two who had dragged her up those steps. 'You should ask her about that,' she said, jerking her chin at Dalesh. 'Sacrificed any orphans lately, Magistrate Dalesh?'

Dalesh sighed. 'Who are these people? This lad looks barely old enough to shave.'

Kantor Witt stood to one side of them, trembling with what Elver assumed was rage. He was sweating and the hand mark on his face was especially clear.

'The girl is a jih creature straight out of the forest to the west. Her touch is poison.' His hand floated up to his cheek, fingers brushing the mark. 'She has tainted me, stolen from me my purity and my connection to Trilot, who has turned his back on me. I demand she be . . . cleansed. The boy is one of the Sleepless, escaped from the monastery in the Broken Path Mountains.'

'That's not true,' said Elver, at the same moment Artair said, 'How do you know that?'

'I followed you.' Kantor Witt grinned at them, his eyes too bright. 'I've heard you talking, at night, and in the morning.' He cocked his head at Elver. 'Does he know? What you two get up to at night?'

'What do you mean?' asked Artair, but Dalesh was already talking over them.

'Isnere, please get your priest back on his leash. I don't have time for this.'

Faceless Isnere sighed and stood up slowly. It was impossible to tell how old he was beneath the regalia of Trilot, but from the way he moved, Elver got the sense of an older man with aching joints.

'Very well. Witt, you are to be commended on trailing and capturing these two unclean spirits. I am sure it will go some way to mending your connection with our lord. We will take these two to the Faceless House now and they will be disposed of as our lord sees fit.'

'Hold on now,' said Dalesh. 'Ashingdown was built with the blessings of the Bloody Claw, the blood of sacrifice poured into its very foundations. By rights, these two should go to Him.'

'And I thought you wanted to get back to your dinner?' said Isnere. 'No, I'm afraid I must insist, Dalesh. Look at this fool's face.' He gestured to Witt, who lowered his head in shame. 'It's the direst insult to Trilot and it must be accounted for.'

'Personally, I think I've improved his face,' said Elver.

'*You will be quiet*,' said Dalesh, her voice as sharp as a whip in the small room. 'Fine. You can take them away, but I want to question them both first.'

'Question them?' snapped Witt. 'What for? I assure you, they are both as monstrous as they come . . .'

'Isnere,' said Dalesh coldly. 'I won't be told my business in my own building. The Bloody Claw has sway here, as I'm sure even this branded idiot knows. I must find out what's behind this sudden influx of jih into Ashingdown.'

The older priest nodded slowly, apparently conceding her point. He turned to Witt, and even through the mask, Elver could tell that the younger man was receiving a severe look.

'We will have them to ourselves shortly, Witt,' he said. 'Let the magistrate work. Dalesh, I will give you a couple of moments, but that is all. Jih are our business, as well you know.'

The pair of them left, Kantor Witt glancing furiously over his shoulder before his superior closed the door behind them. Dalesh blew air out of her nose noisily as she turned her attention to Elver.

'How are you still alive?'

Abruptly, the day she had been thrown into the sea felt so close she could almost smell the salt, and all at once she was newly furious – this woman had held her arm tightly enough to bruise it, had listened to her questions and her protests and ignored them all. And then she'd stood and watched while a twelve-year-old child was thrown to their certain death. Elver tried to yank her hands free from the manacles, but only succeeded in bruising herself.

'You killed me!' she shouted. 'You threw me in the bloody sea, you and that other smirking shithead!'

Dalesh shook her head slowly, her dark eyes piercing Elver. 'Yet here you are.'

'Your mistress tried to sacrifice me, but I belong to another god now,' spat Elver.

'And you're about to be purified by yet another.' Dalesh sighed and went back to the table that sat in front of the fire. There was a black lacquered box there, which she opened and began sorting through. 'I can't help you right now,' she said, 'because as you know, the Bloody Claw's magic is costly and I don't have that tithe to hand—'

'Help us? What do you mean, help us?'

'And the Temple of Trilot is strictly off limits to those dedicated to other gods. They believe the presence of other priests and mages taints their connection. But I will give you this. So you can call me to you, despite their magics. Hopefully, when you use it, I will have the magic to hand.'

She held out a thing that looked a little like a black metal coin. Along the edge of it was a thin line of tiny spikes and in the middle there was a shape like a cat's eye, etched in red enamel.

'Don't take it.' Artair was reaching out for the coin. At Elver's words, he stopped. 'It's a trap.'

'Idiot girl,' said Dalesh. 'The Bloody Claw is a demanding god and being one of his mages often leads us down dark paths. When we chose you, I was young. It was necessary, perhaps, but that doesn't mean I don't feel the weight of that dark path still.' She flipped the black token towards Artair, and instinctively he snatched it out of the air before it could collide with his face. 'Perhaps you crossed my path so I could do something about that.'

'We had an animal with us, a jih spirit,' said Artair quickly. 'We lost him when they took us. You need to get him too—'

At that moment, the door opened, and the faceless priests were there again. It was clear that Kantor Witt had shouldered it open, and he had more guards with him. They swarmed in and Elver felt the first of them grab her bicep none too gently as they began to drag them out of the magistrate's office.

'Wait.' Artair had made the coin disappear somewhere. 'How do we use it?'

'You know,' said Dalesh quietly, before turning away. When she spoke again, her voice was full of impatience. 'I've already seen this little serpent's face more often than I ever wanted or expected to, Isnere. Take it to your prison.'

# CHAPTER 18

The chamber where they were held was clearly meant to house the more traditional kind of jih spirit, the ones that walked on four or six or eight legs, had horns or wings or breathed fire. There were barred windows just beneath the ceiling, letting in light from the fires of the wider temple, and the interior was painted white. There were thousands of scratches on the walls from the monsters that had been kept there before them. Elver shuddered to look at them. Also in the chamber were two deep trenches; one filled with water, the other with piles of what looked like kitchen scraps. She longed to press a hand to her neck, which was bleeding a little, but her hands were still bound.

'What even is it?' asked Artair. He had the black coin in one hand, lying flat in his palm.

'It doesn't matter.' Just looking at the token made Elver angry. 'Some piece of cruelty. She's given you that to make you think there's some hope. The Bloody Claw feeds on suffering.'

'When I asked how it worked, she said I knew.' He tapped the surface of it with his index finger, then picked it up and held it to his eye. He rubbed his thumb over the shape etched into the surface. Nothing happened. 'Maybe she's not ready yet.'

'Or maybe it's a lie.'

'I don't know what she meant. I've never seen anything like this before in my life.' Artair sighed. 'What will they do to us?'

Elver turned to find him looking up at the bars.

'Purify us in Trilot's holy fire,' she said, then shrugged. 'I don't know what that means, but I doubt it'll be a good time. I know that no other monster has ever returned after being caught by a faceless priest. At least, that's what the Queen of Serpents tells us.'

'Perhaps it's a metaphor.' When she gave him a long look, he continued. 'I mean, perhaps it's a ritual they have to do to appease Trilot, and then they'll let us go.'

'Artair,' she said. 'They're going to kill us.'

In the silence that followed, they both heard the distant sound of chanting, the same set of indistinct words over and over. It was beautiful and terrible.

Artair pointed at the water and the food. 'Why feed us then, if they're going to kill us?'

'I don't know, monk.' Elver sighed. 'Maybe they like to keep the ones they burn alive for special feast days. I doubt that will apply to us, though.'

'It's madness! We haven't done anything to them.'

'It doesn't matter.' She wandered over to look at the food. Potato peelings, half-gnawed bones, partially rotten apples. 'They hate us.' She took a deep breath. 'For what it's worth, monk, I'm sorry. I'm the one who burned that priest and got us into this mess. I might be poison, but as far as I can see, you haven't done anything wrong. Apart from try to save your friends.'

He joined her by the food and water trenches and took a folded piece of material from within his robe. He dipped it into the water until it was sodden, then squeezed most of the moisture out.

'Here.' He stepped towards her. 'Let me clean that. The water's good and cold at least, so it should numb it a little. If what you say is about to happen is going to happen, then . . . I don't see why you should be in pain.'

She hesitated. Standing this close to a human – to someone who looked human, she corrected herself – was still difficult. But he could touch her without being in pain, without dying, and that was a bright, curious thing. He leaned in close, carefully cleaning the black blood away, moving the cold cloth down her throat and then dabbing gently at her torn skin. His spare hand settled on her shoulder to steady her and periodically his warm fingers would brush against her collarbone. His touch was different to Lucian's, she noted: when Lucian had taken her hand after they'd freed the monsters in the fair, he had grasped it fiercely – not painfully, but in a way that suggested this touch was the most valuable thing to him in all the world. It was something he craved. Artair, in comparison, was gentle. She watched his face as he worked, so still with concentration. His brown eyes had golden flecks in them, she realized, only visible when she was this close. It felt like being given something secret, something hidden. When he finished and stood back, she felt a small pang.

*Idiot*, she told herself. *You're about to be burned to a crisp for all you know and you're grateful to have a tiny cut attended to.*

That wasn't it, though. The thought of his hands burned in an entirely different way. A way that worried her.

'That's better.' He seemed to notice the way she was looking at him, so she turned her head away.

'Thank you,' she said shortly.

'Elver, that faceless priest you burned. He said something to you about . . . what you get up to at night.' When she looked back at him, he was blushing faintly, his brown eyes very dark. 'What did he mean? I know that you had to hit the evil spirit. Was there something more?'

'His name is Lucian,' she said and watched the surprise that passed over his face. 'I take it you didn't know that.'

Artair looked as though she'd struck him. 'You're talking to him? To *it*?'

'Listen.' She took a step towards him, feeling wild. 'If Lucian is an *it* to you, what does that make me?'

'That's different.'

'How?'

'He is . . . destructive. You don't know what he's done. Why I was put in the Golden Tower of Perpetual Morning in the first place.'

'So tell me.'

'I can't.'

She shook her head. 'Well, I guess if you're lucky, Trilot the Faceless will just burn Lucian away and you'll be left pure finally. Right?'

'Elver . . .'

There was a rattle at the door and a masked priest stepped inside carrying a long spear with a lethally sharp point. Through the eyeholes of the mask it was possible to see a pair of eyes ringed in white makeup.

'Jih creatures,' she said. 'It is time to face your judgement.'

They were taken to another, larger chamber, this one also painted white and lit with what Artair thought must be thousands of candles; they rested on every surface, pale wax in little pools everywhere, dribbling down wood and stone alike. Consequently, it was hot inside the chamber, and he felt sweat prickle across his back and over his chest. When he glanced at Elver, he saw that even her pale face looked flushed, the blue slashes of her scars standing out especially clear. In the centre of the chamber, there was a giant faceted crystal, twice as tall as a human, held in place on its point by a thick silver collar; it was as clear as glass, with a shimmer of golden glitter running through it. Priests with featureless masks ringed the crystal in circles, all on their knees, save for the one called Faceless Isnere, who was watching them approach with his gloved hands folded in front of him. Kantor Witt was there too, a shabby figure at the back of the room.

'There you are.' Isnere gestured to the guards. 'First, we have some outstanding business to attend to. Bring in the creature.'

Belatedly, Artair realized a crowd of faceless priests had entered the chamber behind them and in the midst of the group there was an animal – no, a jih spirit, a monster. It looked a little like the winged cat they had seen in Booster Barnham's fair, only smaller, and its fur was striped rather than spotted. There was a manacle around its neck and chains around its legs, and they were dragging it towards the crystal. The monster hissed and spat at them, thrashing its bat-like wings madly, but there were too many priests.

Next to him, Elver struggled with the guards, her yellow eyes wide.

'No!' she yelled at the top of her voice. 'Let her go! Let her go, you bastards!'

'What are you doing?' Artair shouted at Isnere, but the priest just watched him, impassive.

'Let her go or I'll kill all of you, I swear it!'

'See what a tiny fraction of our lord's power can do,' Isnere said softly, as though neither of them had spoken. 'Watch, and be assured that your souls too will be cleansed.'

The crystal in the centre of the room flickered with light, as though the sun had somehow passed through the room. Rays of white flashed out from it, passing over the jih creature and turning it briefly into a monochrome thing, the stripes on its back washed out, the pupils of its eyes shrinking to dots. It screamed.

'Stop it!' Artair found that he was shouting too. 'Why are you doing this?' He glanced at Elver. 'You're hurting her!'

The white light intensified, and the winged cat curled up on itself, like a creature trying to get out of the rain, while little wisps of smoke-like steam began to rise from its wings and fur. It had stopped screaming, which was somehow worse.

Artair squeezed the black coin in his fist, willing Dalesh to appear. *If you can stop this, then do it!* But nothing happened. Instead, the white light grew so bright he had to look away, and when it abruptly went out he turned back to see a small, shabby shape on the stones where the winged cat had been. He blinked furiously, trying to make sense of it past the after-images that danced in front of his eyes.

'You bastards,' Elver was saying. 'You human scum.'

It was a cat, he realized, just a normal tabby cat that you might see in any tavern in any city, all trace of its jih nature burned from it. And it was dead.

'Trilot be praised,' said Faceless Isnere. 'Now, have them kneel.'

Strong arms forced Artair down. He considered resisting – he was stronger than them, he was sure of it – but the priestess with the spear still had its point resting at Elver's lower back.

*There's a chance we could survive the cleanse*, he thought. *But Elver won't survive a spear in the back. I have to take the chance.*

*And what if the Other was burned away instead?* a little voice in his head replied. *You'd be free, finally.*

The priests were chanting again. Elver was kneeling next to him, her hands still tied behind her back. There was movement within the crystal, a kind of shimmering light that dipped and soared, gradually forming a shape. A humanoid figure. Slowly, it came into focus.

'My lord,' said Faceless Isnere, 'we bring you the tainted jih creatures of the Queen of Serpents, held here for your purifying light.'

'Purifying light, my arse,' Elver said, very loudly. Her chest was rising and falling quickly, anger giving way to fear.

*I'm looking at one of the Twelve gods*, thought Artair. *This is Trilot the Faceless.*

The god was a creature of white cloth, white porcelain and empty space. There was a figure there filling out the shining white robe, and there was a simple clay mask with lips, nose and eyelids, but beyond that . . . nothing. Artair could see no head behind the mask or neck rising from the collar of the robes. The eyeholes of the mask were empty, yet the figure moved and even spoke.

**Twisted, tainted ones,** it said. **Receive my light and be cleansed.**

Trilot the Faceless held out its gloved hands and a bright, white light once again began to grow from the crystal. The shadows of the surrounding priests lengthened, reaching out for the walls of the chamber, their edges painfully sharp, while the priests themselves bowed their heads. The light grew stronger, pulsing like a heartbeat, until it became unbearable. Even with his eyes closed, Artair could see it. Next to him, he heard Elver cry out and he forced his eyes open again. She was curled in on herself, her face a rictus of pain. Little tendrils of white smoke were rising from her skin, and when he looked at his own hand, he saw the same happening to him. Without thinking about it, he leaned over her, trying to shield her with his own body.

'Stop that!' Faceless Isnere's voice came from somewhere above them. 'Separate them. They must be alone for the judgement.'

Before they pulled them apart, Elver briefly pressed her face to his chest, as if finding comfort there, and Artair felt a pang of mingled terror and sadness. *There was so much more to do*, he thought.

The light seemed to hit him with a peculiar weight, like bony hands holding him down, pushing him into the marble floor. He saw his own fist clenched against the stones, bleached of all colour, and he felt a sharp pain in his palm. The coin, he remembered, with its sharp edges, was cutting into his flesh, and when he moved, close to losing consciousness, he saw a red smear against the white – the only colour left in the chamber.

And then there was another light, blood red and somehow familiar. Several priests cried out, and there was a crackling sound, like a fire burning out of control. Artair lifted his head in time to see a portal lined in red fire and Magistrate Dalesh standing in it. Beyond her, he could see darkened countryside and a thin slither of the moon between the clouds. After the unforgiving whiteness of the room it felt like a blessing, like a drink of cold water on a hot day.

'Quickly, you two,' she snapped, 'on your feet.'

Meanwhile, something strange was happening to the floor. Pulsing pink tendrils were oozing up between the cracks in the flagstones, growing at an alarming speed. They were wet and somehow . . . meaty. Artair lurched to his feet as the tendrils began to grasp at the priests, circling their ankles and holding them in place when they tried to run. The light from the crystal was flickering; Artair saw Trilot the Faceless cock his mask to one side in apparent bemusement. Elver was already running for the portal, hopping over the pink tendrils as easily as she did the debris of the forest floor.

'Grab them!' Isnere yelled. 'Magistrate, I will know the meaning of this insult!'

Some of the priests tried to reach them – Artair saw Kantor Witt wrestling fiercely with the pink tendrils on the far side of the chamber, his mouth contorted with rage, but it was too late. Elver hopped through the portal and then Dalesh was reaching through for Artair. He stepped up out of the Temple of Trilot and stepped down into a cold autumn night in the woods.

A handful of seconds later, the portal vanished, leaving behind a faint, wild scent of unwashed beast.

# CHAPTER 19

Elver stood for a moment looking at her hands, which were trembling still, faint wisps of steam or smoke rising from them. Dalesh had released her from the manacles with a small silver key, taking care not to brush her fingers against her hands. The light of Trilot the Faceless had been agonizing, but worse than that had been the emanation of the god's will: she had felt clearly how much the god of purity and truth had wanted the essence of her gone, wiped away like a dirty smudge on a glass. The poison blood inside her, given to her by the Queen of Serpents, had boiled in response. She thought of the jih spirit the priests had destroyed, Trilot's light leaving a small dead animal in its wake.

'You are around a mile outside of Ashingdown,' Dalesh was saying. 'I imagine Isnere will come looking for you first at the magistrate's offices, and then at the Bloody Claw's temple, since he knows I spend much of my time there. But I've no doubt he'll send faceless priests beyond the city walls to look for you too, so you'll want to get moving soon. And I believe this also belongs to you.'

She stepped aside to reveal the cub, who was worrying at a large haunch of roasted meat. He spared them one quick glance before going back to licking his chops.

'Thank you,' said Artair, nearly breathless with gratitude. 'I thought that perhaps . . .'

Dalesh pursed her lips with distaste as the cub rolled over to show his belly.

'The guards found it. Luckily, they brought it to me first.'

'I don't understand.' Artair was looking at the black token in his hand, which was smeared with blood. 'How did that work?'

'You gave me the link I needed with the sacrifice of your blood. And I fuelled the spells from my end.' Dalesh looked faintly smug. 'Easy enough, if you are skilled.'

'What will you do?' asked Artair. 'The priests of Trilot looked angry.'

Elver dropped her hands. 'Never mind her,' she snarled. 'What about the poor soul who paid the price for that portal? Who did you kill to fuel your spells, Dalesh?' She turned to Artair. 'Your saviour here is an apprentice to Mother Maura, the same bloody magpie that took your friends and murdered your monks.'

Artair's eyes widened.

'Maura has done what?' The mage pinched the bridge of her nose with her fingers. 'Listen. Yes, Elver is correct. For many years I studied under the mage known as Mother Maura. I learned a great deal from her. And . . . did many things that were questionable in the name of our god, including what happened to you, Elver. The Bloody Claw demands a great deal for his magic, and because of this his magic is uniquely powerful.'

'He demands blood,' said Elver. 'He demands *lives*.' Being in Dalesh's presence was making her feel feverish.

'If you've fallen into Maura's orbit, then you have my sympathy.' Dalesh sighed. 'I left her service a few years ago. It wasn't easy, but she had done things I couldn't abide.'

'Worse than throwing orphans into the sea?'

'Ouch. Okay. I deserve that. But yes, the price we were paying seemed higher than ever, and the plans she had were, for want of a better word, unhinged. Maura's dreams are blood-soaked and strange, and in my opinion, not achievable. You know, when we dedicated this town to the Bloody Claw and raised the stones that circle it, part of the wall kept falling down. We couldn't figure out why, until one of the masons dug down deeper than the foundations and found that the roots of a tree had crept through the bedrock, making it unstable. Looking at the surface, you'd never have been able to tell those fractures were there.'

'What do you mean? What are you talking about?' snapped Elver.

Dalesh sighed. 'When she was younger, Maura had a family, and through a quirk of fate, she lost them. It changed her. And it wasn't immediately obvious. That's what I mean. We were throwing away lives not for some higher purpose, but for a lunatic's ravings.' She pursed her lips, her already stern face growing harsher lines. 'I remain dedicated to my god, Elver, and I won't apologize for that. But I owe you this much for what happened to you. And I wonder if you can understand better, now that you bear the mark of a god yourself.'

Dalesh's eyes moved over Elver's yellow eyes, her blue scars and white hair. 'There's no missing to whom you belong now, at least. For what it's worth, I'm glad that you survived. Very few people do once the Bloody Claw has set his eye on them.' She sighed. 'Elver, I summoned the portal with a soul globe. We keep them handy in case we need to power a spell unexpectedly, so technically no blood was spilled. Save for a few drops from your young man here.'

'No blood was spilled *today*, you mean.'

Elver considered leaping at the mage, circling her hands around her throat and delivering her to her god early. But Dalesh was already turning away, gesturing at a pack she had left leaning against a tree, and somehow the moment passed.

'You can't return to Ashingdown – and I'd prefer it if you never did, frankly – so here are some supplies for you. About two miles east, there's an inn, although . . .' She shot a look at Artair. 'You may find it a little strange, Sleepless. It's dedicated to the god Enos, the one who watches over sleep, dreams and forgetting.'

'I have heard of her,' said Artair. 'We're taught about her at the Golden Tower. It's said she has a unique dislike for the Sleepless, who are forever outside of her web.'

'It seems you're just endlessly popular wherever you go,' said Dalesh drily.

'And what are you going to do?' asked Elver. Somehow, she felt like this wasn't enough. She wanted something else from Dalesh, something beyond an apology or even a rescue, but couldn't have said what it was. 'You've stolen from Trilot.'

'I'll figure something out.' For the first time, the corner of the mage's mouth quirked into a bitter smile. 'Now get out of here before I change my mind.'

'. . . and they just threw you into the sea?'

Elver nodded briefly, her eyes on the road ahead.

'Then you have just as much reason to hate Maura as me. More, even.' Artair thought of that fierce woman with the red hair throwing a child to their death. It wasn't hard to imagine.

'I didn't know it was her you were dealing with at first,' she continued. 'Maybe you were meant to cross my path, Artair. If anyone was going to help you defeat her, it would be me.' He glanced at her and she looked away, as though embarrassed by this admission.

'She really is ruthless. To buy an orphan just to take their life . . .'

'And they call me a monster. But the Queen of Serpents gave me a new life. She snapped me up and replaced my blood with poison, making me one of her children.'

'Forgive me, but that doesn't sound like an especially kind thing to do either.' She shot him a dangerous look that promised a knife in the dark, or at the very least a kick in the shins. 'Your queen could have caught you, taken you to the shore somewhere. Still alive. Still human.'

Elver made a disgusted noise. It was a quiet night, the moon like a beacon overhead. They were walking along the edge of the road, ready to dive into cover should they hear someone coming; the faceless priests could still be looking for them, after all. Even on the uneven road, Elver walked without a sound, grace softening her every movement.

'And what? Return to the humans who thought so little of my life they sacrificed it to save their own skins?' The cub was trotting along by her feet, and at the sound of her voice he lifted his nose. 'No. I was better off in the forest, living alongside monsters. At least they're honest.'

'I'm sorry,' said Artair. 'I mean, I'm sorry that happened to you.'

The monster girl was quiet for a while. Somewhere in the woods to their left, an owl called, a ghostly, sad sound.

'Well I'm not,' she said eventually. 'And I don't need your sympathy. Save it for the monster that Trilot burned down to nothing.'

'That was a terrible thing,' said Artair. 'The Bloody Claw isn't the only cruel god.'

She glanced up at him with narrowed eyes, seemed about to say something, then shook her head slightly. 'Ashingdown has delayed us a bit, I reckon. We'll have to hurry if we want to get to this Tisk mage in time.' And then she added, 'The sooner this is done, the sooner I can get back to the Jih Forest where I belong.'

The Inn of Enos, when they reached it, was a curious building. It was built of wood and ranged over three floors and a depiction of the god herself sat on the roof, her eight spidery legs running down the walls to clasp the inn beneath her. Soft orange and pink lights glowed from behind the windows. Looking at it, Artair felt a surge of different emotions: it looked like a welcoming, calm place, in stark contrast to Ashingdown and the Temple of Trilot, yet the face of Enos, beaming beatifically from the roof, only served to remind him of who and what he was. His body knew only the illusion of sleep, after all, and since becoming Sleepless he'd not had a single dream.

'Do you want to stay here?' asked Elver. 'We can always risk the woods.'

But as she was speaking, a woman came out of the door of the inn. She wore a shapeless lavender dress with wide sleeves and a soft cap over her hair. She bowed to them both and spoke softly.

'Welcome to the Inn of Enos. The best night's sleep of your life awaits you.'

When Lucian awoke, he found himself bound again, but this time in a warm room with soft lights, the walls painted with undulating patterns like waves. The place felt unnaturally quiet, and when he sat up, even his movements felt muffled. The monster girl was perched on another bed on the other side of the room, the cub curled up on a blanket sleeping soundly. Elver yawned hugely.

'You're awake, then.'

'I am.' Lucian frowned. 'What is this place? I feel like my ears are full of cotton wool.'

'It's weird, isn't it? The god Enos watches over this inn, and she casts a spell of quietness over it to help its patrons sleep better.' She shifted on the bed. 'I don't like it. In the forest, you have to have your wits about you at all times. Artair though – he was straight off.'

'It seems you've had a busy day. Every night, we are somewhere different. What happened today?' His eyes roamed over her, the room, the windows, seeking clues. The girl looked even more watchful than usual. 'The monk must be very glad of your company.

Dear Artair wouldn't survive a morning outside of his precious monastery without help.'

The girl scowled at him, which was curious. 'Nothing happened that you need to know about.'

'You won't even give me a fragment? Where did you get that cut on your neck?' When she didn't reply, he shrugged. 'Elver, I'm tied up. You're the only person I get to interact with. Who am I going to tell?'

She sighed. 'We were caught by a priest in a town near here and we were taken to a Temple of Trilot to be . . . cleansed. We escaped.'

Lucian chuckled, although he wasn't quite as amused as he expected to be. It seemed Elver and Artair were having some interesting adventures while he was locked away in the monk's head. 'Trilot? That old bastard. I was never fond of that grasping little cult, so convinced of their own superiority. Not to mention weirdly obsessed with purity. I wouldn't be at all surprised if they were covering up some unpleasant stuff . . .' He trailed off.

'You've remembered something,' said Elver. 'From your previous life. You disliked Trilot's priests?' She almost smiled. 'Sounds like you had some sense, at least.'

'That's right. I hated Trilot,' he said wonderingly. 'And I didn't care for the Lady Dusk either, too wishy-washy. Imagine being a mage and having to collect *poetry*, of all things.' He blinked slowly. 'It's like I can almost *feel* how I used to feel, Elver. Isn't that extraordinary? I've spent these last years suspended in a kind of numbness and now feeling is coming back. Thanks to you, monster girl.' He blinked again, then yawned. Elver yawned in response.

'What do you think of the other gods?' she asked. 'Tisk, for example? The Hooded Crow?'

'Both respectable enough,' said Lucian. 'In truth, Tisk is the very opposite of respectable, but trickery is as old as blood, and lies are on every human's lips. Powerful. And the Hooded Crow is too sombre for my tastes, but if ever there were a god that has his eye on all of us . . .' He trailed off, and yawned again. His eyes felt like they had weights attached and it would be so easy, so good in fact, to lay down and sleep. So easy . . .

Lucian sat bolt upright, his heart tripping in his chest.

'Gods damn this place, I'm falling asleep! As though I'd give control back to that fool so easily.' He swung his legs down and stood up awkwardly, the bonds around his ankles nipping at his skin. 'Is there somewhere we can go in this place that isn't enchanted? I need to stay awake. I need to remember more – if you'll let me, Elver.'

The girl rubbed an arm over her face and blinked rapidly.

'As far as I know, the whole building exists under this sleep spell, but there is a hot spring in the garden at the back, and guests can bathe in it.'

'A bath! If there's one thing I am sure of, it's that I used to enjoy a hot bath. Untie my bonds and I will swear you the same oath as before, Elver of the Jih Forest – allow me to recover more of myself and I will behave.'

For a few seconds she looked uncertain. When he'd asked, she'd spoken of the Temple of Trilot and their experience there as though it were nothing, but he wondered if it had alarmed her in a way she was trying to hide. He kept his face carefully neutral.

'Fine,' she said eventually. 'The cub can stay here.' She nodded to the cub, who had rolled over onto his back, four little legs sticking up in the air. Tiny fluting snores emanated from his direction. 'He's asleep anyway.'

The spring was a deep, round pool surrounded by large grey rocks and squat, twisted little trees with crimson leaves. The water itself was cloudy, steam rising from it like white smoke. There were no other guests around, and the only sounds were the buzzing of some late-night insects. A handful of moths danced above it, entranced by the moon on the surface of the water. Lucian pulled off his shirt and stripped down to his underclothes, before splashing up to his knees in the pool. The heat was intense, and for a few moments his mind felt entirely blank. How long since he'd felt this kind of warmth? Certainly never in the chilly little cell in the monastery. Grinning, he turned back to Elver.

'This is incredible. Are you coming in?'

The girl was looking at him oddly, and for the first time he became aware of his body. The monk had spent much of his life in training, leaving him lean and well muscled. *Not my body*, thought Lucian, *but it's not a bad one to be stuck with.*

'No,' she said, looking away. 'But you knock yourself out, I guess.'

He waded deeper into the pool until the hot water came up to his chest.

'Ahhhhh. Now this is good. I feel awake again. Are you sure you won't join me?' He moved so that he was leaning against the rocks that circled the pool. 'If you like, I won't look until you're safely in. The water is quite opaque.'

Elver came over to the edge. Did he imagine it or was there a faint blush to her bone-white cheek?

'We have some hot springs in the Jih Forest,' she said. 'A lot of the jih like to swim there, especially in the winter.'

She sat down on the rocks and took off her muddy boots, before rolling up her heavily patched trouser legs. When her feet were bare, she dangled them in the water. Lucian, watching her, found himself wondering what she would look like in finer clothes. He had the idea that once he had been very fond of silk and velvet, and he suspected her white hair would look especially striking against a rich burgundy gown. Once she was settled, she held out her hand towards him.

'If you want to seek out another memory, let's do it,' she said. 'Before another guest turns up to use the spring. But I want you to tell me what you see this time.'

'Why?'

She scowled at him, and he found to his surprise that he liked that fiery little spark in her eyes very much.

'Satisfying my curiosity is the price you pay for retrieving your memories.'

'In that case, it'd be my pleasure to satisfy you.'

He moved through the water towards her, but rather than taking her hand, he slipped his own around her bare foot, sliding his palm over the arch and cupping her heel. She jumped a little, not expecting the move, and then—

He was bound and on his knees. He was in a rocky place, blasted free of all vegetation save for a tiny red root that sprouted between the rocks and boulders. There was a sense of extreme danger, of failure and pain, and around him there were people that meant him harm . . . No, that wasn't quite right. They hoped that he would receive harm instead of them. A woman came forward, holding a torch. She was older than him by decades, and she looked at him with open hate. Red hair blew around her head like a flag of warning.

*Lucian,* she said, *can you guess what happens next?*

When he came back to himself, he was half on the edge of the pool, his lower legs dangling in the water. Elver looked like she'd been splashed herself; her clothes were sodden.

'You slipped under the water when you touched me,' she said. 'I had to pull you out before you drowned, you idiot.' She leaned back self-consciously, away from him. 'What did you see?'

He pushed his dripping hair out of his face. 'A woman with red hair. I think she wanted to kill me. I think . . . I think maybe she *did* kill me.'

Elver's eyes grew very wide.

'I think we should go back indoors.'

# CHAPTER 20

They knew they were on the road to Tisk's temple long before they actually reached it. There were signs dotted on the verge, handmade wonky things that read STOP BY TISK'S EMPORIUM TODAY AND HAVE ALL YOUR DREAMS COME TRUE and LOOKING FOR A WAY TO MAKE YOUR FORTUNE? VISIT TISK, GOD OF ILLUSION.

'Those are some big claims,' said Artair.

'The god of lies,' mused Elver. Already on the road they had seen other travellers, men and women on horses, carts full of goods and once a carriage that appeared to contain an entire family: cousins, aunties and uncles and all. A small child waved at Elver as they passed and, hesitantly, she had waved back. The cub, who had been very difficult to coax from his cosy spot on Elver's bed, had been placed, yawning, back into the sack. He'd consented to be carried by Artair, who, Elver noticed, looked faintly pleased. So far, they had seen no faceless priests.

As they walked, the faint autumn sunshine on the tops of their heads, Elver found her mind returning to the previous night. Firstly, and most annoyingly, the sight of Lucian stripped down to his underclothes, the steam from the pool leaving droplets of water on his smooth skin. When she looked at Artair now, she felt guilty, like she'd seen something she shouldn't have. Secondly, there was the memory Lucian had recovered. With the gaps in what he knew, it was impossible to say whether the red-headed woman was Mother Maura or not, but the idea that he could also have been a sacrifice to the Bloody Claw wouldn't quite leave her. No one knew where the Sleepless came from, after all.

'Did the sleep magic not work on you?' asked Artair. He was looking at her with an expression of concern. 'You seem out of sorts.'

'I'm fine,' she said, thinking of his warm hand slipping around her foot. 'I'm just very ready to be back in my forest, that's all.'

'Remember, if the Other—'

'Lucian.'

'—If he is keeping you awake with chatter, I am happy to be gagged before I go to sleep.'

'I'm not sure that would help.' Ahead of them on the road there was another sign, larger than all the others, and it pointed off down a turning lined with horse chestnut trees. The sign read *THIS WAY TO THE GLORIOUS TEMPLE OF TISK* and next to the elaborately painted words was a relief carving of a fox leaping. 'Looks like this is the place.'

They turned off down the side road, stepping around the green thorny casings that littered the ground. Elver paused to pick up a shiny brown conker, enjoying the silkiness of it against her fingers before slipping it into her pocket: she was some distance from the Jih Forest, but the horse chestnuts reminded her of home – it felt good to take it with her.

The Temple of Tisk looked a lot like a ramshackle cottage; it had a thatched roof with a variety of plants and mosses growing through the straw, and standing in the front garden there were all manner of votive statues – they were all shapes and sizes and colours and depicted the twelve gods in a variety of ways. Elver spotted the Hooded Crow looming over the others, his long beak poking out of his cowl, painted entirely black; there was a statue of Vilon the Many Limbed, their arms and legs caught in the acts of dancing or wielding a paintbrush; there was even a striking figure of the Queen of Serpents, her humped body twisting and curling around the other statues – she had been painted a shining emerald green, which annoyed Elver. *Surely everyone knows she is yellow.* The Bloody Claw was there too in the form of several identical figurines of a lion with one paw raised, its mouth open to expose its fangs. Elver frowned as they stepped past them. It felt like a bad omen.

When she opened the cottage door a bell jingled somewhere, and as they stepped inside she realized it wasn't a temple or a cottage truly – it was a shop. There was stuff of all descriptions everywhere, crowding shelves and the floor, and behind a polished wooden desk a young woman was beaming at them hopefully.

'Welcome to Tisk's temple!' she said. 'How can I make your dreams come true today?'

'This is a temple?' asked Artair. He was looking around at the various goods. There didn't seem to be a rhyme or reason to them that Elver could see.

'It certainly is.' The woman behind the desk – which was itself littered with candles and coins and tiny clay pots – was perhaps a few years older than them, with warm golden-brown skin and black hair. Her eyes were dark and smudged with black pencil, and she wore a heavily embroidered jacket with wide sleeves over a mustard-coloured silk shirt. She was strikingly beautiful. And then her face split into a rueful grin that, if anything, only made her more appealing. She sketched a quick bow, scattering a few little pots with her sleeves. 'I am Sunay Tiskertalia, a mage dedicated to our glorious and benevolent Lord Tisk. Here, in my humble temple, I collect the things that please him.'

'It looks like a lot of things please him,' said Elver.

'Ah, you might well think that!' said Sunay. 'But all of these strange and lovely objects have one thing in common. Can you guess it?'

Elver's eyes had wandered to a painting that hung on the wall behind the woman's head. In it, a fox leapt over a wooden stile in a field, every line of him speaking of speed and agility; gold lines traced it all over like lacework, and when she moved one way or the other, the image changed – instead of a fox she saw a male figure with hair that stood up like a fox's brush, with eyes of a dangerous, searing green.

'All of the things for sale here were once given to another god,' said Artair. 'That's what Tisk desires in exchange for his magic – items that rightly belong to someone else.'

Sunay nodded happily. 'Some of the things I offer him, he takes, but most he just enjoys for a time and gives back. And then I sell them on.' She lowered her voice. 'The idea of making coin from other gods' possessions pleases him greatly. So!' She leaned back, smiling at them both. 'Have you come to buy? Sell?'

'We've come for a spell,' said Elver. 'A spell of illusion. Can we buy such a thing from you?'

'Ah.' Sunay's face became more serious. She left the desk and went over to the front door, flipping the sign that hung there over to CLOSED. 'Come with me,' she said, beckoning to a smaller door to the right of the desk. 'This sounds like something we should discuss in cosier surroundings.'

Beyond the door there was a little sitting room. In here, the items were finer, as though Sunay herself had picked them for their glitter and shine. *Magpie*, thought Elver. The three of them sat on overstuffed chairs, and Sunay poured some fragrant cold tea into three silver cups.

'Tell me then . . . who are you? What's your story?'

Elver spoke before Artair could. 'We are a brother and sister from Addersport. We need an illusion spell to fool the man who is trying to swindle our mother.'

Artair looked at her like she'd grown another head.

Sunay smiled and sipped from her tea. 'Try again. You two are never brother and sister.'

'I—'

'Something you should know about Tisk's mages, my sweet. When your magic is tied to the god of lies, you get very good at spotting them in the wild.'

Elver sat back in her chair a little. Since they had asked about the spell, something about Sunay had changed. She was still warm and friendly, but there was a new perceptiveness about the mage that made her a little uneasy.

'Another mage has kidnapped some friends of mine,' said Artair. 'In exchange for them she has asked me to bring her something . . . but it's something that is not mine to give. We want to give her an illusion instead.'

As he spoke, Sunay's eyebrows inched up over her forehead.

'Oh,' she said, 'but this is *delicious*. Interfering in another mage's business, and therefore another god's business . . . My lord will love this. And how are you involved?' She looked at Elver.

'The thing that he's taken. It belongs to another god. And she has asked me to get it back.'

'Two gods!' Sunay looked absolutely delighted. 'But there's something else you two are not telling me.' She leaned over the small table towards them, her dark eyes liquid with intrigue. 'It's right in front of my nose, I am sure of it . . .'

Artair glanced at Elver. 'There's nothing left to know,' he said quickly. 'Otherwise we are very normal. Very normal people from Addersport.'

'Another lie!' said Sunay triumphantly. 'There, I see it now.' She pointed her index and middle finger on her right hand, indicating both of them at once. 'It's in the way you sit here waiting to be found out. And your stunning golden eyes, of course, my sweet. Jih.

Monster spirits. Which makes me wonder what in Tisk's name it is that this mage wants from you.'

Elver sighed and pulled the neck of the sack open. Inside it, the cub was sleeping with his paws over his nose. Sunay stood up. For a second, Elver wondered if the mage was going to run screaming from the temple to summon the nearest guards or even bring the faceless priests down upon them, but instead she began to walk briskly around the room, as though she couldn't contain her excitement.

'What a day! This is going to be quite the scam. I mean, my Lord Tisk will certainly be interested in helping you, but creating an illusion of a living, breathing creature – a monster, no less – is not easy and the tithe to be paid will be significant. This cannot be any old votive offering snatched from the altar of Barleycorn or the Lady Dusk. Oh no. This must be *special*.' She paused in her scampering and lifted her head. A solid orange glow, like the last light of sunset, rose in her eyes and then departed again. 'Yes. *Oho*, my lord is very clever.'

'What is it?' asked Artair. 'Only, neither of us own very much. We do have some gold . . .'

'No, no, nothing you can simply buy. Tisk asks that you go to the nearby Temple of Threshold, and from there, you procure for him a Frozen Heart.'

'And what is that, exactly?' asked Elver. She had the distinct feeling that every word out of Sunay's mouth was adding days to her time away from the forest. And there were the novices – how much longer did they have left to live?

'The Frozen Heart is one of the key artefacts in the Temple of Threshold, given to those who come seeking the blessing of that particularly powerful god. It has magical properties,' Sunay waved her hand airily, 'but you don't need to worry about that. You will, however, have to lie your way into the temple.'

'Couldn't we just ask for it?' said Artair. 'Perhaps if we explained...'

'No, no, no, the lies are the point, don't you see? If it were given freely, my Lord Tisk would not want it. And you'll have to leave him here, with me.' She nodded to the sack. The cub had woken up fully, his green eyes flashing with their eldritch glow.

'I don't know about that.' Elver frowned. Being asked to trust this magpie with the cub felt like a step too far. 'He won't like it.'

'Nonsense. There's plenty of food. Does he like bacon? I'll bet he does.'

Elver knelt down by the sack and put her hand between the cub's feathery ears. 'We've got to go and fetch something. Will you be okay here?'

*This place smells weird. Lots of weird smells.* The cub eyed Sunay. *Can I bite her?*

'Probably better that you don't.'

The cub's eyes glowed brighter for a handful of seconds, lighting up the parlour.

Sunay gave a low gasp. She turned to Artair. 'Is she talking to the little creature?'

'She is,' said Artair, smiling. 'It's part of her magic.'

*I miss the forest,* said the cub. *I miss my mum. When are we going back?*

A pang of sorrow moved through Elver's chest. 'Soon, I promise.' *Once I've made Maura pay,* she thought. 'And when we're back, we'll go and collect snails together. The really tasty ones. How about that?'

The little creature snuffled with pleasure, and Elver stood up.

'Fine. He'll stay here with you.'

'Marvellous. Quite marvellous.' The mage grinned at them. 'Now then. You're going to need some very specific lies to get into the Temple of Threshold. Don't worry, you're in the hands of an expert.'

# CHAPTER 21

The Temple of Threshold was about as different to the Temple of Tisk as it was possible to get, thought Artair. Aside from the monastery itself, it was the largest building he had ever seen, a vast edifice of pale grey stone cresting the top of a green hill. Slender towers rose from each corner, and a constant stream of couples moved up the path towards it, hand in hand. There were gentle bells ringing somewhere, and as the sun peeked out from behind the clouds the temple seemed to wink back flirtatiously – the windows, doors and the tops of the towers were lined with gold.

'This is never going to work,' said Elver under her breath. 'You'd better hold my hand. Everyone else is holding hands.' Her cold hand slipped into his. 'They're never going to believe we're a couple.'

Artair wasn't sure he agreed. Who was to say what a couple was supposed to look like? Just next to them on the path, pausing to admire the temple, were a pair of elderly women in their sixtieth year at least – one was tall and thin, with deep laughter lines around her mouth, and the other was short and stocky, her ginger hair lined with grey. And a few steps ahead he saw a man and a woman in their middle age chatting amiably with a pair of young men who had their arms around each other's waists. The one thing they all appeared to have in common was that they were glad to be in each other's company.

'I think we fit in well enough,' he said carefully. 'Perhaps if we looked less nervous . . .'

She glanced up at him nervously. 'Do you think I look nervous?'

Actually, he thought she looked beautiful. Before they'd left the Temple of Tisk, Sunay Tiskertalia had made them wash and smarten themselves up and had given them new clothes to wear. Artair wore a simple cream shirt, open at the throat, a pair of dark calfskin trousers and a short, fitted coat of soft brown leather over the top; all of which were tighter fitting than the tunic and robes he was used to at the monastery, but when he'd looked in Sunay's mirror he had been pleasantly surprised. He'd even brushed his hair into a short tail at the back of his head. In the mirror he'd looked older, almost wiser: a young man who'd seen more of the world than he'd been expecting.

The mage had tried to give Elver several outfits, all of which Elver had turned down for being 'ridiculous', until she had settled on a sea-green doublet with tiny fish carved from pearls sewn into the collar and cuffs. Washed and brushed, her white hair lay in soft waves against her cheek, and her yellow eyes – golden really, he thought – looked especially striking framed by Sunay's expertly applied black pencil.

Artair cleared his throat, aware he was staring at her. 'No.'

'Good.' Elver fiddled with the buttons on her doublet. 'I hope the cub is behaving himself. I doubt that mage knows anything about looking after monsters.'

'Look, they're gathering people into groups at the doors.'

The priests of Threshold were difficult to miss. They wore golden surcoats over white robes and they buzzed around the couples like fat golden bees.

Quickly, Artair and Elver were placed into a group with two other couples: another young man and woman, about the same age as them, and the two men Artair had seen on the path.

'Dearly beloveds.' The priest that had been assigned to them was a huge bear of a man, with a barrel-like belly, broad shoulders and a thick, blond beard that curled luxuriously down to the middle of his chest. 'You have come here today to ask the Threshold to bless your unions – to fill your days with a glorious celebration of the love you already share.' His voice was warm, and very, very loud. Artair suspected people could hear it at the bottom of the hill. 'What a joyous occasion. But it will not be easy, oh no.' He looked at each of them in turn, quite seriously. 'You must face three trials before the Threshold will grant their blessing. The trial of truth, the trial of vulnerability, and the trial of connection. My name is Sam, my friends, and as a mage dedicated to the Threshold, I'll be guiding you through those trials today. Now then, don't look so worried,' he said to the young woman clutching her skinny partner's hand. 'I'm sure you'll breeze through each one. After all,' his voice rang with conviction, 'are we not all here in the name of deep, abiding love and the need for connection?'

The other couples looked at each other and chuckled. Artair felt a wave of unreality rush through him: he'd never even held a girl's hand before and now he was at the Temple of Threshold.

'Now then,' continued Sam, 'I assume you all have the appropriate tithes?'

Artair shifted the satchel on his shoulder, feeling the comforting weight of the items inside. This was something else that Sunay had helped them with. In order for the mages of the temple to perform their magics, the Threshold – the god of love, connection and healing – demanded tithes of mended things. In his satchel, Artair had three such items: a tiny sky-blue bowl with herons painted on it and a jagged golden line where it had shattered and been mended with molten gold; a fine silk shawl that had been carefully patched; and a little wooden doll whose face had been repainted several times. When Sunay had presented them with the items, Elver had asked how much they would have to pay and the mage had replied that they were free: they were simply items that Tisk had acquired as part of his own offerings and now they would go towards the acquiring of something much juicier.

With Sam leading the way, they filed into the temple itself. Inside, there was a vast foyer lined with windows that looked out across the hills and in the centre, hanging in mid-air just below the ceiling, was a giant heart of smooth grey stone, complete with chambers and tubes and other things Artair vaguely recognized from his studies. Tiny pink lights, almost like fireflies, moved slowly over the surface. Below that, the priests led groups of supplicants to rows of golden doors that lined the walls.

'Here we are, my friends.' Inside the first room, there was a horizontal hole in the wall that burned with orange flame; it reminded Artair of the ovens in the monastery kitchens. Elver was watching everything very carefully, as though keeping an eye out for possible escape routes. 'This is the trial of vulnerability.'

'We don't have to . . . put our hand in there or anything, do we?' asked the skinny young man. He'd gone very pale.

Sam laughed heartily. 'Young master, the very idea! No. The Threshold consumes their tithe through fire, reducing all the separate pieces into a single flame of connection.'

Elver made a small scornful noise that was for Artair's ear only.

'In the trial of vulnerability, the Threshold's magic will grant you each a vision of your partner's past, a piece of their lives before you were a part of it. Can you accept what your beloved was before this connection was formed? And can you stand to be laid bare in front of your beloved? Only with true vulnerability can a true connection be formed.'

The two young men were the first to complete the rite. At Sam's instruction, they placed their own offering in the fire – a brooch with a newly soldered pin – and then knelt facing each other on a pair of soft grey and gold pillows. The priest told them to lean forward until their foreheads were touching and to close their eyes, and then the priest murmured a handful of words to his god. Tiny pink lights, like those that surrounded the heart, swarmed around the couple. For a few minutes, the rest of them stood and watched, and then the taller man, who wore an eyepatch of soft green velvet, laughed, and the other smiled, shaking his head. The lights vanished. When they got to their feet, they seemed to Artair to be looking at each other with a new level of fondness.

Sam beamed. 'Perfect. I assume that the memories the Threshold gifted you only deepened your connection to each other?'

'I saw Barnard here as a wilful child,' said the man with the eyepatch. 'Sneaking into the kitchens to eat the pastries that had been baked for his brother's birthday. I don't know how his mother put up with him.'

His partner grinned. 'The memory I was given of you was not fit for public consumption, Diamin, so watch it.'

Sam gestured to Artair and Elver. 'Your turn, my friends.'

Elver took the small doll from the satchel and placed it in the fire. It caught immediately, its little face melting, and Artair wished briefly that they had had a different sort of offering. Then they knelt on the pillows, knees together. It was curious, being this close to Elver; normally, she took care to keep herself apart – afraid, no doubt, of accidentally poisoning someone. She sat with a kind of unconscious grace, the line of her neck very white against the collar of her doublet.

'Now then, you two,' said Sam. 'I want you to hold hands and look at each other. This is no place for distance.'

Artair felt his cheeks grow warm. He laid his hands on the tops of his knees, and after a moment, Elver placed her own on top of his. Feeling like something more was needed, he folded his fingers around her hands, and she looked up at him, almost startled. He couldn't quite fathom the expression in her eyes. *Look at her like you are in love with her*, he told himself. *That's how they will expect you to look.*

He smiled, and she frowned slightly.

'Touch your foreheads together and close your eyes,' said Sam. 'And wait for the Threshold to gift you a memory.'

Artair did as he was told. Although he couldn't see the pink lights, he could feel them, a kind of buzzing, excitable warmth that brushed his face and his arms. And then, images began to fill his head, and more than that: smells, tastes, sounds. He was standing on the edge of a rocky piece of coastline, the sea that he had once glimpsed from the monastery windows a vast, heaving presence in front of him, the taste of salt on his tongue as tart and delicious as any fruit. Just below him there was a crowd of rock pools, slick with dark green seaweed and filled with blue and white water that churned with every wave. As he watched, a great yellow serpent rose out of the sea and between its jaws it carried a child, which it deposited on the edge of a rock pool. The girl, who appeared to be around twelve years old, looked bedraggled and pale, but alive. It was Elver. Her hair was dark, save for a wide streak of white at the front, and there were livid bite marks on her face, shoulder and arm. Her sodden clothes were heavy with blood and she was trembling all over. Artair was filled with the urge to go to her, to wrap her up in something warm, but he couldn't move from the rocks where he stood.

*It's her memory*, he reminded himself. *This all happened a long time ago and there's nothing you can do now.*

The girl pulled her knees up to her chest, still shaking.

*Child.* The Queen of Serpents' voice was full of strange music. *Your blood is now my poison and you have left the human world behind. You are a monster spirit, one of my own blessed children. Do you understand?*

Elver lifted her head.

*You will live in the forest that rises behind you and you will be its warden. Elver, poison child – you will always have my blessing and my protection. Do you understand?*

This time the girl nodded and she seemed to have stopped shaking.

'They killed me,' she said. Her voice was almost lost under the hissing and seething of the surf. 'They just threw me into the sea like I was nothing.' Slowly, she rose to her feet, a small defiant figure against the rocks. 'I'm *never* going back.'

With that, the images faded and Artair found himself back in the room with the priest of Threshold and the other couples. Elver was blinking at him owlishly, her hands clutching his tightly. As if she realized what she was doing, she dropped them abruptly.

'There we go.' Sam gestured at them to stand. 'Another connection forged.'

As they got to their feet, Artair found that Elver would not meet his eye, and a cold feeling gripped him. What had she seen? What memory had been gifted to her?

There was the worst of all memories, of course, the one that even he himself did not think about if he could possibly help it. But then, if she had seen that, surely she would have run from the temple, putting as much distance between them as possible?

*The monster cub*, he reminded himself bitterly. *That is who she is here for. Her loyalty to the Queen of Serpents means she can't leave, even if she wants to.*

Meanwhile, the final couple had completed their own rites and Sam was looking around at them all expectantly.

'Shall we move along to the trial of truth?'

# CHAPTER 22

'As soon as we have the Frozen Heart, we should get out of here.'

They were waiting for the priest to finish preparing for the next rite. He was using a small iron tool to sweep away the ash of the previous offerings, while the couples stood together, absorbed in each other.

'Sunay said they don't give it to us until the final trial is over,' said Artair. He was watching the other couples, Elver noticed, openly curious. His curiosity for the world was in every movement and gesture. It both fascinated and annoyed her. 'I don't really understand,' he admitted. 'It's not like we're sneaking in here and stealing the thing under the cover of night. They're going to give it to us because we're doing their tests. If Tisk only takes tithes stolen from other gods, how does that count?'

'Because we're not really a couple,' she hissed back. 'We're taking something to which we have no right.' Her eyes drifted to the young man and woman, who were standing by the pillows, eager to start the next trial. They were holding hands. Her own hand found the conker she'd transferred into the pocket of her doublet. It felt good to have it close to hand; as if somehow the Jih Forest wasn't really that far away. 'And there's a good chance we'll still fail the rites.' She snorted. 'If this god is any good at their job, we should fail. Anyone can see we're not in love.'

'Right,' said Artair. He nodded. 'Well. Let's hope not. We really need that spell.' He lowered his voice. 'Can I ask . . . What memory did it give you? Of me?'

'Oh, nothing that interesting. What did you expect? You've lived in a monastery half your life.' Elver paused. She had seen him standing in front of a tall iron gate that had once been painted red. He was young and skinny back then – fragile – and his face had been wet with tears. Two burly men, guards by the look of them, had been standing at his back, one with a hand on his shoulder that looked less than friendly. Eventually, the gate had opened and a monk in a yellow robe had peered out. He looked cheerful enough, but when the monk reached for him Artair had pulled away, trying to run, and the guard nearest had grabbed him; none too gently, either. Together, they had wrestled the resisting boy beyond the gate, unmoved by his screams. 'You were, I don't know, meditating or something. It was very dull.'

Artair nodded. 'Oh.' He looked relieved.

The priest got the couple to place their next offering in the fire and then they sat facing each other on the pillow, their hands still clasped. Sam stood to one side of them and held his hands over the tops of their heads. A faint pink glow filled the space between.

'The trial of truth,' he intoned solemnly. 'Perhaps the most difficult of the three, for the Threshold looks within each heart and sees what is truly there – truths we sometimes do not even ourselves know.'

A pair of pink lights winked into life, hanging just in front of each human's chest. As Elver watched, they grew and took on familiar forms, until they were two little copies of the humans they hung in front of, like dolls made of pink light. They moved independently of the couple themselves; the tiny pink girl pushed a lock of hair behind her ear, while the girl herself looked down at it in astonishment.

'Speak,' said Sam. 'Let us know the truth.'

The glowing figure in front of the girl went first.

*Markan speaks kindly to me. Sometimes he is late to do his chores and that annoys me a little, but I believe he is my true love.*

The girl laughed nervously. The boy looked a little put out, Elver noticed, but then the figure that floated in front of him was speaking.

*Vellerie is fine for now, but I have my eye on her sister.*

Markan jumped like he'd been pinched, and Vellerie gave a squawk of horror before running for the door, her eyes already streaming with tears. Both the figures of light winked out of existence. All the colour had dropped from the boy's face and when he stood up it was on unsteady legs. He made to go for the door too, but Sam's hand settled on his shoulder, holding him in place. The priest's face was carefully neutral but Elver thought she detected a twitch of distaste beneath the beard.

'Now then, Markan. Best let her go for now, don't you think?'

Sam led the boy out of a separate door, and while he was gone Elver and Artair exchanged an uneasy glance. There was no way, surely, they would get through this trial. They would be asked to leave too, without the artefact that Sunay needed in exchange for the spell.

'I knew I didn't like the look of him,' said Barnard. 'Something shifty about the eyes.'

'Oh come on, Barny,' said Diamin. 'You thought no such thing.'

When the priest came back, he looked cheerful again and gave them all a wry smile.

'It happens more than you would hope,' he said, 'but just think of the wasted years and pain that poor girl has just avoided.' He chuckled lightly. 'Now then. I believe it is your turn next, my dears.'

Trying not to look as doom-laden as she felt, Elver knelt on the grey and gold pillow opposite Artair. Once again, the priest muttered words that she couldn't place, and she felt an odd kind of warmth in her chest as the pink light coalesced in front of her. In front of Artair's chest there was a tiny version of him too, only . . .

She squinted. She half thought she was imagining it, but it almost looked like there were two images, one slightly out of sync with the other – an echo, or a shadow. Elver glanced up at the priest, but he didn't appear to have noticed. Then the figure of light in front of her was speaking.

*When I look at you, I see the one person who might understand what it is like to be me.*

Elver swallowed hard, her heart turning a somersault in her chest. Artair's eyes widened, and she wished fervently that she were somewhere else, anywhere else – even a crowded tavern in Addersport would be preferable to being here, her face burning and Artair's brown eyes seeing the secret, shameful truth. For a wild moment, she wanted to leap up and grab the priest by the hand and poison him, poison all of them . . . But the thought of the cub, and her oath to the Queen of Serpents, kept her in place. She gritted her teeth and stared back at Artair defiantly, daring him to comment.

What he said was, 'Thank you,' and somehow that was even worse than mockery.

The figure in front of him shifted – no, it was definitely two figures, she was sure of it – and then two voices were speaking at the same moment.

*You are brave and fierce and extraordinary,* said the first voice.

*I need to be closer to you,* said the second.

Elver saw her own look of surprise mirrored in Artair's eyes, and above them the priest was spluttering.

'Well, well,' he said, 'I've never known that to happen before.' He looked troubled for a moment, then shrugged. 'We must trust in the wisdom of the Threshold, my friends – it seems that your love for this girl, young master, is so powerful that one pronouncement is not enough, and we should all be so lucky, aye?'

They got to their feet. The remaining couple, Elver noted, were beaming at them happily. She tried not to make eye contact.

'Now, these two,' Barnard was saying to his partner, 'I have a good feeling about. There's a palpable tension. Don't you see it, Diamin?'

Barnard and Diamin passed through the truth test quickly enough, both laughing gently at the small, pink versions of themselves. When it was done the priest bid them rise.

'My friends,' said Sam, 'the final rite, the trial of connection, takes place in the Room of Hearts. There you will go together, without me, and face the Threshold themselves. There, they will reveal to you the moment of deepest connection you have shared thus far and give you a glimpse of what is to come in your future.' He sounded very pleased with himself. 'You will just give me a moment to prepare the room.'

When he had gone, Elver fiddled nervously with the buttons on her doublet.

'One more to go,' she said quietly. 'We're almost there.'

Artair looked flushed and a few strands of hair had come loose from his braid.

'That other voice . . .' he whispered. 'Was it *him*? Or is it like the priest said . . .' He trailed off, his face turning even redder. 'I mean, that both voices were me.'

'I don't know,' Elver said quickly, although both were echoing in her head. *I need to be closer to you.* 'How could I possibly know?'

'Because I *do* think you are brave,' said Artair. Hesitantly, his fingers brushed the back of her hand, as though he meant to take hold of it. 'And kind of extraordinary. And . . .'

Sam came back into the room, his affable face serious again.

'The Threshold awaits.'

# CHAPTER 23

Artair and Elver stepped into the final room alone. At the very centre of the circular chamber there was a firepit, and into this they diligently threw the last of their offerings: the blue heron bowl. Artair felt sure it would shatter in the heat, but it melted away into the fire like it was made of butter, a brief shimmer of gold as the mended parts gave up to the flame. They stood by its warmth, uncertain what to do next.

'We're close now,' said Elver. She was, he noticed, not quite meeting his eye, and she stood just a step too far away for him to take her hand. *You don't have to do that here*, he told himself. *There's no one to pretend in front of.* 'Once we have this Frozen Heart, whatever that is, we can get back to the mage's place and get your spell.' She made a noise almost like a laugh. 'We just have to, you know, fool a god.'

'We've managed it so far,' Artair pointed out.

'Look, the light is changing.'

She was right. The chamber was lit with small oil lamps that ran along the bottom of the wall. One by one they were turning pink. Meanwhile, the air in the room was growing warmer; the warmth, initially, of a pleasant spring day, and then the heat of a hot summer's evening. Artair felt his body warming to it, relaxing by degrees. Elver hooked a finger under the collar of her doublet and loosened it slightly. A pleasant hum filled the room around them, a soft sound that made Artair think of lazy afternoons in the monastery gardens, lying in the grass and listening to the bees. Absurdly, his eyelids felt heavy, and he swayed on his feet.

'Artair?' Elver's cold hand rested on his arm. 'I think the Threshold is arriving.'

He came back to himself, a little thrill of panic making his heart beat faster: in those few seconds he had stepped much closer to sleep than was safe. The chamber was filling up with ghostly figures made of soft pink light, all standing and looking at the pair of them. He could make out no detail in their faces, but he could tell from their shapes and the way they stood that they were all different, and their expressions were kindly. It made him think of walking up to the temple. *Love looks different to everyone*, he thought.

'Two people seeking the truth of their connection.'

The voice of the Threshold was a hundred voices speaking together, yet somehow it wasn't overwhelming. Elver looked like she felt otherwise though, and he remembered that she had spent much of her recent life alone in a forest. He moved a step closer to her.

'I am with you,' he murmured, and she gave him a glance that was almost – was he imagining it? – grateful. It wasn't, at least, actively annoyed, and that seemed like progress.

'First, we will show you your moment of deepest connection, the moment that entangled your lives enough to bring you here to us today.' The Threshold paused, and the glowing figures smiled as one. 'It may not be what you expect. But trust the Threshold to show you what you need to see. And then, we will give you the tiniest glimpse of your possible future – the future that is written by the desire in your blood.'

The magenta light that filled the room began to pulse on and off, like a heartbeat, and in the air over the firepit, an image began to form. It was as though they were looking down on a scene from some high place, and Artair could see a building he recognized. It was the Inn of Enos, the figure of the spider-like god crouched on the roof. Next to him, he felt Elver stiffen.

'Maybe we should just go,' she said quietly. 'This isn't going to work and we can find something else to give Tisk as his tithe.'

The image moved over the roof until they were looking down on a hot spring, clouds of steam rising from the opaque water.

'That's odd,' said Artair. He frowned. 'I don't remember visiting the spring.'

Yet, according to the images, he was there, and so was Elver. As he watched, he strode confidently towards the water, pulling his short robe over his head and discarding it on the grass. The images had no sound, but Artair could see his own face smiling, his own lips moving as he waded into the water. The Artair in the image turned around and gestured to Elver, who was still standing by the edge of the rocks. A horrible suspicion formed in his heart.

'I don't understand.' Except that he did.

Elver said nothing.

In the image, the past version of her had taken off her boots and was sitting on the edge of the spring, while this Artair was still talking away, smiling in a sly way that was . . . *that was not him.*

'You let him out,' said Artair, a plummeting feeling in his chest that made him dizzy. 'You untied Lucian and let him wander about freely.'

'Listen,' Elver was saying, 'listen, Artair, there's stuff you don't understand about him—'

'Do you have any idea what you've done?' Artair took a step away from her, and the figures of the Threshold shimmered as though they were reflections in a pool. 'By the Twelve, Elver, he could have hurt people! He could have done anything and it's *my* responsibility to make sure that he doesn't.' The worst memory, the darkest memory, rose up from where it was always waiting for him. The smell of burning grass, greasy soot on his fingertips. 'He's dangerous, and you gave him his freedom . . .'

In the floating image, Lucian had moved through the water to be closer to Elver, and as Artair watched, his hand reached out and touched her bare foot. It was too much.

'I can't do this.'

He walked stiffly back to the door, ignoring Elver's protests, and found himself back in the room with the priest and the remaining couple, who were waiting for their turn with the Threshold. He felt their eyes searching his face and he turned away from them sharply.

*I have to get out of here. Now.*

As he left the chamber, he heard Barnard speak to his partner, his voice stricken.

'Oh no, I really thought those two would make it.'

Artair let his feet carry him away from the temple, unthinking, while he tried to control the rising panic that threatened to flood through him.

*Here and now, in this moment, I am safe*, he told himself. *The Other is contained.*

The hillside path was still full of couples and groups making their way to the Temple of Threshold, but looking at their happy, hopeful faces only made him feel worse. He kept his head down, trying to recite the mantra even as his mind brought him fact after unpleasant fact.

Firstly, that Elver had untied Lucian's bonds, putting herself in direct danger. Secondly, that she had been talking to him when Artair was asleep – and thirdly, that she had allowed him outside of a locked room, even going so far as to take him outside, putting everyone nearby in danger too.

And fourthly, that she had lied about it.

He remembered what the Trilot priest Kantor Witt had said: *Does he know what you two get up to at night?* Artair felt a soft, insidious pain blossom behind his breastbone. Gods, was it even worse than he thought?

Belatedly, he realized he could hear the patter of rapid footsteps on the path behind him. He frowned, looking resolutely ahead of him.

'Artair.' Elver appeared at his shoulder. 'Artair, please. Listen to me for a moment, will you?'

'I trusted you,' he said.

'Lucian is like you. He's like *us*. He's a jih spirit.' Artair began walking faster, and she scurried to keep up. 'What did the monks tell you about him? Did they tell you anything at all? You've never spoken to him, so how can you know what he's like, truly?'

Other couples on the path were giving them unsettled glances.

'I don't need to know him,' said Artair. 'I only need to know what he's done.'

'And what was that, exactly?'

Memories threatened to rise, and he clamped down on them viciously. He couldn't think about that on top of everything else, so he shook his head roughly.

'We've failed to get the heart,' he said, still not looking at her. 'We'll have to go back and see if there's something else Tisk will accept. There has to be something.'

Questions were rising in his throat and he was swallowing them back down with difficulty. *What did the two of you talk about? Did he threaten you? Did he mock me? Were you both laughing at me, the idiot monk tasked with keeping an evil from the world? And why did he touch your foot? What happened in the part of that memory I didn't see?*

'I bet anything from that place would do,' Elver said. 'I'll go back. Steal something. I'm used to stealing things from humans.'

Artair glanced at her. Her head was down and her hair was hanging in her face so that he couldn't see her expression.

'What are you talking about? The place is teeming with priests and couples. You can't just wander in and steal things. What even would you take?'

She shrugged. 'I'll wait until it's dark. The sun's going down already. There's bound to be something. Listen . . .' In the pause, he heard bells ringing from the temple above them. It seemed they were finishing for the day. 'When I touch Lucian, he gets part of his memories back. Because he has them, Artair, like you and I do, which means he can't be just an evil spirit, right? He has a past—'

'You do whatever you want,' Artair snapped, already regretting the sharpness in his voice but hopeless to prevent it. 'I'm going back to Sunay. She might have some idea of what I can do next. *I'm running out of time.*'

He carried on down the path as Elver's footsteps faltered and stopped, and for a second he wanted to turn back, to look at her. Instead, he looked down at his feet and kept on walking. It was growing dark and he needed to be undercover: whatever Elver might think about it, Lucian was dangerous.

# CHAPTER 24

Darkness came swiftly to the hill. Elver only had to wait a little while for the last supplicants to file out of the temple, and then one by one each lit window fell into darkness until the only light was a faint pink glow, which she suspected must come from the great heart in the foyer. She wondered where the priests of the Threshold went at night; whether they had rooms inside the temple somewhere, a place where they all gathered and ate their supper together. She imagined Sam sitting with his fellow priests, sharing with them the stories of Markan, who had secretly preferred his girlfriend's sister, or the strange couple who made it all the way to the rite of connection before being shown something that caused the handsome young man to flee the temple in a huff. She imagined them chuckling over it, shaking their heads. They would see such things every day, she supposed.

There was a woman standing by the grand entrance that Elver initially took to be a guard, but as she drew closer she saw that it was one of the priests: an older woman with a mop of soft grey curls and a pair of silver spectacles on her nose. She was smoking a pipe and leaning against the wall, puffs of white smoke rising to form a small cloud over her head.

This was annoying. Elver had expected guards, and had been prepared to poison them to make her way inside the temple, but an old woman taking the night air?

*Mother Maura*, she reminded herself. If they could get this spell from Sunay, then she could destroy the mage's plans and have some small taste of revenge for what had been done to her. And as much as she hated to admit it, the idea of letting Artair down at this point was . . . uncomfortable. He'd trusted her and she'd already failed him once. She needed to get the Frozen Heart, if she could find it. So what was one Threshold priest in the face of all that?

But when Elver crept towards the woman, keeping to the darkest parts of the shadows and moving silently, she did not slip the knife from her belt, and when she reached out to brush her fingers to the back of the priest's neck, she gave her only the briefest touch. And when the woman gave a gasp and sank to her knees, Elver made sure to catch her and deposit her out of the way of the doors, on a patch of grass that looked soft enough. She even picked up the woman's pipe and left it near her outstretched hand.

Inside, the place was quiet, the lamps dimmed so that the shifting pink lights from the vast magical heart gave the impression the temple was caught in a silent, magical storm. There was no one around that she could see, although she could hear a number of people nearby talking. Perhaps upstairs somewhere, the priests were indeed enjoying the supper she had imagined. She crept over to the chamber where she and Artair had been ushered through the rites earlier that day, until she stood once more in the Room of Hearts.

The firepit was cold, and the place was empty, the little oil lamps at the edges of the room dimmed down to tiny fireflies of light.

Except, she realized, it wasn't entirely empty.

There, on the floor by the firepit, was an object where previously there had been nothing. It looked like a tiny version of the heart that had been hanging in the foyer of the temple, its tubes and chambers made of white clay and glazed with a faintly glittery sheen. It had to be the Frozen Heart.

Hardly able to believe her luck, Elver ran over to it and scooped it up, but the second her fingers touched the slick surface, she saw—

She saw a forest filled with the mauve shadows of twilight, moss as green as emeralds and as thick as flesh underfoot. Artair was there, but he looked pale and dishevelled, his shirt soaked with blood, and Elver stood opposite him. She was clutching a posy of poisonous flowers in one hand. As Elver watched, her future self stroked Artair's cheek and then his jaw, brushing the hair back from his face in a gesture of tenderness she barely recognized. She said something that Elver couldn't hear and then she kissed him, dropping the posy. After a moment, his free hand buried itself in her hair, they were pressed close, and—

The images faded, and as Elver came back to herself, her heart thundering in her chest, she saw that the chamber was once more filled with magenta light and the Threshold had reappeared: a hundred beings of soft pink light, watching her with identical rueful expressions.

'What was that?' she demanded. 'What did you just show me?'

'What you came here to find,' said the Threshold in their many voices that were one. 'A glimpse of your future. You left without taking your Frozen Heart, so we have placed it here for you to collect. We knew that you would return.'

The Threshold hummed. If it was possible for a hum to be smug, she thought the Threshold was managing it.

'You mean we passed your stupid test?'

'Child, you can hardly deny the truth of the connection between the three of you, now that you have seen the vision granted by the Frozen Heart.'

'You don't expect me to believe that was *real*, do you?'

'We are only capable of the truth, Elver of the Jih Forest. Whether you are capable of seeing it is another matter entirely.'

Elver treated the god to a recitation of every curse word she'd ever read or heard on the streets of Addersport, and, with a chuckle, the Threshold faded away.

'So full of yourselves,' Elver said to the empty chamber. 'Well, we fooled you, so you're obviously not that wise.'

She bent to pick up the Frozen Heart and once again her mind was filled with the scene in the forest – the bloodstained shirt, the fingers threaded through her hair, how closely they were pressed against each other – and she snatched her hand away like it was a hot coal. This time, it occurred to her that the person she was kissing in this glimpse of the future wasn't necessarily Artair . . . It could be Lucian. She had no way of knowing. Swearing again, she pulled the sleeve of her shirt down over her hand, picked up the heart and put it in her pocket.

They had the Frozen Heart, which meant they had the spell. Supposing that Artair ever spoke to her again, they were a step closer to foiling Mother Maura's plans, which meant she was a step closer to returning to the woods and solitude. Yet, as Elver made her way to the door, she found that her mind was full of other thoughts entirely.

# CHAPTER 25

'She's resourceful, that girl. It's written all over her. Imagine how resourceful you have to be to live and survive in a forest full of monsters.' Sunay shook her head in a wondering fashion. 'I wouldn't put it past her to return with the Frozen Heart after all, you know.'

'And how many people will she have poisoned to do it?' asked Artair. They were sitting in the mage's cosy study, drinking hot black cups of something Sunay called kopi. When he had returned and she had seen his face, she had immediately put a pot on to brew, saying it would help him think clearly. From the way his muscles were twitching Artair strongly suspected that kopi was a stimulant of some kind, something that the Golden Tower of Perpetual Morning strongly disapproved of – to rely on stimulants to stay awake was to invite disaster, that was their teaching. But he found he was glad of it, savouring the bitter tang on his tongue. It was unlike anything he'd tasted before.

'You can't make an omelette without poisoning a few eggs,' said Sunay in a musing tone.

'Pardon me?'

'Look, the business of gods and mages is a messy one, my friend, full of dark deeds and dubious decisions.'

'You would poison someone if Tisk asked you to?'

'Well, quite aside from the fact that doesn't sound like my lord's style at all, yes of course.' Sunay paused to take a sip from her own cup. 'The bond between mage and god goes bone deep, Artair. I owe all to my lord, and the price for my pretty little spells is a lifetime of devotion. It's not really something that can be danced around or negotiated – once that deal is made, often in early infancy, there is no throwing off the yoke. Which makes me wonder about the bond between our Elver and the Queen of Serpents. Famously she does not make mages, and no one performs magic in her name – the only one of the Twelve to avoid humans in this way – yet she has her children, the jih that she has transformed over thousands of years, taking their ordinary natures and making them extraordinary. Which makes me wonder what Elver is, exactly, to her. As far as I know, she has never transformed a human so directly before. Isn't that interesting?'

'What about me?' he asked quietly. 'They say the Sleepless are jih spirits too. Did she make us? And if she did, why?'

Sunay took a loud slurp of her kopi and grimaced. 'An excellent question. I don't have the answer for you, I'm afraid. Perhaps no one knows, save for the Queen herself.'

Artair looked into his cup of kopi. Perhaps he would never know the truth of his own nature.

'What do you know about Mother Maura?'

'I've heard the name, and I have heard that she is as ambitious as the day is long, but she is a mage of the Bloody Claw – calling them ambitious is like calling a fox devious. Of course it is, that's its nature.' She leaned back in her chair, cradling the cup in both hands. 'Some names have a dark reputation attached to them without bringing with them any details, so when you and Elver went off to the Temple of Threshold, I took the liberty of asking my lord if he knew anything.' Sunay paused, pursing her lips. 'Normally, he loves to gossip, so I was surprised when he had very little to say about this Maura. Claimed that he knows little more than a name. Mentioned that her hair often clashes with her choice of gown.'

'Nothing else?'

'When he told me so little, I asked around the village just east of here. Most had not heard of her, but a few had. The rumour was that some years back she dedicated the town of Ashingdown to her god, a bloody ceremony that raised its walls and brought it prosperity. The rumour on the heels of that was that the sacrifices were not willing.' Sunay sighed. 'I don't envy you dealing with this one, Artair. Darkness and tragedy cling to her like blood to a cloth.'

The door opened and Elver was there, blinking in the lamplight. Sunay nearly jumped out of her skin.

'By the Twelve, do your feet even touch the floor when you walk?'

Artair found he could not look away from her. On some level, he'd thought she wouldn't come back.

'I've done it,' she said. 'I've got the Frozen Heart.' The cuff of her shirt was cupped around it, as though it were too hot to touch.

'Oh, well done!' Sunay stood up and crossed over to her. 'How? Artair tells me that your final rite was somewhat, uh, curtailed.'

'I stole it,' said Elver quickly. 'Easy enough. Those idiot monks don't lock their doors.'

Sunay reached out and plucked it from her grip, and as she did Artair saw the pair of them exchange a look, Sunay's thick black eyebrows raising in something that looked like surprise.

'Well. This will do nicely. Let's get this to my Lord Tisk and then you'll have your spell. Come on, it's a little walk to the temple.'

'You mean this isn't the temple?' Artair downed the last of his kopi with something like regret.

'This? Goodness me, no,' said Sunay happily. 'Did you really think that Tisk's temple would be out in the open? The hidden and the secret, those are my lord's domains.'

She led them out the front door of the cottage, past the rows and rows of votive statues; in the moonlight they looked a little uncanny, as though they might come to life at any moment and rush at their ankles. From there, they ploughed through an overgrown copse of horse chestnut until they emerged into a small clearing carpeted with autumn leaves of red, gold and brown. In the centre, there was a stone basin filled with water reflecting the starry sky above, its edge carved with leaping foxes. There wasn't a single leaf floating in it, despite the hundreds crunching underfoot.

'My Lord Tisk,' said Sunay. Unlike most of the other mages and priests they had encountered, she did not sound solemn or meek. Her voice kept its cheerful cadence. 'I have an extra-special offering for you today, for the unrivalled knock-down price of one slightly fancy illusion spell. How about it?' She placed the heart into the water and it seemed to vanish immediately – Artair could not see a bottom to the basin, only more sky, which wobbled and reformed at the mage's touch. They all stood there for a moment in silence, listening to the sound of an owl hooting somewhere in the trees behind them.

'So,' said Elver eventually. 'Did that work, or . . . ?'

'He can be a little tricksy sometimes,' said Sunay. She dipped her fingers into the water again, causing a few ripples. 'A bit more background on this one, my lord – the illusion spell is needed to fool a mage of the Bloody Claw, at the request of the Queen of Serpents. The mage in question is Mother Maura, the one I was asking you about. Juicy, right?'

A second later the small ceramic heart bobbed back up to the surface and Sunay plucked it from the water, smiling. Orange light oozed from the object like syrup, sinking into the skin of her hands.

'Oh yes,' she said. Sunay held out her free hand, watching as the magic flowed over her fingertips and across her palm. 'That's the stuff. I will just keep . . . Oh.' Her eyes flared with the orange light, filling the clearing with a bonfire glow.

'What is it?' asked Elver.

'My lord has made an unusual request of me. Nothing to worry about. It happens, every now and then.' When Elver made to reach for the ceramic heart, the mage closed her hand around it. 'I'll just keep hold of this for the time being, if you don't mind.'

Again, they exchanged a look that Artair didn't understand, and then Elver shrugged.

'Sure. Fine. Makes no difference to me.'

'Now then.' Sunay put the heart inside her wide-sleeved jacket and rubbed her hands together. 'You two can bed down in the cottage tonight and we will get going in the morning. I would say bright and early, but I will be honest with you, I like to avoid dawn where possible. My bed calls me too strongly at that hour.'

'What do you mean, we?' said Elver.

'I mean we, us three,' said Sunay. She grinned at them, her dark eyes sparkling.

'You can't just . . . give us the spell?' Elver was looking more uncomfortable by the second.

'Us?' Artair said, looking at Elver. 'I thought you were only coming as far as this temple. You said you would take the cub home again from here.'

'I've changed my mind,' Elver said shortly, giving him a pointed look. 'I've more reason than anyone to see Maura stopped.'

'My lord insists I accompany you,' said Sunay, brushing over the awkward pause. She was still all smiles. 'As I might have mentioned before, he has a taste for the business of other gods and this positively whiffs of it. So. You get the pleasure of my company. Come on, I don't know about you two, but dealing with gods makes me ravenous, and I make a passable chestnut stew. Just don't ask what's in it.'

'Is it chestnuts?' said Elver, a pained tone to her voice.

'It is.' Sunay looked delighted. 'However did you guess?'

When Lucian opened his eyes that night, it was to look up on a ceiling that was strung with tiny glittering objects – he could see silver acorns, tiny, bejewelled figures, porcelain hands with blue lines painted across their palms, dozens of coins that had been pierced and hung from golden threads. He sat up and found that he was lying on a bed in a small attic room. There wasn't much else of note in there, aside from a storage chest at the foot of the bed and a small round window that looked out onto a peaceful night forest.

'It's a bed at least,' he said aloud. 'That is an improvement on the stony ground of a dismal little clearing.'

There was no sign of the monster girl, and he was surprised to find himself disappointed.

'I need her to help me reclaim my memories, of course I'm put out when she's not in easy reaching distance,' he told himself. 'Not to mention the fact that she's about the only person I've had to talk to in recent memory. I can hardly afford to be fussy about company at the moment.'

Through habit more than hope, he tested the bonds around his wrists and ankles and found them to be especially tight, and when he lifted his legs into the air to get a better look, he realized there was something different about them – they were magical in some indefinable way. A whiff of another god, someone sly and slippery . . . In fact, this whole room smelled of it. He looked again at the items hanging from the ceiling. They had been tithes to someone, once.

'So, I can smell magic. That's something I didn't know before.' He swung his legs to the edge of the bed and looked at the door. There was magic there too and he didn't need to rattle the handle to know it was locked. 'Looks like I'm not going anywhere this evening.'

Yet, when he shifted to swing his legs back up onto the bed – may as well get some rest in that case – he heard the stealthy tread of someone trying not to make any noise.

'Elver?' he called softly.

There was the faintest sigh and then he heard her voice from somewhere just beyond the door.

'I can't talk to you.'

'Why not?'

He slid off the bed and hopped awkwardly towards the door until he was resting his head against it. He could feel her on the other side, a cold slip of a girl with sharp golden eyes.

'Artair knows I let you out at the Inn and he's angry about it.'

'Why do you care what he thinks?'

'I don't,' she said quickly. 'But this journey is annoying enough without travelling alongside someone with the permanent hump.' She paused. 'And he has a point. He trusted me and I made him a promise. I might not have any loyalty to humans, but he is jih, and I owe him that much.'

'Elver . . .' Lucian's mind was racing. If she wouldn't untie him, that was one thing, but if she wouldn't even be in the same room as him, he'd never discover who he was. He decided to do the thing he would normally avoid at all costs: tell the truth. Or something like it. 'The memories you've uncovered have given me part of my life back. I have to have more than just those tiny scraps. I need to know who I am. What I am.'

There was a long silence on the other side of the door. Lucian held his breath.

'I can't,' she said eventually.

'Elver, at least talk to me,' he said, trying to keep the desperation from his voice. For one strange, elastic moment, he wanted to reach through the door and take her hand. Not, for once, to rouse the forgotten memories that were still sleeping inside him, but simply to feel the touch of someone else. The touch of the monster girl. 'I just want to hear your voice.'

'I can't,' she said again, and he heard the soft creak of a floorboard as she moved away.

Dispirited, Lucian hopped back towards the bed. A familiar rising panic tinged with fury was flooding his chest. Was this it? He'd been given a few glimpses of his life before this imprisonment and that would be all he would get – just enough to make this living nightmare an especially painful torture. He wrenched at the bindings on his wrists, relishing the pain as they cut into his skin.

'You don't want to do that. You'll do yourself a mischief.'

Lucian's head snapped up. The voice came from a shelf that ran along the top half of the wall, filled with bric-a-brac similar to that hanging from the ceiling. Crouching among the figurines and decorative glass was a fox, his brush as red as an autumn leaf.

'Who are you?' Even as he said it, Lucian knew it was a ridiculous question. This was a god. It could hardly be anything else.

'I think you know me, Lucian.' The fox jumped down from the shelf silently, sooty black feet somehow delicate against the floorboards.

'Do you know *me*?'

The fox laughed. 'I like mortals, but they're very self-involved, you know? Always assuming they're at the centre of every story.' He paused. 'Well, perhaps you are, Lucian, but that doesn't mean I know who you are. And that's the question, isn't it?'

'Can you tell me who I am?'

The fox came and sat around a foot away from him, long tail curling neatly around his legs.

'Why would I do that? It seems you've found a much more interesting way of getting that information. Elver's another story-fated mortal. Interesting, how you all group together. Besides, haven't you heard? You can't just ask a god for a boon. Not one you're not dedicated to, and not without paying the price.'

Lucian leaned back, considering.

'Then why are you talking to me at all?'

'Because it's all so *interesting*.' The fox's ears pricked up. 'I thought when Sunay paid the tithe it would be your usual peasant shenanigans, but oh no. There are other *gods* involved.'

'Look, I'm not asking for magic. I'm asking for knowledge. All I want is to know who I am and have a chance to re-join the world. I used to be someone. I can feel it. I wasn't always a prisoner locked in some idiot monk's head.'

'Listen, kid, I'll tell you what I'll do.' The fox paused to lick the soft wad of fur on his chest with a bright pink tongue. 'I have sharp teeth. I can chew through those bonds for you. How about that?'

'You will?' Lucian sat up, his heart beating so fast he forced himself to take a slow breath. *Remember who you are dealing with.* 'And what's the price?'

'Ha. You're smart. I like you.' Lucian saw a flash of white teeth, a foxy grin. 'At some point soon, you're going to find yourself in the domain of another god. Steal something for me. That's all.'

'Consider it done.'

'Good.' The fox began walking towards the door.

'Wait!' Lucian half stood, the bonds pinching at his ankles. 'Aren't you going to let me out?'

'Oh no, not yet.' The fox's tail swished back and forth. 'It needs to be exactly the right moment. And this isn't that. Sit tight, kid.'

And with that, Tisk the god of mischief and lies disappeared through the closed door as though it were made of smoke.

# CHAPTER 26

The next morning was cold and grey, a thick frost on the grass that crunched underfoot as they walked. Artair had consulted the map that Mother Maura had given him before they left and they were perhaps a handful of days away – enough time to get there before the mage made good on her threat and killed his friends, but it would be very tight, and as he glanced at the yellowing clouds overhead, he found himself thinking of the bloodstains on the monastery stones, the look on Reah's face as she was pulled back into the portal.

Sunay Tiskertalia was wearing so many clothes she looked almost comical; her thick knitted scarf came up to her nose, but he could still tell she was smiling when he glanced at her.

'I feel the cold,' she said. 'Too used to staying in my cosy little cottage.'

Elver paused to crouch by the cub, removing a crunchy brown leaf from his ear feathers. 'I told you already,' she said to him. 'We're going on an adventure to fool a mage. A bad one.' She paused. 'If you get close enough, you can definitely bite her. I might bite her too.'

She and the cub didn't seem to feel the cold at all. Elver had accepted one of the woollen hats Sunay had offered and was wearing a cloak over her sea-green doublet, but otherwise she seemed unconcerned, her hands and face and neck bare to the icy morning air. The pair of them walked on ahead while Sunay and Artair came along behind. He found that his eyes settled frequently on her slender figure, and each time they did he felt something catch at his heart. Since the Temple of Threshold, they had said very little to each other. Luckily, Sunay appeared to disagree with silence on a fundamental level and had dedicated herself to keeping up a running commentary.

'I prefer to travel in the spring and summer, and often I will do so for months at a time, so that I can offer my services to the little towns along the coast. I'm fond of the seaside. They do these little potatoes sliced and roasted with fish cooked in this crispy batter, have you ever had it? There's something about the coast that appeals to my lord, I think, because it's difficult to know where it begins or where it ends, because of the tides, and that's his cup of tea entirely – the uncertain, the tricksy, the shifting. Do you see?'

'Mmm?' Artair dragged his eyes away from Elver. 'I have never been to the seaside.'

'What?' She slapped him lightly on the arm. 'What? You have to try these roasted potatoes. Delicious little devils, believe me.'

'I believe you.'

It was an interesting thought, with many sharp edges. Yes, he would like to see the sea up close, to walk along the edge of it and eat the things sold there by the vendors of colourful little stalls. But supposedly he was on his way to rescue the other novices, and would ultimately be returning to his cell high in the mountains, to be locked away from the world again. No sea, no freedom, no delicious little potatoes. No walks through a glade turned white with an early touch of winter, and no monster girls.

The lands they were currently travelling through were beyond what he'd been able to see from the monastery windows, a completely unknown place where the landscape itself seemed to have a different character. It was a rocky place, not barren exactly, but littered with stones and boulders, some as big as houses, and through many of them ran seams of quartz that glimmered like ice despite the lack of sunshine. He had the impression it was a land that had been violently upturned at some point in the distant past: frequently, they would come across ravines, or great cracks in the earth.

By the late afternoon, the frost was long gone, although the air remained icy, and ahead of them Artair was shocked to see a range of mountains that were not his own. They glowered under the clouds like purple bruises.

'Let's have a rest,' Sunay said, although she did not look tired to Artair; certainly she had not grown weary enough to stop talking. 'Make a campfire or whatever it is you ruffians do when you're out in the wilds. I prefer an inn. A hostelry. Hot breakfasts and fluffy towels. That sort of thing.'

Without speaking, Elver began gathering wood for a fire, the cub circling around her constantly, and when they found a suitable spot out of the wind – nestled under one of the vast boulders that littered the place – Sunay began brewing tea in a little tin pot she had retrieved from her bags. The cub settled himself down by the fire, rolling over onto his back to bear his blue scales to the warm flames, but Elver hovered at the edge, not sitting down.

'Will you have a cup of tea?' said Sunay. 'I've got a little honey somewhere if you prefer it sweet . . .'

'I'm just going to go for a walk,' said Elver, not looking at Artair as she spoke. 'I'll be back in a bit.'

With that she was gone, disappearing behind a row of pine trees. Sunay sighed.

'Are you going after her then?'

'Why would I do that? She's angry with me.' Artair leaned closer to the fire, holding out his hands to warm them. 'The last thing she wants is me trailing after her.'

'Lord Tisk, give me strength. She's not angry, Artair, she's *guilty*.'

The mage took a sip of her tea. 'Oo, that's too hot. And, anyway, I thought it was you who was angry with her?'

'I . . . Yes.' This was true. She had let Lucian roam free when he was incredibly dangerous, and she had lied to him about it. Yet this morning, under a grey sky with the silence of the wide-open world around them, Artair found that he didn't really know how he felt. He only knew that he did not like the prickling silence between them.

'Your fate is tied up with hers, my friend, and there's no escaping that.'

'What do you mean?'

'I've seen things.' Sunay shrugged. 'I'm a mage after all.'

'A mage dedicated to the god of lies.'

She laughed at that, delighted. 'That is true enough, I'll give you that one. But if I told lies all the time I'd hardly get anywhere, would I? Get after her, lad. Trust me on this one.'

He stood up a little reluctantly. 'Will you keep an eye on him?' He pointed at the cub.

'I feel that me and this little creature bonded permanently when he chose to eat three pairs of my favourite socks,' said Sunay. 'We'll be fine.'

Artair set off towards the pine trees. It was not hard to follow Elver. Although the frost was gone, water droplets still clung to every leaf and blade of grass, and he could see her footprints as darker shapes among the green. Eventually, he came to a thicker row of pine and cedar trees, their scent like the ghost of winter, and beyond that he saw a wide lake covered in pale green ice. Elver was crouched by the edge of it, her arms around herself and her head down, and he wondered if she were cold after all. She looked very small and alone, framed against the ice of the lake.

*This is a mistake*, he thought. *Sunay is wrong. Elver wants her time alone, and I should give her that. If we never share a smile again, so what? At the end of all this, she goes back to her forest and I go back to the monastery, and that's that.*

He half turned to go and then a sound rose from the lake that made him pause. It was a strange, high-pitched hum, followed by several ear-splitting cracks that made him jump. The ice on the lake broke and then shattered apart as a huge serpent's head rose out of it. The creature was a searing golden yellow, the colour of the laburnum blossoms in the monastery garden – they were poisonous, he remembered – and it had rows of spikes and thorns that trailed down its back. Horns a little like deer antlers sprouted from its narrow head, and its eyes were black from lid to lid and dusted with tiny points of light, like stars. Elver had scrambled to her feet and snatched the woollen hat from her head. She was not afraid, but she was respectful. Artair felt frozen in place.

This was the Queen of Serpents.

*Poison child.* The god's voice was a scratch against a drowned stone, a claw drawn slowly over a piece of slate. *You have been long missing from my forest. Do you have what was stolen?*

'I have the cub,' said Elver. 'He's safe.'

*Then you are returning to us?*

Elver hesitated. 'No, not yet. There are other jih creatures in need of my help. The woman who threw me into the sea has them and she'll kill them if I don't do something.'

The serpent rose up, its long body flexing to raise the head so that it hung over Elver. Jaws lined with sharp golden fangs fell open, revealing a split purple tongue. The sight filled Artair with terror. It would take less than a second for this creature to swallow her whole, but Elver seemed undaunted.

*Child, let me taste your blood so that I would know the truth of it.*

Artair tensed. He didn't know what he would do if the god

attacked Elver, but he knew it would be unthinkable to stand by while it happened. Elver took her dagger from her belt and did something that he couldn't see from where he was standing. She raised her hand above her head, palm facing the serpent, and the long purple tongue flickered out and back again. The Queen of Serpents moved serenely backwards, sinking its golden coils back into the water.

*Poison child, there is much you haven't told me,* said the serpent. Artair thought he detected a new, dangerous tone to her words, like thin glass ready to splinter into lethal shards. *There is this human boy. This Sleepless.*

'He's not human,' Elver said quickly. 'He is jih, one of your own, my queen. Artair – and Lucian – they need my help. I want to help them. You said . . . you said something about tasting a destiny in my blood. Maybe this is it.'

*They are not jih enough,* said the serpent. *They smell human, taste human, only their minds are jih. You will treat them as you would any human, poison child.*

'What do you mean?'

*You will kill them.*

Artair watched Elver's shoulders go rigid. He couldn't see her face from where he stood, but he saw when she shook her head.

'My poison doesn't work on them.'

*Then you will take that dagger in your hand and draw it across their throat.* Impatience had crept into the Queen of Serpents' voice. *He is full of human stench and not worth your notice. Kill the boy and return, with the cub, to the forest.*

'No,' said Elver.

The movement was so fast that Artair almost missed it. A tail as thin as a whip lashed out of the water, briefly churning it from green to white, and abruptly Elver was on the ground, curled up with her arms wrapped around her waist. Artair broke cover, no thoughts in his head save for the terrible idea he might be about to watch Elver get eaten. But the Queen of Serpents was already drawing away, sinking back beneath the water.

*You have become too accustomed to human touch, poison child. Remember who made you. Remember who saved your life.*

The serpent sank beneath the water and was gone. Artair reached Elver and helped her into a sitting position. She gave him a brief, surprised look that was half lost in a wince.

'Are you hurt?'

'How long have you been there?' she said, not answering him. 'I don't— Ow.'

She tugged at the bottom of her shirt and Artair had a brief glimpse of her stomach; there was a livid red mark across it, already bruising. Quickly, she covered it back up again.

'You are hurt. Let me help you back to the fire.'

He thought she would pull away from him, but instead she nodded, and carefully he got her standing upright. Her hand was in his briefly and she squeezed it once before letting it go.

'This is the god you're so devoted to?' Once the words were out of his mouth, he realized how harsh they sounded. Elver blinked. Her eyes, he realized, were the same searing gold as the Queen of Serpents' scales.

'She saved me. She pulled me out of death and gave me a different kind of life. I owe her everything.'

'You don't owe her your pain, Elver.'

'And you don't owe the world your freedom, Artair, but you still gave it up, didn't you?'

He found he had nothing to say to that. They walked slowly back through the pines together.

# CHAPTER 27

They were travelling through a town called Tarflin when the faceless priests caught up with them.

Sunay didn't seem to need an explanation: she just saw the look on their faces and began hurrying them down a side street. Elver glanced over her shoulder, catching sight of a slice of white robe as it disappeared around the corner. There had been a small group of them and they were carrying something heavy between them, although she couldn't see what it was.

'Down here, look,' said Sunay, shoving them without ceremony down a narrow alleyway that was slippery with mud. 'You see those blue doors there?'

The pair of doors looked as though they had seen better days and were partly covered with pasted-up advertisements for a nearby tavern. Artair touched one hesitantly.

'In you go, in you go.'

They stepped through into a darkened space and a large man loomed out of the shadows. Elver had an impression of barrels lined up against the walls, dusty crates covered in blankets.

'Who's that?' snapped the large man. He had an equally large beard and a puckered scar that wound its way from his left ear to the bridge of his nose. 'What are you doin', just walking in like you own the place?' To Elver's alarm, she saw that he was carrying a heavy club, the end of it blackened and smooth as though it had been dipped in tar, and he was eyeing up Artair like he'd be happier with his brains spread over a wall. She raised her bare hands – at least there was plenty of skin on display to poison.

'Oh Creg, I'm glad it's you,' said Sunay, rushing up to the man and patting him familiarly on one enormous bicep. 'I just need a place to hide these two idiots for a moment. Do you mind?'

'Sunay?' The man – apparently called Creg – visibly relaxed. 'I didn't think we'd be seeing you until next month. The boss is still working on the tithes . . .'

'Yes, yes, I'm just passing through on a bit of other business.' From outside, Elver could hear people shouting. She couldn't be sure it was the priests of Trilot, but whoever it was, they didn't sound friendly. 'Somewhere to hide these two, my friend?'

'What they done?' Creg looked genuinely interested, as if he hoped they were a pair of passing murderers.

'*Creg.* You know better than to ask those sorts of questions,' Sunay replied brightly.

He chuckled. 'Follow me.'

The man led them along a squalid corridor and down a short flight of steps into what was clearly some kind of storeroom. There were more boxes here, taking up most of the space, and a set of long narrow windows that looked out onto the pavement above at foot level. They were dirty and scratched; Elver wondered if the people walking past them outside even knew they were there.

'Perfect,' said Sunay. Creg, for his part, was already stomping back up the steps.

'What is this place?' asked Artair.

'Just the business premises of another client of mine,' said Sunay rapidly. In her brightly embroidered coat she looked very out of place among the boxes and dirt. 'You can lie low here for a while, and I'll have a little peek outside and see what's going on.'

'We don't have time,' said Artair. 'We have to keep on towards Mother Maura's sanctum or she'll . . . We need to hurry.'

'If we go out there now, they'll catch us,' said Elver. She glanced at the windows again. She could see a pair of feet, clothed in sandals, and the hem of a white robe. 'Look.' She lowered her voice. 'Sunay's right. We have to wait until it's clear.'

The cub, who had been in her arms, wriggled abruptly, demanding to be put down, so she tipped him out of his sack. Immediately, he went over to the boxes and began sniffing them with great enthusiasm.

*Blood*, he said happily. *Blood has been spilled near these things.*

'I'll be back when I know the coast is clear,' said Sunay, already heading back out the door. 'Keep your heads down, my lovelies. I'm going to lock you in, just in case any faceless priests come rattling doorknobs.' She closed the door behind her and they heard the key turn in the lock.

'What is this place?' asked Artair.

'I guess it wouldn't be surprising that a mage dedicated to the god of lies would do work for . . . less than respectable clients,' said Elver. She nodded to the crates. 'I think those things are stolen.'

Since there was nowhere else to sit they made seats for themselves on the boxes. The cub settled down to sleep at their feet, his nose on his paws.

'We don't have long now,' said Artair quietly. 'A handful of days.'

'I know,' replied Elver. From somewhere above their heads, she heard a slow chanting. Quiet at first, as though it were some distance away, and then growing closer. Gradually, the words became clear and a cold feeling settled over her like a shroud.

*Father of purity*
*Father of justice*
*Let us not be tainted by those with ill blood*
*Send your light*
*To burn the monsters away*

The worst thing about it, she thought, was that it made her feel guilty, like she had genuinely done something wrong, when all she was really doing was existing. That was the insidious evil of Trilot: it made a home under your skin and stabbed at you from the inside.

'What is that light?' asked Artair sharply.

It was early afternoon on an overcast day outside, yet the strip of street they could see was growing brighter and brighter, as though the sun itself was edging towards them. It was a hot, white light, illuminating the street and the other buildings so that every tiny detail was exposed: in a glance, Elver saw the marks made on a brick by a stonemason that told the world who had shaped the stone; a broken bottle that had been thrown into the gutter; green glass as clear as lake water; and the elaborate knot tied in a pair of laces as the owner of the boots scampered away along the cobbles. And then a beam of pure white light flashed across the pitted surface of the road towards them. She had a second to see that the bulky item the priests of Trilot were carrying between them was a vast iron lantern and then the beam of Trilot's light sliced across her arm – it burned like she'd been dashed with boiling water.

She yelped, scrambling backwards, and then Artair was there, shielding her body with his. Smoke rose from them both.

'Quick,' she said through gritted teeth. 'Get directly under the window. It won't be able to reach us there.'

They pressed themselves against the grimy wall, the cub twined around their feet. The little creature was trembling with terror. Artair crouched and placed his hand on top of the monster's head, scratching behind his ears.

'They're scouring the streets.' Her anger felt very close, like a hand around her throat, slowly squeezing. 'The Twelve cursed shower of dung beetles. The faceless priests talk a lot about purity and justice and safety, but all they really want is for all jih spirits to suffer. Trilot feeds on our pain.' When Artair didn't answer, Elver found herself searching his face. The lamp had passed on by and much of him was hidden in shadows again. 'Why do you hate your own kind so much?' she asked quietly.

The cub looked up at Artair, pushing his snout into the boy's leg.

*I have decided I do not want to eat you*, he said. *So you shouldn't hate us.*

'I don't hate our kind,' said Artair. 'I just hate . . . me. Or what's inside of me.'

'Why?'

Artair shifted on the box. In such a small space there wasn't a lot of room for his long legs.

'Five years ago, I lived far, far to the south of this place. Far enough that even in the monastery's library, I never found a map that showed it. My people were a travelling people, living out of tents and caravans, always moving with the seasons. I spent so much time outside then. I knew the sky overhead better than I knew my own face.' He paused. 'I don't remember that much of it these days. I think what happened fractured all those memories, somehow. We made our living from the breeding and selling of a particular type of pony. They were hardy and fast, perfect for getting around the plains where we lived, and we'd take them to markets and sell them, or people would come to us – they were famous, those ponies, and they were the heart of our wealth. And our lives, really. Just after we took our first steps, we'd learn to ride.' He smiled a little. Even in the gloom, Elver could see that smile contained very little that was happy. 'One summer, my last summer, it was so hot all the grass died and the plains were full of dry, inedible white grass, and we kept moving, looking for a place for them to graze. Usually, we'd let the ponies roam a little – they always came home – but that summer we were keeping them all together, paddocked in a herd so we could be sure that they were regularly watered.'

Artair stopped, his head down. He scratched the cub between the ears again, and the silence spooled out between them.

'What happened?' Elver asked eventually.

'I wish I knew, but in truth I have no memory of it.' He sighed heavily and looked up at her. 'I woke up to the smell of horse flesh cooking. My father was shaking me by the shoulders. At that time, fires were strictly forbidden, even for making our food, because the danger of the grass catching was so great . . .' He trailed off again.

'It's alright,' she said quickly. Seeing him in this much pain was unbearable somehow. 'You don't have to tell me.'

'No, it's better that you know,' he said. 'That you know what I did. What I let out into the world. Lots of people saw me, including my family. In the middle of the night, I lit a torch and took it into the pony paddock and threw it onto the grass. It caught terrifyingly fast – that's what my mother said, afterwards. It was one of the last things she said to me. That it caught in a great whoosh and then the ponies were screaming as they burned.'

For a long moment, neither of them spoke.

'How did they know . . .?'

'That I was Sleepless, and hadn't just lost my mind? Well, I had no memory of it, for a start. They found me afterwards in a dried-out creek on the edge of our camp. I'd run away once the horses started burning and everyone was occupied trying to save them. And when I eventually fell asleep again, the elders of my people had a long talk with this Lucian. He was a furious creature, they said, full of the need to destroy things, to kill things, and he told them he'd do it again if they didn't let him go. So they wrote to the Golden Tower of the Perpetual Morning and I was sent away.' He rubbed the pad of his thumb along the line of his jaw and Elver heard the rasp of his stubble. 'What you have to understand, Elver, is that losing the ponies destroyed my people. It was their wealth, their future, everything they had invested in for generations. Lucian may as well have burned them all too. My parents sent me to the monastery and I never heard from them again. I don't know what happened to them in the end. Perhaps they died, too.'

He hung his head and Elver saw a single tear track down his cheek, a pure glint of silver in the dirty little storeroom.

'Artair.' She shuffled over so that she was sitting next to him on the boxes and she put her arms around him. It felt awkward, and she was acutely aware that she had never held someone this way before, but the impulse was undeniable. She looped an arm around his neck and pulled him to her so that his head rested against her cheek. His head was warm and his arms circled her back, pulling her closer. Her heart fluttered, a bird trapped in her chest.

'I'm sorry,' she said. Being this close to another being felt like nothing else she'd ever known. She blinked, caught between sorrow for him and a sudden roaring hunger for this feeling to last for ever. *My queen told me to kill him*, she reminded herself. *This is exactly what she was afraid of.* As if in rebellion at that thought, she pressed her lips to the top of his head, giving him a quick, dry kiss, and she didn't let go until they heard the key rattle in the door. Creg appeared at the top of the steps, silhouetted by the light in the corridor behind him. Reluctantly, Elver and Artair drew apart.

'Less of that,' he said cheerfully enough. 'This is a reputable place.' He laughed at his own joke, then placed a battered tray on top of the crates. 'I've brought you some lunch in case you were getting hungry.'

'Where's Sunay?' asked Elver as Artair said thank you.

'She's been and gone – your faceless lads are out there in force, apparently. Whatever you did got them mightily ticked off.' This seemed to please Creg enormously, and for that Elver liked him more. 'She'll be back in a while, don't you worry, but you best eat while you can. You might be leaving here in a bit of a hurry.'

Creg left and they set the tray between them. There were large sausage rolls, heavy enough that Elver thought they could potentially double as a weapon, as well as hard-boiled eggs wrapped in pork meat and seasoning. There were four green glass bottles filled with a clear liquid that definitely wasn't water.

'What is this stuff?' asked Artair after taking a swig. 'It tastes funny.'

Elver shrugged. She was feeding pieces of the sausage roll to the cub, who was snapping them up hungrily.

'Sunay must be looking for a safe route out of this place,' she said.

They finished the food and the drink in short order, and made themselves comfortable on the crates once more. Outside, the daylight had grown mellower as the afternoon marched on.

Artair yawned, and she looked at him sharply. 'Are you alright?'

'I'm fine,' he said, giving her a brittle smile. 'I've not had an afternoon nap in five years.'

The cub was nosing at her for more food.

*More of that, please,* he said. *That was good. There's a lot of interesting food outside of the woods. Why doesn't Mother take us here?*

Elver thought of the white light of Trilot, burning the monstrous right out of them. What would be left of the cub if that happened to him? Would he be reduced to a dead fox cub? A dead bird, perhaps? Her hand brushed her arm, which was still tender from the burn.

'We're not welcome here, little one.'

*That's rude,* said the cub. *I'm great company. Why are we still in this small, bad-smelling room?*

'We're hiding,' she told him. 'Don't worry, we'll be out in the fresh air soon enough. Although you might be back in the sack again for a little while.'

The cub snorted. *The sack smells of poo.*

'That's your own fault.' She paused. 'Perhaps we can get a new sack from this place, though. It seems like the sort of thing they'd have hanging about. Artair, do you think . . .?'

But Artair was asleep, his chin resting on his chest and his hair falling forward to cover his face.

# CHAPTER 28

Lucian heard Elver get up and run across the room, heard her rattle at the door handle. He let himself droop forward a little further, giving himself over to the illusion of sleep. Elver was hissing through the door, calling for someone called Creg to come and unlock it. There was a version of this plan where Lucian leapt up the moment the door opened and forced his way out. He didn't know where they were, but that hardly mattered – his arms and legs weren't bound and he could run. Yet he stayed where he was, and when Creg came into the room – Lucian got the impression the man was large from the thump of each booted foot – he didn't move, letting the man grab his arms and legs and tie them with rope, only lifting his head slowly, blinking sleep out of his eyes. He needed to get her trust back, and he hadn't forgotten Tisk's promise. There was a chance the fox would return to release him from these bonds.

'What was in that drink you gave us?' Elver was asking.

'Just a bit of grog,' Creg said in an apologetic tone. 'What, is he allergic to it or something?'

'No, but he's probably never had it before and he drank it like water.' She cursed in a colourful way that Lucian found quite delightful.

'Elver?' He squinted against the light. 'Where are we?'

'By the Twelve,' said Creg, 'he really is plastered.'

Elver sighed. 'You can leave us now.'

When Creg had gone, Lucian sat up, looking around. Elver had retreated to the far side of the room, watching him with a sharp expression that caused a worm of worry to burrow in Lucian's gut. He had the sudden idea he had made a mistake.

'You're angry,' he said. It wasn't a question.

'I know what you did to Artair's people,' she said. In the gloomy light from the dirty window her eyes were almost silver. '*Why?*' The monster cub was curled tightly on her lap, its face buried in its paws.

'Can you imagine,' he said slowly, 'the pure terror of waking up and not knowing where you are, or who you are? Just sudden, terrifying existence, with no context and no familiarity. No one with a kind word or touch – just a dizzying sense of . . . dislocation. Of being violently thrown . . .' He stopped. He realized he didn't quite feel himself and the room felt like it might spin away if he turned his head too quickly. Had the monk been *drinking*? 'Here and now, speaking to you, monster girl, I am lucid, or close enough to lucid that it makes no difference, because I have had years to come to terms with what has happened to me.' A sour laugh forced itself up his throat. 'No, that is the wrong phrase. There is no coming to terms with something you do not understand, Elver.'

'So, what?' snapped Elver. 'You confused yourself into setting that fire?'

'I told you before that there were only two things I knew for certain,' Lucian said, keeping his tone even. 'That my name was Lucian, and that this,' he tipped his head to one side, indicating himself as best he could, 'wasn't my body. Well, that wasn't entirely true. There was a third thing I knew, and it was this: that death is power. So I sought it out.'

Elver was quiet. She had leaned back deeper into the shadows, letting the dark claim her.

'In truth,' he said, 'that idiot monk is lucky I only killed his horses.'

'I thought I knew what monsters were,' said Elver. 'That we were misunderstood. But you truly are the thing they are afraid of.'

Lucian grinned around the strange pulse of sorrow that moved through his chest – it was almost a physical pain.

'We had a deal,' he reminded her. 'I'll behave, and you'll give me my memories back.'

'Deal's off.'

'You can't do that.'

'I can do what I like,' said Elver.

'This is . . .' Lucian made to stand, but the bindings on his ankles forced him to sit again. He expected to feel the usual fury rising, but instead he only felt tired. 'This is the closest I've ever come to finding out who I am, Elver. How can you take that away from me?'

Something flickered in her eyes at that, but when she spoke, her voice was made of flint.

'You took Artair's whole world away from him.'

After that, she wouldn't speak to him. Outside, the daylight was leached from the sky until only the soft glow of moonlight lit the cramped storage room, filtered through a fine layer of dirt. He saw Elver glance at the door repeatedly, clearly expecting someone to return at any moment. When that didn't happen, she drew her legs up under her, and when the cub came and lay down next to her, she went to sleep. Or, at least, she grew very still and quiet; he couldn't hear her breathing at all.

'She *is* asleep,' came a soft voice at his shoulder. 'I imagine if you live in the woods like some grubbing little insect you get used to sleeping in uncomfortable places.'

A figure stepped out of the shadows. Lucian leaned away from it, his skin crawling with unease. The shape was a man with sharp features, a shock of red hair and a neat little beard and moustache. Narrow green eyes twinkled in the dark. He grinned at Lucian, his teeth a little too sharp.

'You,' said Lucian.

'Me,' agreed Tisk. 'Are you ready for your freedom, little ghost?'

'I am,' he said. And then, 'Why now?'

'Because this is the time that will cause the most mirth.' Tisk pointed at his bindings and they slithered away like snakes, falling onto the floor. Lucian stood, rubbing at his wrists. 'And will you take your memories before you go?'

'She doesn't want me to,' he said. It felt strange, saying those words aloud, as though he had made himself vulnerable somehow.

'They are *your* memories,' said Tisk. 'And you'll need them, where you're going.'

Lucian hesitated. Standing over the girl, he remembered being in the hot spring, one hand curled around her bare foot; he remembered being in the tent with the caged monsters, how she had sat and spoken patiently to the frightened creature – had given it kind words, the softest touch, when it had needed such things the most.

'If you're going to do it, hurry up,' said Tisk. 'I only have patience for tricks and tall tales, and this is neither.'

Very gently, Lucian reached out his hand and placed a single finger on the back of her hand. He felt the chill of her skin, and—

He was in a temple lit with red flames. In front of him was the vast golden figure of a lion, its eyes clusters of rubies. Blood ran from its mouth like a fountain, and Lucian was knelt before it. This was, he knew, his biggest test so far; he was to ask his god for a boon and use what he was given to work a spell. It was dangerous, and all eyes were on him, but he was good at this. He had talents beyond the rest of them and his only concern was how long he'd had to wait to get to this point. That he had been forced to wait like the rest of these talentless magpies-in-waiting was an insult, one he intended to pay back one day.

He glanced to the right of the lion and saw *her*, hair the colour of the blood that ran from their god's mouth, her cheekbones pressing at her skin like knives. *Mother.* The gaze she pinned him with was speculative, sharp, but not necessarily unfriendly. *She sees my power,* he thought, filling with pride. *She recognizes that I will be her equal, one day. Maybe sooner than she thinks.*

Directly in front of him was a thin glass globe filled with a shifting violet light. A soul, taken and kept for just this purpose; precious and unimaginably valuable, and his to do with as he wished. As he picked it up, feeling a faint vibration from the thing inside it, he caught a glimpse of his own face in the glass: black hair, tawny hazel eyes, skin the colour of cream – he spent too long in poorly lit temples.

'My lord the Bloody Claw,' he said aloud. 'Consume this soul and grant me a boon.'

He smashed the globe on the stones in front of him and he heard the thin shriek of the soul as the violet light streamed up and into the mouth of the lion. In response, his hands filled with red fire, unimaginable heat and pain and *power*—

Lucian came back to find himself sprawled on the floor, with Tisk the god of lies standing over him.

'Well?' Tisk asked brightly. 'Was it all you expected and more?'

Lucian got to his feet shakily. He knew who he was. He knew *what* he was. Once, he had had a connection with one of the gods powerful enough that he had been able to use its power for himself and now that he was aware of it he could feel it – a thin line of fire deep within his bones, banked down to embers. To claim the rest of himself he needed to reawaken it, reforge that connection, and to do that he had to get to the nearest temple of the Bloody Claw.

He pointed to the door. 'Make yourself useful and open that.'

# CHAPTER 29

'Wake up, child, you've misplaced your sweetheart.'

Elver came around slowly, her whole body heavy with a tiredness that felt deep and unnatural. Sunay was leaning over her, one hand tugging at her sleeve. Elver pulled her arm away sharply. She could tell from the quality of light in the room that she had slept through into the late morning and the door was standing open. The cub was prowling around the little storeroom, and Artair . . .

She sat up abruptly, her head spinning unpleasantly.

'Where is he?'

'That's the question, isn't it?' Sunay plucked at her sleeves. 'I hate to say this, but I can smell my lord's magic all over this room – on the door, on the ropes we used to tie up Artair and on you, too. That's no normal slumber you're fighting your way out of.' The mage looked unsettled, a frown creasing her normally smooth brow. 'The problem with serving Lord Tisk is that he delights in things like this. Sowing chaos, throwing plans out the window. It can make getting anything done a trial, let me tell you.'

'He's gone.' Elver rubbed her hands over her face, willing herself to wake up. Artair wouldn't have just disappeared, not when they were so close to reaching Prideful Leap, which meant that Lucian had waited until she was asleep and got out of the room somehow. 'And Lucian is in control. When did he go? Do you know?'

Sunay shrugged. 'I've been out all night, and Creg wasn't here – he does most of his work at night, as I'm sure you can imagine.'

'Then he could be anywhere.' Her heart felt like it was sinking through the floorboards, which only made her angrier. He was nothing to her – he was worse than nothing; he was a thief who had come into her forest and harmed her kin. So why did the idea that she'd never see him again make her feel like her stomach had been flipped upside down?

'And he won't be easily caught. Now then, Trilot's faceless donkeys have all cleared out, so let's get you out into the fresh air. I think my lord's magic has knocked you for six and I don't like the lack of colour in your cheeks.'

'They're always like that.'

'Even so, I don't like it. Let's be having you.'

They wrestled the cub into a fresh sack and ventured outside. It was a bright, fresh morning, the sky a great upturned bowl of blue, one of those autumn mornings that welcomes winter with open arms. Elver took a few deep breaths, trying to banish the lingering threads of sleep.

'So what will you do, Elver of the Jih Forest, child of the Serpent Queen?' Sunay said grandly. 'Because what you *could* do is have a slap-up breakfast, hoick that sack on your back and return home. The monster will be returned to his forest and that was your promise to your god, wasn't it? You'll even have a boon from Tisk in your back pocket to use in the future, should you ever need it.'

The magpie was right. There was nothing tying her to the novices, and she wouldn't be able to find Artair now even if she wanted to – she had no doubt that Lucian would have taken them as far away as possible, on whatever dark errand he had in mind. Yes, it was true that part of her had cherished the idea of destroying Mother Maura's plans, a slice of vengeance for her curtailed childhood and her stolen life. But the Jih Forest waited for her. She saw herself walking the road back from Addersport, stepping off the packed dirt into the trees, never to be seen by human eyes again. Her old life was waiting there for her. Of their own accord, her fingers found the conker in her pocket and squeezed it.

And then she thought of Artair tending the cut on her neck, of kneeling before him in the Temple of Threshold, and the pain he carried with him. She remembered how, when Trilot had attempted to burn the monstrousness out of them, he had tried to shield her with his own body.

And she thought of the Queen of Serpents, striking her down because she wouldn't do as she was told.

'No,' she said. 'I'm not going to do that. With Artair out of the picture, there's no one to save those novices. And I know what it's like to be left to the mercy of Mother Maura.' Her mouth twisted as she spoke the mage's name. 'Sunay, if you will come with me, I will attempt to save them.' She cleared her throat. 'I could use your help.'

'And you shall have it.' Sunay made to clap her on the back, then seemed to think better of it. 'I owe you for the Frozen Heart. Now then, I seem to remember that it was Artair who had the map. Do you know where Mother Maura's sanctum is?'

Elver nodded. She had committed the location to memory the first moment she had seen it scrawled in Mother Maura's own handwriting.

'Good. Then let's get out of here. We'll grab that slap-up breakfast on the way.'

When Artair initially awoke, he thought he'd been buried alive.

He was in a small, dark space, without even enough room to stretch his legs. The walls of the place pressed in on him and there were things brushing against his face, soft cloying things like fur or feathers.

And his wrists and ankles were bound.

Panic bloomed in his chest like ink dropped into water, contaminating everything. He tried to stand up, failed and crashed against the wooden wall, smacking his temple hard enough to produce a handful of bright stars across his vision. He grasped after the words of his mantra, the ones the monks had taught him to recite whenever things became too much, but they scattered away from him. He didn't know where he was, and he was tied up, which meant that Lucian was in control. And if Lucian was in control, then Artair had failed and everyone was in danger.

'Elver? Elver!'

She was not with him and did not answer him. But he did hear a noise; it was the sound of a wooden chair being pushed across floorboards as someone stood up.

'You're awake.' The voice was silken and dangerous, and coming closer. Belatedly, Artair realized there was a little light in that dark space. Just above his eyeline there was a keyhole, and the light it was letting in sketched out the circumstances of his incarceration: he was leaning against the wooden panels of a wardrobe, and the soft things that were draped across his head and shoulders were hanging clothes. Awkwardly, he shuffled over to the keyhole and pressed his eye against it. 'I imagine you've had quite the shock.'

The room beyond the wardrobe was lavish. He saw a four-poster bed piled with embroidered blankets, thick rugs on the polished floor and elaborate tapestries hung on the walls. There were leaded windows too, letting in sunshine bright enough it caught the motes of dust in the air and transformed them into points of shifting gold. From the voice, he expected to see a man standing in the room, but he could see no one. And then, a moment later, an orange shape moved across the floor in a flash and jumped up onto the table. It was a fox, its eyes full of yellow fire.

'Who are you?'

'Come on, you can do better than that, Artair. You know who I am. Unless you'd like me to lie to you? Would that make it more obvious?'

'You're Tisk.' Artair swallowed. He was talking to a god. 'What are you doing here?' and then, 'Can you let me out?'

'To answer your first question, I am here to protect my investment, and to answer your second, no, because that would jeopardize my investment.'

'You don't understand. The other me . . . He can't be allowed to roam the world freely. He's dangerous. People will get hurt.'

The fox shook himself, puffing up the heart-shaped patch of white fur on his chest.

'Do you really believe such things, Artair?'

He ignored that. 'I have to be at Prideful Leap in three days. If I'm not there, she'll kill the other novices.' A wave of frustration and horror moved through him and he thumped his shoulder against the wardrobe. Why was he wasting time talking to a god who clearly had no intention of helping him? He could break this door down himself. It was a start, at least. He slammed himself into the door again, but although he felt the whole structure rattle, the door itself didn't budge.

'I wouldn't bother,' the fox said drily. 'I've been doing a little reinforcing.'

'*Why?* Why are you on *his* side? He's an evil spirit, a thing meant to cause misery and chaos. How can you help him?'

'I refer you to the answer I gave to your first question.' The fox dropped back down to the floor, his sooty black paws making no noise at all. 'But I do have something for you. Your counterpart left you a missive. And I am to read it to you.'

To Artair's astonishment, where there was once a fox, there was suddenly a man. He was wiry and lean, with a shock of red hair and sharp green eyes. He wore a deep burgundy velvet suit lined with peach-coloured silk and he had a walking cane topped with a silver fox head. The man grinned in his direction, as if he could see Artair's surprised expression. For all Artair knew, he could. Tisk crossed back to the table and picked up a piece of paper that had been left there, neatly folded.

'My sweet idiot monk,' he read aloud, his voice taking on a slightly pompous tone. 'How does it feel to wake up with your wrists and ankles tied together, unable to move or even sit up without discomfort? How does it feel to know that you will spend hours in that tiny space, with no break from the monotony, and, even better, that every day for the rest of your life will look exactly the same? I wish I were able to see the look on your face when you realize that this is your fate, but I suppose if I could, we wouldn't be in this mess in the first place.' Tisk paused to stroke his moustache, nodding faintly. 'You think of me as the evil creature that has stolen a place inside your head, monk, but the reality is, I will be much kinder to you than you ever were to me. I am a mage of the Bloody Claw. I know this now, thanks to Elver – her unexpected sweetness has been one of the few highlights of this miserable existence.'

Artair lowered his head, trying to ignore how those particular words made him feel.

Tisk continued reading. 'I should have liked to taste more of it, but there was no time. Now, I must travel to the nearest temple to my god, and once I am there, I will reforge the connection that was once mine, reclaiming my talents as one of the greatest of the Bloody Claw's mages . . .' Tisk sighed. 'He does go on a bit, I'll give you that.' He resumed the pompous voice. 'For I am destined for greatness and power that you could not possibly imagine, blah blah, a little more here on how important and powerful he's going to be, yadda yadda . . . Oh, here we go. The juicy bit.' Tisk cleared his throat. 'Once I have reforged that connection, I will make whatever sacrifice the Bloody Claw requires to: firstly, give me back all of my memories, and secondly, to cast *you*, pious, grubbing little monk, out of this head and into eternal nothingness. I might not be able to return to my own body, but if there's a chance to fully inhabit yours, I will take it. Do you understand the kindness of this act, Artair? I will not keep you prisoner for ever, a creature trapped in a cage, slowly losing its mind – I will simply cast you into oblivion.'

Tisk stopped reading and folded the paper away into his pocket. He twirled the cane briefly.

'There you have it.'

Artair pressed his face to the door so that his mouth was close to the keyhole.

'You *have* to let me out,' he said. 'Lucian is dangerous. Can't you tell?'

'Oh my goodness, I don't *have* to do anything. Not unless you're willing to pay for my services. And you, boy, don't have anything I want.' Tisk grinned, a sharp, foxy expression that raised the hairs on the back of Artair's neck, and then he vanished, leaving behind the scent of burning leaves.

Artair picked one of Elver's many colourful curse words, said it as loud as he could and then slid down the wardrobe door to sit with his head between his knees.

# CHAPTER 30

'Trust me, this will get us there so much faster and I've practically walked my legs into little stumps. See?' Sunay stuck out one leg dramatically. 'Please, Elver, think of my shoes.'

Elver hesitated before the steps. The coach was the biggest she had seen, with enough seats inside for around ten people, and at the front were two powerful black horses with white socks. She had pulled her hood up over her head, but there was no avoiding the fact that the cabin was *crammed* with humans. They would be able to see her scarred face and her yellow eyes, and, even worse, she would have to expend so much energy to avoid touching them – because humans certainly didn't seem to have any sense of personal space. It was dusk, the temperature around them dropping swiftly, and she could see from the expressions of the people already inside that they would dearly like her to stop dithering and get in so they could close the door.

*It'll get us there quicker,* she told herself. *Which means I'll be home all the sooner.*

She bent her head to the sack in her arms. It was just possible to see the faint green glow of the cub's eyes.

'We have to get in a human carriage now,' she whispered. 'Are you going to behave yourself?'

*Can I bite them?*

'No.'

*You are very boring.* The cub yawned. *I will make things more exciting. I will jump out, and bite.*

'Listen.' Elver pressed her head into the sack, so that her nose almost touched his. 'This is a big scary thing for me, okay? Being this close to humans. So I need you to be brave for both of us. Just be brave and very . . . quiet. Can you do that for me?'

It was too dark to see, but she felt the cub's feathers puff out with self-importance.

*I will do it. Because I am very brave and tough.*

Elver closed the neck of the sack and nodded at Sunay. She followed Sunay up the steps, which were then folded away by the driver. The humans inside were a varied bunch, as far as she could tell; there was an older couple, one of whom was wrapped with enough blankets and shawls to see them through the darkest winter in the Jih Forest; a broad-shouldered woman with a broken nose and large, labourer's arms; and a family – a mother, father and three smallish children. She and Sunay found seats in the corner, where Elver attempted to hide herself away as much as possible – she could already see the smallest kid staring at her with big, blue eyes – but Sunay leaned forward and greeted everyone in the carriage, merrily introducing herself and solemnly shaking hands with each of the children. With a lurch and a mild protest from one of the horses, the coach started on its way. Elver placed the sack on the floor between her feet, giving the cub a surreptitious pat as she did so.

'I should tell you all that I am a mage dedicated to Tisk, lord of tales, tricks and tribulations.' Sunay produced a large silver coin from somewhere within her sleeve and spun it expertly across her knuckles, making it flash like the moon. The children immediately turned their attention away from Elver to the mage. 'So this carriage ride is truly blessed.'

'It had better be,' said the broad-shouldered woman mildly. 'I've got work in the next village and I can't have any tricks delaying me, magpie.'

'Of course, of course,' said Sunay, bowing her head. 'I merely offer some minor entertainments to keep us merry on the journey.'

'At what price?' asked the older man. His voice was dry, but he was smiling faintly as he spoke.

'Why, only your souls . . .' Sunay paused, then laughed uproariously. 'Just kidding. Any godly trinket you might have on you would do. My lord isn't fussy.' She made the coin dance and the children began to tug at their mother's skirts until she gave her husband a meaningful look. He sighed and pulled a small item from within one of his bags. It was a tiny carving of a mouse inscribed with letters too small to make out. He passed it to Sunay.

'We had this token of Milik the Small for our cottage – it kept the mice out of the pantry, but we're moving, so I don't suppose we need it any more.'

'Perfect,' said Sunay. She tapped the top of the wooden mouse's head and suddenly it was real, eyes like little beads of black glass, nose twitching inquisitively. The children gasped, and when Sunay held out her hand towards them, the mouse turned several somersaults before transforming into a silver button, which she passed to the littlest kid. The child cradled the button in her hands as though it might turn back into a mouse at any moment. Elver caught herself smiling. Annoyed, she looked down at her own boots.

Something in the carriage seemed to shift then and several conversations broke out. The mother of the children brought out a number of sweet buns from her own bag and passed them around the little cabin, while the old lady who was so thoroughly wrapped up against the cold bent to tie the laces of one of the children.

The woman with the broken nose leaned towards Elver with a smile, holding out a small silver bottle which she had produced from somewhere within her coat.

'Want a sip? It'll keep you warm.'

For a long second, Elver didn't move. The human woman was completely at ease with her, despite the way she looked, and was offering something of her own for no reason that Elver could see. Carefully, so as not to brush the woman's fingers with her own, she took the bottle and had a cautious sip. It tasted of honey and elderberries. When she passed it back, the woman winked.

'My name is Halla,' she said. 'Pleased to meet you.'

'I am Elver.' She cast about desperately for something to say. 'The drink is . . . very good.'

'Thank you.' Halla flushed with pleasure. 'I brew it myself and I always take a little with me when I'm away for work, especially when it gets cold. I deal with timber, you see, and I'm out in all weathers.'

Halla offered the bottle to the elderly man, and got chatting to him too, and Elver felt a strange mixture of relief and disappointment. It occurred to her that Artair would have loved this; would have been thrilled just to sit and hear other people's stories. He was so curious about the world. Through the window to her left she could see warm lights burning in the darkness. They were passing through a village or a town and these were the welcoming lamps of a human space. For the first time that she could remember, she felt almost comforted by it.

When Sunay paused for a moment in her relentless charming of the children, who were now arguing among themselves over who got to hold the mouse button, Elver leaned over and spoke into the mage's ear, as close as she dared.

'Do you still have the Frozen Heart on you? Can I . . . look at it for a moment?'

Sunay's dark eyes found hers immediately. They were twinkling with amusement.

'Missing him already, are you?'

'I don't—'

'I'm afraid I'll have to disappoint you,' said Sunay without pausing. 'I popped that little trinket inside Artair's pack, so wherever he is now, that's where the Frozen Heart is.'

'I . . .' Elver's skin prickled all over. The thought of him seeing the vision that was contained in the clay heart filled her with horror. 'Why did you do that?' She cleared her throat. 'I mean, don't you sell Tisk's used-up tithes in your shop?'

Sunay shrugged. 'I just have the feeling that Artair – or maybe even the other one – might need it before long, that's all.'

At that moment, there was an angry shout from the coach driver. Halla half rose in her seat.

'What's going on? Does he need help or something?'

A second later his cry was answered by two screams from the horses, and the carriage lurched alarmingly one way and then the other. The children screamed too, clutching at their parents, and suddenly they were all falling sideways into the wall of the carriage, belongings flying everywhere. Elver landed awkwardly a second before Halla crashed into her, knocking all the air from her lungs.

*I can't touch her*, she thought, panic and anger closing her throat. *I mustn't touch any of them.*

There was a chorus of shouts and cries as the carriage came to a stop, punctuated by the crying of the children. Next to and slightly beneath her, Elver heard Sunay swearing colourfully. She reached out for the sack, which was still somewhere near her feet, and placed her hand on the rough hessian weave. Beneath it she could feel the cub's heart beating wildly.

'Are you alright?'

*I am being brave*, said the cub, too quickly. *Not like all these shrieking humans.*

The window of the carriage was now above them, providing

a glimpse of the night sky. As Elver watched, there was a flash of blindingly bright light, there and gone again in an instant. Her stomach turned over and she began scrambling towards the door, climbing over the others as best she could without pressing any part of her skin to theirs. She had a terrible feeling she knew what she'd see outside. Behind her, Sunay was trying to comfort the children as well as help the old lady to her feet. Someone had grazed themselves – Elver could smell the blood. She pushed the door until it swung open and slowly raised her head out of the opening.

The coach was on its side at the edge of the road, the two wheels in the air still spinning. One of the horses had moved some distance away; there was no sign of the other one. All around them were small cottages with smooth clay walls and just beyond them stood one taller building with a tower and a bell. The carriage driver was lying face down in the dirt, unmoving. Elver couldn't see anyone else, so she clambered down the side of the vehicle, dropped to the ground and ran over to him. Behind her, she could hear the others climbing out of the coach.

'What in the bloody Twelve happened?' shouted Halla. Her voice was full of the anger that emerged when a tough person was frightened. 'Did we hit something?'

The older man climbed down the side of the coach. He glanced around at the cottages.

'I'll go and get help,' he said. 'There has to be someone awake here.'

Hesitantly, Elver pressed her fingers to the man's back, waiting for the rise and fall of his breath. When it came and she was sure he wasn't dead, she turned back to the coach in time to see Kantor Witt rising from behind it, where he'd been hiding out of sight. He had a small Trilot lamp in one hand and his formerly white robes were grey with dirt and streaked here and there with wet mud. His fine golden hair hung in his face in greasy clumps, her livid handprint still unmistakable even in the dark.

'You ride with a monster!' he screamed, pointing with his free hand at Elver. 'A dirty jih spirit has tainted you all!'

Sunay, who had followed Halla and the first of the children out of the carriage door, rolled her eyes. 'Oh good, a priest of Trilot, said no one ever.'

'What are you talking about?' shouted Halla, squaring up to him as she climbed down the side of the carriage. 'Who are you?'

'I am here to save you,' raved Witt, his voice rising. 'The spawn of the Queen of Serpents has slipped in among you, turning everything good to filth—'

'Did you startle those horses deliberately?' asked Halla, her tone distinctly dangerous. 'Because if you did—'

'I did it to save you from the monster!'

'There are no monsters here, you wheezing little turnip.'

Kantor Witt, his face twisted with a rage that seemed to edge beyond the sane, threw the lamp overarm at Halla. It missed her entirely and smashed into the smallest child, who was being lifted out of the open coach door by her father. There was a tinkling sound of shattering glass and a high-pitched scream of pain and fright from the child. The lamp had smashed on her dress and set the hem of it aflame. Elver had time to see Sunay leap at the child, smothering the fire with her own embroidered coat, and then she found that she was running, hands held out in front of her and her teeth bared. She sped past Halla, who gave her a surprised look.

'You see it now!' Witt yelled triumphantly, jabbing a finger in her direction. 'Witness its true form, its poisonous, filthy form as it—'

Elver collided with him at full force, sending him flying into the mud with a thump. She made to press her hand to the other side of his face, the one yet to be marked, and then she paused, her fingers hovering less than an inch from his cheek.

'Those people have done nothing to you,' she hissed.

Kantor Witt squirmed beneath her. 'They've sat and breathed the air that you've poisoned, monster, so they are a lost cause. Trilot will never turn his grace upon them again. If I put them out of their misery I'd be doing them a favour.' His eyes were glassy and unfocused. 'You are death to everything you touch.'

Elver thought of Artair then, and Lucian, who had both felt her touch and lived to tell the tale. Perhaps there was another way to live, after all.

'Not to everything,' she told him. '*Not to everything.*' She took her hand away.

'What are you doing?'

'You don't know me,' she said. 'You don't know me at all, or any of the creatures you choose to hate so much. Remember that I, a monster, could have killed you tonight, and chose not to.'

Halla appeared at her side, frowning deeply. She held out a hand to help her up, which Elver did not take, but once she was on her feet she carefully patted the larger woman on her sleeve in a gesture of thanks.

'Who is he?' asked Halla. 'What sort of monster deliberately spooks horses and throws a lit lamp at a child?'

'The human kind,' said Elver.

There was a shout from behind them, and the older man came jogging over with a pair of burly men, one of whom was in some kind of guard's uniform.

'You need to arrest this man,' Halla said, pointing at Kantor Witt. 'He deliberately spooked the horses and caused us to overturn.'

'And he threw a lit lamp at my child!' called down the mother of the children, her voice still hoarse with panic. 'He could have killed her!'

'No, no, you are wrong!' bellowed Kantor Witt, flecks of spittle flying from his mouth. He lifted himself up onto his elbows and pointed at Elver. 'That is a jih creature. An abomination. Have it tied up and I will escort it back to the Temple of Trilot. The monster must be burned, must be cleansed!'

Halla placed her booted foot on his chest, pushing him back into the dirt.

'That's enough from you,' she said, her voice stony. She nodded to the guard. 'He's mad or something. Do you have a jail in this village?'

'Well,' said the guard in a musing tone. 'We have a pit. Will that do?'

'I'd say so,' said the father of the children.

When Kantor Witt had been dragged away, still screaming about monsters and abominations, a number of people appeared from the cottages and together they righted the coach and collected the missing horse, who had made his way into someone's garden and started eating their crop of tomato plants. The coach driver was taken to the small village tavern and given a jot of rum, while the second burly man offered to drive them the rest of the way. Elver watched it all happen from the edge of things. They came together seamlessly, she thought, with no questions or suspicions. They joked with each other and smiled frequently. Someone brought them out cups of hot tea – Elver accepted one cautiously – and an old woman from the village gave the smallest child a new dress to replace the burned one; it had belonged to her own daughter when she was small, she told them. And not once during all this did anyone look at her and consider Witt's words. They saw her, saw her scars and her yellow eyes, and instead of a monster they saw someone who had put herself in harm's way for them.

'We'll be on our way again shortly,' said Sunay, appearing at her elbow, with the sack containing the cub held firmly in her arms. 'I apologize, Elver. This coach ride was a little more eventful than I was expecting. Perhaps we would have been better off walking after all.'

'No, it was a good idea.' She watched one of the children gently pat the newly returned horse on the nose. 'It was the right way to come.'

# CHAPTER 31

'I'm not sure about this.'

They were standing at the foot of a cliff, in front of a cave entrance. The wall of the cliff was orange with clay, broken up here and there by a creeping plant with pale blue leaves that Elver didn't recognize. To one side of the cave there was a tall pile of stones, each carefully balanced on top of the other, with a deer skull sitting on top. Elver found her eyes were drawn again and again to its empty eye sockets. It was not a place that she could picture Sunay spending much time in – this was wild country, far from the road – but she seemed completely comfortable. At their feet, the cub prowled through the grass, chatting to himself about interesting scents.

'It's the best course for him,' said Sunay. 'I know the little sneak well enough now that I can create the illusion without having him close by, and Prideful Leap will not be safe for him. I think you know that too.'

'Yes,' Elver said reluctantly. 'If she sees through the illusion, if she guesses we're hiding him close by . . . But leaving him in the care of a stranger? A magpie?'

'I'm a magpie too,' Sunay pointed out. 'And Bawric owes me a favour.'

As if summoned by his name, a figure emerged from the shadows of the cave. He did not step blinking into the light, as anyone else might, but seemed to adjust instantly. He looked calmly at them both in a considering way, while a pair of wolves, their pelts grey and shaggy, appeared at his side.

'The Pack welcomes you,' he said.

Bawric was a wiry man in his forties, with brown hair that fell to his shoulders and a neat, dark beard. His eyes were a ruddy brown too, almost red, and there was a scent to him Elver thought she almost recognized: he smelled a little like the forest.

'My friend, how are you?' Sunay said warmly. As she spoke, three more wolves emerged from the cave, their noses twitching. Elver was not concerned by wolves – she lived in the monster forest, after all – but she did not know how they would react to the cub. She tensed, not sure what she would do if they went for him. Her poison skin would not reach them through their thick fur pelts.

'Busy.' Bawric was watching the cub too. 'Your message mentioned that you needed an animal tending to. I feel like you left out some important information, Sunay.'

'You just need to watch him for a day or so,' said Sunay. 'You'll barely notice him among all these fine fellows.' She gestured to more wolves, who were beginning to crowd the entrance to the cave. 'What do you say?'

'Jih monsters are outlawed, by order of Trilot,' he said evenly. 'If I was found harbouring one, I'd be fined. Locked away. Perhaps worse.'

'And you follow what Trilot says, do you?' said Elver. She was thinking of the small dead cat they had left behind in the Temple of the Faceless God. 'I thought the Pack was your lord, magpie.'

Sunay laughed nervously. 'My friend is keen to see the cub safe, you see, and it makes her seem *less than friendly*.' She shot Elver a look.

'I would be less than friendly too, if I were a jih spirit wandering the human realm,' said Bawric. 'Yes, I know what you are, girl. One of the gifts of running with the Pack is that I can see the true nature of things. To hunt, you must see clearly.'

Elver stood up a little straighter and lifted her chin a touch.

'If you are too afraid of Trilot to help, then tell us now so that we can find another solution.'

One of the wolves gave a sharp yip, briefly exposing yellow fangs. Bawric, though, shook his head, the smallest suggestion of a smile at the corner of his mouth.

'I've no love of Trilot,' he said in his calm voice. 'And no hatred of the Queen's kin either. Even monsters must hunt, locked away in their own forest.' He nodded to the wolves, and they retreated back into the shadows. 'But it's not me that little chap would be spending his hours with. Come in and we will see how my companions feel about your proposal. Then I'll give you my answer, Sunay Tiskertalia.'

Inside, the cave mouth drew into a narrow bottleneck before widening out into a much larger chamber. Hanging on the craggy stone walls there were around a hundred bleached animal skulls, some of them decorated with flowers and strings of black and gold beads. Running near the length of the chamber was a long, narrow firepit that gave off a pleasant warmth and the scent of cooking meat. To her surprise, Elver found that she was drawn to it; the urge to go and sit by the hearth – to rest, and talk, and eat – was powerful. *Humans like to gather together.* She thought of the people in the carriage, and the way Halla had offered her a swig from her own bottle. The wolves, of which there had to be at least twenty, were either standing near the back of the cave or sprawled on stony ground beyond the hearth. A few of them stayed close to Bawric, and in this space Elver had a better idea of how big they were; their long snouts rested at the same level as the mage's chest. She pointed to the skulls.

'All animals you've taken?'

'Hunted, killed, dressed and honoured.' Bawric nodded to the skull of what looked to be an elk. Its antlers were strewn with loops of glass beads. 'We remember those who made us work for it. Now then.' He sat by the hearth. 'Let's have a look at this chap.'

But the cub was still cowering by the entrance to the wider chamber.

'Come on,' Elver called to him. 'You need to come and meet this magpie.'

*I shan't.* The cub wagged the brush of his tail back and forth, scarlet feathers bristling. His eyes burned green. *I don't feel like it.*

'We don't really have time for this,' she replied through gritted teeth. Bawric was watching her with interest, and she could feel her cheeks growing pink. 'You can have the last of the dried meat from my pack. Or I can just come and pick you up and bring you over myself.'

The cub scampered back a little further, his claws skittering on the stone. *You wouldn't dare! I will bite you! I will snap your human fingers off!* He danced about. *This cave smells like dung and you are all made of dung.*

'He is still a very young animal,' commented Bawric.

Elver turned to him in surprise. 'You can understand him?'

The mage shook his head. 'Not as you do, jih, but I know the behaviour of pups better than most.' He nodded to the crowd of wolves. 'He's frightened, and he doesn't want us to know he is. Perhaps he'd be more forthcoming if you called him by his name?'

'His name? He is a keltraxia cub. That is what he is.'

Bawric leaned down towards the firepit and picked up a small clay bowl that had been resting near the heat. From its colour, it was made from the same clay that made up the cliff face. There were walnuts inside, which Bawric crushed open with his fingers before picking out the sweet pieces of nut inside.

'All creatures have their chosen names,' he said. 'As a mage of the Pack, I can see what they are, although I will admit I've never attempted that magic with a monster.'

Sunay, who had been uncharacteristically quiet, crouched to take a nut from the bowl. 'Will that truly help us, my friend? To know the creature's name?'

Bawric shrugged. 'Help you? The point is not to help you, Sunay, but to treat this little creature with respect. The respect all animals deserve, even those who have been touched by the Queen of Serpents.'

Elver frowned. She couldn't decide if she liked this human or not.

'What does it cost? This magic?'

'Something with a sharp edge. A blade, a tool, a knife. I would take a worked piece of flint, if you had it.'

Elver's hand drifted towards her belt. What did she need a weapon for, after all? She *was* the weapon.

'Here.' She took the dagger from her belt and passed it to the mage, taking care to keep her fingers out of reach of his. 'Take it. Do the spell.'

Bawric examined the blade, then nodded. 'It has seen a lot of blood, this blade.' She thought for a moment he would accuse her of something, but instead he seemed pleased. 'Some of it in the pursuit of prey. Good.' He slipped the dagger into his own belt and the firepit glowed with a sudden brightness, as though someone enormous had breathed on it. There was a murmur that seemed to come from all around them, and the skulls began speaking.

*His name,* they intoned in old, dry voices, *is Fleet. Now you know his name, now you know his nature.*

*Oh, that's right,* said the cub. *That's who I am.*

'You never thought to mention it?' cried Elver. 'We even asked you, once . . .'

*Well, I wasn't sure,* said Fleet. He trotted down into the chamber, his tail held high. *But now I am. I'm Fleet, that means I'm fast and I'm clever and you can't catch me.* He glared around at all the wolves, his eyes very wide. *When I am grown, even you won't dare challenge me!*

'Those who run with me, this is Fleet.' Bawric was talking to the wolves, his voice taking on a rhythmic, musical quality. Every pair of wolf eyes turned to him. 'He is young and hasn't learned to hunt yet. Will you teach him, my friends? Will you let him run with us for a while, to learn the ways of scent, and mark, and tooth?'

There was a moment of busy silence. Elver looked at Sunay, who shrugged ever so slightly before popping another piece of walnut in her mouth.

*Me? Learning to hunt?*

Elver crouched by Fleet and scratched him behind the ears in the way that Artair did sometimes.

'I have to go somewhere for a little while, with Sunay, and it's dangerous for you to come with us,' she said quietly. 'So I want you to stay here until we come back for you. It'll be safe here.' As she said it, she wondered how true that was.

*Elver, how long will you be gone?* There was a note of fear in Fleet's voice that caught at her heart.

'Not long. A day or so. You'll hardly know I'm gone, and then when I come back, we'll be going home.'

*I'll miss you.*

This felt like a slightly outrageous statement from the creature that had spent much of his time sleeping, running away, eating all their food or dramatically going to the toilet at awkward moments, but even so Elver smiled. Around them, the wolves were lifting their long snouts to the ceiling and howling in unison, a strange, eerie sound that made the hair on the back of her neck stand on end.

'They say they will gladly run with him,' said Bawric. 'So I'll take him into my care for as long as you need.'

Elver pulled the cub closer and buried her face in the feathers that sprouted between his ears.

'I'll miss you too, Fleet.'

# CHAPTER 32

Lucian arrived on the outskirts of Ashingdown in the early hours of the morning, his whole body thrumming with the need for sleep, but he resisted it, taking big gulps of frigid dawn air to drive the urge away. For the last two days, Tisk had been the one to tie him up when he couldn't stay awake any longer, the wily god appearing just when Lucian needed him every morning, but today he was close to his goal, the Temple of the Bloody Claw within reach, and the idea of waiting another day to reclaim who he was – and to banish Artair from this body – was unthinkable. He let his feet lead him, passing the pillars with their lion statues and following grubby streets and alleyways until finally he stood in front of the temple. It was a striking building, and even at the last dregs of his patience he took a moment to admire it: the whole thing was carved from cloudy red marble, giving it the appearance of a towering slab of fresh meat, and every inch was covered in depictions of his god. The Bloody Claw prowled over the arch of the entrance, leapt from the walls onto unsuspecting victims, stood proud and numerous along the roof. Many of the lions had golden eyes, painted with a careful hand, and they flashed like tiny suns in the early-morning light.

Inside, the place was quiet. There were lamps burning red, and there was a wild, spicy scent that made the hair on the back of Lucian's neck stand on end. With that scent came a flood of emotions he didn't understand: reverence, excitement, fury, terror. He swallowed hard, suddenly filled with the urge to leave the temple and never return.

'Can I assist you, child?'

A priest had appeared from behind a screen. He was bare-chested, a tattoo of the Bloody Claw sprawling from his stomach to his collarbone. He wore a bronze lion mask that caught the light from the lamps and turned it into a liquid fire that flowed over fangs and whiskers.

Lucian felt his hands ball into fists. To be called a child by a mere priest . . . Priests were the grubbing servants of his lord, whereas he was a weapon, a sword forged to do His will. But as much as he'd like to show this idiot the meaning of power, this was not the time to lose his temper.

'I am here to give my thanks to our lord.'

The priest cocked his head. 'He has blessed you?'

Lucian smiled, feeling a genuine burst of pleasure at the thought.

'He has brought me back into His light,' he said. 'And shown me the path to power.'

The priest nodded seriously. Lucian knew this was the sort of thing they liked to hear. The Bloody Claw was the god of ambition, influence, potential and strength. You did not enter the temple if these weren't the things closest to your heart.

'Then you should come to the place where He is strongest, child.'

The priest led him out of the main chamber into a smaller, darker space behind it. In here, the wild animal smell was almost overpowering, and the room was dominated by a huge marble bust of the god, its mane flowing down onto and into the floor; it looked as though the whole space had been carved from a single, enormous piece of marble. Its jaws were open, exposing teeth as long as Lucian's forearm and a broad tongue covered in gold leaf. There was a tarnished spot on the end of its tongue. This would be where supplicants would leave their offerings. Lucian knelt before it.

'I will leave you in contemplation of His glory,' said the priest. There was a whisper of sandals against stone and he disappeared back through the door. Lucian waited for a moment longer, to be completely sure he was alone. And then he lifted his head.

'My lord, I've returned,' he said. Dimly, he was aware that his hands were shaking. 'Give me back what is mine.'

The room remained silent. Lucian reached inside himself for that thin line of fire and willed it into a living flame.

'Speak to me, lord.'

*Blood.*

The voice was a low, purring growl, deep enough that he felt the stones under his knees hum faintly. Lucian took the knife from his belt – stolen from the last tavern he'd stayed in – and cut the palm of his hand, barely feeling the hiss of pain. Blood flowed across his skin, black in the smoky light. He pressed his hand to the statue's tongue.

'Give me back what is mine, lord.'

There was a feeling of slight pressure under his hand, as though the marble were eagerly drawing the blood away from him. And then it stopped, and for a few breaths nothing happened.

*Blood*, said the Bloody Claw again. He had never been the easiest god to speak to. Lucian knew that other mages could have whole conversations with their patron god. Tisk, certainly, was talkative enough. But the Bloody Claw was, at his heart, a beast, an animal, and speaking to mortal humans was below him.

Lucian sat back on his haunches. It wasn't enough, he knew that. His own blood was freely given and therefore worthless. But to give the Bloody Claw what he wanted here, in this place, was incredibly risky. He looked down at the knife in his hand, the blade already slick with blood.

*What are you going to do?* he asked himself, his own voice slick with contempt. *Slink away with your tail between your legs and admit defeat because what He asks of you is too hard? You've spent too long in the body of this soft monk.*

The Bloody Claw was right to ask this of him. After all, if he couldn't do this one, simple task, he was hardly worthy to be one of the lion's most celebrated mages. Lucian stood. The hand that gripped the knife was no longer shaking.

'Priest?' he called. 'I need your help.'

Blood flowed freely over the lion's tongue; not black now but a lurid crimson, its mineral scent combining with the wild animal funk of the temple to create something terribly familiar.

Lucian pushed the priest's body to one side, breathing heavily. Such a quick, simple little murder, but it had left him exhausted, even drained. *You're tired*, he told himself. *That's all.*

He placed his hand in the blood, which was still obscenely hot.

'You know me, lord,' he panted. *'Give me back what's mine.'*

Something stirred in the depths of the lion's throat. Lucian shivered, suddenly very aware of the huge teeth that surrounded him. If this were a real lion, it could bite him in two with one decisive chomp. For a moment, he wanted to pull his hand away, to remove himself from that circle of danger, but he knew that to do that would be to walk away from the Bloody Claw forever and accept this broken, diluted version of himself. Instead, he forced himself to look at the dark space at the back of the lion's throat. There were noises coming from it. Soft, dangerous noises.

'You know me,' he said again, his voice firmer this time. 'Let me wield your power as I once did.'

In the depth of the shadows, a pair of yellow eyes opened, slitted pupils thinning with an emotion Lucian couldn't place. A flood of memories rose up, washing him away.

*Blood dripping onto stone for a thousand, thousand years . . .*

He was Lucian Prideson, a foundling child left on the steps of a temple and raised under the watchful yellow eye of the lion. Others were talented, but Lucian was a prodigy, guessing the ways and wants of the Bloody Claw with an accuracy that alarmed the priests, until he was sent to be taught by one of their lord's most feared and respected mages: Mother Maura. Under her tutelage he blossomed, the line of fire within him burning brighter and brighter every day. He saw Maura presiding over sacrifice after sacrifice, wielding power and parcelling it out to her acolytes, but most of all to him, her favourite. Her most trusted.

'My Lucian,' she called him, pushing a strand of black hair behind his ear. 'My little lion cub.'

And then he saw her watching him in a different way, her green eyes narrowed.

There was a plan, something years in the making, that Maura had been piecing together since before he had come to her as a potential apprentice. Only her most trusted inner circle knew of it and when they did speak of the plan, they did it in high, lonely places, far away from the other acolytes, and far away from the presence even of their god . . .

Eventually, Lucian was brought into that circle. He remembered a clifftop overlooking a city, the sea a twinkling line in the distance, and her robes snapping in the wind.

'Lucian, my lion cub,' she had said to him. 'Have you ever thought what it would be like to have power without the price?'

She had explained to him the idea of a poisoned sacrifice. A tithe with thorns. A life that the Bloody Claw would greedily consume, only to find it was a false life, something twisted and dark. The lion would become an eater of the dead, the very opposite of his holy purpose, and he would die . . .

'He would die in sacrifice to *me*,' Mother Maura had said. 'And I will take His place among the Twelve. No more grubbing around for magic or begging for power. It will simply be mine.'

Lucian had shaken his head. This body, his real body, had hazel eyes and hair as black as the wing of a raven.

'I don't understand,' he had said to her then. 'What sort of sacrifice could possibly poison a god?'

'An exceptionally rare one. One that has died once already,' she had said. 'Secretly, carefully, I have been searching for such a thing, Lucian, and I am sure we are getting close.' The wind had blown her red hair away from her face and she had closed her eyes, as though making a wish. She had looked beatific, almost peaceful in that moment, yet Lucian had been anything but. The idea that she might try to strike down their god – the being that he had devoted all his life and training to – wasn't just ludicrous, it was insulting. An abomination. What did she expect them to do? Shatter the statues of the Bloody Claw and put up new ones, statues of Mother Maura, *a mortal*? And then would the acolytes be expected to go on bended knee to her? The idea of grovelling to Maura for his magic . . . The reverence and respect he had always carried for his mistress had splintered on that clifftop, becoming something lethal and sharp.

He had known better than to say any of that to her, though. He had waited instead, hoping to speak to their lord himself – perhaps by revealing Maura's treasonous plan he could win the Bloody Claw's gratitude.

But he didn't make it.

He never knew what had given him away. Perhaps he just wasn't as good at hiding his true emotions as he thought. Maura might have looked at him in an unguarded moment and seen his treachery brewing there as easily as she saw his tawny eyes. Or perhaps he simply wasn't enthusiastic enough when she conducted her searches for this so-called poison sacrifice. Either way, one night he was dragged from his narrow bed in Prideful Leap and brought to a piece of the shattered mountain, the night sky wheeling overhead. The rest of her inner circle had been there, fear and caution on every face, and she had . . . not killed him, no, but drawn his soul out of his body and cast it to the winds. As good as dead, really, her last words to him ringing like a bell.

*You'll serve me or you'll die. Perhaps one day you'll learn that lesson.*

Never.

Lucian lifted his head slowly. It felt heavy with the sheer weight of memories that had been reawakened within him, and he found he barely had the energy to sit up, which was a problem, because there was a dead priest next to him and someone could walk in on him at any moment. With effort, he rubbed his bloody hand on the trousers of the priest, cleaning it as best he could.

There was too much to take in. He was a mage, yes, and once he had been the most promising mage dedicated to the Bloody Claw, but Mother Maura had seen what he was and severed his mind from his body. He didn't know how he had ended up inside Artair's body, but it hardly mattered, because Mother Maura had found him at the monastery and in a final act of humiliation, had forced him to do her bidding again. Maura, who had sent Artair into the forest to find a monster . . .

Several things slotted into place at once, and despite his weary limbs Lucian scrambled to his feet, his heart thudding in his chest.

'What have you figured out?' asked Tisk, who had appeared next to him in a wink of orange light. 'Something exciting, by the look on your face.'

'It was never about the monster cub,' said Lucian, barely looking at the other god. 'It's about *Elver*. She died that day at Addersport, but the Queen of Serpents brought her back and filled her with poison. *Elver* is the poison sacrifice, and Maura knew she had to draw her out of the forest, away from the protection of the queen . . .' He trailed off. 'And I bet the monster girl is on her way there right now. Damn the Twelve into oblivion.'

'I'll try not to take that personally,' said Tisk. 'So what are you going to do about it?'

There was a squeak from the chamber beyond the altar, a boot moving over a polished surface, and Tisk vanished just as a figure appeared in the doorway. It was a woman in her late twenties, her brown skin lined deeply around the eyes, as though she spent a great deal of time frowning. She frowned now as she took in the scene around the lion, and Lucian realized he knew her.

'You,' she spat. 'I thought I told you not to come back to Ashingdown, you idiot.' She strode over to the altar and shook her head. As a mage of the Bloody Claw she was largely unconcerned at the sight of dead bodies but she did look increasingly agitated. 'What pretty mess is this now?'

'Dalesh!' Lucian grabbed her arm and shook it, half laughing. 'It's me! I mean, I don't look like I used to, but don't tell me you've forgotten already. You were like a sister – or at least a sister I didn't like very much. It's me, it's Lucian.'

Dalesh shrugged his hand away abruptly.

'Artair, you want to start making sense pretty sharpish or I'll have you back in the Temple of Trilot before you can spit.'

'I'm not Artair, I'm Lucian. Look, I . . .' He paused, wracking his brain for the thing that would convince her, and convince her quickly. 'Mother Maura once sent us to set a snare to catch a deer. She wanted to sacrifice it, but your trap caught a rabbit, and you set it free even though we knew she'd have taken that instead. You said that . . . You said that Milik the Small would see it as a grave insult and you didn't want your room infested with mice for ever after, but really, you thought the bunny too adorable to die. You swore me to secrecy and I truly never told a soul.'

Dalesh was very still.

'Lucian is dead,' she said, although she did not sound at all sure.

'You're only half right,' he said. 'Listen to me, Dalesh. I need your help, and we have very little time.'

# CHAPTER 33

'We are honoured, of course, to have such a revered mage living so close.' The guide, who had told them his name was Liamat, nodded his head so deeply it was almost a bow. 'It will be my pleasure to take you to the path that leads to Prideful Leap, where you may find Mother Maura. For the nominal fee of three gold pieces.'

Elver wandered a few steps away, letting Sunay handle the negotiation. The little shed where the guide waited for potential customers was painted a dusty pink and there were rows of shelves inside covered with figurines made of clay. Most of them were of the Bloody Claw, and you could buy them, according to the sign, for a few coppers each. A number of the ornaments were of the shattered mountain itself. Elver's eyes drifted to the window where the real thing waited for them; a range of stone so dark it was almost purple, where some huge cataclysm had reformed it into a series of jagged, lethal-looking shapes that almost seemed to defy gravity in places. Looking at it made Elver uneasy. Something had happened to this place, something unnatural.

'Mother Maura my wrinkled old arse.'

Elver startled. The bundled shape she'd taken to be a pile of cloth and furs was in fact a tiny old woman. A face like a pickled apple glared at her from within a rabbit-skin scarf.

'Nana, please,' said the guide. 'We've talked about this.'

'All I'm doing is telling the truth that you don't dare tell these wandering idiots.' The old woman almost seemed to bounce to her feet. Elver had the impression of a tiny, coiled spring, ready to erupt.

'The *truth* about Mother Maura.'

'And what truth is that?' asked Elver. Sunay had paused in the act of handing over gold coins, her eyebrows raised.

'Do not listen to her,' said Liamat, a faintly pained smile on his face. 'Mother Maura is a very respected mage and *we would not want to besmirch her good name* . . .'

'Balls,' said Nana. She sprung across the little hut and snatched a gnarled walking stick from where it leaned against the wall. 'Pay my idiot grandchild and I will take you to Prideful Leap myself. Not all the way up to it, mind. I don't have a bleedin' death wish.'

'That's enough, Nana. Please, I will gather my things and we can set off immediately,' said Liamat, in what he clearly thought was a no-nonsense tone, but Sunay had already pressed the coins into his hand.

'We will take this one,' she said, nodding at Nana. 'Thanks all the same.'

Outside, the sky was filled with dark clouds, glowering as though in competition with the mountain, and a row of leafless trees stood like a skeletal chorus against the horizon; winter had come early to this part of the world. Nana led them along a path of small white stones, the brightest thing in that darkened landscape. As she walked, she stabbed the ground with her stick as though it had done her a personal insult.

'How long will this take?' asked Elver.

'Patience is a virtue, did you know that?' Nana looked her up and down. Her eyes were blue and very, very sharp. 'No, I don't suppose you do. It'll take all of this morning and mayhaps most of the afternoon, because the shattered mountain is not a sensible place to take a leisurely stroll. But I'll keep you entertained on the way, don't you worry none.'

'Yes,' said Sunay brightly. 'The truth about this Mother Maura is something we are very interested in.'

They moved down the path into a ravine where the little white stones ended. Here the earth was raw and red, like a wound. Elver spotted a weathered wooden sign planted in the dirt, carved with signs she didn't recognize and an arrow pointing east.

'Why are you two going there?' asked Nana. 'You don't look like her usual type, if you'll pardon me for saying so. You're too cheerful,' she said, jabbing the end of her stick in Sunay's direction, 'and this one looks as though she'd sooner chew her own arm off than ask for help from anyone.'

'I am setting up a new business,' said Sunay with the smooth delivery of an accomplished liar. 'And my good friend Elver here is my business partner. We seek a spell to outfox our rivals and the blessings of the god of ambition. We've heard that ambition is Maura's speciality.'

Nana snorted. The ravine twisted up through the landscape like a snake. Splintered boulders as big as houses towered on every side. Elver wondered again what kind of violence had shaped the place.

'You got that much right,' said Nana. 'But it wasn't always the case. Would it surprise you to know that when she was a young woman, she laughed a lot? Always laughing, that one. She took very little seriously, did Maura, when she was a slip of a thing, but she was a natural mage.'

'Her reputation is, uh, not for laughter,' said Sunay, glancing quickly at Elver. 'It is hard to picture a mage of the Bloody Claw with a sense of humour, I must admit.'

'Oh, she wasn't dedicated to the Bloody Claw then, oh no. It was Tisk, the god of lies and mischief.'

Elver watched Sunay blink several times and then give a hearty chuckle that didn't quite convince.

'Haha, I see now why your grandson was keen to keep you in the shed, Nana.' Sunay wagged a finger at the old woman. 'You're quite the jester it seems. Everyone knows that the god you form a bond with is for life. It's not something you can change as you see fit, like your trousers or your haircut or your feelings about blue cheese.'

'Even so, she did it,' said Nana. She came to a halt, using the pointy end of her walking stick to scratch an itch on her shin. The path was taking them steeply up at an angle, and thanks to the looming rocks of all sizes it was hard to see where they would be heading next. Elver thought of Artair and wondered where he was and what he was doing. Or what Lucian was doing. It was impossible to say who might be in control, but she guessed that if he had any choice, Artair would have been on their trail. She strongly suspected he had no choice.

'How?' said Sunay.

'Why?' asked Elver.

Nana made a satisfied little noise.

'Well, Maura of old, you see, she was young, and she had a sweetheart, and in time they had babies, like sweethearts sometimes do. Happy, they was, for a while. Oh, Maura would do little pieces of magic for those that needed it – a little glamour for the girl hoping to catch a young man's eye, a story for a man who needed to wriggle his way out of some commitment, an unbreakable alibi for a miscreant—'

'All good, honest spells,' put in Sunay.

'But her real love was for those kiddies.' Nana had grown quieter, and not, Elver sensed, because the road was harder. 'Maura doted on them, and her husband. You never saw her without one baby or the other in her arms.'

'You knew them, didn't you?' said Elver.

Nana sighed, and they started walking again.

'We lived in a village not far from here. One tavern, two horses and a blacksmith's sort of place. You won't find it on any maps now, because, well . . . I used to watch the babies for her sometimes, when she was away and her husband was busy. They were good little mites really, better than Liamat was at that age anyway.'

They turned a corner and to their left the world dropped away, giving them a view of the guide's shed. From their vantage point it looked tiny, like a fingernail dropped onto the landscape.

'What happened to them?'

'Thirty years ago, long before either of you were a twinkle in some rogue's eye and I had a rear end you could bounce a gold piece off . . .' The old woman paused while Sunay had a coughing fit. 'Thirty years ago, there was a minor spat between the Twelve. Now then. A minor spat between the gods can have devastating consequences for us lowly mortals, right? If they've set their minds to knocking seven flavours of shit out of each other, there's little we can do but watch and hope we survive it.'

'Which gods?' asked Sunay.

'The main players were Trilot, the faceless one,' said Nana. 'And himself, the Bloody Claw. What the disagreement was about, I don't know, and I reckon no mortal does, but it was our world that bore the brunt of it alright. Maura was away, doing some elaborate illusion for a minor duke, when Trilot shattered the mountain with a blast of his purifying light – a blow meant for the Bloody Claw that missed. You can see what happened to the place.' She gestured with her stick at the near-purple boulders that clustered around them on the mountain path. 'We had an avalanche,' she continued. 'Half the mountain turned to powder and dumped on our heads. And, well . . . It could have been me, that's what I always think. If her husband hadn't been home to look after those kiddies, I would have been the one inside their little cottage when it was flattened.'

Silence pooled between them for a moment. Overhead, Elver heard the call of an eagle and she thought of Fleet, out running with wolves somewhere. Her hand closed over the conker in her pocket.

'What I remember,' said the old woman, 'and I reckon I'll remember it for ever, is the sound she made when she found out. Such sorrow, such horror. It turned her mind on a pin, that moment, that's what I think, and she went to her Lord Tisk and asked him, *told* him: bring them back. *I'll pay any price, but bring them back.*'

'Tisk cannot do that kind of magic,' said Sunay. All the usual humour had leached from her voice, leaving it wan and pale. 'None of the gods can, not even the Hooded Crow.'

'Maura wouldn't accept it. She was convinced that there had to be a power large enough to bring her loved ones back from the Shadowed Lands, and her need for that power changed her. She was a child of the fox and she became a creature of the lion. Instead of laughter on her lips, it was blood, and a dagger in her hand.'

'It's not possible,' Sunay insisted, although she sounded much less certain. 'At least, it shouldn't be.'

'Seems to me that lots of things are possible that shouldn't be,' said Nana. 'What I know for certain is that Maura changed and that laughing girl was never seen again. Fury and a lust for power are what drive her now.'

'She'll destroy as many lives as she likes to get what she wants,' said Elver. She was thinking of the novices they intended to save. And herself, thrown from the top of the Tumble Stone.

'So, are you sure?' Nana stopped and turned to them both, her eyes narrowed so that they looked to be caught in a fine net of wrinkles. 'Are you sure this is the path you must take? Because the price for her bloody work is a high one.' She cleared her throat. 'This is why Liamat doesn't want me guiding travellers up here, but I think you should know. You should be warned.'

Elver exchanged a look with Sunay. 'We're sure, Nana,' she said. 'This is the path we have to walk.'

They came within sight of Prideful Leap just as the sun touched the western horizon, flooding the valley below with golden light. It was a rambling building of white marble seen from this distance, a pearl wedged in the midst of the mountain's shattered purple heart. Elver looked at it and wondered what it meant that Maura had chosen to build her sanctum here, among the very stones that had buried her old life.

'This is as far as I'll go,' said Nana. The old woman had barely broken a sweat during their long climb. 'By all reports she don't like to be reminded of what went before, so I prefer to keep out of her sight. But you can see the path easily from here.' She pointed, and, sure enough, there was a jagged and meandering way, punctuated here and there with stunted, wizened little trees clinging to the rock.

'Thank you, Nana,' said Sunay, slipping the old woman an extra gold piece. 'It's been enlightening.'

'Don't say I didn't warn you,' said Nana as she turned to go. 'That magpie has nothing but rage left in her heart.'

# CHAPTER 34

'Come with me.'

Lucian stood up wearily. The act of explaining everything to Dalesh had drained his last reserves of energy and sleep weighed on his brow like a heavy hand. Yet he had to keep moving.

Dalesh led him from the altar – away from the dead priest – and along a corridor into a room dominated by a large iron door set into the wall. There was magical writing over every inch. Lucian tried to read some of it but his eyes would not keep the letters in the right order. Dalesh, meanwhile, had unlocked the door with a key that glowed a faint red, and when it swung back he saw rows and rows of shelves that were mostly empty, save for three small glass globes containing a faint luminescence. With his memories once more intact, he knew that mages of the Bloody Claw collected souls in magical glass globes so that when they were in sudden need of a tithe to work some magic or other, they would have something appropriate to hand. They would be the souls of animals mainly, but the most valuable would contain the spirits of mortal humans. His eyes skittered across the globes, taking in the pale lilac fire they contained. Was that how he had looked when Mother Maura cast him from his body?

'Right.' Dalesh plucked one of the globes from the shelves and held it up to the light, frowning slightly. 'This place is not as well stocked as I'd like, but this should be enough to power the portal. Mother Maura's sanctum is in the middle of the shattered mountain and that place is riddled with old magic that'll play havoc with my spells. I can get us to the foothills but no closer – I wouldn't want to risk emerging from the portal with our guts on the outside.'

'Why don't we just tell him?' said Lucian. The words seemed to take for ever to leave his mouth. He blinked owlishly. 'Tell the Bloody Claw what she's up to so he can tear her to pieces.'

Dalesh gave him an impatient look as she pressed the globe into his hands. 'Load the soul globes into your pack. Do you remember so little of our lord, Lucian? He has no patience for fighting between magpies. Imagine how it will look to him if we claim that Maura intends to kill him? It sounds ludicrous enough that he may just kill us for wasting his time. I'll be back in a moment. I need to have your mess attended to and fetch some things.'

And with that she was gone. Lucian stood looking at the soul globe in his hands. There was a wink of orange light and then Tisk was leaning against the giant iron door, twirling his fox-headed cane in one hand.

'Do you remember,' he said, 'that you promised to steal something for me?' He nodded at the globe. 'That'll do nicely.'

'Why do you want it?'

Tisk grinned and rolled his eyes. 'Because it doesn't belong to me, of course. Do I need to remind you that without my help you'd still be trussed up like a festival pig?'

Lucian gave him the globe and then collected the last two from the safe. He placed one in his pack, taking care to wrap Artair's old shirt around it.

'If you can unlock doors, I don't see why you couldn't have just taken that for yourself whenever you wanted.'

'That would spoil all the fun, handsome boy.'

Dalesh returned. Lucian didn't need to look to know that Tisk had vanished before she got a look at him. The mage had a small pack slung over one shoulder and a knife pushed through her belt. She took the glass globe from his unresisting hand and then dashed it on the flagstones, muttering words as she did so. With a rush of hot fur scent and a crackling noise, like parchment thrown on a fire, a doorway stood lined in fire before them. Through it, Lucian could see a desolate-looking patch of countryside scattered with chunks of purple-grey stone. A cold trickle of recognition moved through him. It wasn't far from this place that he'd been turfed out of his own body. And what had happened to it then? Had Maura just left it there under the sky, to be picked to pieces by birds? Did his bones lie there somewhere, underneath that uncaring sky?

'Be quick.' Dalesh was already stepping through the portal. 'If what you said is true, we've very little time.'

Lucian followed her. As he passed through the doorway of ruby flame, however, a strange rushing sensation moved through his body, as though he were falling from a great height, and when he got to the other side he stumbled, dropping to his knees. *Stupid monk body*, he thought. *Why is it failing me when I need it the most?*

Dalesh watched him slowly get back to his feet. It was one of the things he remembered the most clearly about her, that scrutinizing gaze. He had always found it difficult to hide things from her.

'You're practically dead on your feet,' she said, before glancing up the path that rose behind them. The fiery portal snapped out of existence. 'We're not too far from Prideful Leap, but you need to rest first.'

'I can't,' snapped Lucian. 'If I sleep, *he* will come back.'

'If you don't, Maura will chew you up and spit you out.' Around them, the wind picked up, bringing with it a brief scatter of raindrops that felt icy against his face. Dalesh pulled her cloak closer around her shoulders. 'Are you so sure that this monk will obstruct you? He wants to save these other monks, doesn't he?'

'That's not the point.' The idea of giving control back to Artair when he finally had it was unthinkable. This body was now his, this life was his, and he wasn't giving it back. But it was true that Artair needed to confront Maura as much as Lucian did, and if he spent the whole of this day tied up and imprisoned, they would make very little progress. He had the horrible feeling he might have to . . . trust the monk. He grimaced.

'Besides which,' Dalesh continued, 'I saw those two together. He's half in love with that monster girl. I doubt he would want to leave her facing a sacrificial knife alone.'

Lucian's grimace turned into a scowl. He found himself thinking of the way she had looked at him when he'd waded into the hot spring. It was hard to accept that it was Artair's body she was looking at – she had never even seen Lucian's face. Except, he realized with a strange tightening in his chest, she had. She just didn't know it.

'Fine. I will rest. But you will tie me up beforehand and explain to him exactly what is at stake. He must agree to work together on this and to give me back control when we face Maura.'

'Can he do that?' Dalesh asked, frowning. 'Just give it back to you?'

'He'll have to,' said Lucian hotly. 'What use is a monk going to be against a powerful mage?'

In the end, they found a spot out of the wind and made a makeshift camp. Lucian sat and began pulling things from his pack, looking for something to eat before he gave up to sleep, and his hand brushed against a solid object wrapped in a silky cloth. At first, he thought the soul globe had somehow changed shape, and then when he unwrapped it, he saw that it was in fact a small, porcelain heart, anatomically correct and covered with a glaze that gave it a faint shimmer. He picked it up between finger and thumb, meaning to examine it more closely, but when he did, his mind filled with an image: a forest at dusk, and Artair standing under the trees in blood-soaked clothes. Elver was looking up at him, a vulnerable expression on her face, and as Lucian watched, she stroked his face and kissed him. In Lucian's chest, something tightened painfully.

*Is she kissing me or him?* Somehow, it seemed a more important question than why his clothes were soaked with blood.

He watched the scene again and again, examining the young man's eyes to see if he could spot something of himself in them, but wherever they were, it was too dark. Eventually, Dalesh nudged him with her boot, and he stashed the heart away in the pack again.

'Enough stalling. You need to sleep.'

It felt strange to be instructing Dalesh in how to tie him up and he was half convinced that his blood was running too hot to sleep, but when he laid his head down darkness came up to claim him as swiftly as falling into an old well.

When Artair woke, it was to find himself on the edge of a freezing mountain, gazing out across a dizzying drop. He gasped and tried to wriggle backwards away from it, his wrists and ankles bound tightly together, but a hand took hold of his shoulder and dragged him away slightly. A vaguely familiar voice spoke.

'You're safe, monk. Calm yourself.'

He rolled onto his back to see Dalesh, the magistrate from Ashingdown that Elver had had such an alarming reaction to; the mage who had delivered her to Mother Maura in the first place. The woman's lips were pressed into a thin line, as though she had received bad news, or was about to deliver some.

'What are you doing here? Where am I?' That was, he realized, one of the things he hadn't expected about losing control: all the questions he awoke with every day. It was exhausting.

'I am here to help you idiots,' she said drily. 'Although the Twelve only know why I'm getting mixed up in this.' She sighed. 'I have only a little time to explain, so I'm going to need you to listen and actually take in what I'm telling you. Now. Do you know who Lucian is?'

Artair sat up. 'Can you at least untie me?'

'Not yet. Answer my question, monk.'

'Lucian is what the Other that lives inside me calls himself. He is a spirit of evil and chaos.'

'Hm. Chaos I might give you, but Lucian is, or was, a real person and not a dark spirit. He's someone that I knew when I was an apprentice to Mother Maura. He was also an apprentice – one of her most promising, in fact.'

Artair shook his head. 'That's not true. It's not possible.'

Dalesh continued as though he hadn't spoken. 'I had thought for all these years that Maura had killed him outright, but it seems she merely displaced him from his body. Removing souls from mortals is something mages of the Bloody Claw can learn to do – it lets us save tithes for when we need them. The last thing you want is to be in desperate need of a spell only to have nothing to give to our lord in exchange for the power. Somehow, he ended up in your head – but that, perhaps, is a mystery for another day.'

'That's just not true,' Artair said again. 'It can't be. If that were the case . . .' If that were the case, it meant that he had helped imprison someone. It would mean that Lucian had endured years of torment at his hand, denied simple things like walking under the summer sky, the pleasure of eating a hot breakfast on a cold morning or speaking to a friend as the sun set. It was unthinkable. And yet . . . Elver had also believed Lucian to be more than a dark spirit. 'Why would the Brothers and Sisters of the Golden Tower lie to me?'

Dalesh shrugged. 'It's likely they didn't know. Maybe the Sleepless demons are real, or maybe all of these so-called dark spirits are simply misaligned souls. It doesn't matter. This is what you need to know, Artair. Artair, are you listening to me?'

'I am,' he replied, although it was difficult to fix on her words. A cold rush of horror was moving through him, threatening to drag him away like a rip tide.

'Mother Maura doesn't care about this monster cub she had you steal. The cub was bait to get Elver out of the Jih Forest and into Maura's sanctum. Maura intends to use Elver as a sacrifice to trick the Bloody Claw—'

'What?' This brought him back to the present sharply. 'What do you mean, sacrifice her?'

'I mean exactly what I say.' Dalesh was losing patience. 'She needs the life of your friend to throw down and depose a god. Elver is on her way there now – and a sacrifice that walks right up to the knife is so much more powerful than one that is taken by force.'

'Then we have to go.' He made to stand up and remembered his ankles were tied. 'She could be there already!'

'Wait.' Dalesh took hold of his forearm, holding him in place. She fixed him with dark brown eyes. 'Lucian needs to know if you will work with him. If, when the time comes, you'll let him take control. It annoys me to say it, honestly, but he was a talented mage when I knew him. He could be our best chance at stopping Mother Maura.'

'Give him control? I . . .' Artair shook his head. 'Why does Lucian even care?'

'Mother Maura means to kill our god, Artair.' Dalesh sighed. 'And I strongly suspect Lucian is quite fond of your friend, as much as he would like to hide it.'

'He is?' Artair swallowed. He thought of the vision he'd seen at the Temple of Threshold, his counterpart's hand curling gently around Elver's bare foot. *Does he know what you two get up to at night?*

'Can I trust you then?' asked Dalesh. She shook his arm lightly. 'Can we trust you not to run off down this mountain when I untie you?'

There was no question, not really. If there was a chance of saving Elver, he would have to take it. He held out his bound wrists.

'You can trust me. Lucian can trust me. Cut me free.'

# CHAPTER 35

'So,' said Sunay, her voice significantly deeper than usual. 'Do you like me better this way?' They had decided that since Maura would be expecting Artair, they would have to produce him, and Sunay – as a professional liar and spinner of tall tales – was the best choice to play the monk. She had used the illusion spell on herself and the sack, filling it with an illusion of the cub. It was, she had explained to Elver, not quite enough magic to create two living, breathing illusions at once, but she could give Maura a glance inside the sack and hold the image of the cub there for a brief moment. It would have to do.

The illusion of Artair, though, was remarkably convincing. It was like having him standing in front of her again, although his usual stoicism was missing, replaced with Sunay's cheery optimism. It made her miss him.

The mage struck a pose, hands on hips and chest thrust out, and despite herself, Elver laughed.

'I will admit, Sunay, you are suddenly much more appealing.'

'I knew it.'

The entrance to Prideful Leap was a wide path paved with stones so white they were almost translucent, at the end of which stood an elegant doorway leading into the main building, which looked something like a cathedral made of ivory. A flock of birds, tiny flecks of black at this distance, moved restlessly around its towers, as though they couldn't quite bear to touch the sheer white marble. It was beautiful, and extraordinary, and remarkably out of place in the strange, magic-blasted landscape, as though it had been plucked from some fairy tale city and dumped on the shattered mountain.

Lining the path were statues, also crafted from the shining white stone. Each of them, Elver realized as they passed, were of Maura, at different ages and in different poses. Here she was as a young, slim-hipped woman, her hair loose down her back and a lion cub held in her arms. Here, a Maura Elver recognized more readily: an older woman with her hair partially tamed, one hand reaching to the sky as though she wanted to rip the moon from it. The statues made her uneasy, but it wasn't until Sunay spoke that she realized the reason why.

'Not much sign of the Bloody Claw here, is there?'

'No. That's odd, isn't it? You have images of Tisk in your temple, right?'

'I certainly do. He'd get the hump otherwise, the vain fool. My beloved lord, I mean.'

The last statue they passed was of another version of younger Maura, this time kneeling with her arms around two small children. Elver paused at this one, her stomach churning. Whatever her relationship with her own, Maura had no love for children. Elver was certain of that.

'We've been expecting you.' They both turned at the voice. A young man dressed in scarlet was coming out of the narrow entranceway. He wore a black silk mask over the lower half of his face and his eyes betrayed no emotion. 'Although there was only supposed to be one of you.'

'They're not easy things to wrangle, monsters,' said Sunay, briefly holding up the sack so that Maura's apprentice could see it. 'I needed help, that's all.'

'Very well. Follow me.'

Inside, Prideful Leap gave way to darker stone and somehow the place felt colder than it had out on the mountain itself. There were a handful of other men and women dressed in scarlet, who watched them pass with pointed interest.

Elver's heart began to race. This was it. Soon, she would be in the presence of the woman who five years ago had chosen to throw her to her death. She felt sick with a strange mixture of dread and excitement; they would get the novices away and perhaps then she might have a chance to say what she'd always wanted to say to the woman who had killed her. Perhaps she'd get a chance to show her just how poisonous this monster girl was. There was little chance the mage would recognize her and the thought of seeing an expression of shock on Maura's face was delicious – she only wished that Artair could really be there to see it.

The apprentice mage led them down a set of stone steps and the temperature dropped even further. There were torches in the sconces burning with a smoky, red light. Sunay hung back to speak into her ear, and Elver tipped her head away a little to avoid hurting the woman: she didn't know how the illusion worked, but she didn't want to accidentally poison her.

'This place is gloomy, isn't it? My lord prefers the open air.'

'I don't like it,' said Elver. 'It feels like walking into a tomb.'

They emerged into an underground cavern, the strong mineral scent of water in the air. At the back of the chamber, there was a semi-circular seating gallery carved from the dark stone and on it sat Maura.

Elver's poison blood pulsed in her chest as though it were rising up in anger, or fear. Here, finally. This was the moment – she was facing the woman who had murdered her.

Mother Maura was wearing a white dress made of many layers of thin silk, each heavily embroidered with things Elver couldn't make out. Her hair lay against all that white like a spray of fresh blood. The mage was looking at something she held cradled in her hands, but when they entered the chamber she looked up sharply. Spotting the pair of them, she leaned back, settling one elbow on the step behind her.

'Thank you, Warnick,' she said, gesturing to the apprentice. That voice: a purr that promised violence. It hadn't changed.

'We've brought you the cub,' said Sunay, Artair's voice leaving her throat with confidence. 'So you can let my people go now.'

Maura nodded, although she made no move to get up. Elver noted that the novices were nowhere to be seen.

'Show me,' said Maura.

Sunay walked forward until she was a few feet away from where Mother Maura sat. Anyone who knew Artair well, Elver thought, would note that he was swinging his hips an unusual amount. Sunay opened the sack at the neck and revealed the contents to Maura. The mage's eyes brushed over the illusion of the cub and returned instead to Elver. A quick slither of a smile moved over the woman's mouth, a movement that put Elver in mind of a lizard skittering across a stone. The apprentice named Warnick came forward and took the sack from Sunay.

'Very well. A deal is a deal,' said Maura. 'I can't deny that you've done what I asked.' She stood, placing what had been in her hands on the seat next to her. It appeared to be a child's toy: a bear carved from wood and painted with bright colours. It had little pearl buttons for eyes and at some point it had been broken and glued back together with care. Maura lifted one hand and made a kind of twisting gesture in the air, as though taking hold of an invisible rope, and two portals appeared in the air, just like the one Dalesh had used to get them out of the Temple of Trilot. Through one of them, Elver could see a group of people crowded together. They looked frightened out of their wits but otherwise unharmed. They all wore the same yellow shirt and robe that Artair had been wearing when he'd entered the Jih

Forest. The other portal looked out onto a peaceful garden; she could see plants in neat rows and heaps of autumn leaves that had fallen and not been swept away. *The monastery*, she thought. *Artair's home.*

Maura clapped her hands together three times, startling the group of novices who were staring at her with wide eyes. Suddenly, she had the air of a teacher with little patience left at the end of a long day.

'Out of one door and into the other!' She clapped again. 'Get a move on, children, we don't have all day.'

Hesitantly, the first of the novices stepped down out of the portal. The boy paused, glancing shyly at Artair before scampering across to the other fiery door. Quickly, the rest of them followed. Elver could see from their faces that the garden was known and beloved to them and she felt a pang of something deep in her chest.

Once they were all through, Maura made the gesture again and both portals vanished in a flash of red fire. *We've done it*, thought Elver. *Wherever you are, Artair, we got them home.*

'It seems our business is concluded,' said Maura smoothly. Now that she was closer, Elver could see that the white embroidered shapes on her dress were all small human figures – children at play, children sleeping, children chasing each other. The sight of those tiny pretend children made her skin prickle all over. 'It's quite a journey up that mountainside. The pair of you must be famished. Will you stay for some dinner?'

Sunay in her form as Artair sketched a deep bow. *Careful*, thought Elver. *Don't overdo it.*

'Alas, we have other places to be,' said Sunay. 'And we must take our leave.'

'Surely not.' Maura smiled. Her nails were painted red, obscenely bright against the white of her dress. 'Such a long journey for a fleeting visit. Prideful Leap isn't the sort of place you visit without properly taking it in.' She turned her head towards Elver slowly, like a bird of prey spotting something that had previously been hiding. 'Forgive me, but don't I know you, child? I'm sure I have seen your face somewhere before. Although perhaps back then it wasn't so torn and poorly mended.'

Elver swallowed. Rage poured into her like a river, flowing through every part of her like the waterways that flowed through Addersport.

'You should know me,' she said, each word venom on her tongue. 'You killed me, once. Threw me into the sea like I was nothing. I am Elver, the child you murdered to banish the serpents from Addersport.'

To her surprise, Maura did not look shocked. She did not gasp and her eyes didn't widen. Instead, she turned back to the steps, a sweet little smile on her face. She shook her head a fraction.

'Oh Elver,' she said. 'What a prize you are. So proud and angry and full of poison. I am *so* glad you made it. There was always the chance that you'd refuse to leave the forest, or that someone would capture you on the way here – those priests of Trilot are such beasts. And there is your own cold-blooded mother, your *queen*, who might have moved against me if I'd struck directly at you. But no, you've fought your way here for the privilege of being used again.' Maura laughed, a single bark-like noise that sent cold fingers of dread down Elver's back. 'What a cruel little joke your life has been. And your death. Or should I say, deaths.'

Sunay was backing away slowly, heading towards the door on the far side of the chamber.

'What are you talking about?' Elver snapped. 'I came here to help Artair.'

'You came here because *I willed it*,' said Maura. 'It's true that I thought you were dead. Why would I think anything else? So you can imagine my surprise, after years of searching for the perfect poison sacrifice, when my spells brought me your face. And now you'll die for my lord a second time and give me everything I need. His life, his power, and my . . .' For the first time she faltered. 'My family. Once I am a god, nothing will be denied to me.'

It was a trap. Elver lunged for the mage, her bare hands reaching for the exposed skin of the woman's face and throat, but Maura snapped her fingers and abruptly Elver was falling through a hole in the air – one that dumped her back out onto the stone floor of the chamber. For a moment she lay there, the force of the impact knocking all thought from her head.

'It might please you to know, Elver, that it cost me five of my best apprentices to perform these little feats of magic for you today. If you don't stop resisting, I will have to have more killed. Would you like that?'

Elver opened her mouth to spit some sort of acid reply but managed only a wheeze.

'And *you*.' Maura rounded on Sunay, who had been continuing to creep towards the door. 'Don't think I've forgotten about you, Lucian. I know you're in there.' She grinned wolfishly. 'How have the last few years been? Absolutely horrid, I hope. It was such a treat when my spells revealed where your soul had ended up. And what a delicious pleasure it is for me to have you witness the success of the plan you thought yourself too good for. In fact, let me put your counterpart to sleep so you can witness its full glory.'

The mage lunged for Sunay, meaning to place her hand – which was suddenly full of ruby fire – on Artair's forehead, only for her hand to pass through it and beyond, as though Artair were a thing made of air and light. There was an orange shimmer, a sudden scent of autumn leaves, and Sunay was standing before her instead. The mage of Tisk raised her hands, grinning sheepishly.

'So,' she said. 'You probably have a few questions.'

# CHAPTER 36

The path was steep and the air was thin, but Artair was used to living on a mountain, and he had to stop occasionally to wait for Dalesh to catch him up. Every time he did so he felt a prickle on his back, as though he could feel the danger Elver was in breathing down his neck.

*Let us get there on time*, he thought. *Let her be alright.*

Eventually, Prideful Leap stood before them. There was no one at the entrance, and to Artair the place looked abandoned. He glanced at the statues of Mother Maura as they made their way down the final path. They looked like ghosts of the woman he had met in the monastery.

'We are here,' said Dalesh unnecessarily. She was looking at Maura's sanctum as though she'd rather be anywhere else. 'Are you ready to turn over this body to Lucian?'

'I don't know how to do that.'

Dalesh briefly looked like she wanted to throttle him. 'Lucian seemed to think you could.'

'He comes forward when I lose consciousness. But I have to tell you, I don't think I've ever been less sleepy in my life.' A cold wind blew up, as though reinforcing his words. He didn't want to give control over to the Other – *Lucian*, he told himself, *his name is Lucian* – but if that meant they had a better chance of saving Elver, he was willing to do it. He just didn't know how. 'You could try knocking me out?'

'You are a sturdy-looking lad, Artair. I'm not sure I could manage it without using a stone or a stick, and then I risk smashing your brains in.'

'Time is running out.' He kept picturing Elver on a stone altar, her blood flowing across white marble, her yellow eyes dimmed for ever. 'Can't you use magic to make me sleep?'

Dalesh sighed. 'There are the soul globes, but I've no doubt we'll need every one of those to stop Maura from killing the Bloody Claw.' She hesitated for a moment and then shook her head. 'You will have to trust me.'

It happened so fast that Artair was on his knees before he truly realized what had happened. Dalesh's knife had torn through his shirt and sliced a ragged path across his stomach. An agonizing pain pierced him from front to back. He made an odd, strangled noise.

'I'm sorry. It has to be relatively deep. My lord doesn't accept paper cuts as payment.'

She raised her hand, which was now overflowing with ruby fire.

'I'll bind the wound as best I can. You'll be fine.'

'Elver . . . the novices . . . you have to help—'

'My lord, I send you this offering of blood and pain in exchange for a boon . . .'

Dalesh leaned down and pressed her glowing fingers to Artair's eyelids. There was a strange, rushing sensation, as though he were a leaf pulled along in a forest breeze, and then sleep came up to claim him.

'What in the name of all that is reasonable and good . . .' Lucian gasped with pain. *'What have you done?'*

'What I had to,' said Dalesh shortly. She helped him up with one hand and he stumbled, pressing his hand to his stomach. The wound was tightly bound, but there was a darkening stain on the fabric. 'You're here, aren't you? There's no way I could face her on my own. Her power goes beyond all of us.'

'Beyond you, perhaps,' spat Lucian. He took a deep breath, trying to concentrate. That Artair had let this woman stab them seemed incredible. *You need to take better care of this body, monk,* he thought. *I don't want it poked all full of holes.* When he felt like he had a better handle on the pain, he patted the pack at his side, checking for the shape of the remaining soul globe. It was their one chance to stop Maura. 'Let's get in there before I lose any more blood or you get another urge to stab me.'

'The urge is rising, believe me.'

Inside, the bright white stone ended and Prideful Leap became a place of shadows and dark corners. From nowhere, Lucian remembered walking across the cold floor with Maura. He had been very young, little more than a baby really, and he had asked her why her sanctum was so different inside. *Sometimes*, she had told him, *how we are on the outside has to be very different to what we carry within. Sometimes we have to hide our true selves.* As he walked across those stones again, his soul carried in an alien body, those words seemed painfully prescient.

A few of Maura's acolytes came over to them, their red and black uniforms familiar to Lucian, but Dalesh gestured them away brusquely and none challenged her directly. After all, thought Lucian, once she had been an apprentice too, and now she was a mage of the Bloody Claw in her own right. They would assume that she and Maura were colleagues.

The two of them walked together to the steps that led down into the under-altar. They both knew, without discussing it, that this was where Maura would be conducting her magic. When they had been fresh-faced apprentices with only a little blood on their own hands, this was where their mistress had performed her darkest rites. Lucian picked up the pace, the pain in his stomach fading. This was where it all came to a head. Maura would pay for what she had done to him, and when he stopped her from killing the Bloody Claw, the god would have little choice but to make him first among his mages. And Elver . . . He thought of that kiss again. Well, perhaps if he saved her, he'd know who that kiss was for.

They ran down the final steps into the under-altar and Lucian paused, taking in the scene in front of him. Elver was curled on the floor as though she'd been thrown there. Mother Maura, eerie in a flowing white dress, was standing over her. There was also a figure that briefly looked like Artair, but in a shimmer of orange magic – *Tisk is here*, thought Lucian – she was revealed to be a young woman with black hair and big dark eyes. She said something to Maura that he didn't catch and then Elver was up and running at the mage, her arms outstretched. Maura leapt back, making a gesture in the air as she did so and a fiery portal opened up, casting Elver back onto the floor. The monster girl rolled onto her side, panting, then dragged herself into a crouch.

'Another life spent, Elver,' said Maura, grinning. 'You're running through these lives like water. It's time to stop resisting.'

Lucian tried to run forward but the wound in his gut slowed him to a rapid limp.

'Maura!' he shouted. 'Mother, it's me! Your favourite bloody pupil.'

She rounded on him, her teeth bared in something between a grimace and a grin. Her teeth looked too sharp.

A handful of acolytes melted out of the shadows and converged on Elver, but when they got close she lashed out at them. Lucian saw her grab the hand of one long enough that he fell away in a dead faint, and after that the others hung back. She looked like a cornered animal, her golden eyes wild and fury in her heart – she looked glorious.

'Lucian Prideson.' Mother Maura sounded pleased to see him,

which felt like a poor sign. 'There you are, finally.'

'All these years I've longed to burn the world down for what happened to me, but it was you I should have been dreaming of killing.' He grinned. 'You couldn't bear it, could you? That I was a better mage than you. More powerful, more skilled.'

'Always so arrogant.' Maura nodded as though he were confirming this for her. 'I did take a great deal of satisfaction in flinging you out of your body. You should take it as a compliment, Lucian, that I kept an eye on where your soul ended up. I knew you'd be a problem again. Some said I should have just killed you but . . .' She smiled. 'I am sentimental, I suppose. And you were like a son to me.'

'You're a terrible *mother*, and a mediocre mage,' said Lucian hotly.

Maura appeared to ignore that. 'This is quite the reunion, you know. Elver, let me introduce you – Lucian is the boy who picked you from the orphanage for me and set you on this path. Without him, you might have lived a normal life. Without him, you wouldn't be dying for a second time in my name.'

Lucian met Elver's gaze. He saw shock there, and confusion. She would hate him now, of course, and why not? His whole life had been hatred and pain. Cold fury pulsed through him, and he drew the soul globe from his pack. He hadn't cast a true spell in years but he could feel the lines of banked fire within him glowing with anticipation. Lilac light bathed his face as he held the globe in front of him. He'd command the Bloody Claw to spirit Elver away somewhere safe, somewhere off this gods-forsaken mountain, and then Maura would have no poisoned sacrifice. What happened from there, well, he'd work it out.

'My lord,' he began, 'I gift you this soul . . .'

Someone punched him in the stomach, close enough to the stab wound that for a second the edges of his vision darkened. He bent over double, gasping, and the soul globe slipped from his hand to shatter on the flagstones, a wisp of light glowing like an ember before dissipating. He peered up through watering eyes to see Dalesh standing over him.

'I brought him to you, Mother,' she said, still looking at him. 'I knew you'd want him to witness your triumph.' She crouched, bringing her face level with his. 'I always thought you were a pompous little prick, Lucian.'

Lucian opened his mouth to speak but managed only a wheezing croak.

'Good girl,' said Maura warmly. 'Did you incur the wrath of those Trilot fools for saving my little sacrifice, Dalesh? It would have been such a waste to see her purified before she got to fulfil her true destiny.'

'Nothing I couldn't handle, Mother,' said Dalesh, clearly pleased with herself. 'The priests of Trilot have all manner of dark secrets and I happen to know enough of them to keep them under my thumb.'

Maura smiled. 'Good. Now. What else do you have for me?'

Dalesh snatched his pack away from Lucian's side and began digging around in it. As she did, her face fell.

'Where is it?' She was angry, but there was a note of fear underneath it that Lucian found very delicious indeed. 'Where's the other globe, you little sneak?'

'I must have mislaid it,' he replied through gritted teeth.

She punched him a second time, connecting heavily with his side. Dark stars burst in front of his eyes again but he just about managed to stay on his feet.

'Stop it!' Elver's voice, sharp as a knife. 'Leave him be, or I'll pull your guts out myself.'

Lucian lifted his head. The monster girl had backed away against the wall. Maura's remaining acolytes had hold of the woman with black hair and were holding a blade to her throat. Just as he registered this, he felt the cold kiss of steel press against his own neck. Dalesh's breath was hot in his ear. 'Forget the globe,' she said. 'If we need another life, there's always yours to give.'

'Well, Elver, here we are.' Maura retreated to the stone gallery, pinching the skirt of her dress to lift it before seating herself. 'It's time for you to make a choice, poison girl. I'm not entirely without feeling, after all. I know what it is like to love someone and lose them. So. Behave yourself, succumb to your fate quietly and without any further tantrums, and I will let these two go. Your life, for two others. Three, technically. And what kind of life is yours, anyway? A filthy recluse living in the forest, unable to touch or be touched, doing the will of a *wyrm*.' Mother Maura's nose wrinkled as though she could smell something bad. 'You should have stayed dead, what was left of your bones rotting in the waters of Addersport. Let your life achieve something great, after all – save the lives of your friends and see me ascend to my rightful place among the Twelve.'

Elver was breathing hard, her white hair plastered to her forehead and cheeks. Lucian wanted to shout at her to run, to fight Maura with everything she had, but his energy was all but gone. He could feel the wound bleeding freely again, a hot stream of blood soaking his shirt and the waist of his trousers. Oddly, it seemed as though Artair were very close; he could feel the monk's own feelings of horror and fear suffusing his own. *In these final moments, we are one*, he thought in wonder.

Elver stepped forward, her hands held in front of her, palms facing out.

'I'll do it. Let them go. *Let them go.*'

Mother Maura's grin was so wide it almost seemed to split her face in two. She looked, Lucian thought, very like the god she was determined to kill.

'Wonderful. Let's give my lord his final meal, shall we?'

# CHAPTER 37

She had to get close enough to the magpie to touch her. Poison her with the weapon the Queen of Serpents had infused into her skin. Once she was dead, the acolytes of the Bloody Claw would scatter. Elver was almost sure of it. Maura just needed to believe she had given up; then she might let her guard down.

'Stand in the pool,' Maura snapped. 'It is the Bloody Claw's sacred place. In here, he is the strongest of all the gods.'

Elver took a few steps towards the shallow pool that waited in the centre of the chamber. The water there was shifting and strange; sometimes it looked like blood, and other times it looked like lake water, green and deep and silent. Maura stood at the edge, already murmuring magpie words.

Lucian had slumped in Dalesh's arms, the blood loss finally catching up with him, and Elver considered what Maura had said. The handsome boy with the hazel eyes who had been with Dalesh that day had had no sympathy in his eyes when he had picked her from among the orphans; there had only been a certain sharp satisfaction, an eagerness for power. It would be easy to hate him. Except that she had seen his desperation and his fury. She had seen, to some small degree, what Maura had done to him – not just casting him from his body, but moulding him to be a weapon, a tool, a thing to be used and discarded. She knew it wasn't the sort of thing that was easy to recover from. And then, as she watched, awareness flowed back into the boy's body and it was Artair slumped there instead. He sat up, surprising Dalesh, who pressed the blade back towards his throat.

'Don't move,' she hissed.

'Elver!' She saw the confusion and pain surface on Artair's face as he took in what was happening around them, and somehow that was the worst of it. 'What are you doing?'

'I'm sorry,' she said. She glanced back at Maura, to see if the mage was taking this in. 'Look after the cub for me. Take him back to the Jih Forest. I think I . . . I'm glad I met you, Artair.'

'What's happening?'

'That's enough,' Maura said sharply. 'Get into that pool, girl. The time has come. I have promised the Bloody Claw the rarest and most delicious of meals, and He is going to grace us with His presence. Prepare yourself.'

Elver stepped into the pool. It was blood, she thought, but blood that wanted to be other things, stranger things. She frowned at it. Around her, the room was growing warmer, the lamps glowing a deeper, darker red, and there was an overpowering scent: of raw flesh, of fetid pelt, of animal sweat. A dark shadow was growing, a looming shape that stood on the far side of the pool. She was ankle-deep in blood, and in its still reflection she could see things that shouldn't be there: the trees of the Jih Forest, the lazy trickle of insects through the air, a sky scudded with clouds. It was as if she stood by her own lake, looking at its reflection.

*You are close, my queen*, she thought. *But are you close enough?* Maura had wanted to draw her here for a reason, and she suspected it was because in this place the Queen of Serpents was greatly weakened.

There was a cry from Sunay, drawing Elver's attention away from the pool. Maura lifted her arms in welcome.

'My lord!' she cried. 'I bring you the child of another god, one touched and blessed by the queen of monsters, the Queen of Serpents. Yours to devour.'

Reluctantly, Elver lifted her head to look at what had appeared in the pool with her. It did look like a lion, a lion as tall as the oldest oak and as wide as a house, with a mane that cascaded around its proud head and eyes that burned like twin, green stars; but instead of being covered in golden fur it was a raw and bloody thing, made of twisted flesh and sinew. She had the sudden, awful idea that each piece of the Bloody Claw was made from the blood and flesh of everyone and everything that had ever been sacrificed to him. *He takes us and makes us part of himself, adding to his own power*, she thought. *No wonder Maura wants to feed me to him.*

'Maura means to kill you!' This was from Artair, who received a shove from Dalesh in payment.

'Mother Maura is my most dedicated, my most blood-soaked mage,' rumbled the Bloody Claw. His voice was thick and deep, a clotted rumble. 'The one mage in all of Tlevrae who ripped her allegiance from a lesser god to be in my service. Her loyalty is absolute.'

'It is my honour to serve,' said Maura, bowing her head. The mage came forward, stepping into the pool of blood. She produced a long, serrated knife from somewhere in the folds of her dress. Elver felt the woman bury hard fingers in her hair, pulling her head back to expose her throat.

'That's it, accept your fate,' Maura murmured into her ear. 'Be a good girl and do as Mother says.'

Elver waited for a heartbeat, waited for the knife to appear in the corner of her vision. She saw Maura's hand clasped around the handle, the freckles on the backs of her fingers.

'My lord, devour this gift and grant me a boon!'

The point of the knife touched the skin under her jaw. Elver grabbed Maura's wrist, the one part of her arm not covered by the sleeves of her dress, and the woman gave a single high-pitched shriek, yanking herself away so that Elver lost her grip. She stumbled in the pool of blood, scrambling to get another purchase on the woman, but Maura was already summoning more magic, her free hand shaking slightly as she drew shapes in the air. The skin around her wrist was the colour of a sweet red apple.

'*Spiteful little snake.*'

Ropes of fire appeared out of nowhere, looping around Elver's body as quickly and as tightly as a snare. She fell into the pool, unable to move her arms or her legs.

'Have it your way,' Maura said, shaking her wounded hand. 'My lord can eat you alive instead.'

Elver lifted her eyes to the god that towered over her. She could see his jaws opening, revealing yellowed fangs of bone and gristle, each as big as she was tall. She tried to bring the Jih Forest to mind, its cool breezes and the extraordinary creatures that lived there; in particular, she thought of the serpent's lake, the one where the Queen of Serpents would come to visit her. *This isn't blood I'm lying in*, she thought, *this is lake water, fresh and green and ready to welcome me. I am always home, because I carry it with me.*

With some difficulty, she turned her head back to face Maura. 'Let them go. That was the deal.'

'The deal, poison child, was that you went to your fate willingly.' Maura grinned. 'But you just had to lash out, didn't you? Like the little snake you are.'

Elver swallowed and looked up at the lion god.

'I hope I stick in your throat,' she said.

Artair watched, helpless, as the Bloody Claw lowered his head and snapped Elver up in one bite. His knees gave way and he slumped to the floor.

'No.'

He could feel Lucian close and knew that his dark spirit – except dark spirit wasn't what he was, he knew that now – had seen what had happened somehow, had dreamed it or tasted Artair's own horror. *We've lost her*, he thought. *After all this, she's gone.*

The Bloody Claw himself was shaking out his mane in apparent satisfaction.

'A fine meal,' he said. 'A rare flavour indeed. I can taste the fury of the Serpent Queen, notes of curtailed potential. Except . . .'

Mother Maura lifted her head, her eyes hooded. Her shoulders were rising and falling quickly.

'Hmm. Perhaps I do not feel . . .'

There was a flash of orange light, and the god Tisk appeared in his handsome human form. He looked up at the Bloody Claw, shaking his head.

'You always were an old idiot,' he said mildly. 'No real interest in humans beyond what they could feed you, when I could have told you they're full of so many interesting things, so many complications and complexities. Learn how to eat *those* and you'll never be hungry again.' Tisk grinned. 'That's certainly what I've found, anyway. And I strongly suspect you should have listened to the mortals today.'

The effect of Tisk's appearance on Maura was electric. The colour had drained from her face and her lips were drawn back from her teeth as though she were ready to bite him to pieces. Meanwhile, the Bloody Claw was lowering his body to the floor, shaking his head as though he had a bee in his ear.

'You!' screamed Maura, jabbing a finger at Tisk. 'You dare show your face to me again?'

'A fine way to talk to a god,' said Tisk. In speaking he seemed to become larger, more dangerous: rather than a fox or a man, he was something else, something much older, with sharper edges. He nodded to Sunay, whose eyes were very wide. 'Do you hear this,

Sunay? Are you not going to defend my honour?'

'You've always been cheerfully dishonourable, my lord,' she said in a very small voice. 'It's one of the things I like best about you.'

Tisk chuckled at that. 'It's you, Maura, who are the dishonourable one. I gave you my blessings at birth, just like Sunay here, but you threw them away. Pledged yourself to the big idiot cat. How am I supposed to take that as anything other than an insult?'

'*You failed me.*' Tears were streaming from Maura's eyes and there were patches of hectic colour on her cheeks and lips. 'I gave you everything I had, everything I could, and you *wouldn't bring them back.* None of you could.' She took several deep ragged breaths. 'All of you, useless. So I must become my own god.'

'I do not feel . . . I feel wrong, somehow.' The giant lion of flesh had lowered his head to the pool and yellowish drool was running from between his jaws. Tisk continued as though he hadn't spoken.

'But that's not entirely true, is it, Maura, my dear? There is one god who could have brought them back. Only one god who ever had the power to bestow new life . . . but you couldn't bear the thought of your children being reborn as jih.' He laughed. 'You should have gone to Trilot, faithless one – it would have suited you better.'

'Shut up. Shut up! It's done now, and you can't stop me. The Bloody Claw is dying in sacrifice to me. Nothing can stop it now!'

'Whoever said I wanted to?' replied Tisk. He turned to the monstrous lion, who was now lying on his side, enormous chest rising and falling with effort. Tisk poked him with his cane. 'I hope this hurts, old friend. You do not take what is mine without consequence.'

'I cannot . . . I cannot die . . .'

'You can and you will,' spat Maura. She waded through the pool of blood towards the fallen lion, her white dress soaking scarlet from hem to knee in an instant. 'It was your idiotic war with Trilot that killed my family, and now you will know what it is to suffer.' She rested her hands on his fleshy leg, digging her fingernails in like they were talons.

'I am a god...'

'Not for much longer. Soon, you will be little more than a pile of rotting flesh and your power will be mine.' From his vantage point, Artair could only see a portion of her face; it was wet with tears. 'And I will have them again. My darlings.'

The Bloody Claw began to convulse. Behind him, Artair felt Dalesh gasp and step away from him. There was a clatter as her dagger fell to the ground. Similarly, the remaining acolytes of Mother Maura were backing away towards the walls, dragging Sunay with them.

Artair stood up carefully, one hand pressed to the wound in his stomach. The pain there was bad, but it was nothing compared to what he felt in his heart. He took a slow, deep breath, remembering the teachings of the Perpetual Morning – not to master fear this time, but to banish pain.

*Here, in this moment, I am safe.*

'It's happening,' murmured Dalesh. 'It's really happening.'

The body of the lion twitched and shivered, and then abruptly its side split open and a vast yellow serpent burst out of it, shining with its own golden light. For a handful of heartbeats the cavern was lit up as though it were a midday afternoon, and all of them felt the lash of the Queen of Serpents' fury.

WHO DARES TO HARM MY POISON CHILD?

The serpent had Elver in its jaws, Artair saw, and before he really knew what he was doing he was sprinting across the short space, the agony in his gut forgotten. Once, in the monastery gardens, Brother Benzin had found an injured wild cat, its back leg hanging broken and useless, yet when they had tried to move it, to try to bind its injury, the creature had lashed out at them, hissing and spitting without thought. Artair thought of this as the mortally wounded lion god rounded on the giant golden serpent, his jaws sinking into her scaly hide once, twice, three times. The Queen of Serpents dropped Elver into the pool and lashed out at the lion, her hook-like teeth tearing more ragged holes in his raw flesh. Yet despite his injuries, the Bloody Claw knocked her away with one blow from his enormous paw.

'You have no power here, wyrm,' he said. The lion sounded weak, and confused. 'Begone.'

The serpent writhed in the pool for a few seconds, poisonous black blood oozing from between scales that glittered like gold coins, and then she vanished, leaving Elver behind. A second later Artair had the girl in his arms, lifting her out of the blood.

'Elver?'

Her golden eyes were still and unseeing. She wasn't breathing.

'No.'

Behind them, the Bloody Claw collapsed.

'It's happening!' Maura's voice was shrill with joy. The Bloody Claw did not yet appear to be dead, despite the gaping hole in his body, but a ruby-red fire was leaking out of him, oozing from his flesh like sweat, and it was surging towards Maura. She held out her hands to it, and the fiery energy surged over her, running over her skin and filling her eyes. As Artair watched, she began to rise off the ground, her feet hovering a good foot or so above the stones. He turned away from the sight, clutching Elver closer to him, and kissed her on the forehead.

'I'm sorry,' he murmured. 'I'm so sorry I brought you here.'

'All is not yet lost.' A cold nose poked him in the ankle. It was Tisk, now in his fox form.

'Maura is becoming a god,' Artair pointed out. 'And Elver is . . .'

He couldn't finish the sentence. 'What can we do?'

'A great many things,' said Tisk. 'There are always a great many things we can do, boy. You two, for example, are capable of extraordinary feats, if only you would work together.'

Artair felt sick. 'She's *dead*, you fool.'

'Not her, my handsome young idiot. Is it me or is everyone much too comfortable with disrespecting the gods these days?' Before Artair could reply, Tisk spoke over him. 'I'm talking about the soul you carry with you. For some reason, the pair of you are under the illusion you are entirely separate beings. Now, illusions are rather my area, so let me give you a little glimpse of what I mean.'

'What are you talking about?'

Maura was a being of pulsing red light, rising up towards the ceiling of the chamber.

'Here, I will show you.'

The fox bit his hand. Not hard, but firmly enough to send a little electric shock of pain through Artair that seemed to jolt something loose. He shook his head; he felt abruptly dizzy, and the room around him shimmered and wavered, wobbling into double vision and back again.

'What was . . . What was that?'

His own voice sounded strange and he realized a moment later that it wasn't his voice. Or at least, not his voice alone.

'What are you doing here?' snapped Lucian. 'What in the name of all the gods . . . She's done it, she's taken the Bloody Claw's power!' Artair winced as Lucian looked down at Elver's body in their arms, feeling the other spirit's own pain and horror. 'You let her die, monk?'

'There was nothing I could do!' He took a breath. 'And you told me you could stop Maura if I gave you control! What happened to that?'

'I can see that you two are going to be incredibly popular with this party trick. You should take it on the road, sell tickets,' said Tisk. 'But can I suggest concentrating on the current mess you're in? Because when Mother Maura has finished siphoning off that beast's power she will be eager to tidy away any loose ends. And you and my mage are the loosest of ends, if you will beg my pardon.' The fox vanished and instead the foxy-faced man was crouching over them. He had a soul globe in his hand – Artair saw the knowledge in Lucian's memories – and he passed it to him with a wink. 'Here you go. I've been saving this for you.' He paused. 'There's still time, Lucian.'

Lucian held up the glass ball and reached for the line of fire within him. It was barely there, banked down to nothing as the life force of the Bloody Claw drained away, but he grasped after it anyway, holding onto that connection like it was a lifeline.

'My lord,' he said aloud. 'I give you this soul in exchange for a boon – I ask for the last of your power . . . enough for vengeance.'

He cast the globe onto the floor where it shattered. The faint lilac light within it swirled around the pieces of broken glass and flew through the air towards the Bloody Claw, slipping through the great beast's open jaws.

'It's too late,' said Artair. 'He's already dead.'

'No,' said Lucian. 'This *has* to work.'

Maura was turning slowly, her arms outstretched. When she spoke, her voice rang like a bell.

'I take my place among the Twelve. And you will all call me Mother!'

Lucian felt it first as a warmth in his chest, a faint touch of heat that caught and began to burn more brightly. The line of fire quickened and smouldered even as the connection it represented faltered and died.

*Take it.* The Bloody Claw's voice in his head. *Take it and keep it from her as long as you can. She will never be complete without it.*

Lucian made to stand up, intending to carry Elver with him, but the pain in his stomach was too great.

'Artair, you have to get us up. I can't do it.'

The pain was bad, but Artair remembered the words of the monks – *you exist here and now, and in this moment, you are alive* – and he pushed the pain far away from himself and Lucian. Instead, he concentrated on what needed to be done. He stood, Elver still in his arms. Lucian's gratitude felt like the faint touch of the sun on a winter's day.

'Thank you.' Power surged within them, ruby red and volatile. A great deal of anger was driving it: his, Lucian's and the Bloody Claw's. He felt Lucian's sharp mind rubbing up against his own, so precise and ambitious and strange.

'I will summon a portal,' said Lucian, and a second later it was there, a fiery doorway hanging in front of them. Meanwhile, Sunay had slipped away from the other acolytes and she appeared at his elbow, her face the colour of ash. She went to touch Elver's hand where it lay lifelessly on her chest, then thought better of it.

'Quickly,' said Artair. Sunay went first, ducking her head as though to avoid the flames, and Artair and Lucian followed after, Elver still held in their arms. When they were through, standing on cool green grass, they turned back to get one last look at the chamber where Mother Maura had killed the Bloody Claw. Because he was dead now: both of them could feel it, a broken connection deep inside.

Beyond the doorway, Maura hung suspended in her own shimmering luminescence. The red glow had transformed into a powerful white light that dipped and waned like dappled sunshine on a wooded path, and her red hair too had turned entirely white.

Her face was beatific, peaceful, contented, the face of someone who had finally achieved everything they wanted. Except . . .

Her cheek twitched, and her eyes flickered open.

'There is something missing,' she said. 'Some piece of his power that has slipped away. *How is this possible? Why am I not complete?*'

For half a heartbeat, her eyes found Artair's, and they widened with sudden furious knowledge before Lucian closed the portal.

'Lucian!'

# CHAPTER 38

Elver awoke standing on a grey shoreline. Behind her was a shadowed land brooding under a silver sky. Ahead of her, a calm sea the colour of sleep. In the surf, strange objects stood in a row, churning water frothing around them as the waves moved silently in and out. There were twelve of them, and although they seemed to bear no relation to each other she realized she had a pretty good idea what they meant. There was a large anatomical heart carved from mud-coloured clay; a silver trident glowing with white light; a brace of logs that despite the surrounding seawater burned with a cheerful flame; a mirror of black glass; an axe with leaping lions carved into the handle . . . This last was broken and dull, a deep crack running through the steel head. These were avatars of the gods, which probably meant she was in big trouble.

She waded out into the surf, feeling the warm waters soak her trousers, and pressed her hand to the slick surface of the mirror. A moment later, the Queen of Serpents rose from the sea.

'Where am I?' asked Elver.

*You are on the very edge of things, poison child. The place where the shadowed lands meet the realm of the Twelve.*

'Then I'm dead.'

*Death, for you, is complicated. I brought you back once before and made you my creature. I made you jih. Your life is not for others to spend, but for me to weave.*

Elver frowned. 'I feel like you could have made that clearer at the time.'

The Queen of Serpents slid forward, bringing more of her body out of the sea and hanging her long head over Elver. Idly, Elver wondered if she was about to be eaten again. It seemed to be that sort of day.

*You have changed*, said the Queen of Serpents.

'Yes,' agreed Elver.

*There was always anger in your heart, but now you nurse it towards me also.*

'You struck me,' Elver said. 'I have only ever done what you wanted, and my thanks was a lashing.'

The Queen of Serpents' long jaws fell open, revealing rows and rows of serrated teeth.

'And you've kept me away from the world, all these years. I've missed so much.'

*The world hates your kind*, replied the god. *It was dangerous for you. Elver, you have seen how the world treats jih, and you've suffered because of their hate. Why would you expose yourself to that?*

'Because hiding isn't living.'

*The faceless priests nearly burned the jih from you. The rogue magpie fed you to the Bloody Claw.*

'I can handle myself.'

*Child, you are dead again.*

'Why do you care so much? Make another poison child.'

Water droplets glistened on the serpent's whiskers, clear as diamonds.

*Your life is mine to weave, poison child, and I have a purpose for you. But if you would prefer, I could make you human again and send you back to the mortal realm. You would be dead, but you would be human, and accepted by humans. They might even bury your body where they keep their own dead. Is that what you want? To be human?*

Elver laughed. 'No, of course not. There's nothing wrong with what I am. Apart from the dead bit.' She thought of Artair, and Lucian, even Sunay. She wondered what had happened to them, if they were safe. Being dead was one thing, but never seeing them again was something else. 'I don't want to be human again. But I want to live. Remake me, like you did before.'

*I can grant you a new life,* said the Queen of Serpents, *but it is not without cost. You will be more jih than ever. Humans will not accept you.*

'Some of them will. The ones that matter, anyway.'

For a long time, neither of them spoke. The silent sea moved on, rushing and retreating, rushing and retreating, while a sun the colour of bone rose slowly over the horizon. Elver wondered how many mortals made it to this beach and what other deals had been struck with gods on the edge of the shadowed lands.

'This purpose you have for me. Will you tell me what it is?' she asked eventually.

*In time you will come to know.*

'I won't be struck again. Not even by you.'

The Queen of Serpents lowered her great head until the tip of her snout touched Elver's forehead. She was gentle, and her breath was warm.

*I was a fool. I sensed love for another in your heart and I was afraid for you.*

Elver felt her cheeks grow hot. It was strange, she thought, that even when you were dead you could blush.

'That's no excuse,' she said. 'And I won't forget it.'

*I will earn your forgiveness, poison child.*

Elver nodded.

'Why do you hate them so much? They are jih too, the Sleepless. Artair and Lucian, they are both yours.'

*They are not my chosen. They are a shadow of what you are, child.*

'What do you mean?'

*Sometimes, a human soul becomes lost on its way to the shadowed lands and I snap it up, before the Hooded Crow can harvest it. It pleases me to hide them inside living human bodies. It vexes the old Crow that he cannot find them.*

'Why?' Elver shook her head. 'Why would you do something like that?'

*To vex the old Crow. Was that not clear? He did me a grievous injury once, and he must pay for it for ever.*

To her own surprise, Elver felt a wave of anger move through her, banishing the cold of the bleak shore.

'We're not just . . . bargaining chips for you to move around. We're not pranks you can play on other gods. We are alive! Well, usually we're alive. You've no right.'

*I have every right*, said the Queen of Serpents. *I am a god.*

Elver sighed. The anger left her abruptly, leaving a weary kind of exhaustion in its wake. When she did not reply, the serpent's long purple tongue flickered out, tasting the air.

*You sulk, poison child, but every moment away from the mortal realm makes sending you back harder. Do we have a deal? Will you accept this new life?*

'Yes. Send me back. Remake me.'

*Very well. I will give you a new heart, Elver of the Jih Forest. Do with it what you will, but remember always that it belongs to me. One day, I will tell you to leave the human world behind entirely and become fully the creature you were meant to be. On that day, you will not defy me.*

It didn't feel like much of a choice: remain in the shadowed lands forever, never seeing Artair or Lucian again, or get to live for a little longer in the human world, with the knowledge that some day it would end. Nothing lasted for ever, after all. Not for mortals. She put her hand in her pocket and closed her fingers over the conker.

'Do it.'

Elver gasped. There was a soft pain in the very centre of her chest, like a knife of glass sliding through her breastbone. The poison that served as her blood seemed to teem just under her skin, as though this new heart had set it aflame.

'What did you . . .?'

*Remember, monster child. Your heart is my own. One day, you must leave them.*

When Elver woke again, she was lying on the softest moss, the light of dusk lying sweetly all around. Next to her, there was a creek running with clear water, and she knew in her bones that she was home, that she was back in the Jih Forest. Someone had placed a posy of flowers on her chest, which she picked up and sniffed: inkwort, seven-petal and monkshood. All poisonous. She could hear voices coming from nearby. Carefully, feeling strangely unused to her own body, she got to her feet and followed them, the posy held in one hand.

The forest felt closer than it ever had, the green life of it pressing on her from all sides. Somewhere close by, she could smell the sharp tang of water – a river, running sweet and strong, the shape of it clear to her without having to see it. And somewhere to the north, a wider, deeper place, where the water sat cold and black and unmoving. Somehow she knew that lake, had a new awareness of its watery depths, and she longed to go there, to let the water close over her head and sink herself into the living mud.

*Not yet,* she thought fiercely. *I will live under the sun for a while yet.*

It made her wonder though, what other changes were coming.

Artair and Sunay, when she found them, were sitting by a small, smoky fire. Both of them looked worse for wear. Artair's face was pale and his eyes were red, and his clothes were blood-soaked. The black lines that circled Sunay's eyes were hopelessly smudged.

'. . . it's always been his delight to mess around with things, to tweak and flip-flop and shock. I suppose we shouldn't be surprised that this change was temporary.'

'I can still feel Lucian there, a little,' said Artair. At the sound of his voice, Elver felt her heart beat faster. 'We're aware of each other in a way we weren't before.' He paused. 'Elver knew. She told me he was no demon and I didn't listen.'

'Does that mean you'll listen to me now?'

It was gratifying to see them both jump out of their skins, but when Sunay burst into tears Elver felt a sharp pang of guilt.

Artair got to his feet unsteadily, the last of the colour draining from his face.

'Elver?'

'I'm okay, I'm okay.'

Sunay jumped over their small fire, embraced her, then leapt away as though she'd touched something hot on the stove.

'Ouch! Gods, Elver what happened? We thought you were dead, I collected flowers for you and we put you next to the stream because we thought you'd like that . . . Oh gods, we talked about *burying* you and putting up a marker but we couldn't do it because we kept crying and you looked so peaceful . . .'

Elver laughed. 'As far as I can tell, I *was* dead. But the Queen of Serpents wasn't happy with that, so here I am, back again.' Her eyes caught on Artair's blood-soaked clothes. 'Wait, are you hurt? How badly?' She went to go to him and caught herself. 'What happened?'

'I'm fine,' said Artair. He seemed unable to look away from her. 'That is, I was hurt, but Sunay called up a spell to heal me.'

'It's not Tisk's usual magic and I had no tithe to pay him, so . . .' Sunay turned around to reveal a bright orange fox's tail peeking out the bottom of her embroidered jacket. 'My lord's little joke. I'm sure he'll get tired of it eventually. Maybe. Artair and Lucian were bleeding a frankly worrying amount, so it seemed like the only thing to do.'

'Thank you,' said Elver, and meant it. 'Where is the cub? I mean, where is Fleet?'

'Don't worry, he still runs with the Pack,' said Sunay. 'He's perfectly safe. Probably learning a few unsavoury habits, if I'm honest.'

'Oh, I . . . That's good, I suppose.' Privately, she wondered what the Queen of Serpents would think about one of her children learning the ways of another god, but she found she cared less about the Queen's ire than she once had. 'And what happened back there, at Prideful Leap . . . after I . . . ?'

Artair opened his mouth, shook his head, apparently lost for words. Sunay looked between the two of them, a small smile touching the corner of her mouth.

'What we need is food,' she said firmly. 'With Artair being recently injured and you being recently dead, I think I should be the one to go and do some foraging.' She brushed her sleeves down briskly, tail twitching. 'I'll be back in a little while.'

She scampered off between the trees and Elver watched her go with a faintly troubled smile of her own. There was a reasonable chance that Sunay would meet other jih, or bring back something inedible, judging by her choice of flowers. But Artair was looking at her and she found that she was very glad that they were alone.

'You came after me, didn't you? You realized it was a trap.'

'Lucian did.' Artair took her hand and held it gently between his own. 'Tisk brought us together for a little while, and I saw his memories . . . Mother Maura took the Bloody Claw's power, but Lucian stole the last dregs of it. I don't know what that means, but I suspect it changes things. Elver, I've spent all this time thinking he was a mindless dark spirit intent on chaos and destruction. But he was a real person, with his own life. *Is* a real person.'

'I suspect chaos and destruction still aren't far from his agenda,' she replied, thinking of how, all those years ago, he had led her up the steps of the Tumble Stone and given her over into Mother Maura's care. 'He has done some terrible things, Artair. It could be that you were closer to the truth than you realize.'

'I don't know,' he said. His thumb moved over the delicate skin of her wrist. It was good to be touched, she thought. It seemed impossible that she'd spent so long without it. 'I think that maybe he deserves his own life as much as I do. Maybe there's something we can do about that. I don't know what, but I want to try.'

'Artair . . .' This was who he was, she realized. Someone who thought of others first; someone who opened himself up to the world, even if that risked pain and failure. 'The novices made it back to the Golden Tower. You don't have to worry about them any more. What are you going to do now?'

He grinned suddenly, as though surprised by his own freedom. 'I don't know. There is no order of the Perpetual Morning now, and if everyone who is Sleepless is like Lucian, someone who has been forced out of their body . . . I'm not sure there should be an order at all. We're all free now, for better or for worse.' His hand squeezed hers. 'What about you?'

'The forest is my home, but I know there's more to life than staying at home. If Lucian has stolen power from Maura, there will be more trouble on its way. I don't know. It feels like I'll be seeing her again soon, somehow. But I know I won't be alone.' She glanced up at him, hoping he would take her meaning. 'Right?'

Her heart thumping steadily in her throat, she reached up with her free hand and stroked his cheek, his jawline. There was stubble there, delightfully rough under her fingers. His eyes seemed to lighten a shade, as though inside him a delicate flame had burst into life.

'Elver, can I . . . kiss you?'

'I think that would be great, actually.'

They came together hesitantly at first, Elver marvelling at the softness of his lips, and then the kiss became warmer, sweeter and a little more urgent. His hand slid around the small of her back, drawing her closer, and she buried her fingers in his hair. Unbidden, she found herself thinking of Lucian. The sly way that he smiled, every glance like a knife that knew where to cut you . . . She pushed the thoughts away, alarmed by how they made her heart beat faster, and for a little while, there was nothing else. The sounds of the forest fell away, and there was Elver and Artair, caught in a kiss that felt like it could lead anywhere. And then they heard Sunay singing, her voice a little louder than it needed to be perhaps, as though she were warning them of her arrival. Then she stopped singing and called out in a slightly indignant tone:

'I could have sworn the fire was here! Where are you two? All these trees look the same to me.'

They broke apart, laughing softly.

'I'm going to find her,' said Elver. 'Before she gets herself eaten by a jih creature that wants a bit of peace and quiet.'

Lucian watched the monster girl walk away, his heart hammering in his chest.

# EPILOGUE

There was a chamber at the heart of Prideful Leap, one that only Maura had ever been inside. It was small, no bigger than a large wardrobe, and the walls were painted white, so that it more closely resembled the outside of her sanctum. On a wooden plinth there were three yellowed skulls, each of them less than complete. The smallest was broken clean in half, a scattering of teeth – painstakingly collected from the rubble – placed neatly next to it. This was all she had left of them.

Maura knelt in front of the skulls. She took the largest into her hands and turned it over and over, as she had done many times before. Despite her power, despite her godhood, when she reached for their souls, they did not reach back.

'This should be enough,' she whispered. 'I've done everything I planned to do. The old lion is dead, I have his power, so *why isn't this working?*'

She placed the skull back in its spot and stood, turning around to find herself on a grey shoreline, a churning sea spreading out in front of her. A sun the colour of old bones hung high in the sky, and several strange objects protruded from the surf. One in particular caught at her heart and drew her to it, as heedless as a moth to an oil lamp. It was a bear carved from wood and painted with bright colours, standing on its rear legs, but the pearl buttons she knew made up its eyes were missing, and in comparison to the other objects it was dreary somehow, without its own interior glow. Maura reached out and ran her finger along its snout. *Incomplete.*

'You are unfinished, Mother.'

She spun at the sound of the voice, her white hair falling forward over her shoulders. A fox sat watching her from the sand, his coat all the colours of autumn.

'You.' Maura felt the white-hot heat of her hatred gathering in her chest, fuelling her power. She raised a single hand, an orb of boiling magic gathering there. 'This is your doing.'

'Please,' said Tisk. He paused to scratch his ear with a back foot, eyes half shut with pleasure. 'All of this you have brought upon yourself. It has nothing at all to do with me. And if you're going to be one of us now, Mother, you have to play by our rules. We do not fight in the sacred places.'

Against her will, the power faded from her hand as quickly as it had arrived.

'Why are you here?' she spat. 'Why have you involved yourself in this at all?'

Tisk flicked his tail, the foxy equivalent of a shrug. 'I gave you all the gifts I could give, Mother, and you threw them all away. Some would call that wasteful. Insulting. And still I was prepared to forget about you. Until I stumbled upon the strands of your plan. The patronage of two gods really wasn't enough for you, Mother?'

'You know it wasn't. And you know why.'

'They won't be pleased.' He twitched his tail in the direction of the other gods' avatars. 'How do you think these ancient beings will react, Mother, when a mortal takes the place of one of the Twelve? They will try to stop you.'

'Let them. I have nothing to lose.'

'On the contrary, you have gained an awful lot. And has it brought you everything you ever wanted?'

'If I have to burn every god to the ground, if I have to see every child in Tlevrae die to have mine returned to me, I will do it.'

'Do you hear yourself? You sound like a madwoman.' Tisk sniffed with something like amusement, but Maura thought she could sense fear underneath it. She was something new, something the gods hadn't dealt with before, and they were right to fear her. 'And you dare name yourself *Mother*.'

When she didn't reply to that, the fox began to fade from view, a shadow thing cast into nothingness by the light from an ivory sun. Maura watched him go, then stared at the patch of sand where he had been for a long, long time.

She was thinking of Lucian, his heart filled with a power that rightfully belonged to her. He was a mage with no master, a half god trapped in the body of a mortal.

He shouldn't be too hard to find.

# ACKNOWLEDGEMENTS

Huge thanks to Emma Jones, for her enormous enthusiasm for this project and her excellent edits – each comment made this a better, hotter book and I'm tremendously grateful. Thanks also, as ever, to Juliet Mushens, genuinely the best in the business and a dear friend; everyone should be lucky enough to have that one person in their life who will look them in the eye and say: 'You can do this.' I'm in debt to the wider teams at both First Ink and Wednesday Books for all the love lavished on *The Sleepless*, and I've been very lucky to be blessed with two extraordinary covers: big thanks to Pablo Hurtado de Mendoza and Tom Roberts for their incredible work on them. My disaster children look so beautiful!

My family continue to be the rock I stand on – even if they are not aware of it – and I must give thanks especially to my mum, who tolerated (possibly even supported) my sudden move to the west last year. The last year or so has been a wild one, to put it mildly, and the usual suspects kept me sane – thank you Andrew, Den, Boo, Adam and Jenni.

I suspect no one wants to hear a love story in the acknowledgements, even in the acknowledgements to a romantasy novel, so I will resist that indulgence, except to say that it's fortuitous to be falling in love when you suddenly need to write convincingly about these things. So perhaps the most heartfelt thank-you goes to Peter Newman, not just the sweetest person I know, but also a wildly talented writer whose first reactions to *The Sleepless* were incredibly valuable. I couldn't have written it without you, babe.

# ABOUT THE AUTHOR

Jen Williams is a writer from London currently living in Bristol. A fan of witches and dark folklore from an early age, these days she writes character-driven fantasy novels with plenty of banter and magic, as well as horror-tinged crime thrillers with strong female leads. She was nominated for Best Newcomer in the British Fantasy Awards and her books *The Ninth Rain* and *The Bitter Twins* both went on to win Best Fantasy Novel, which she won again in 2024 for *Talonsister*. *The Sleepless* is her first novel for YA readers.